Clad in Armour
of
Radiant White

Rosaline Riley

Published by: Braxted Books

12 Braxted Park, London SW16 3DW, UK

Copyright © 2015 Rosaline Riley

A CIP catalogue record for this book is available from the British Library

ISBN: 978-0-9932122-1-5

For Martha, Ben, Amy and Matthew
who sent me on a writing retreat.
Thank you.

Contents

School Song

Notre Dame 'neath your banner we proudly stand
Clad in armour of radiant white . . .

King James Bible (1611), Book of Ecclesiastes 3: 1-4

To every thing there is a season, and a time to every purpose under the heaven:
. . . .
A time to weep, and a time to laugh; a time to mourn, and a time to dance;
. . . .

SEPTEMBER

1966

The train gave a sudden jolt, causing Ellen, who was standing by a door in the corridor, to momentarily lose her balance. As it began to move away she steadied herself and raised her hand in farewell. Her mother and sister – Mrs McCann attempting a brave smile, Christine with carefree abandon – started walking along the platform, waving back to her as they went. For a few yards they were able to keep pace with the train but as it picked up speed they were soon left behind. Ellen, leaning out of the window now, carried on waving until they disappeared from sight.

Mrs McCann had been very emotional when they'd said their goodbyes a few minutes ago, embarrassing Ellen – and taking her by surprise too. After all, her mother had always wanted her to go to university. And she couldn't remember her getting this upset last year when Mick had gone off to Liverpool, but perhaps she just hadn't noticed then.

'She's not emigrating you know!' Christine had said, obviously feeling that all this emotion was misplaced. 'She'll be home at Christmas.'

Which was true, Ellen thought. She wasn't really leaving home. She would be back in the holidays (or vacations as they would be called now). Nonetheless, she could see that this was a poignant moment for her mother. Fighting back her own tears, she stood in the corridor for a few more minutes before going into the compartment where earlier she'd deposited her suitcase on the overhead luggage rack.

There were two other people in there already; an elderly man sitting by the door, and a woman by the window. Ellen stepped over the man's outstretched legs and sat down opposite the woman. Seated here, with her back to the engine, she stared out of the window and watched as first the station and then Turneley itself receded into the distance in front of her. Her eyes filled with tears. Her mother would be all right; she knew that. So why, she wondered, was she herself feeling upset now, when just a short while ago she'd been so happy and excited? A new chapter in her life was beginning, and all she could feel was overwhelming sadness.

PART ONE

SEPTEMBER

1959

September meant the start of a new school year, and this year the start of a new school, too.

Ellen opened the wardrobe door, unable to resist having yet another look at her new school uniform. It would have to be a quick look, though, because she was about to go for her piano lesson and it'd already gone six o'clock. Any moment now her mother would be shouting up the stairs urging her to get a move on or she would be late. And last night she'd dreamt about being late – one of those annoying dreams where she'd been trying and trying to get to Mrs Walker's house but obstacles kept getting in her way and slowing her down. She didn't want this to happen now so she shut the wardrobe door, dashed down the stairs and snatched up her music case from the side of the piano in the front room.

'I'm off now,' she announced, pausing only to pocket the lesson money her mother had left out on the sideboard before charging out of the back door and down the yard.

As she flung open the gate, she nearly bumped into her friend, Jennifer Chadwell, who'd just been on the point of opening it from the other side. 'I can't come out now,' she told her. 'I've got my piano lesson. I'll see you later.'

Leaving Jennifer standing there, she set off down the

backs at a rapid pace. The hard leather music case kept knocking painfully against her bare leg as she hurried along, but she didn't mind. Because she, Ellen McCann, could play the piano. And tomorrow she, Ellen McCann, would be going to her new school. In every respect, her life was just so much more exciting than Jennifer Chadwell's.

This was her first piano lesson after the long summer holiday; the first since the music exam, in which, much to her and Mrs Walker's delight (and that of her mother too, of course) she had gained a distinction in Grade Two (having skipped Grade One altogether – 'and after only eight months of lessons!').

Over the past few weeks, inspired by this achievement, she'd been entertaining the idea of becoming a world famous pianist. She'd been playing her exam pieces and then rising from the piano stool to acknowledge the rapturous applause of an imaginary audience. As the piano was in the front room where these performances – although audible – were not visible, she could practice bowing deeply, again and again, without anyone seeing her.

The piano was also audible to old Mrs Chisnall-next-door who was always saying how much she enjoyed hearing it. So Ellen had decided that when she was famous she was going to invite Mrs Chisnall to one of her recitals at the Royal Albert Hall.

Nearly an hour later, she returned home bearing the Grade Two certificate that was destined to be framed and hung on the wall over the piano.

'Just look at this!' said her mother, taking it out of its envelope. 'Distinction!'

Ellen's brother Michael, the only other person in the room, gave the certificate the slightest of glances before turning back to watch the television.

'Are you all ready for tomorrow, then?' Mrs McCann asked, putting it back into the envelope.

Ellen nodded. She'd been ready for days. And now, at

long last, 'tomorrow' was almost here. 'I hope me and Joan'll be in the same class,' she said, feeling – for the first time – a little bit nervous.

'Well don't worry if you're not,' said her mother. 'You'll soon make new friends.' She glanced at the envelope containing the certificate, only just managing not to add: cleverer friends, girls with distinctions in piano playing, perhaps. 'You will,' she said confidently. 'Just you wait and see.'

She made it sound so easy, new friends effortlessly replacing old ones. But Joan Grady was irreplaceable. She was Ellen's best friend at school (Jennifer Chadwell being her best friend at home) and they'd sworn to remain best friends for ever. 'Even when we're married,' they'd said. Well, never mind! They could still be best friends even if they were in different classes. They could still travel to school together and spend dinner times and playtimes together. Except, Ellen reminded herself, they weren't going to be called playtimes anymore. They were going to be called break times from now on.

Forgetting all about Jennifer, who might well still be waiting for her outside, Ellen went up to her bedroom and opened the wardrobe door again. And there it was, her new uniform: the brown gabardine mac; the brown gymslip sharing a coathanger with the brown cardigan; the two cream blouses hanging side by side, and sitting on the shelf above the hanging rail, the brown velours hat with the school badge embroidered on its striped hatband.

She reached up, took this down and stroked its velvety smoothness. Most of the uniform was too big for her – some of it only slightly, some of it a lot. 'You'll grow into it,' her mother kept saying, and no doubt she would – sooner or later. But it would seem that her head had stopped growing because the hat was a perfect fit. Turning towards the dressing-table she put it on and stood gazing at herself in the mirror. She was still there a few minutes later when her sister came bounding up the stairs.

'Oh, no!' said Christine, bursting into the bedroom. 'You're not trying things on *again*, are you?'

'Shut up, you,' said Ellen.

'No, I won't. And I'm going to bed now, so you can go away.' Christine drew the curtains and the room darkened.

Ellen peered at her shadowy reflection in the mirror for a moment longer, then took the hat off and put it back on the shelf.

'I can't wait for tomorrow,' she said with a little shrug of excitement.

Ellen's old junior school – St Wilfrid's Girls' School – was a small, single-storey, stone building set on the very edge of the small town of Makerton. It had just four classrooms, one cloakroom and a row of outside lavatories. The infants' school was across the playground, and the boys' school was a few hundred yards down the road, near the church.

Her new school – the St Thérèse High School for Girls (or the Convent as it was universally known) – was very different. It stood right on the main road running northwards out of the much larger neighbouring town of Turneley, five miles away. It was a tall, red-bricked building with many windows and a double arched doorway set back slightly from the street.

This doorway, though, led directly into the nuns' quarters and was never used by the pupils. Instead, and more interestingly, they entered the building down a long flight of shallow steps that ran parallel to the pavement outside and led into the basement below, where all the cloakrooms were situated.

On their first morning, Ellen, Joan Grady and the two other girls from St Wilfrid's who had also passed the eleven-plus – Margaret Latham and Sheila Murphy – walked down these steps together. Once inside, and still wearing their coats, hats and outdoor shoes, they were ushered upstairs and into the school hall where the headmistress, Sister Marie-Pierre, standing on a dais at the front, was waiting to begin the process of sorting them into their classes.

Starting with 1A, she began reading out names in alphabetical order, and the owners of these names began to line up accordingly. Ellen, clutching her shiny new satchel, listened carefully. There was no 'Joan Grady', no 'Margaret Latham'. Her heart was pounding.

'Erica Latimer,' called out Sister Marie-Pierre and another girl moved into line. And then: 'Ellen McCann.'

Stifling a triumphant smile (she was in the top class – her mother would be delighted!) Ellen gave Joan a rueful glance before moving away from her little group of friends and going to stand behind Erica Latimer. The next name to be called was 'Angela Norris'. So no 'Sheila Murphy' either. But then, no-one could've possibly expected Sheila to be in the top class. She had been lucky to have even passed the eleven-plus.

When all the girls in 1A were assembled, they were marched out of the hall, and so it was only later – at break time – that Ellen learned the fate of the other three: Margaret Latham was in 1B; Joan and Sheila were in 1C. She felt a tinge of anxiety, hoping that her friends wouldn't hold the fact that she was in the top class against her now. She felt sure that Joan wouldn't – or Margaret – but she wasn't so sure about Sheila Murphy.

She couldn't help remembering what had happened back in May when the eleven-plus results had come out.

'You're snobs now,' they'd been told by their classmates at St Wilfrid's.

'No we're not!' they'd protested.

'Yes you are. Everybody who goes to Turneley Convent's a snob.'

It was, it seemed, as simple as that.

'My sister goes to the Convent and she's not a snob,' objected Joan.

'Yes she is.'

'No she's not!'

'She is.'

It was pointless arguing.

'Take no notice,' Sheila Murphy had said then. 'They're just jealous because we're clever and they're not.'

But being clever was one thing. Being cleverer might well be a step too far.

Ellen loved the Convent – just as she always knew she would. She felt as if she had been transported into the pages of one of those girls' school stories of which she was such an avid reader. She had never felt like this at St Wilfrid's.

She loved the oak staircases, the parquet floors and the stained glass windows. She loved the enclosed courtyards, the nuns' garden at the back of the school and the tiny chapel where, twice a week, each class went for morning prayers. She loved the school hall, the science labs, the geography room, the gym, the library. She didn't mind the inconveniences – the fact that the dining hall was some distance from the main building, or that the playing fields were over a mile away in the grounds of La Maison, the Convent's preparatory school. She loved the new routines and rituals, the new subjects, the teachers (only a few of whom were nuns).

And in 1A, where the alphabetically-ordered pupils sat at desks that were arranged in pairs, she was captivated by her desk-mate, Erica Latimer.

'What school did you used to go to?' Erica asked that first morning, looking at Ellen with her strange grey-blue eyes which one minute looked quite dark and then the next seemed disconcertingly pale. Ellen felt a bit intimidated by her.

'St Wilfrid's,' she replied, her voice hoarse with nerves.

'Where's that?'

'In Makerton.'

Erica looked blank.

Ellen cleared her throat. 'What school did you go to?'

'St Peter's.'

Ellen nodded meaningfully, although she had no idea where this school was either. But Erica, tossing one of her long plaits of dark hair over her shoulder, had already turned away.

Erica Latimer exuded confidence. She had older sisters in the school and seemed to know everything and everyone right from the start. She had an impressive command of the geography of the building and was the one to follow whenever they changed rooms. There were eight other girls from her junior school in 1A, so she was never short of friends. Although her best friend, a girl called Sally Wagstaff, was – like Joan Grady – in 1C.

Bit by bit, Ellen got to know more about Erica and each new piece of information made her even more interesting. Her three older sisters were: Georgina who had just left school and was now at a teachers' training college; Rachel who was in 4A; and Maria (who everyone thought was very beautiful) who was in 2A. She also had two younger brothers, Tom and James.

But the most interesting thing of all was something Ellen learned some time later – and from another girl, not from Erica herself. Three years ago, Mrs Latimer, Erica's mother, had died in a terrible accident. She had lost control of her car and had crashed into a tree.

Ellen was stricken by this. She tried to imagine what the loss of a mother would feel like. Her heart ached for the Latimer children. She could hardly bring herself to look Erica in the eye after hearing this sad story, but it had happened three years ago and Erica herself had never mentioned it.

Ellen told Joan about this, going home on the bus that afternoon. They sat in silence for a while and then Joan said: 'Well, I'm glad our mothers don't drive, aren't you? Or our dads.'

But driving cars wasn't really the point. After another silence, Joan asked: 'Who would you rather die, your mam or your dad?'

'I don't know,' lied Ellen. 'Who would you?'

'My dad,' said Joan instantly. 'I couldn't bear having no

mam, could you?'

'No,' said Ellen – resolving to be especially nice to her father from then on to make up for this betrayal.

Her chance to begin doing this came later that evening. She and Michael were sitting at the table doing their homework when suddenly Michael burst out laughing.

'He's done it again!' he said, pointing to his father through the window. 'He's walked straight past it again.'

He was referring to the back door. Not long ago the McCanns had had a bathroom built on to the back of their kitchen and part of the building work had involved removing the old back door and reinstalling it further down the yard. It'd taken a while for them all to get used to this new position, but now they had – all except Mr McCann who was taking longer to adjust.

Ellen glanced up from her books and Christine wandered over to have a look too. Their father, who had been chopping firewood at the bottom of the yard, was already retracing his footsteps.

'He'll never get used to it,' said Christine.

'Yes, he will,' said Ellen, refusing to join in the laughter. 'Leave him alone. It's not funny anymore.'

But it was – and even Mr McCann had to smile when he came into the room.

Ellen had desperately wanted this new bathroom to go upstairs. That had been the original plan; it would go in Michael's bedroom and he would sleep downstairs in the front room. But then the newly acquired piano had been put in there so that idea had been abandoned. The bathroom would have to go downstairs instead, even though it would make the yard much smaller and would mean losing the shed and the outside lavatory (although that would be no great loss now).

It was a compromise she'd been reluctant to accept. She'd suggested that they should move to a council house instead. Joan Grady lived in a council house on the new Greenside estate just outside Makerton which had a proper upstairs bathroom – and a front garden with a small lawn, too. And their Auntie Annie also lived up at Greenside now. She couldn't understand why her parents were so scornful of the idea, why they thought that their house (even if it was an end-of-terrace) was better than a council house.

Once built, however, the bathroom, was a great success. Having it downstairs might not be ideal, but – like having a best friend in another class at school – it was much better than not having one at all.

Because she had homework to do, Ellen didn't go out to play on weekday evenings anymore. At first, Jennifer Chadwell, who was still at St Wilfrid's and didn't have homework, kept calling for her, but after constantly being told: 'She's doing her homework,' she stopped doing so.

Michael McCann and Jennifer's brother (also called Michael) had homework to do too, but they rarely let that stop them from going out. Their school was eight miles away in Ashburne and they went on a special bus which picked them up at eight o'clock every morning outside Makerton library and delivered them back there just before five o'clock every afternoon. Often, when he was challenged about his lack of homework, Michael McCann would claim that he had done it already on the bus coming home, or would do it on the way to school the next morning. Ellen would smirk in disbelief at this before settling down virtuously with her own books.

Friday evenings, however, were different. After she had done her piano practice she could go out. And Jennifer was always glad to see her and be brought up to date with all the details of life at the Convent. So, on the Friday after she'd heard about Mrs Latimer's death, Ellen rushed out as usual, eager to tell Jennifer all about it, only to find her sitting on the McCanns' front step with another girl.

This was Sandra Crompton who lived about a hundred

yards away up Turneley Road and who every now and then condescended to come down to their end of the backs to play. Sandra was twelve and 'a little madam'. Sometimes even, 'a *knowing* little madam'. Ellen didn't like her.

'Was that you playing the piano just then?' she asked accusingly as Ellen, who had come out the back way, appeared round the corner.

'Yeah?'

Sandra sniffed.

'Have you done your homework?' Jennifer asked, obviously forgetting what day it was.

'It's Friday,' said Ellen, sitting down on the pavement in front of them and crossing her legs.

'Those are funny socks,' said Sandra.

'They're my school ones,' said Ellen, wishing that she had changed out of them along with the rest of her uniform.

Sandra sniffed again, more loudly this time. Ellen's dislike of her intensified.

There was a short silence and then Sandra said: 'Have you started your periods yet?'

Ellen blushed. 'No.'

'Have you, Jennifer?'

'Don't be stupid! She's only ten!'

'So what? I know somebody who's only nine and she has periods.'

'No you don't.'

'Yes I do.'

Ellen pulled a disbelieving face.

'Well . . . anyway . . . I've started mine,' Sandra announced wriggling about on the step. 'And I'm having one now, if you must know. Can you tell?'

'No,' said Ellen, hoping that the conversation would end here.

But Sandra, as befitted one who was 'knowing', was determined to share her knowledge and began telling them all the intricate and intimate details of her condition. Ellen, in spite of herself, was interested, and she could tell that Jennifer was too.

Then, having dealt as comprehensively as she could with the female body, Sandra began talking about boys and their bodies. If girls had periods, she said, did they know what boys had?

Jennifer shook her head.

'Do you know?' Sandra asked, looking at Ellen.

Ellen had no idea what she was talking about. 'I think I do,' she muttered, leaning over to readjust her socks.

But Sandra wasn't fooled. 'No you don't,' she said. 'I can tell you don't.'

And so she proceeded to enlighten them, talking graphically about white stuff shooting out of their you-know-whats in bed at night. Ellen glanced at Jennifer. They both had brothers and she felt sure that they would have heard about such strange events if what Sandra was telling them were true. Nevertheless, although she couldn't imagine her mother tolerating such unacceptable behaviour, she felt momentarily relieved that Michael's bed wasn't downstairs in the front room, near her piano, after all.

When she had disseminated all this information, Sandra stood up. 'I'm going home now,' she said. 'I've got to change my sanitary towel. I'll see you tomorrow.' And she set off up the backs and disappeared into the dusk.

Ellen checked the step carefully before relocating herself next to Jennifer. Neither of them spoke for a while. Ellen was wondering whether listening to Sandra talking like that was a sin. Was it being impure? If so, then they would have to mention it in Confession. But what would they say? She sighed to herself. Because that was the tricky bit - finding the right words to describe their sins so that the priest would know what they were on about. Jennifer, she remembered, had had problems with this before.

* * *

A few months ago, on their way to Confession one Saturday evening, they'd been talking about how hard it was to think of interesting sins to confess. It was always the same boring

few every time. Ellen had been telling Jennifer how she tried
to counter this by varying the words she used when saying
how many times she'd committed each sin. Being disobedient
sometimes; telling lies *once* (or more often, depending on the
eventfulness of the two weeks since her last confession);
laughing and talking in church *a few times*; missing night
and/or morning prayers *several times*; having uncharitable
thoughts (this was a good sin) *occasionally*. The trick, she'd
said, was not to repeat the same words in any one confession.

Jennifer didn't seem too impressed by all this. 'Well,
anyway. . . I've got a new sin,' she said, 'but if I tell you, you
can't have it too.'

'I can if I've committed it,' said Ellen.

'Well . . . Miss Long said we should always be modest.
And I've not been. So I can say that I've been immodest,
can't I?'

'Why, what've you been doing? You mean boasting or
something?'

'No. My mam's always saying I spend too much time in
front of the mirror. That's not being modest, is it?'

Ellen wasn't so sure. She thought this might be vanity.
Was being vain the same as being immodest? And anyway . . .
just how much time in front of a mirror was considered to be
too much? After all, mirrors were necessary. And what if you
spent ages, not admiring yourself, but thinking how horrible
you looked? That couldn't be a sin, could it? Well . . . yes, it
might be, it might be a sin of despair, but that was straying
from the point. She decided, wisely as it turned out, that she
needed more time to think about this before adding
immodesty to her list of potential sins.

'Father Maloney's mad,' said Jennifer as they walked
home afterwards. 'Do you know what he said?'

Ellen shook her head.

'I said I'd been immodest sometimes, and he said, have
you been immodest in thoughts or in deeds? So I said in
deeds. And then he said, how many times have you been
immodest? And I said, nearly every day. And he said, nearly

17

every day for the past two weeks? And I said, yes Father. (I didn't tell him that I'd been doing it before then, too.) And then do you know what he did?'

Ellen shook her head again.

'He moved the curtain and had a peep at me! But I put my head down so he couldn't see my face. That's not right, is it? He's not supposed to do that, is he?'

Ellen shrugged.

'And then he said, were you on your own or with someone else?' Jennifer paused to let the stupidity of this question sink in. 'So I said that sometimes I was on my own and sometimes there were other people there. And then he didn't say anything for ages – I thought he'd gone. And then he said I should think of Our Lady and pray to her for guidance.'

Ellen had a brief vision of Our Lady putting on her veil without looking in a mirror.

'And do you know what he gave me for my penance?' Jennifer went on.

Ellen shook her head for a third time, but she knew that it'd been a considerable one because she'd had to wait a long time for Jennifer to complete it.

'A whole decade of the rosary!'

Ellen suspected that immodesty meant something quite different to Father Maloney than it did to Jennifer. Otherwise, why would it have attracted such a big penance? For him, it probably had something to do with boys and things. But then, how could it be done on your own, she wondered?

* * *

Ever since then, although she knew there had been a misunderstanding, she had never felt comfortable attending to her appearance in a mirror when there were other people around.

'We shouldn't have listened to Sandra talking like that,' she said now to Jennifer.

'Well, we didn't know she was going to say rude things,

did we?'

'No, but we shouldn't have listened when she started to. It's bound to be a sin.'

'Well if it is, I'm not confessing it,' said Jennifer.

I have been listening to Sandra Crompton, *once*, Ellen rehearsed. Were you on your own with her or were there others present, asked Father Maloney? And she pictured herself and Jennifer standing in front of a big mirror, with Sandra Crompton hovering over their shoulders, whispering rude things in their ears.

It was getting darker now, and chilly. Ellen wrapped her cardigan around her bent knees and was about to launch into the sad story of Erica Latimer's mother when their two brothers hove into view. (Outside of their respective homes – to avoid confusion – Michael McCann was generally called Mac, while Michael Chadwell was Chad. But between themselves, Ellen and Jennifer always referred to them as 'our Michael' and 'your Michael'.) Colin Hurst, who lived next door to the Chadwells, was with them. They'd been playing football on the rec but the failing light was driving them to the lamp-post in front of the McCanns' house. As they approached, the girls studied them with renewed interest.

'What are you two staring at?' demanded Colin.

'Nothing,' they said in unison. Then they glanced at each other and began giggling. Colin was visibly annoyed but the two Michaels just ignored them.

When they'd controlled their mirth, Ellen looked again at Michael Chadwell. She'd been looking at him a lot lately, she realised. He seemed to be getting quite handsome. And why hadn't she noticed before what a really nice smile he had? She wondered if she might be falling in love with him; it was certainly an interesting thought.

'Is this what you're laughing at?' said Michael McCann. 'Who's done all this?' He pointed at the side wall of the Chadwells' yard and began kicking the football against it.

Ellen got up to look but Jennifer stayed on the step. 'Sandra Crompton did all that,' she said.

Chalked on the wall were several new 'equals' signs. These consisted of two sets of initials, one on top of the other, separated by the sign = which stood for 'loves'. 'Loves' meant that the owners of the initials were 'going out' with each other. 'Going out', however, was something of a misnomer. You didn't actually have to go anywhere – or, indeed, do anything other than agree that you were a couple. You could hold hands and kiss if you wanted to, but this was not an absolute requirement. Different couples dealt with 'going out' in different ways.

Whenever these signs appeared, it was the custom to deny that you liked the person you were paired with – even if you did – just in case the feeling wasn't mutual. You didn't want to find yourself in the sad position of 'going out' with someone who wasn't 'going out' with you. So, if you saw your initials displayed like this, you had several options. You could rub them out, cross them out, or leave them alone to fade slowly over time.

It was a game that required skill. Only if the assertion was positively unthinkable (your name linked with Colin Hurst's, for example), would you go to the trouble of rubbing the initials out completely. Leaving them, but with a line drawn through them, was much more interesting. It allowed for the possibility but withheld the confirmation. And for a girl, leaving the initials totally unchallenged was considered a bit 'forward' and wasn't really an option unless you were already part of an acknowledged couple.

Sandra Crompton was always doing these equals signs when she was around. She seemed to have a compulsive need to pair everyone off, even little children like Christine McCann and Colin's brother, Paul. The most prominent sign on display now, and the one which Michael McCann was attempting to rub out by kicking the football at it, was written in extra large letters and had an elaborate heart drawn round it. It proclaimed that S.C. = M.M. Sandra Crompton obviously didn't mind being 'forward'. Neither did she seem to mind that hers was an unrequited love. This wasn't the first time she'd declared her love for Michael McCann – and it probably wouldn't be the last.

Ellen scanned the rest of the signs. And yes, there was one that said: E.M. = M.C. She felt deeply gratified. But it could only have been a lucky guess on Sandra's part, she thought, because she'd only just realised this herself.

'She's got a cheek!' she cried indignantly, feeling herself blush. She stole a sideways look at Michael Chadwell. He had the football now and was kicking it against the wall, obliterating more of the chalky declarations. But if he was aiming at E.M. = M.C. then he was being unusually inaccurate. It remained untouched. Her heart soared.

They stayed around the lamp-post for a while longer, until Jennifer, complaining that she was cold, went in. Reluctantly, Ellen did so too. As she walked by herself down the shadowy backs, she felt suddenly overwhelmed by the singularity and significance of her life. She was Ellen McCann, here, on earth, now; she was going to the Convent; Erica Latimer's mother was dead; and yes – she was definitely in love with Michael Chadwell!

Resonating with self-awareness, she opened the gate, closed it behind her and walked up the yard, coming to an abrupt halt in front of the brick wall where the back door used to be. Fortunately, the living-room curtains were drawn, so no-one inside witnessed her mistake.

She found it hard to get to sleep that night. Her mind was full of what Sandra Crompton had been talking about earlier – and with what she had written on the wall. Ellen couldn't quite articulate the connection between the two things, but she was aware that there was one. It was pleasantly exciting. And just in case it was sinful too, she tried to think about Mrs Latimer instead; about death and loss.

But her mind kept wandering back – again and again – to Michael Chadwell.

'Have you got a boyfriend?' Erica asked Ellen, the following Monday morning as they were putting on their little white veils to go to the chapel.

'No. Have you?'

'He's not my boyfriend,' said Erica. 'We're not going out or anything like that, but there is someone I really like. Actually . . . I'm in love with him.'

Ellen, in love herself, was interested. 'What's his name?' she asked.

'Joe Wagstaff.' Erica was whispering now. 'He's Sally's brother. But you must swear not to tell her what I've just told you.'

Ellen nodded. She was thrilled that Erica was confiding in her. 'There's someone I like, too,' she said, and immediately wished that she hadn't. It sounded so unconvincing, as if she were trying to copy Erica.

'Yeah?'

Ellen could tell that Erica wasn't really interested though. She, on the other hand, would have loved to hear more. But: 'Stop talking! Line up in silence, please,' ordered their form-mistress.

Joe Wagstaff would have to wait.

OCTOBER

1961

Posters had gone up all around the town advertising the imminent arrival of Millington's Fair.

This fair came to Makerton twice a year, every May and October. Huge maroon-coloured caravans, brightly painted trucks and an assortment of trailers and generators would arrive on a Tuesday at the waste ground adjoining the market, and over the following few days all the rides and stalls would be erected ready for the weekend. The following Tuesday they would be dismantled again and the fair would move on to Turneley. No-one knew exactly where it went after that, but it always came back the next May and October.

The first time she'd been taken to the fair, when she was very small, Ellen had been frightened by the noise. 'I don't like it! I don't like it! I want to go home,' she'd cried – apparently. (It was a story her mother enjoyed telling – over and over again every May and October!) But Ellen had grown out of this fear long ago; she loved the fair now. And she loved it best of all in October, when the nights were dark and the bright lights showed up to best effect.

As soon as she saw the posters, she began counting down the days. And she wondered – as she always did when the fair came – whether she would see Hilda Millington again.

It was years ago now since the exciting occasion when Hilda and her cousin Lillian had attended St Wilfrid's School for the few days that the fair was in Makerton, but Ellen had never forgotten it.

* * *

The Fair girls had been put in Miss Long's class, and Ellen and Joan Grady had been given the privileged task of looking after them. Lillian, the younger of the two, with an Italian-sounding surname that no-one (not even Miss Long) could pronounce properly, was dark-haired and pretty, and had small golden hoops in her pierced ears which made her seem very exotic. She was very friendly and quite willing to answer the many questions the girls put to her about life on the fair. Yes, they lived in caravans. No, they didn't keep going on the rides all the time. No, they were not sisters but some sort of cousins. They went to school sometimes but not every week, and Lillian didn't mind whether she went or not.

The other girl, Hilda Millington, seemed much older – too old really to be in this class of nine and ten year olds. She had short, dusty-looking light hair and green, slanted eyes like a cat's. Whenever she looked at anyone – pupil or teacher – she would narrow these eyes slightly as if struggling to make sense of what she was seeing. Whenever she was asked a question she just shook her head or shrugged her shoulders. Lillian could read and write and do her sums, but Hilda sat impassively through all the lessons and activities – listening, watching blankly, attempting little. She hardly spoke a word all week. Everyone liked Lillian the best, but Ellen was fascinated by Hilda.

October, as well as being the month when the fair came, was also the month of the Holy Rosary and Miss Long had instructed all the girls in her class to bring their rosary beads to school every day so that they could say a decade of the rosary at the start of each morning and afternoon session. This didn't apply to the Fair girls, of course, but to Ellen's surprise, on their second day at school, Hilda produced a pair too. These were strange, scary beads – large black wooden ones, on a tarnished silver chain, with a rather too-graphic bleeding Jesus stretched out on a beaten metal cross. They were the sort of beads you might use to ward off Dracula were he ever to make a nocturnal visit to Millington's Fair.

'They're her grandma's,' said Lillian, no doubt feeling that some explanation was necessary.

As they were saying their decade of the rosary that morning, Ellen opened her eyes and, with a sidelong look, watched Hilda wielding the beads. It was obvious that she didn't know how to use them properly.

'I don't think they're really Catholics,' she whispered to Joan at playtime. 'I think they're just pretending to be.'

Whereupon Joan, much to Ellen's embarrassment, turned to the Fair girls and asked: 'Are you two really Catholics?'

'Yes!' said Lillian.

Hilda just shrugged.

Ellen's own rosary beads were her most prized possession at the time. Her Auntie Annie had given them to her recently as a present from Lourdes. They were beautiful – iridescent blue in colour, with oval shaped beads, a silver medal of Our Lady and a beautiful silver crucifix. They lived in a little pearlised box with a blue velvet lining.

That afternoon, while Miss Long was doing the register, Hilda suddenly reached across and took this little box from Ellen's desk. She opened it carefully, picked up the beads by the crucifix and let them fall into a coil in the palm of her hand. She placed the crucifix on top of the pile and then sat gazing into her palm as if she were reading her future.

Ellen was transfixed. A quiver of pleasure ran through her body. 'You can lend them if you want,' she said.

The class stood up, ready for the afternoon decade of the rosary. Hilda handed Ellen the black beads and began to finger the beautiful blue ones herself. All through the prayers Ellen worried that Hilda might have misunderstood her – that she might be thinking the swap was more permanent than had been intended. She didn't want to lose her lovely new rosary beads. And so immediately the prayers were over she put the horrible black ones back on Hilda's desk. With a slight sigh, Hilda dropped the beautiful blue ones into their box and, giving Ellen a long, grave look, passed this back too. Ellen smiled, and for a brief moment she thought Hilda was going to return the smile. There was the slightest of flashes in the green eyes . . . but they failed to light up and the blankness returned.

Lillian and Hilda left the school the following Monday afternoon and they'd never been back since. Every time the fair came Ellen looked for them and, on a couple of occasions, had caught glimpses of Lillian, but never of Hilda. Perhaps she no longer lived on the fair, she thought. But where else could a girl like Hilda Millington go?

* * *

This October, Ellen was also intending to go to the fair in Turneley – on Saturday afternoon, with Erica Latimer and some other girls from school. Erica had also invited her home for tea afterwards, which was something else to look forward to. But all that was over a week away. First there was the Makerton Fair, and she was hoping that this would provide the opportunity – at long last – for 'something definite' to happen between her and Michael Chadwell.

When Sandra Crompton had first started chalking up their initials, it'd seemed right to deny the charge. But, for reasons which now seemed ridiculous to Ellen, they'd persisted with their false denials to the point of paralysis. They'd had their moments, it was true: looks exchanged; little smiles; last year's Bonfire Night of course, and for a long time she'd been content with these. But she was thirteen-and-a-half now, she told herself. She'd been in love with him for two whole years. Something much more was needed.

On Friday evening, after tea, Ellen could hardly wait to get out of the house.

'What about your piano practice?' said her mother.

'There's not time now. I'll do extra tomorrow,' she said,

already on her way upstairs. She changed out of her uniform and then, kneeling down to see better, applied her eye-shadow in front of the dressing-table mirror. This done, she licked the tip of her little finger and flicked it under her eyelashes. She repeated this procedure a few times on both eyes until she was satisfied with the results.

Jennifer and Michael Chadwell were already waiting in the darkening backs for the McCanns to come out. But they didn't want to get to the fairground too early, before the big rides were switched on, so they all loitered there for a while, waiting for the right moment to leave. There was one place near Mrs Chisnall's back gate, where the top of the Big Wheel was just visible through a gap in the houses, and when they saw that going round it was time to go.

With Christine in tow, Ellen and Jennifer went on ahead of their brothers who had now been joined by Colin Hurst. It was a nuisance having Christine with them; there were some rides she was too young to go on, and someone would have to take her home early. But it was Ellen's intention to look after her for the first part of the evening and then get Michael to take her home. This would then leave her free to focus all her attention on Michael Chadwell . . .

First, Ellen took Christine on the swinging boats, and then all three of them went on the Noah's Ark. After this they walked around for a bit looking at the stalls. They bought some candy floss for Christine, which she was expected to stand and eat while Ellen and Jennifer went on some of the bigger rides. When she started complaining about this, they ignored her and so, bored with watching them whirling around on the Waltzer for the second time, she wandered off on her own.

When they came off their ride, she was nowhere to be seen. They started looking for her but the stalls and rides were so close together and the spaces between them so crowded with people that it was difficult to see very far or move very quickly. Ellen began to panic. I'll kill her when we find her, she promised herself, she's always doing this.

They came across the boys but none of them had seen Christine.

'She'll be all right,' said Michael McCann, with brotherly unconcern. 'She's not a baby. She'll find you herself.'

But this casual attitude only made Ellen even more agitated.

'Come on then, Mac,' said Jennifer. 'We'll go on the Big Wheel while Ellen keeps looking for her.'

She and Ellen had been on the Big Wheel many times before but neither of their brothers had, and the girls had agreed that tonight was the night to remedy this pathetic situation.

Mac hesitated, pretending now that he, too, was a bit worried about Christine.

'He's scared,' said Colin Hurst. 'I'll go on with you, if you like.'

'No I'm not!' said Mac.

'No you won't!' said Jennifer. She seized Mac's arm and started propelling him towards the very long queue for the Big Wheel.

'I'll help you look for your Christine if you want,' said Chad.

'Thanks,' said Ellen, wishing that Colin Hurst would go away.

It didn't take much longer for them to find Christine, but it seemed like an age to Ellen. As soon as she saw her sister, her anxiety gave way to fury and she grabbed hold of her and shook her hard. 'Where have you been, you - stupid - little - girl?' she shouted, above the noise of the fair.

People were turning round to look at them. Ellen, aware that Michael Chadwell was also witnessing this unseemly behaviour, stopped shaking Christine, who then proceeded to cry as loudly as Ellen had been shouting. It was a sound strategy because, in an effort to shut her up – and, presumably, to calm Ellen down – Chad offered to take her on the Dodgems, the nearest ride to where they were standing, and which just happened to be stationary. Christine immediately stopped crying and clambered aboard a car with him.

'Shall we go on too?' Colin Hurst asked Ellen.

'No! Go away!'

She was trying to regain her composure, but it wasn't easy. Each time their dodgem car went past, Christine, her head on Chad's shoulder, kept smirking pointedly at her, and Ellen, glaring back, was getting more annoyed by the minute. She would send Christine home after this, she thought. Then she could concentrate on Chad. 'Go on! Go away!' she said again to Colin Hurst who was still hanging around.

When the ride was over, Christine got out of the car, promptly lost her footing and fell flat on the floor of the Dodgem track. A collective murmur of concern arose from all the onlookers. Chad rushed over to her and lifted her back on to her feet. Fortunately, only her dignity was hurt – but the tip of her nose, her chin, hands, knees and the front of her coat were all covered in oil. She began to cry again.

'You stupid girl. Just look at you!' shrieked Ellen, horrified at this devastating sight. 'Look at your coat. My mam'll kill you.' People were still looking.

'She'll kill you for not looking after me properly,' wailed Christine, putting the final touches to her woeful appearance by wiping her tears with an oily hand.

'Go and get our Michael,' Ellen ordered Colin Hurst, who, having ignored her previous commands, was looking on with malicious glee.

Mac and Jennifer were hauled out of the queue just as it was nearly their turn to get on the Big Wheel.

'Just look at her!' cried Ellen to her brother. 'You'll have to take her home now. I've had enough of her!'

Mac pretended to be reluctant but didn't put up much resistance.

'I'll come with you,' said Chad, looking ruefully at his own oil-smeared hands.

Ellen could have wept.

'Shall we all go on the Big Wheel now, then?' asked Colin

as the trio disappeared off in a homeward direction.

'Why don't you take a running jump?' Ellen said, disappointment making her vicious.

Taking the hint at last, Colin wandered off into the crowd.

Jennifer did still want to go on the Big Wheel, though, so they went to join the queue. The fairground was packed now: music was blaring out above the thrumming noise of the machinery; lights were glaring and flashing; people on the Big Wheel were screaming in fright and delight. Ellen began to cheer up a bit.

A group of girls were walking towards the queue. Jennifer saw them first and nudged Ellen, nodding slightly in their direction. Amongst them were Joan Grady and Sheila Murphy. They were all laughing loudly about something but Joan stopped as soon as she caught sight of Ellen. Their eyes met, and instantly they both looked away. In doing so, however, Ellen inadvertently found herself looking straight at Sheila Murphy, who had also stopped laughing and was now staring back at her in an exaggerated way, curling her lip as she did so. Ellen flushed and turned away.

Oh, how she hated Sheila Murphy! She wished she would fall off the top of the Big Wheel and get broken into pieces. Well . . . perhaps not quite that. She wished she would be sick on the Waltzer, then – all over herself. I hate her! I hate her! I hate her! she thought, feeling miserable again.

The group of girls moved on, and the queue began to edge forwards. Soon she and Jennifer were on the Big Wheel, and as they soared up high above the fairground, things began to take on a different perspective. She would forget about Joan Grady and Sheila Murphy. She would enjoy the ride. And tomorrow she would try again with Michael Chadwell.

'I've spent too much money, tonight,' she said to Jennifer when they came off the Big Wheel. 'I'm going to win some back on a Roll-a-Penny stall and then I'm going home.'

The Roll-a-Penny stalls were a good remedy for overspending, if only you could make yourself walk away when you were winning. Ellen took four pennies out of her purse; she would use these and no more. She put the purse back into her jacket pocket out of temptation's way and, followed by Jennifer, walked over to the nearest stall. She placed her first penny on one of the wooden slides that poked through the wire mesh barriers separating the players from the playing boards. These boards were covered in numbered squares, and if your penny landed on one of them, you got that number of pennies back.

Ellen's penny rolled down the slide, went in a straight line and fell over on to a number three. Without waiting to be paid, she angled the slide and rolled her next coin. This one circled round casually before coming to rest on a number two. Feeling lucky now, she launched her third penny. It left the slide, described a wide arc, stayed balanced on its edge for an exciting moment and then toppled over just inside the one-shilling square. This was the highest paying square on the board. But was the penny in it – or was it just on the line?

The woman stall-holder, who was circling round, raking up pennies and doling out rewards, arrived at Ellen's segment. She was wearing a big dark coat with the collar turned up and black woollen gloves with the fingers cut off. She began to dole out the winnings. Three pennies, two pennies . . . Ellen held her breath, her eyes on the board. Would she get the shilling? There was an agonising delay . . . and then twelve pennies, in rapid succession, came shooting towards her. She gathered them together, looking up to smile gratefully at the woman. But it wasn't a woman; it was a girl. A girl with dusty fair hair whose green, slanted eyes flickered, almost imperceptibly, before she turned away.

Ellen, her own eyes wide now, turned to Jennifer: 'Did you see who that was?' she said. 'It was Hilda. Hilda Millington who came to our school that time. Don't you remember?'

Jennifer did, but only vaguely.

Without rolling any more pennies, they waited for Hilda to turn again in their direction. Yes, it definitely was her. Ellen was all ready to smile again, but Hilda just glanced at the empty board and continued her clockwork rotation. Ellen rolled her fourth penny, but her luck was over. It rolled right off the board and on to the ground. Exercising great discipline, she pocketed her winnings and, taking one last look at Hilda, she and Jennifer set off for home, leaving the bright lights, the throbbing noise and the loud music behind them.

There was, of course, more loud music to be faced when she got home, but her head was too full of Hilda Millington to be much bothered by this. She'd always envied Hilda her life on the fair, but now she wasn't so sure. How shabby and sad she'd seemed tonight, trapped in her stall. Poor Hilda.

She wondered if Joan Grady had seen her too.

It rained all day on Saturday and Mrs McCann, who hadn't yet fully recovered from the previous night's disaster and was not in the best of tempers, forbade all fair-going. So now, all Ellen's hopes in relation to Michael Chadwell rested on the final night of the fair. It was essential that nothing else should go wrong.

On Monday afternoon she hurried out of school, half ran to the bus stop and just managed to catch an earlier-than-usual bus home. Still wearing her school gabardine mac and her scarf, she went straight into the unheated front room to do her piano practice before tea. Her hands were cold and her playing was awkward. She needed some gloves like Hilda's, with the fingers cut off. But this probably wasn't the moment to go ruining a good pair. Her mother would undoubtedly see it as an act of provocation.

She ate her tea as quickly as she could and left the table while her mother, Michael and Christine were still eating. Seated in an armchair, with her books balanced on her lap, she did some conspicuous homework.

'You're rushing that,' her mother objected.

'I'm not. I've only got a bit to do, and I've nearly finished.'

'What about your homework?' Mrs McCann said to Michael.

'I did it on the bus.'

'I did it on the bus,' Ellen mouthed with a sneer, but Michael took no notice.

Thankfully, Mr McCann was taking Christine to the fair this time, so that was one less thing to worry about. Ellen packed her books away in her satchel and ran upstairs to get ready. After taking great care with her preparations, she ran back down again and, grabbing her jacket from the hall, managed to get out of the house before her mother had time to make her usual comments about her appearance. (The blue eye-shadow had been around for several months now, but Mrs McCann still hadn't resigned herself to it.)

Jennifer was determined to get the two, somewhat reluctant Michaels on to the Big Wheel this evening. 'You're frightened, aren't you?' she goaded them. 'They haven't got the guts, have they?' she said, trying to enlist Ellen's support.

What Ellen wanted, though, was proof of Michael Chadwell's love, not his courage. For her, it was a matter of the heart, not the stomach. And as Jennifer, holding on to Michael McCann's arm as if he were her prisoner, marshalled them into the queue, her own heart began to beat faster. Colin Hurst, however, was threatening to spoil things by assuming that he would be joining them.

'There's no room for you,' she protested.

'Yes there is. You can have three people on one seat. Look, there're three on that one, and that one,' he insisted, pointing.

This was true.

'Well you're not sitting with me and Ellen,' said Chad, and Ellen's heart pounded even more.

'OK then. You can come on with me and Mac,' said Jennifer who was not on a romantic mission.

Ellen and Chad got on first. It was all a bit of a scramble. As soon as the previous riders got off, they had to take their places quickly before the man in charge clicked the safety bar into place and off they went. Ellen readjusted her position slightly so that she was sitting a little nearer to Chad who was holding on to the bar with both hands. They went rocking backwards for a few feet before they stopped again and the other three piled on. Then, one seat at a time, they moved slowly onwards and upwards as more new riders got on board.

They rose into the air and came to a halt at the very top of the Wheel where the noise and the lights of the fairground seemed, momentarily, very far away. And where, if you looked over your shoulder, you could get a good view of the town. Ellen, well practised at this, twisted round to point out where their houses were, causing their seat to rock alarmingly and Chad to clutch the bar more tightly. Beneath and behind them, they could hear shouts and screams coming from Jennifer and Colin Hurst.

Ellen always found stopping at the very top of the Wheel to be the most disconcerting part of the ride. There were no points of reference to steady yourself by – just the night sky and the feeling of being suspended in space. Sometimes, if the stop was prolonged, she could begin to feel slightly panicky. Tonight, however, there were stars in the sky and Michael Chadwell was sitting beside her. Tonight she felt she could stay up there for ever.

The worst bit of the ride was coming over the top for the first time and dropping down towards the ground, but on their first revolution they didn't experience the full thrill of this as they were still stopping every few moments to let people off and on. The other three were above and slightly in front of them now and Jennifer turned round to wave down to them. Colin started doing the same and their seat began to rock violently. Mac's head, Ellen noticed, never moved. She smiled and waved back – but very carefully, so as not to alarm her own companion.

'Here we go!' she said as they moved on, slowly but without stopping this time. The Wheel gathered pace and they swung to the top and swooped down in an arc of pure sensation. Screams filled the air. Ellen hadn't intended to scream herself this time, but she couldn't help it. She could hear Jennifer screaming too. The next time round was even better as the Wheel was at full speed now. She abandoned herself to the moment.

After a few revolutions, the intensity of the thrill lessened and they settled down to enjoy the exhilaration of being scooped up into the darkness, of soaring through the air and then almost scraping the ground before rising again. Each time they swept past the control box with the enormous speakers the music was deafening. Then, when they rose into the air again, it seemed to fade away.

'Do you like it?' she asked Chad.

'Yeah, it's great,' he said, relaxing now. He put his arm across the seat behind her. She leaned back slightly and his hand closed on her shoulder.

All too soon, though, their ride was coming to an end. Ellen tried to ignore the deceleration but it was no use. The Wheel slowed to a stop and the process of disembarkation began. They had a last few moments at the summit before beginning their jerky descent.

Elvis was singing now, informing them that it was now or never. They glanced at each other shyly. Chad's arm tightened around Ellen's shoulder. Neither of them moved. Tomorrow, Elvis warned them, it would be too late, but it was already too late now, tonight. With one last lurch they reached the bottom of the ride and were unceremoniously tipped out of their seat. Before they had time to adjust to the situation, the other three came tumbling off after them and they were a group again.

None of the others seemed to notice that 'something definite' had almost occurred.

That night in bed, Ellen relived the Big Wheel ride over and over again. At first it was enough just to keep savouring the memory of it, but after a while she began to embellish it, adding little details here and there until, just before she fell asleep, it had become the most romantic interlude imaginable.

When she woke up the next morning, and the memory of the night before came surging back, she couldn't understand why she had wasted the night having that stupid dream about being late for her piano lesson again.

The following Saturday afternoon, Ellen had arranged to meet the other girls outside Higham's department store in Turneley. This was a popular meeting place as several buses, including the one from Makerton, stopped there. Angela Norris was already there waiting. She was wearing her school gabardine mac.

'Hi-ya,' said Ellen, registering this fact. She checked her own reflection in Higham's shop window and made a slight adjustment to the collar of her maroon wind-cheater jacket.

A few minutes later Erica arrived with Sally Wagstaff. Sally was wearing black ski-pants and an expensive-looking brown suede coat. Erica, her hair in a high pony-tail and not its usual plait, was wearing a chunky blue cardigan instead of a coat. Her eyes seemed much bluer than usual, which might have been due to the colour of this cardigan, or to the blue eye-shadow they were all wearing. Swiftly, but comprehensively, they all absorbed these details about one another before setting off in the direction of the market square.

'Where did you get that jacket from?' Erica asked, in such a neutral tone that Ellen couldn't tell whether she approved or disapproved of the garment.

'Manchester,' she replied – which wasn't strictly true. She'd got it out of her mother's catalogue, but she didn't want Erica to know that. The catalogue had a Manchester address though, so it wasn't really a lie. But it was definitely – and deliberately – misleading.

(It was like when Erica had asked her what her father did

and she'd said that he worked for the National Coal Board. She'd wanted Erica to think that he had an office job, whereas, in reality, Mr McCann worked at the pit. She supposed that Erica's father could be said to work for the National Health Service. But he was a doctor – a surgeon, at Turneley General Infirmary. And again, the other day, when they'd been talking about how difficult it was to get enough time in the bathroom without other people banging on the door and telling them to hurry up, she'd been very careful not to reveal the location of their bathroom. She'd definitely not wanted Erica to know that it was downstairs.)

Turneley's fair was much bigger than Makerton's. There were more rides and more stalls and Ellen kept looking for Hilda but she was nowhere to be seen. Sally seemed to have lots of money to spend but Erica had even less than Ellen, which was a relief. When their money ran out they lingered a while longer but it was getting colder as the afternoon wore on and Erica – who was coatless – decided that it was time to go. They said goodbye to Angela and set off for the Latimers' house.

Erica lived in Church Walk, only a short distance away in the direction of Turneley's large and splendid Jubilee Park. There was no church in Church Walk now but it was called this (Erica had once told Ellen) because in 'the olden days' it used to stretch all the way to the Parish Church, which was in the town centre, behind Higham's. When the park was built it bisected the road which became Church Street on the town side but remained Church Walk on the other.

It was a wide road lined with trees and, on this late October day, bestrewn with autumn leaves. There were several parked cars on both sides of the road. The houses were large, bay-windowed, three-storey terraces with small front gardens and big front doors.

(In the first year, when they'd been doing maps of their streets in a geography lesson, they'd had to go round the class stating their addresses and saying what type of house they lived in. Ellen, who answered before Erica, said her house was an end-of-terrace and blushed because most of the people who'd already answered had said theirs were semi-detacheds. She would've said semi-detached, too, (which strictly speaking an end-of-terrace was), had not her address been the somewhat incriminating King's Terrace. Erica, answering next, said hers was a mid-terrace. She only said 'mid' because Ellen had said 'end', which made it sound as though 14 Church Walk was a slightly more humble abode than 2 King's Terrace. Ellen knew that this definitely wasn't the case, even though she hadn't yet seen Church Walk. There were terraces and terraces. And from all the things that Erica had told her, it was obvious that there was a huge difference between their two houses. But Erica was totally unaware of this. She just assumed things; and Ellen was happy to let her.)

Sally lived just across the road from the Latimers, at number 17, but it seemed that she'd been invited for tea as well. Erica had a front door key, which impressed Ellen. None of the McCann children had a key because there was always someone in whenever they arrived home. There didn't seem to be anyone in this house now, but it was possible that there were people upstairs. Ellen's eyes swept up the rather grand oak staircase. The stairs at King's Terrace were wedged in between the living room and the front room and had just a modest handrail on one side.

Erica led them down the spacious, tile-floored hall, past the telephone on the hall table, and into the large kitchen. 'We're having tea, toast and honey – and cake!' she said, lifting the lid off a cake tin and looking pleased with its contents. She filled the kettle and put it on the stove to boil.

Sally took off her suede coat and draped it over the back of a chair, before going to help Erica make the toast. She seemed very at home here. Ellen removed her own jacket and stood around feeling awkward. There was a kitchen table with a long bench and four chairs around it, which was where they were going to have their tea. She sat down on one of the chairs.

They were busy devouring toast and honey when Maria
Latimer wandered in – the beautiful Maria, who (Erica had
told Ellen recently) was going to be a nun when she left
school. She was wearing navy-blue slacks and a black jumper.
Her long hair, which was brown but not as dark as Erica's,
was tied back loosely at the nape of her neck. She looked
almost demure, but there was something in the way her hair
was coming loose from its elastic band, and in the way she
held herself, that slightly belied this description. Ellen had
seen her often in school, but always at a distance. Close up
now, she could see three little chickenpox scars on her face.
She couldn't take her eyes off her. Maria, however, didn't
acknowledge Ellen's presence in any way. She took an apple
from the fruit bowl on the table, looked at it intently for a
moment, and then put it back again.

'Don't eat all that cake,' she said to Erica, glancing into
the open tin, 'or you'll be in trouble.'

'Do you want a piece?' asked Erica, lifting the cake out
and on to a plate.

'No thank you.' Maria reached for another cup and
saucer from the cupboard and poured herself a cup of tea
from the enormous teapot sitting in the middle of the table.
And then, hearing the front door opening, she went off,
taking her tea with her.

Mr Latimer and Erica's two younger brothers came in
carrying bags of groceries. They were accompanied by a
woman who, having hung up her coat in the hall, followed
them into the kitchen. This woman was wearing a black dress,
a chunky silver necklace and several large rings. Her hair was
in a French pleat and she was quite heavily made-up. Ellen
had no idea who she might be.

'Oh, you're home then,' said Mr Latimer, depositing his
bags on the table. 'Hello, Sally.' Sally, whose mouth was full
of toast, raised her hand in greeting. 'And hello . . .?' he
smiled turning to Ellen.

'Ellen,' she said.

'Hello, Sally. Hello, Helen,' said the woman.

'Hello,' said Ellen nervously. Feeling confused by the 'Helen', she heard herself breathing far too heavily on to the aitch of her own 'hello'.

Mr Latimer and the boys departed but the woman stayed and began unpacking the shopping.

'Why didn't you use the cake stand for this?' she said to Erica, picking up the knife and cutting the cake into six pieces.

Erica shrugged.

The three girls continued to eat in silence. When the woman had finished unpacking, she helped herself to a cup of tea from the pot and then, smiling brightly at them all, went out of the kitchen too.

'Who's that?' asked Ellen instantly. Erica didn't say anything.

'That's Maggie,' said Sally. 'She's a friend of the family.'

'She's not my friend,' muttered Erica, lifting the lid and peering into the depths of the tea-pot.

When they had finished eating they went into the dining-room. As well as a sideboard, and a large table and eight chairs, there was also a piano in here. Ellen went over to it and began fingering the keys. There was some music open on the stand but it looked very difficult. She sat down and began to play one of her last exam pieces from memory – Mozart's Sonata in C. The opening bars were very melodic with two small but impressive trills. The next bit, however, involved a series of fast runs which could be precarious without the music in front of her, so she stopped there. She knew that all the Latimer girls except Erica could play the piano. Erica had started to learn, but then had stopped. She hadn't said as much, but Ellen knew that this must have been when her mother died.

There was a gramophone in the dining-room too and Erica wanted them to listen to the new record she'd bought last week. It was Helen Shapiro singing Walking Back To Happiness. She sang along with this, very loudly, and they began to giggle. When they had had enough of Helen Shapiro they went into the sitting-room. Tom and James were in the kitchen now having their tea and Mr Latimer was with them. Erica must have thought that Maggie was in there too, but she wasn't. She was sitting on the sofa reading a magazine.

There were lots of photographs displayed around the room, some on the walls, others on tables and shelves. Ellen wondered if Mrs Latimer was in any of them, but didn't like to look too closely.

'Was that you playing the piano, Sally?' asked Maggie, smiling again.

'No, it was Ellen,' said Erica.

'Oh, really?' said Maggie, turning her smile on to Ellen. 'You should play some more for us.'

'She can't. She's got to go home soon.' Erica's tone was unmistakeably hostile now.

'And where is home, Helen?'

'Makerton,' said Ellen, trying not to make it sound like a confession.

Maggie nodded, slowly. 'Well, you must come again and play for us properly next time.'

Before Ellen could reply to this, the doorbell rang and the awkward little conversation came to an end. Erica, accompanied by Ellen and Sally, went to open the front door, and Claire Wagstaff, Sally's older sister, rushed in. With a quick 'hi' she dashed past them and bounded up the stairs. The three younger girls followed her up and into the big front bedroom that Maria and Erica shared.

'Go away,' said Claire. 'We've got things to discuss.'

'It's my room, too,' said Erica, sitting down on her bed. 'You go away.'

'We'll be going out soon,' said Maria.

'So will we.'

'You're just being tiresome now.'

'Yeah-ay-yeah!'

Maria sighed. 'Come on,' she said to Claire. 'Let's go up to Gina's room.'

They brushed past Ellen, who was standing in the

doorway, and disappeared up another flight of stairs to Georgina Latimer's unoccupied bedroom on the second floor.

(*'Combien de chambres à coucher y a-t-il dans votre maison?'* Mlle Perkins had asked them when they were in the first year.

'Il y a cinq chambres à coucher dans notre maison,' Erica had said.

'Il y a trois . . . ,' Ellen had replied, wondering how many she would have said if the sale de bain had been put upstairs and Michael's chambre à coucher had been downstairs in the front room.)

Claire Wagstaff, as well as being Maria's best friend, was also Joe Wagstaff's twin sister. Erica was still in love with Joe Wagstaff, but this was something that only Ellen knew. Sally had no idea. In fact, Sally must never know, because it was imperative that Joe Wagstaff should never know either – well, not yet, anyway. Some day, in the future, all would come to pass. In the meantime, she could brood over him, in secret, to her heart's content.

Erica went over to the bedroom window and looked out into the darkness. There was a very good view of the Wagstaffs' house from here and Ellen imagined that she was looking for Joe. She herself often did this at home. If she stood at the extreme right hand side of her bedroom window and squinted down to the left, she could just see the Chadwells' back gate (which was actually a side gate). It was a bit of a strain, though, and if she stood there for long, waiting to catch a glimpse of Michael, her eyes would begin to ache. She envied Erica her easy vantage point.

A few minutes later they heard Maria and Claire going back down the stairs.

'They're going to the fair,' said Sally, settling herself on Maria's bed. 'They won't bother us anymore.'

'Yeah-ay-yeah,' said Erica, turning away from the window and jumping on to her own bed. They began giggling again.

But soon Ellen had to go. This was the first time she'd

been allowed to stay in Turneley into the evening and she didn't want to jeopardise further outings by being late home. Erica and Sally decided to walk to the bus stop with her. She went to say goodbye to Mr Latimer and Maggie who were both in the kitchen now.

'Goodbye, Helen. It was nice to meet you,' said Maggie.

'Her name's Ellen, not H-Helen,' said Erica.

'Oh, I'm sorry, Ellen,' said Maggie. 'I thought . . .'

'You thought she couldn't pronounce her haitches,' said Erica.

'I thought she said Helen.'

'No. You thought she meant to say Helen but said Ellen instead.'

Ellen shifted her weight from one foot to the other, feeling awkward and embarrassed.

Maggie gave Erica a long, neutral look. 'I thought she said Helen,' she said again, very quietly this time. And then, a little less neutrally: 'And it's aitch, not haitch.'

Erica laughed. 'Is it?' she said. 'His – hit - really? Eey, by gum!'

'Erica!' said Mr Latimer.

'Yeah,' said Erica defiantly. 'Yeah-ay yeah!'

As they were walking down the road towards the town centre, they caught up with Maria, Claire and . . . ! Erica clutched Ellen's arm and nudged her meaningfully. So the boy walking with them must be Joe Wagstaff! But it was dark and Ellen, not wishing to be caught staring, only managed to get a glimpse of him as they scuttled past. Tall, fair-haired, possibly handsome.

She did, however, get a better look at Maria. Her long hair was loose now and hanging round her shoulders. She was wearing eye-shadow and lipstick. She looked very grown up, very attractive. But was this how a prospective nun should look? It seemed inappropriate, somehow – sacrilegious almost.

Ellen sat upstairs on the bus feeling very grown up. Most people were coming into Turneley at this time of evening, not leaving it, and the bus was nearly empty. Across the road, she could see lots of people waiting outside Higham's for their dates to arrive. She imagined a future time when Michael Chadwell would be waiting there for her – but that didn't make sense, really, since they would both be coming into Turneley on the same bus from Makerton.

She spent the homeward journey thinking about Maggie. Who was she? Was she Mr Latimer's girl-friend? Why hadn't Erica ever mentioned her before? Did she live with them? She would have to wait until Monday for answers to all these questions. But she would have to get Sally on her own and ask her, because she felt sure that Erica wouldn't tell her what she wanted to know, otherwise she would have done so already.

Maggie was obviously not a subject for discussion. Like Mrs Latimer, whom Erica also never mentioned.

NOVEMBER

1963

November, the month of the Holy Souls and Guy Fawkes, was the month of death.

In spite of its grim undertones, however, Bonfire Night was a festive occasion and for Ellen it used to be the highlight of the month. When it was over – which all too soon in the month it was – there was little else to look forward to until Christmas. Every year, she used to pray for good weather because a wet or windy fifth of November could mean that there would be no bonfire at all in their backs. Sometimes her prayers were answered; sometimes they were not.

'Guy Fawkes was a Catholic, remember,' her father had said one year when God (also a Catholic) had blighted the night with storm and tempest. This fact, however, did not account for all the other fine Bonfire Nights.

Remember, remember the Fifth of November, Ellen thought as she stood at her mother's bedroom window and looked down on to the croft – the small piece of waste ground where the Ashburne Road, King's Terrace and Turneley Road backs converged. In previous years they'd had some great bonfires here, but tonight it was in darkness because Mrs Chisnall, their next door neighbour, was dying.

Yes, there had been many wonderful Bonfire Nights. But one in particular had certainly been a night to remember. She smiled as the memory of it came back to her now, so vividly that it seemed to light up the dark croft below. She'd only been twelve at the time – and still very much in love with Michael Chadwell.

* * *

They'd started collecting stuff for this bonfire in October, as soon as the fair had left. Colin Hurst's father, who was a plasterer, was a good source of material. He brought home vanloads of old doors, floorboards and skirting boards and stored them at the bottom of their yard in the small outhouse known as the cubby-hole, next to the outside lavatory. Once this was full, other cubby-holes were required. Storage was always a problem. Backyards were small, and space – especially covered space – was limited. And it was covered space that was needed because if it rained and things got too wet, the fire wouldn't light on the night.

When the McCanns had had their bathroom extension built they had lost their cubby-hole and Mac, who was one of the commanders-in-chief this year, felt this lack of space keenly. It was hard giving orders to other people when you couldn't lead by example.

There were other bonfires round and about and sometimes rival gangs of children would come and raid their yards and steal their wood. One such gang, from further up Turneley Road where Sandra Crompton lived, was always doing this. It was infuriating.

After one particularly bad raid they all congregated in the backs to assess the damage. Quite a lot of wood had been taken from two of the Ashburne Road yards and, of course, the Turneley Road gang were the chief suspects.

'We'll have to raid them back,' said Colin Hurst. 'We can't let them get away with this again.'

'We don't know for certain it was them,' said Ellen, surveying their depleted stock. 'It could have been that lot up Kimberley Road.'

'We'll raid them as well,' said Mac recklessly. 'We need to get back as much stuff as we can.'

Ellen felt that this might be unfair. Just retribution was one thing; pillage another. But it was no use appealing to the boys' moral sensibilities. This was war now, in which all things were fair.

Days of reconnaissance followed before it was agreed that they should forget about Kimberley Road (which was too far away) and just concentrate on Turneley Road. Mac was sent on an information gathering exercise to Sandra Crompton, to find out where they were storing their wood. With very little prompting she told him what he wanted to know, and then he beat a hasty retreat.

They decided they would launch one main attack on the yard where, according to Sandra, a huge amount of wood was being stored. A date was set and a plan drawn up.

'Me and Ellen are coming, too,' said Jennifer, 'so don't think we're not.' There were mutterings of male dissent.

'They'll be all right,' said Chad.

Ellen gave him a little smile.

'Well you can't come looking like that,' protested one of the boys from Ashburne Road, pointing at Jennifer's bright pink scarf and her shocking pink socks. 'They'll see us coming a mile off. You'll have to wear something else.'

'Of course I will. I'm not stupid, you know,' she retorted.

'And you'll have to do what we tell you. And no arguing,' said Colin Hurst who had been even more overbearing than usual recently but had been getting away with it because his father had been such a good supplier of wood.

Jennifer shrugged.

'Can I come, too?' asked Christine.

'No! You're too young. No-one under ten can come,' ruled Ellen. 'It's too dangerous.'

On the night of the raid Ellen and Jennifer appeared in their darkest clothes. Jennifer was carrying two balaclavas.

'Look at these,' she said. 'I remember our Michael

wearing these when he was little.' She put one on. 'Here,' she said, offering the other to Ellen. 'You wear this one, then they can't say we're not properly dressed.'

'No, I don't need it,' said Ellen, reluctant to look so unbecoming in Michael Chadwell's presence. 'My hair's dark anyway, and I've got my scarf.'

'OK,' said Jennifer, putting the superfluous balaclava on the McCanns' front hedge, to be retrieved later.

After one last briefing they all set off. The backs were very dark. Once beyond the range of the lamp-post outside the McCanns' house they could hardly see where they were going. Jennifer had a torch but had been forbidden to use it yet. It was for unforeseen circumstances only. As they advanced further into enemy territory, they kept bumping into each other in the darkness and the two girls began to get the giggles.

'Shut up!' hissed Colin. 'They'll hear us coming.'

Another few yards and they'd arrived at their target. Ellen pulled her scarf up over her nose. Jennifer switched on the torch and held it under her chin. She nudged Ellen, who started giggling again when she saw the weird effect this was creating.

'Shut up!' said the commander-in-chief. 'And turn that stupid torch off!'

The plan was for Mac to climb over the gate which, according to Sandra, would be bolted on the inside. Once over, he would unbolt it and Chad and Colin would go into the yard with him to locate the booty. Then, forming a chain, they would pass out planks of wood to the others. When they were loaded up, they were to run back home as quickly as they could. 'Don't try to carry too much,' Mac had warned the girls. 'You'll only drop it.' But they were determined to carry as much as the boys.

Ellen began clenching and unclenching her gloved hands in readiness for the task ahead. They all stood and watched as Mac climbed on to the gate, using the latch as a foothold. This released the catch, and the gate – which wasn't bolted after all – swung open, taking him with it into the yard. Ellen and Jennifer began to giggle again. Swearing quietly, he dropped to the ground. Chad and Colin slipped in after him, and then two unplanned things happened in quick succession.

First, two small figures emerged out of the darkness. Jennifer fumbled for her torch and shone it on to Paul Hurst and . . . Christine, who was wearing the abandoned balaclava and so wasn't immediately recognisable. Unable to resist the lure of adventure, they'd disobeyed orders and had followed their elders at a discreet distance.

'What're you doing here?' said Ellen in a rasping whisper. 'Go away! Go on! Go back home!'

But before either of them could respond, the second thing happened. Loud barking was heard coming from the house next door to the one they were raiding. This was followed by the rattle of a door opening. Then the dog, barking all the while, rushed down the yard and threw itself at the gate. It sounded enormous.

'Run!' said Colin, appearing with a plank of wood in his hands. He thrust it at one of the other boys and then, obeying his own command, proceeded to lead the retreat.

Mac grabbed hold of Christine's hand, Chad grabbed Paul's and they all began to run as fast as they could. It was very exciting, running so quickly in the darkness over the uneven cobble-stones. Ellen's heart was pounding in her ears almost drowning out the sounds of footsteps, shouts and frenzied barking from behind them.

They were nearly back on home territory when the dog caught up with them. Still barking, it began circling round Ellen, snapping at her ankles. She stopped running and started screaming. Three boys came panting on to the scene. One of them grabbed the dog; another one grabbed Ellen.

'Get – off – her,' shouted Jennifer, hitting him with her torch. She looked very threatening in the balaclava.

Chad let go of Paul Hurst and came rushing over. 'Get off her,' he shouted too, thumping the boy on the shoulder with one hand and grabbing hold of Ellen's arm with the other. Disconcerted to discover that it was a girl he'd caught, the boy let go of her and advanced upon Chad instead. The dog, which wasn't as big as it'd sounded, was still barking furiously.

'What were you doing in our yard?' this boy said, thrusting his face into Chad's.

'Getting our own back,' said Colin Hurst, taking a few steps forward, full of bravado now. The boy ignored him and continued to stare at Chad who held his gaze and began pushing him away up the backs.

'Stop picking on girls,' he said, glancing sideways at the dog which was growling now. 'Coward!'

There was a brief moment of suspense, when anything might happen next, and then the three boys moved away into the darkness, uttering threats as they went.

'Are you all right?' Chad asked Ellen, touching her on the arm.

She nodded. She was shaking – from a mixture of shock and elation. Jennifer came and put a protective arm around her.

'I'm all right,' Ellen assured her. (I'm in love with your brother!)

They congregated around the Hursts' back gate and by the light of Jennifer's torch surveyed their loot – one solitary plank of wood. But Ellen didn't care. For her the evening had been a great success. She was in love with Michael Chadwell. He had rushed to her rescue. He was in love with her, too.

On the night itself, they'd all agreed that they wouldn't light their bonfire until seven o'clock but at twenty past six, when they could see the glow of other fires in the sky, they couldn't wait any longer. And as the flames took hold and fireworks began to go off all around, Ellen felt a great surge of happiness. This was what she had been looking forward to for weeks.

Lots of people came out and gathered in groups round the fire, ooh-ing and aah-ing at the many firework displays on show. Rockets whooshed up into the night sky; gold and silver fountains cascaded on to the ground, and sparklers danced in the air. Catherine Wheels, pinned to gate-posts, whirled round and round, furiously at first before gradually fizzling out, and bangers exploded with a heart-stopping violence which Ellen hated (although it didn't do to admit as much). Fathers attended to the fire and set off the bigger, more dangerous fireworks, while mothers hovered and fussed. And the bonfire roared and blazed, sending out sparks and the occasional cloud of smoke that made their eyes water and their throats tickle.

After a while, the fire settled down to a comfortable glow. Chairs were brought out and food and drink began to appear. There were fewer fireworks now, from theirs as well as neighbouring sites.

At about eight o'clock, Sandra Crompton appeared with an older boy. His arm was draped nonchalantly around her shoulder; his hand (they couldn't help but notice) was dangling perilously close to her right breast, which, alongside its partner, was thrusting out proudly from beneath a tight jumper. When Sandra saw Michael McCann looking at her, she reached up and took hold of this hand whilst simultaneously sliding her other arm round the boy's waist.

'What do *you* want?' Mac asked. They all gathered in a group, closing ranks to prevent her advancing any further. She looked scornfully at their bonfire.

'It's not as good as ours, is it?' she said, looking up at her consort. He shook his head. 'It'll be out soon,' she continued, sniffing.

'We've got loads more stuff to put on it,' said Mac. 'We've got enough to last till midnight.'

'I bet you've not!'

'Yes we have!'

'Ours is much better than this, isn't it?'

The boy nodded again.

'Well shove off back to it, then,' said Jennifer. 'We don't want you hanging round here.'

Sandra sniffed again and with a mocking smile began to steer her companion away. As the amorous couple were departing, Mac lit a large, loud Jumping Jack firework, which zigzagged up the backs after them, forcing them apart as they leapt out of its way.

Ellen stood watching them go. She glanced at Chad, wishing that he would put his arm around her shoulder like that, or at least hold her hand. But perhaps not here with everyone looking.

Jennifer went off to get some of her mother's treacle toffee and the others drifted back to the fire. But Chad lingered.

'I bet their fire's useless,' said Ellen, looking up to where they could see its glow in the sky.

'Shall we go and have a look?' Chad said, just as Jennifer returned with a bag of the toffee. He didn't take any, but Ellen did – realising too late what a dreadful mistake this was. Within seconds, her teeth were stuck together in its vice-like grip. Jennifer moved away to offer the toffee to other people, and Chad stood waiting for Ellen to reply to his suggestion. She tried to speak but her jaw was immobilised. She tried to start chewing, but it was almost impossible.

'We could go up Turneley Road and have a look from Benson's entry, and then they wouldn't see us,' said Chad tentatively, obviously not quite knowing how to interpret her silence.

Ellen tried again to say 'yes' but couldn't. She nodded instead and, just in case he hadn't seen this, began walking in the direction he'd just suggested. All the time, she was trying hard to dislodge the toffee with her tongue, but to no avail. Before they reached the lamp-lit street she made a surreptitious – but equally futile – attempt with her finger. It felt as if her teeth were being extracted along with the toffee and so she gave up. She wondered how long it would take to melt away of its own accord. Weeks probably. She could have wept. Wiping her sticky finger on the side of her jacket, she tried chewing again.

They were on Turneley Road now, well away from everyone. Chad had his hands in his pockets but Ellen kept her left arm by her side, all ready should he decide to make a move and take her hand. She tried to will him to do so. A series of rockets went up in front of them and when they looked up into the sky to watch their progress, they bumped into each other slightly. They moved apart at once, but Ellen's arm was on fire.

'Look at that!' said Chad, taking his hand out of his pocket to point towards another part of the sky where another spectacular display was taking place. He didn't return this hand to his pocket but left it hanging stiffly, an inch or so from hers. She could feel the magnetic force between them. He was going to hold her hand, perhaps kiss her! But the treacle toffee was still in her mouth and she panicked and crossed her arms over her chest. They continued up the road, Ellen chewing furiously.

The toffee was nearly gone by the time they reached the narrow entry at the side of Benson's shop. They were in enemy territory now.

'Let me go first,' said Chad, stepping in front of her off the street and into the dark alleyway.

At the other end of this they had a good view of the rival bonfire. It was all right – but definitely not as good as theirs. Sandra Crompton and her friend were nowhere to be seen. There were a lot of other people around though and so, unnoticed, they stepped out of the entry and began to make their way home down the backs, passing the house they'd tried to raid on the way.

Once away from the brightly lit scene, they slowed their pace. Their hands touched again but this time neither of them moved away. He's going to hold my hand now, thought Ellen, slowing down even more. And the slower they walked, the faster her heart raced. Should she take his hand? No, he had to be the one to make the first move. Would he? Yes, he was holding her hand! They had stopped walking altogether, neither of them noticing that Colin Hurst and Jennifer were coming towards them in the darkness, until they heard Colin's voice.

'What're you two doing here?' he said, and they leapt apart. 'Have you been to look at their bommy?' Then, suspiciously and with a leer: 'What are you up to, eh?'

'Nothing,' said Chad. 'It's not worth looking at, is it?'

Ellen shook her head.

'It's nearly out, isn't it?'

Ellen nodded.

'Come on, let's go back then, if it's not worth it,' said Jennifer, taking hold of Ellen's arm. 'Do you want some more toffee?'

'No! – thank you.'

Ellen, getting ready for bed later that evening, gazed at herself in the bathroom mirror. Her eyes were bright and her face was flushed from the combination of the cold night air and the warmth of the bonfire. She looked very nice. She moved closer to the mirror and kissed her reflection, her breath steaming up the glass. She looked even better like this, she thought, all misty and romantic. Then the word 'immodest' flitted across her consciousness and she wiped the mirror with the sleeve of her pyjamas.

She raised her toothbrush to her mouth and then gazed – in horror this time – at the two rows of bared black teeth that were confronting her in the mirror. Oh, no! The treacle toffee! They looked awful! When she'd smiled at Michael Chadwell across the dying embers of the fire, just before coming in, had she smiled with her lips parted or closed, she wondered? She smiled now with them shut tight, but it felt awkward; it was not her usual way of smiling. But then neither was the double-rowed grimace she adopted when cleaning her teeth. She tried her usual lips-slightly-parted smile. No, no! She moved as far away from the mirror as the dimensions of the bathroom would allow, and smiled again. Would he have noticed them from this distance? It was hard to say. In despair, she brushed the offending teeth as hard as she could, soon restoring them to their usual shade of white. No amount of brushing, though, could erase the tragic image from her mind.

Thinking things over as she lay in bed, she decided not to let the memory of her black teeth haunt her. When Chad had held her hand he couldn't possibly have seen them. It had been a beautiful moment. She loved him so much, and now she was absolutely sure that he loved her too.

Assuming the authority that went with authorship, she re-ran the story of the evening again, this time transferring the black teeth on to Sandra Crompton. And in this revised version, where Colin and Jennifer hadn't interrupted them . . .

* * *

Ellen's smile widened, amused by these memories of her younger self. She turned away from the window and studied herself in her mother's dressing-table mirror. Michael Chadwell had been her first love, but she hardly ever saw him these days, hardly ever thought about him anymore. He had been her childhood sweetheart – but she was no longer a child. She'd stopped 'playing out' ages ago. And there were other boys claiming her attention now.

Since the beginning of term – since they'd been in the fifth year – she and Erica had been spending Friday and Saturday evenings in Turneley. Sometimes they went to the pictures, but mostly they went to the Cellar Bar. This was a below-ground establishment on Duke Street. It was two bars really: a large, alcohol-serving one, that had a small stage area upon which 'acts' of various kinds performed at intervals throughout weekend evenings; and – somewhat incongruously – further along a narrow corridor, a rather dingy coffee bar whose only attraction was its rather edgy, subterranean ambiance. It had a rather claustrophobic atmosphere but Ellen and Erica, used to their basement cloakrooms at school, felt very much at ease there.

They'd started going to the Cellar because Sally had told Erica that Joe Wagstaff and his friends were often to be found there. So they would go and sit at a nearby table, from where Erica, with a great show of nonchalance, could observe his every move. He hadn't been there for a few weeks, though, which was disconcerting for her. But there were other boys. And you could spend the whole evening surveying them and being surveyed, all for the price of two glasses of orange juice – one even, if the woman behind the counter wasn't being vigilant.

Strictly speaking they were under age, the coffee bar in the evenings being an extension of the main bar, but they'd never been challenged on this point. Indeed, no-one there knew just how young they were (except Joe Wagstaff, of course). Everyone else was at least sixteen, and they said they were nearly seventeen if anyone asked – which they rarely did.

Yes, she was grown up now, she thought, turning away from the mirror. She had outgrown bonfires; and she had outgrown Michael Chadwell.

She knew she should go and do some homework, but she wandered into her own bedroom and lingered a while at the window in there, watching the aerial firework displays in the distance. Then she closed the curtains and went downstairs. There was nobody else in the house. Her father had taken Christine to a bonfire at the Makerton Labour Club, and her brother was out somewhere – probably with Michael Chadwell. Her mother was next door sitting with Mrs Chisnall.

Poor Mrs Chisnall had been ill for quite some time, but she was much worse now. Everyone was saying that it was just a matter of time, the end was in sight. It made Ellen shiver whenever she heard this – just as it did when her father said, every autumn, that the nights were drawing in. It sounded so portentous.

Mrs Chisnall had been a widow for as long as any of them could remember. She had a son, but he lived away and hardly ever visited her. 'We don't see much of your Frank these days,' Mrs Entwistle from across the road kept saying, but Mrs Chisnall wouldn't hear a word against him. 'He's got an important job,' she would say. 'It's hard for him to get away.' Ellen had no idea what this important job might be.

Apparently he had always been the apple of his mother's eye, a late child upon whom she had always doted. Out of her hearing, though, Frank Chisnall was spoken of with contempt. 'He'll be up here fast enough when she's dead and gone and there's a house to be sold,' Mrs Entwistle said. And no-one disagreed with her.

Mrs Chisnall was bed-ridden now, a prisoner in her downstairs front room, and the job of caring for her was shared out among those of her neighbours who were willing to help. They took turns to take meals in for her and to do her little bits of shopping and washing. They administered her medication and emptied her commode in the outside lavatory (Mrs Chisnall had no bathroom extension). And sometimes they went in just to sit with her. The district nurse had taken to calling every day, and the doctor every few days. She dreaded the thought of ending up in hospital, or, even worse, in a 'home'. 'Don't let them put me away,' was her constant plea.

On several occasions over the past few months she had fallen in the night and been found on the floor the next morning, bruised, cold and confused. Following these falls, she had been in hospital a few times, but had always wanted to get back home as soon as possible. 'She won't be coming out this time,' people said after the last such incident – but she did.

Every evening her fire would be banked up in the grate and the fireguard fastened in place, and then she would be locked up alone in the house until morning when one or other of her neighbours would go in early to see to the fire and make her breakfast, ever fearful of what they might find.

'Don't let them take me away again,' she said, one day at half-term, when Ellen and Christine had been sent in with her dinner. Christine, embarrassed, began to giggle.

'You won't let them take me away again, will you, love?' she repeated, clutching at Ellen's arm.

'No. No, I won't let them,' said Ellen, upset and horrified.

Mrs Chisnall also had a nephew, Alan Bentley, a big, bluff, middle-aged man who lived in Ashburne and who, unlike Frank, did come to visit her from time to time. He came to 'cheer her up' though, not to help with the chores.

He came once when Ellen was in there.

'I wish the good Lord would take me, Alan,' Mrs Chisnall whispered to him.

'Now you know you don't mean that, Auntie Mildred,' he boomed, 'because He does keep coming for you, but you won't go with Him!'

'I'll go when I'm good and ready,' she retorted, with a flash of her old spirit. She had been cheered up.

But the doctor had begun saying that if she got any worse she would really have to go into hospital: she needed round the clock care, now.

'Poor old soul,' said Mrs McCann. 'It'll break her heart.' And Ellen knew that her mother was hoping and praying that the end would come sooner rather than later so that Mrs Chisnall might die in her own home.

Often, when they got home from school, their mother wasn't there.

'She's not in Mrs Chisnall's *again*, is she?' Christine complained.

None of them liked coming home to a motherless house but Ellen was moved by her mother's care and compassion. 'It's not her fault,' she snapped. 'Don't be so selfish!'

But Christine continued to moan.

'You'll be old, yourselves, one day,' said Mrs McCann, later, when she came home.

Ellen tried to do some homework but the noise from the fireworks was distracting. She wondered if Mrs Chisnall was being disturbed by all the commotion. Her mother, she knew, was staying with her longer than usual tonight so that she wouldn't be afraid.

'Poor old soul,' Mrs McCann said again, when eventually she did return. Ellen's eyes filled with tears. She felt her mother's profound sadness and her own unworthiness. She vowed to herself that she would do more to help from now on.

Less than a week later, however, the good Lord came again for Mrs Chisnall, and this time she slipped away with Him in the night. She was found the next morning by Mrs Entwistle who reported that in death she looked very peaceful; there were no signs of suffering. Everyone was relieved.

'It's for the best,' said Mrs McCann. 'God rest her soul!'

But to Ellen it seemed so very sad that poor Mrs Chisnall had died all alone, locked up in that dark house, with the fire going out in the hearth.

For the rest of the week, like all the other neighbours, they kept their curtains drawn at the front of the house. Also, no piano playing was allowed, even though Mrs Chisnall's body was not next door but at the chapel of rest – and even though she'd always liked hearing it when she'd been alive.

This didn't affect Ellen who, a few months ago, had given up having piano lessons. Her initial enthusiasm had long since waned and she'd been wanting to give up for ages. Yet, in spite of the fact that her reluctance to practise had become a constant source of strife in the household, Mrs McCann had wanted her to continue, and it'd taken Ellen a long time to go against her mother's wishes. Eventually, though, she did. She sent a note with Christine, who was having lessons now, too. *Dear Mrs Walker,* she wrote. *Due to pressure of schoolwork I have decided to discontinue my piano lessons. Thank you very much for teaching me. Yours sincerely, Ellen McCann.*

'Hmmph,' her mother said when she found out. 'What a waste of time and money that's been, then. And talent.'

But Ellen didn't care.

There would be no Albert Hall outing for poor Mrs

Chisnall now, anyway.

Ellen took the morning off from her Saturday job at Teller's Confectioners so that she could accompany her mother and Christine to Mrs Chisnall's funeral.

Alan Bentley had taken care of all the arrangements. The mourners had been instructed to congregate in Mrs Chisnall's house – some in her front room where the bed in which she had died was still lodged under the window – to await the arrival of the hearse. As they filed in, an array of floral tributes impeded their progress along the narrow hallway.

Frank Chisnall, who had arrived the night before, greeted them as they arrived. ''Ow do, Cyril . . . Mrs Entwistle,' he said.

Mr Entwistle grasped Frank's hand in both of his own. 'Now then, lad,' he said gruffly.

'I hardly recognised you Frank, it's been that long,' said Mrs Entwistle.

'Not that long,' Frank protested, grinning and winking at Ellen whom he had not immediately recognised at first sight, thinking that Christine, who had preceded her into the house, was her. Ellen smiled back. Frank Chisnall, she could see, was a bit of a charmer.

'It's been long enough,' persisted Mrs Entwistle. 'Too long, if you ask me.'

'Leave the lad alone,' said her husband. 'This isn't the time or the place.'

'How's your Jack?' asked Frank. He and Jack Entwistle had been childhood friends. Ellen had seen one of Mrs Chisnall's photos of them, taken at school. Two skinny lads in short trousers. Frank had certainly bulked up since then.

'He's doing all right,' said Cyril. 'He sends his condolences.'

The hearse arrived bearing the wreath-strewn coffin and they all spilled out of the house and into the funeral cars. The procession moved slowly along King's Terrace and on to Turneley Road. People stopped to stare and older men removed their hats and caps as it passed. It continued into the High Street and on to St Luke's Parish church.

The service was short (no Requiem Mass in this Protestant church) and fairly anonymous (Mrs Chisnall had never been a great church-goer). They sang *Abide With Me*, which Ellen loved, and then went outside and gathered round the open grave for the burial. It was a bitterly cold, grey day. Ellen felt herself shaking with cold and emotion.

In Loving Memory of a Dear Husband and Father
she read on the headstone.

Alfred William Chisnall
1883 – 1927

Mr Chisnall had died in an accident down the pit when Frank was only a baby. 'They'd not been back five minutes,' she remembered hearing Mr Entwistle saying to her father once, referring to the Miners' Strike. 'She took it bad. It was only having their Frank that pulled her through and kept her going.' But after the War when Frank was demobbed (so the received wisdom had it) he'd never settled down. He'd become 'a wanderer'. So what, Ellen wondered, had kept her going since then?

Poor Mrs Chisnall! She'd always made a fuss of the McCann children when they were little. They'd loved going into her house to eat scones and Eccles cakes when she'd been baking. She'd had a dog, too, that they used to play with. But Buster had got old and died (Ellen and Christine had cried for hours when they were told) and then Mrs Chisnall had been all on her own. And after she'd got ill they hadn't been so keen to go in anymore. They hadn't wanted to keep her company when she'd most needed it. And now it was too late.

The tears ran down Ellen's face – the mascara had been a mistake, but she hadn't foreseen this access of emotion. As the coffin was lowered into the gaping hole in the ground, she gave a shuddering sob and felt her mother's steadying hand on her arm. Christine began to cry too. Ellen looked across at Frank Chisnall who was standing with his head bowed, for the moment locked in grief. Mr Entwistle, who was standing just behind him, had his hand on Frank's shoulder. Ellen sobbed again, more loudly this time, and covered her face with her hands.

Straight after tea on the Friday after Mrs Chisnall's funeral, Ellen began her usual getting-ready-to-go-out ritual. The bathroom, in spite of the paraffin heater in there, was very cold in the winter and so after she'd bathed in the bath salts specially reserved for these going-out nights she went into the warm living room to put on her make-up and do her hair.

Mr McCann and Christine were watching the television, and Ellen was half watching it too through the mirror on the wall above the sideboard as she attended to her face. Lips had to be very pale and eyes very dark now. She began applying her brown eye-shadow, black eye-liner and black mascara. Christine turned sideways on the couch and watched her critically.

'She's putting too much black round her eyes again,' she reported to no-one in particular.

Mrs McCann, coming in from the kitchen, tutted reflexively. But Ellen just spat into her mascara again and made a paste with her little brush. She wasn't going to rise to this provocation.

She saw the newsflash through the mirror. President Kennedy had been shot in Dallas in Texas. Arrested, she turned round to stare directly at the television screen. Mr McCann, who had been dozing off, sat up straight in his armchair.

'The Lord have mercy on us,' said Mrs McCann, sitting down heavily on the couch beside Christine.

Ellen missed her usual bus and was ten minutes late arriving outside Higham's to meet Erica. It was a sombre evening. They sat in the depths of the Cellar Bar, their dark clothes matching the solemnity of the occasion, feeling shocked and uncertain. Was the president dead, they wondered? 'Yes, he's dead. It said so on the telly,' someone told them. What did it mean? What would happen now?

Just before nine o'clock, Sally Wagstaff and her boyfriend, Steve, arrived. They'd been intending to go to the pictures but had stayed at Sally's to watch the news and now it was too late, so here they were instead. Erica looked at Ellen, flaring her nostrils and raising an eyebrow slightly. Ellen gave her the faintest of smiles in return. The message was clear enough. Sally, with her pale blue jumper and matching eye-shadow, her hair back-combed high on her head, and Steve, with his short, neat hairstyle and smart clothes, were not in tune with the surroundings. They were an embarrassment and Erica was not pleased to see them.

Sally, happily unaware of this, took out a gold packet of Benson and Hedges cigarettes and offered them round the table, while Steve supplied them with more details of the motorcade death in Dallas. Erica sat with her head bent and her hair falling forward, hiding her face. She wasn't smoking the cigarette she had in her hand but kept flicking ash from it into the ashtray. Ellen, watching her, wondered if she was thinking about her mother's car death.

The evening wore on.

'God, this is depressing,' said Steve, looking round with distaste.

'Don't stay here then,' said Erica, stubbing out her second cigarette.

'Everywhere's the same,' he said. 'Nothing ever happens in Turneley.'

'It does sometimes,' said Ellen, annoyed by this feigned cynicism. 'The Stones are coming on Wednesday night, for one thing. And – me and Erica have got tickets!'

But Steve, not a fan of the Rolling Stones, was unimpressed. 'Turneley's hell,' he persisted.

'No, it's not,' said Erica. 'But if you really hate it so much then go and live somewhere else. Please.'

'I will, as soon as I can. Don't you worry.'

'Good,' said Erica, and then, in a half-hearted attempt to

gloss over her rudeness: 'You can always get out of Turneley, you know, but you can't get out of hell. Once you're there, you're there for ever.' She paused. 'For ever and ever,' she intoned ghoulishly.

'Turneley's purgatory, then,' said Sally.

But Steve, probably unfamiliar with the concept of purgatory, ignored this remark. 'Let's go and have a drink in the other bar,' he suggested.

Erica and Ellen didn't want to do this. It was too expensive, and if they got caught drinking in there their evenings in the Cellar Bar could come to an end.

'Thank goodness for that,' said Erica as Sally and Steve departed on their own. 'My definition of hell is having to spend a Friday evening with Steve. I really don't know what Sally sees in him.'

Putting sorrow aside, they spent the rest of the evening anticipating the forthcoming Wednesday night at the Palace Ballroom – and speculating on their chances of ensnaring a couple of Rolling Stones. Ellen tried to imagine how her brother would react if she were to succeed in this. He'd been beside himself with envy when she'd told him that she and Erica had managed to get tickets. He was such a big fan of the Rolling Stones that not long ago he'd announced that he wanted to be called Mick from then onwards.

Just before this, he'd been going out with Sandra Crompton – much to everyone's surprise and his mother's profound dismay. Sandra was a big 'little madam' now and might easily lead her son astray. But the relationship hadn't lasted long. Although Sandra had spent years pursuing him, it only took a few weeks for her to get bored with him. He was heartbroken for days after she finished with him, then he went into the sixth form at school, transformed himself into Mick McCann and forgot all about her.

So . . . if she were to go out with Mick Jagger, Ellen thought, it would be really funny. 'Mick, this is Mick,' she would say, introducing them to each other and trying not to smirk.

When Ellen got home that evening the television was full of the president's assassination. And over the course of the next few days they all watched the newsreels from Dallas, replayed again and again. They watched in fascinated horror as the assassin, Lee Harvey Oswald, was shot in turn by Jack Ruby. And they watched the president's funeral in Washington with its heart-rending scenes of his two little children.

At school they prayed for the soul of President Kennedy: *'Eternal rest give unto him, O Lord.'* And at home, Ellen prayed for Mrs Chisnall too: *'And let perpetual light shine upon her. May she rest in peace. Amen.'*

Praying for specific souls like this reminded her of the November, years ago, when she was in Miss Long's class.

* * *

The souls of the dead, Miss Long had reminded them, couldn't pray for themselves – *'Their lips no prayer can utter / No suppliant psalm'* – so they had to rely on the living to do it for them – *'Good Christian pray.'* And these prayers would reduce the time they spent suffering in purgatory.

You could pray for them at any time of the year, of course, but November had been specially designated as the month for making a really concerted effort. And so, dutifully, they prayed and sang hymns just like they did every year – *'Requiescant in pace.'* But rather than just praying for the holy souls *en masse* like this, Miss Long favoured a more personal approach. They could, she suggested, pray for specific souls. Dead relatives, for example. Their grandparents, perhaps.

Well yes you could, thought Ellen, but how did you know they were in purgatory? Her grandmother had been dead for fifteen years. Surely she was in heaven by now? And her grandfather McCann – who had died when she was six, which was only three years ago, so he could easily still be in purgatory – had been such a disagreeable old man that whenever she tried praying for his soul she could never quite rid herself of the thought that he might be in hell. Prayers for either of these grandparents, then, could well be wasted ones.

65

'Or,' said Miss Long, in more creative mood, 'you might pray for the soul who is the next one to go to heaven. And when that soul gets there it will remember you when it's your turn in purgatory.'

Yes, having such well placed friends was certainly an attractive proposition and, glancing around at her classmates, Ellen could see that this would be a popular suggestion. Moreover, if they all undertook to pray for this particular soul, it wouldn't take long to get it into heaven, and then their prayers could be directed towards the next nearest, and then the next, and so on, and before November came to an end they would all have several new friends in this highest of high places. Ellen reckoned that if she were to spend every November for the rest of her life praying for these next-into-heaven souls then her own stay in purgatory would be little more than a flying visit.

But that night, having just prayed for that soon-to-be-fortunate soul, she was overcome with unease. Wasn't this being too selfish? Wouldn't it be better to pray for the soul who was the furthest away from heaven (another of Miss Long's suggestions) or (yet another), the most forgotten soul? She got into bed and began pondering these matters.

Just because no-one on earth remembered a soul, it didn't mean that it still had a long time to go in purgatory. It all depended on how bad it'd been while alive. And anyway, once prayed for, this soul would immediately lose its most forgotten status. But then . . . so would the one furthest from heaven, too. Or would it? Her head began to spin. And wouldn't opting to pray for these souls be just too selfless? If she did this she wouldn't make any friends at all, because one fleeting little prayer wouldn't be remembered by someone who might still have years and years to go in purgatory, would it?

The next day she asked Joan Grady who she was praying for. 'My granny,' was the prompt reply.

'But what if she's already in heaven? Then you'll be wasting your prayers.'

'Miss Long said no prayers are ever wasted,' said Joan confidently.

Ellen wasn't convinced. How could Miss Long know that for sure? How did she know any of these things? How did anyone know? 'Are you going to keep praying for your granny for ever?' she asked. 'Every November for the rest of your life?'

Joan shrugged. 'It only takes a minute,' she said.

Yes, but even so. All those minutes added up over a lifetime.

A few nights later, something else began to bother her. That day they'd been singing a hymn about the Holy Souls which contained the lines:

> *Those Holy Souls they suffer on*
> *Resigned in heart and will*
> *Until Thy high behest is done*
> *And justice has its fill.*

While she had no idea what God's 'high behest' was, she did know the meaning of 'justice'. The Holy Souls were in purgatory to atone for their sins. The ones who were in there for the longest time had obviously been the greatest sinners. Was it *just*, therefore, to give them an unfair advantage over others who had sinned less? If God had sentenced them to a certain length of time in purgatory, then who were they to plead with Him to change His mind? Surely He would give them 'eternal rest' in His own good time?

No, all things considered, she decided that she would stay with the soul who was next into heaven. Interceding for this one wouldn't interfere too much with God's wishes. It also had the added advantage of keeping things moving, speeding things up. It would reduce overcrowding and make life (death) more tolerable for everyone in purgatory – including the very long-term residents.

She turned over in bed and tried to go to sleep but all these complexities were playing on her mind. What if Miss Long was wrong to ask them to pray for specific souls? Shouldn't they just be praying for all of them together *('may they rest in peace')* like they'd always done? Or – and had the Pope thought about this, she wondered – perhaps they shouldn't be praying for any of them at all? Perhaps they should let justice run its course? She tried to keep track of her thoughts but kept losing the thread of her argument until, thoroughly exhausted by all this theological turmoil, she fell asleep at last.

It was a relief when the month ended and the religious imperative switched to the more joyful one of preparing one's soul for Christmas.

* * *

Ellen had no time for these niceties now. Except that all over the world people would be praying for President Kennedy, while probably only she and her mother would be praying for poor Mrs Chisnall.

She wondered whether Joan Grady was still praying for her granny. Or Erica for her mother – who, as it had turned out, might well still be in purgatory atoning for her sins.

DECEMBER

1963

We long to see Thee, so,' they sang in morning assembly.
To see Thee newly born
We long for Christmas morn
The sands of time run slow.

And then, without warning, Erica began to sing the next line with great operatic gusto: '*Oh come, oh come, oh come*' she trilled, her voice vibrating and rising higher with each repetition. She kept quiet for the next line – '*Our Saviour dear to be*' – and then '*Oh come, oh come, oh come,*' she warbled, joining in again. Ellen, who was standing in front of her, shook with silent mirth.

As with most things of a religious nature, the Advent hymn reminded Ellen of Miss Long. 'You'll enjoy Christmas Day all the more if you're in a state of grace,' she'd told her class of little girls, all those years ago. And to help them achieve such a state she'd outlined an Advent plan of action that involved making extra church visits, saying additional prayers and – most importantly of all – making sacrifices. She'd been a great believer in the spiritual value of self denial. Each day, during the month of December, she'd presented them with a list of things to do or not to do, and on Fridays she'd added a few extra ones for the weekend.

Ellen concentrated on the words of the hymn now, trying to mean them. But fervour couldn't be forced. She was, she realised, well past her spiritual peak. That year in Miss Long's class had been the most grace-filled one of her life and she would never rise to such heights again. And, just for a moment, she was quite overcome with nostalgia for those spiritual days of yore. Perhaps, as an Advent sacrifice now, she thought, she could forego the pleasures of the forthcoming school dance. What, she wondered, closing her hymn book, would Erica have to say to that?

This was going to be the first dance ever held at the Convent. It was going to be on the last Friday of term, in the dining hall – well away from the main school building and the nuns. There would be no live music, only records. And there would be teachers present, along with the elderly school caretaker and a handful of volunteer fathers, in case of trouble.

It was to be a tickets-only event. Fifth and sixth-formers were eligible to attend and could purchase two tickets each, on the understanding that any guests they brought along should be male ones. A sufficiency of boys was vital to its success. A predominantly female dance would be deemed a disaster.

Ellen and Erica weren't inviting any of their Cellar Bar friends, though, because a school dance wouldn't be groovy enough for them – especially not coming as it did so soon after the spectacular night at the Palace Ballroom with the Rolling Stones. And they didn't want to advertise the fact that they were still schoolgirls either – or even worse, convent schoolgirls.

In spite of its non-grooviness, Erica had decided that it was going to be the social event of the season for the simple reason that Joe Wagstaff was going to be there. He, apparently, had been given no choice in the matter. Claire Wagstaff, who was chair of the dance committee and very keen that the evening be a success, had shamelessly flouted the two-per-person rule and had issued Joe with a pile of tickets and instructions to bring along as many of his friends as he could muster.

'At least there'll be some reasonable boys there, then,' said Erica, on hearing this. 'Thank goodness they won't all be like Sally's stupid Steve!'

No one had any doubt that Joe Wagstaff would be able to fulfil his mission because, in spite of its many shortcomings, this dance had one obvious attraction – a guaranteed abundance of girls. And it was this that was attracting Mick McCann too. He asked Ellen if she could get tickets for him and Chad, but Ellen, taken aback by this unexpected request, pretended that this might be difficult. He kept on pestering her, though – as did her mother. Mrs McCann hadn't completely recovered from the Sandra Crompton episode and thought that a nice girl from the Convent was just what Mick needed.

Eventually, Ellen gave in and agreed to get the tickets. But she was uneasy. Did she really want Erica to meet her brother? Although she herself often went to the Latimers' house, Erica had never been to hers, or met any of her family (apart from Christine, who was in the first year now). Ellen had never wanted to invite her. It had never seemed necessary. Erica's interest in the McCanns was minimal, and Makerton was not on her map. And this suited Ellen.

So, if Erica were to meet Mick now, would he be presentable enough? She cast a critical eye over him, trying to be objective. What if Erica were to regard him with the same contempt she did Sally's Steve? And then there was Michael Chadwell. Did Ellen want him to go to the dance? Erica knew nothing about him, so, as far as she was concerned, he would just be Mick's friend. And that was all he was now, anyway. Her brother's friend. Her friend Jennifer's brother. He didn't mean anything else to her anymore. Did he?

Michael had left school last July and was working at Browning's brewery in Ashburne, training to be an electrician. He and Mick were still the best of friends, but their social life rarely took them into Turneley. On Fridays, though, he did go to Turneley Technical College on day release and occasionally, if Ellen had stayed late at school or had been doing something with Erica afterwards, they would get the same bus home. But whenever this happened neither of them ever acknowledged the other's presence. There was no hostility involved here – not like there was between her and Joan Grady and Sheila Murphy. It was merely a show of casual indifference. Their long love affair was over.

But was it? Now that she knew he was going to the school dance she wasn't quite so sure anymore. He began to reappear in the little dramas she acted out in her mind, in bed at night, before she fell asleep. The first time this happened he only had a small part, but she knew that if she didn't exert more directorial control he could – very easily – become the romantic lead again.

'I see our Michael's going to your school dance,' Jennifer Chadwell said as they walked home from church together the following Sunday morning.

'Yeah,' said Ellen.

'He's really looking forward to it,' said Jennifer. 'He's pretending he's not, but I can tell he is.'

'Mmm.'

Apart from these Sunday morning chats, Ellen didn't see much of Jennifer nowadays. But theirs was an easy, uncomplicated friendship and over the years they'd always managed to keep each other up to date on most of the more interesting details of their separate lives. And one day, probably quite soon now, Ellen would make Jennifer laugh by telling her how – when she was little – she used to be in love with Michael Chadwell.

On Friday afternoon, a week before the dance, Ellen was on a later bus going home from school when Margaret Latham, carrying a shopping bag as well as her satchel, came struggling up the stairs and sat down next to her. She had been buying new shoes and was about to show them to Ellen when

Michael Chadwell appeared at the top of the stairs. Automatically, Ellen transferred her attention to the scene outside the bus window. Margaret stopped what she was saying too, until he had sat down several seats in front of them.

'That's Jennifer Chadwell's brother, isn't it?' she whispered to Ellen.

'Where?'

'There, in front.'

'Oh . . . yeah.'

'He's nice, isn't he?'

The bus lurched away from the stop and Ellen's heart lurched with it. 'He's all right,' she said. 'Do you fancy him?'

Margaret gave a little shrug and smiled. 'He's nice,' she repeated, in an ordinary voice now, as the noise of the moving bus ruled out any possibility that he might hear what they were saying. They both stared at the back of his head for a few moments. Then Margaret turned her attention back to her new shoes.

Ellen admired them politely but without enthusiasm. Both she and Erica had acquired new boots recently. Knee-high black leather ones. Hers had zips up the back and low stiletto heels; Erica's had zips at the sides and the heels were a bit higher. Compared to these boots, Margaret's shoes were very ordinary. But then, Margaret Latham was very ordinary, too, so it wasn't surprising.

'Do you know him?' Margaret asked, putting the shoebox back into its bag and the bag on to the floor by her feet.

'Who?'

'Michael Chadwell!'

'Yeah. He lives near us. He's a mate of my brother's.'

They stared at the back of his head again.

'Do you think he might be coming to our school dance?'

'Who? My brother?'

'No! Michael Chadwell! Well, both of them.'

'I don't know,' said Ellen, who only last night had given

Mick the two tickets he'd been begging for. 'You do fancy him, don't you?'

Margaret smiled again.

'Do you want me to invite them?' said Ellen, suggestively. After all, she thought, trying to ignore the dismay she was feeling, why should she care if Margaret Latham fancied him?

As the bus was approaching Makerton, Margaret suddenly whipped her school hat off. This was against school rules and something she never usually did. It was obvious why she'd done it now. It was so that Michael Chadwell would see her to better advantage when he got up to get off the bus. But, to Ellen's satisfaction, when the moment came he instinctively avoided looking at either of them. She knew, as she followed him down the stairs, that Margaret (who had another stop to go) would be disappointed, would be thinking that he hadn't noticed her. But he had definitely noticed Ellen – he wouldn't have avoided looking at her if he hadn't!

As soon as the bus stopped, Michael leapt off and disappeared up the backs. Ellen followed behind, feeling more confused than ever now. But it was Friday night, and a couple of hours later she was on the bus again, going back to Turneley where there were other boys to think about.

Erica wanted Ellen to stay at her house on the night of the school dance, but Ellen had her Saturday job the next morning and so she said no.

'Have the day off,' said Erica, impatiently. They were in between lessons and the conversation could come to a halt at any moment.

'I can't. I've already had one Saturday morning off for that funeral I told you about. And it's too near Christmas. They'll be too busy. They wouldn't let me.'

'Say you're ill.'

'No.'

'Why not?'

'Stop talking please,' said their teacher, sweeping into the classroom. Erica, thwarted, pulled a face.

Ellen wondered why she was making such a fuss about it. Probably something to do with Maggie, she thought. Having Ellen to stay overnight could be something else with which to annoy her. Annoying Maggie was one of Erica's favourite past-times these days.

('You didn't tell me you'd asked Ellen to stay for tea,' Maggie had said, a few weeks ago, one afternoon after school.

'I didn't think I needed your permission,' said Erica.

'I didn't say you needed my permission. I just think you should've told me, that's all.'

'Should I have?' said Erica, staring at her. 'Well, I'm telling you now.'

'Erica!' said Mr Latimer warningly.

'I'm sorry, Dad, but I don't know what my stepmother's getting so upset about.'

'I'm not upset,' said Maggie, returning Erica's stare. 'It's just that I would've made more if I'd known.' She transferred her gaze to the shepherd's pie that would need stretching seven ways now. And then, noticing Ellen's discomfiture: 'Ellen knows she's always welcome.'

'Does she?'

Ellen really wished that Erica wouldn't keep doing this.)

'My stepmother won't mind, if that's what you're thinking,' said Erica, resuming the conversation at the end of the lesson. 'You'd be no trouble. There's an empty bed in my room now that Maria's moved upstairs.'

Ellen, busy rummaging in her desk, said nothing. There was a short pause.

'Well, perhaps it's better if you don't stay,' said Erica, changing tack, 'because Joe's going to walk me home after the dance and you'd only be in the way.'

Ellen stopped rummaging and raised her eyebrows in mock disbelief.

'No, I mean it,' said Erica. 'Sally says she thinks he's got a girl-friend, the way he's been behaving, but she's always saying that. Anyway, I think I've waited long enough. It's time

I made a move before someone else claims him by mistake.'

'So what exactly are you going to do?' Ellen asked, trying to banish from her mind the unwelcome image of Margaret Latham claiming Michael Chadwell by mistake.

'I'll just be my usual irresistible self!' said Erica. 'That usually works.'

'It hasn't worked with Joe Wagstaff so far, though, has it?'

'That's because he thinks I'm still a kid,' said Erica. 'He never looks at me properly. All I have to do is make him notice me.' She paused. 'And I will, at this dance. But don't say anything to anyone,' she added, just like she always did whenever she spoke about Joe.

Only Ellen (and Jennifer Chadwell, but that didn't count) knew about this grand passion. Only Ellen knew why Erica would never go out with anyone else for very long. Her heart, she would declare, belonged to Joe, and it was no use trying to pretend otherwise. No-one else, it would seem, could compare with him. Her belief that they were destined to be together one day was unshakeable. But Ellen wondered about Joe Wagstaff. Admittedly, she'd only seen him a few times, but it seemed to her that he wasn't so much unaware of Erica, he was just totally indifferent to her. She might make him notice her at the dance, but then what? His indifference might well remain intact.

Some loves, Ellen felt, were doomed. Some things were just never meant to be.

The night of the dance was cold and damp. Erica had promised Claire Wagstaff that they would help with some of the preliminary preparations so they'd arranged to meet at quarter to seven – instead of the usual half-past – outside Higham's. The shop's windows were ablaze with Christmas lights and on the façade above the doorway there was a row of Christmas trees. When Ellen's bus arrived, Erica was already there, waiting impatiently in this festive setting, her head swathed in a headscarf to stop her hair from going frizzy in the damp air. As she stepped off the bus, Ellen, too, took similar precautions, tucking her own long hair inside her coat and turning her collar up as far as it would go. It was essential to maintain as sleek a look as possible.

'Come on, let's go. I don't want anyone seeing me like this,' said Erica, keeping her head down. 'I look like the Queen.'

'Whereas I, on the other hand,' giggled Ellen, pulling her collar across her face, 'look like Olga, ze beautiful spy.'

But it was early, the streets were almost empty, and they didn't see anyone they knew. It felt strange going this way in the evening, to school, rather than the other way to Duke Street.

The dining hall was at the bottom of a small terrace of houses that ran along one side of the school. When they arrived there, everything was nearly ready. The walls and ceiling had been decorated with holly and paper chains and fairy lights. The Christmas tree, which up till now had been standing in a corner, was on the stage between two huge speakers. There was a table up there too with a gramophone on it and a pile of records. Someone's father was fiddling with knobs and a microphone.

Erica looked round the room. 'It's too bright in here,' she announced. 'Can't we turn some of these lights off?' She walked over to the switchboard and flicked off half of the switches. The room was instantly transformed.

'I think we'd better have a few more on than that,' said Claire, switching some of them on again before walking away. Erica went to switch them off again, but Maria, who was standing nearby, gave her a warning look.

Erica turned to Ellen and pulled a face. 'Did you see that?' she said. 'Just for a minute there I thought she was going to say something to me. But no. Just the look. I don't think she's said more than two words to anybody in the last week. I think she's practising for her vow of silence.'

Maria had wanted to leave school last summer and go into her convent. Only her Latimer grandmother had supported her in this, and so, against the united forces of her father, Maggie, her other grandmother in Birmingham and the headmistress, Sister Marie-Pierre, she'd given in – seemingly without too much of a fight – and had agreed to stay at school and do her A-levels. But she was, according to Erica, withdrawing from the world in her own way. She'd moved out of the bedroom they'd always shared and into Gina's old room at the top of the house. And, as Caroline Latimer was away at college now, her bedroom up there was empty most of the time too, so Maria had the attic all to herself and spent most of her time up there alone.

Ellen looked at her now. Her long dark hair was loose around her shoulders. She was wearing a charcoal grey dress with long sleeves. She had fish-net stockings on and black shoes with low stiletto heels. And she was wearing quite a lot of dark eye make-up. As usual, she looked almost – but not quite – demure. There was something about her that was hard to define. It was this habit she had of looking down. But then, when she looked up and shook her hair from her face it was difficult to keep your eyes off her. As far as Ellen was concerned, Maria Latimer was a continuing source of fascination.

Above the dining hall, next to the domestic science and needlework rooms, there was a small cloakroom which tonight was to be for the girls. The much larger one downstairs had a Gents sign fixed to its door now.

Sally Wagstaff opened this door a few inches: Look at this!' she said, pointing towards where someone had draped a cloth over the ancient machine on the wall which disposed of used sanitary towels.

'Oh, God!' said Erica. 'How embarrassing!'

They went upstairs to hang their coats up. Some sixth-formers were already in the little cloakroom and Erica joined them in front of the mirror, eager to repair any damage the walk through town might have caused.

'Come on. You look fine,' said Ellen, glancing briefly at her own reflection.

But Erica was not to be rushed. When she'd finished with her hair she turned her attention to her boots. There was a bit of dirt on one of them and she bent down to wipe it off with her finger. The other girls began to leave, and Maria slipped in through the open door as they were doing so.

Erica, who had failed to notice this, straightened up and proclaimed in a husky voice: 'OK, I'm ready. Tonight he will be mine. All mine.'

Ellen cleared her throat in warning.

'What?' said Erica, then seeing her sister, opened her eyes wide in mock horror. But she hadn't said who 'he' was, so she smiled sweetly at Maria who gave her another level stare, shook her head and disappeared into a toilet cubicle.

'God! That was a close thing,' gasped Erica once they were outside the cloakroom. She put one hand on her brow and the other on her heart. 'My secret! Nearly out!' she intoned. They giggled all the way down the stairs.

They had been assigned the task of collecting tickets at the double outer doors of the building. It was very draughty there and Ellen wished she'd kept her coat on.

Margaret Latham arrived with a group of her friends. 'Is he here yet?' she asked Ellen.

Ellen shook her head.

'He is coming, isn't he?'

Ellen shrugged. 'They've got tickets,' she said. 'They've probably gone to the pub first.'

It was ten past eight before Mick and Chad made their appearance. Ellen took their tickets and turned to Erica who was peering out into the darkness, still waiting for Joe Wagstaff to arrive.

'Erica,' she said, 'this is my brother.'

Erica was momentarily diverted. She looked Mick up and down, her eyes deepening in colour as she did so. 'Hi -ya,' she said, smiling at him. 'I'm Ellen's best friend. But then, I expect you've heard her mention me.'

'Once or twice,' said Mick (sounding very Lancashire to Ellen's ears). He took Erica's hand and kissed it. 'Pleased to meet you, Erica.'

Oh, no, thought Ellen. He's showing off! She glanced at Michael Chadwell who grinned at her and shook his head. This brief, yet all too familiar, little moment of intimacy between them added to her agitation.

'Unhand me, sir,' said Erica. 'I am but an innocent Convent girl!'

Ellen's heart sank even further. The possibility that Erica and Mick might get together hadn't occurred to her until now. Then, out of the corner of her eye, she saw Joe Wagstaff and his cohort coming down the terrace.

Erica saw them too. 'And I have work to do,' she said, removing her hand abruptly. She turned away from Mick, all her attention now on Joe.

Ellen directed Mick and Michael Chadwell into the hall – where, she knew, Margaret Latham was lying in wait. Was she going to allow Margaret to succeed in her quest, she asked herself? Could she stop her? Well of course she could, she reassured herself – if she wanted to. But did she really want to? Was she still in love with Michael Chadwell, like Erica was with Joe Wagstaff?

She turned her attention back to the doorway and watched Erica go into action, laughing, joking and flinging her hair about as she welcomed the new arrivals and took their tickets. Joe Wagstaff didn't seem to be taking much notice; some of his friends, though, were definitely showing an interest. Ellen could foresee complications.

She studied Joe. He was wearing a black polo-neck sweater and a leather jacket. His hair was longer than it'd been when she'd last seen him. There was no denying that he was good-looking (was he better looking than Michael Chadwell?) but there was something about his manner that she didn't like. What was it? Was he conceited? Was he 'cock-sure'? This was something she'd heard her father say about Frank Chisnall – 'He's too cock-sure, for his own good, that one.' But Joe Wagstaff wasn't cocky like Frank. He did seem very sure of himself, though, very confident, very self-contained. Ignoring her welcoming smile, he gave Ellen the slightest of glances as he went past her and into the hall. No, she decided, she didn't like him. She didn't 'warm to him', as her mother might say.

'You didn't tell me your brother was so gorgeous,' said Erica, calming down a bit now that Joe was out of sight.

'Is he? I don't see it myself.'

Erica didn't seem to have noticed Michael Chadwell at all. But then, why would she? And Ellen wondered, for the millionth time, why – apart from that very first 'there's someone I like, too' – she'd never, in all these years, mentioned him to her friend.

Being on the door held no attractions for them now, so Erica declared that everyone who was coming must have arrived by now. They closed the doors and handed the tickets to a volunteer father.

'I'm freezing,' said Ellen, hugging herself to get warm.

'Come on, then, let's go in,' said Erica, opening the door to the dining hall. 'Joe Wagstaff, here I come!'

It was hot and noisy in the hall. They pushed their way through the dancers, each looking for someone different. They saw Joe first, talking to one of Claire's friends. Erica positioned herself so that she could watch him while she and Ellen were dancing. Ellen felt obliged to dance with her, although she would have preferred to continue her search for Michael.

It wasn't long before two of Joe's friends came to join them. Unfortunately, neither of them were ones that Ellen would have chosen. She shuffled around half-heartedly, and then caught sight of Margaret Latham who seemed to be dancing with Mick. But where was Michael? He must be there somewhere. Her dancing partner said something to her but she couldn't hear what it was and couldn't be bothered to ask him to repeat it. She gave him a weak smile, hoping this would suffice.

She turned to Erica, intending to convey her displeasure, but Erica was concentrating on other things. Usually she danced in a very self-absorbed way, with her head down, lost in her hair. But now she was waving her arms about flamboyantly in the very limited space. Her head was up and her eyes were fixed firmly on Joe Wagstaff. Ellen felt vaguely embarrassed. Sometimes she worried about Erica.

When the music stopped, they tried to disengage themselves from their partners, but with only limited success. As they moved away, the two boys continued to follow them at a distance.

'Oh, for God's sake!' said Erica. 'What's the matter with them? Some people can't take a hint, can they?'

It was only halfway through the evening and already Ellen was exhausted. Erica's vigilance was driving her mad. 'What's he doing now? Who's he dancing with? Where's he gone?' But it was clear, even to Erica, that her plan wasn't working. Despite her best efforts, Joe Wagstaff was taking no notice of her at all.

'Come on,' said Ellen, who had just seen Margaret Latham leaving the hall. 'Let's go to the cloakroom.'

Reluctantly, Erica allowed herself to be led away.

When they got there, Margaret was busy combing her hair in front of the mirror. She smiled at Ellen. 'Thanks for getting him to come,' she said. Her eyes were shining; she'd obviously had some success.

Ellen looked at her through the mirror and tried to smile back.

'Who? What's she talking about?' asked Erica as Margaret glided away.

'She fancies that boy with my brother,' said Ellen. Then, as she caught the flicker of interest in Erica's eyes, she wished that she hadn't mentioned Mick.

'Let's go and find your brother,' Erica said. 'I'm fed up with bothering about Joe Bloody Wagstaff.'

They re-entered the dining hall to the strains of Cliff Richard.

'Oh God! This music's so grotty!' complained Erica. 'We

can't dance to this.'

They went to stand at the side of the room.

'What's Joe doing now?' she asked.

'I thought you weren't going to bother with him anymore.'

'Oh, it's all right,' said Erica, ignoring this last comment. He's only dancing with the nun.' She looked round the hall and, seeing Mick in the distance, began waving to him.

He came over and held out his hand to her. 'Come and dance,' he said – and Ellen found herself abandoned.

She could see Margaret Latham dancing with Michael Chadwell now, and turned away quickly to avoid looking at them. A group of her classmates were standing nearby so she went over to join them.

'Who's that boy Erica's dancing with?' asked Angela Norris.

Mick was well and truly into his Jagger stride now, and Erica, diverted at last from Joe-watching, was responding with equal enthusiasm.

Ellen shook her head. 'That's my brother,' she said ruefully.

When the music stopped, Mick and Erica stayed together. The next record was a slow one and Ellen watched disapprovingly as Erica draped her arms around Mick's neck. '*I can't stop loving you,*' lamented Ray Charles as they swayed together harmoniously. Ellen, caught up in the words of the song, didn't dare look to see if Margaret Latham and Michael Chadwell were similarly entwined, so she looked at Joe Wagstaff instead.

He was still dancing with Maria, although they were hardly moving at all. He had his arms around her and she had her head turned away from him. Her hair was like a veil around her face and her eyes were downcast. She looked very beautiful and very sad. She reminded Ellen of a holy picture of Our Lady that her mother kept in her prayer book. Our Lady of Sorrows. Except that, unlike Our Lady, Maria Latimer didn't have her heart displayed on the outside of her dress for all to see.

The dance, scheduled to end at half-past ten, went on five minutes longer. But now the last dance was over and all the lights were back on. Ellen had been dancing with one of Joe Wagstaff's more attractive friends – a boy called Pete – but she was anxious to get away.

'Can I walk you to your bus-stop?' he asked.

'No, it's all right,' she said. 'I'm going home with my brother.'

She scanned the hall, looking for Mick and Erica.

'Come on Mick,' she said when she'd tracked them down. 'We've got to go.' She turned to Erica. 'I'll see you tomorrow.'

But Mick was in no hurry to leave. 'I'll walk you home,' he said to Erica.

'You can't! You'll miss the last bus,' said Ellen.

'I have to stay and help clear up, anyway,' said Erica, looking round. 'You go home with Ellen.' Now that the dance was over, Ellen could see that she was reverting to her original plan of walking home with Joe Wagstaff.

She went upstairs to the crowded cloakroom.

Margaret Latham was already up there, struggling into her coat. 'Are you coming home with us?' she asked.

Ellen nodded.

When they got back down, Michael Chadwell was waiting by the door and Mick was still talking to Erica. People were streaming out all around them.

'Come on, Mick!' said Ellen, exasperated. 'We're going to miss that last bus if you don't come now.'

Pete was still hovering. He asked her if she would be in the Cellar Bar tomorrow night.

'Yes, probably,' said Ellen.

'I'll see you there, then?'

'All right,' she said, glancing at Michael.

Mick put the same question to Erica.

'Yeah, OK,' she agreed, her attention elsewhere.

'I'll see you tomorrow night, then,' he said, moving away.

Not if I can help it, you won't, thought Ellen, steering him out of the door.

The road outside was dimly lit. It was drizzling, but so slightly that the rain was only visible in the glows of light around the old-fashioned gas lamps. As they walked towards the main road the Convent loomed up out of the darkness on their left hand side. Somewhere inside, the nuns would be asleep in their beds, except perhaps for Sister Marie-Pierre who might be lying awake wondering if all had gone well and whether they were all safely on their way home.

They had to hurry. If they missed the eleven o'clock last bus they would be in trouble. Ellen, striding along miserably behind Margaret and Chad, could tell that Margaret's new shoes were hurting her now and took what satisfaction she could from this observation. They arrived at the bus-stop with only moments to spare. The bus was about to leave and while they were still clambering up the stairs it pulled away. The upper deck was nearly full and they couldn't all sit together. Margaret and Chad found two seats together near the back and Ellen and Mick sat, separately, a few rows in front of them.

Once the bus had emptied sufficiently, Mick got up and went to sit in front of the other two. He sat with his back to the window and his leg across the whole seat so that he could talk to them. Ellen, who felt obliged to move also, had to sit across the aisle from him. Margaret and Chad, she noted, were holding hands.

'Why don't we all go to the Cellar Bar tomorrow night, then?' said Mick, looking as pleased with himself as Margaret was looking with herself.

'I don't think that's a good idea,' said Ellen.

'Why not?' I've told Erica I'm going.'

'Well, I don't think you should,' said Ellen. They were all looking at her now. 'Erica's not interested in you, Mick.'

He looked at her in disbelief. 'It didn't look like she wasn't interested,' he said.

'She looked interested to me,' said Margaret, leaning her head on Chad's shoulder. 'She was all over him.'

'She was just using him,' said Ellen. 'She was trying to make someone else jealous.'

Mick looked far from convinced.

'She's crazy about this other person,' Ellen went on, looking at Michael Chadwell and blushing. 'She's been madly in love with him for ever. She couldn't care less about you, Mick. Forget about her.'

'You make her sound horrible,' said Margaret. 'I thought she was your best friend.'

'She is. But sometimes she's not a very nice person.'

'Why are you friends with her then?'

Ellen shrugged. Turning her back on them, she slid closer to the window and spent the rest of the journey gazing out into the night and contemplating her last statement. It was true; sometimes Erica wasn't a very nice person. But it didn't matter. What Erica had to offer was complicated. Ellen couldn't really put it into words – not words that Margaret Latham would understand, anyway. When she was with Erica, life was more intense somehow, more vivid. Even when they were bored it was an interesting boredom. No, what Erica had to offer had nothing at all to do with being nice. Margaret Latham, she supposed, was a nice person. She was just the kind of nice girl that Mrs McCann would like Mick to go out with. And, no doubt, just the kind of nice girl that Mrs Chadwell would like too.

When the bus stopped at Makerton Library, Chad stayed on to take Margaret home. Ellen and Mick got off and walked up the dark backs without speaking.

'Now, did you have a good time?' asked Mrs McCann when they got in.

'Yeah, it was all right,' said Ellen.

Mrs McCann turned to Mick. 'Did you meet any nice girls?' she asked.

He made a disparaging sound. 'Apparently not,' he said sullenly, sitting down in front of the television.

When Ellen went up to bed, Christine was still awake and full of questions.

'Ssh. Go to sleep,' said Ellen who didn't want to talk.

'Did Mickey Mouse chat up anyone?' asked Christine. 'Just tell me that.'

'No he didn't. Now shut up and go to sleep.'

But Ellen couldn't get to sleep herself. She lay awake for ages, going over the events of the evening in her mind. She constructed an alternative ending to it. In this version, Michael Chadwell had his arm around her shoulder as they were all walking to the bus stop. 'I'm afraid I'm not a very nice person,' she said, turning to a distraught Margaret Latham who, weeping (and limping) was being comforted by Mick.

When eventually she did fall asleep, she dreamt that she was standing in the backs with Michael Chadwell. He had his arms around her and was just about to kiss her when the six o'clock Angelus bell at St Wilfrid's began to toll.

'Oh, no! I 've got to go for my piano lesson now,' she said, in dismay.(Her music case was already in her hand.)

'I'll wait here for you,' he promised. 'I'll wait for you for ever.'

But Ellen hadn't been practising and Mrs Walker, angry at her poor performance, kept her long past her designated time. She tried to hurry home, but her progress was slow. She was running, running, her music case slamming painfully against her leg. I'm going to give up the piano, she vowed.

When she did finally reach the dark backs she couldn't see Michael anywhere. She thought he must've got tired of waiting for her, but just as she was about to go in, he appeared out of the shadows by Mrs Chisnall's back gate.

'I didn't know you lived here, Ellen,' he said, enfolding her in his arms. And to her horror she found herself gazing into the mocking eyes of Joe Wagstaff!

'No, no!' she cried, struggling to get free. 'No!' And in the process, she woke herself up.

The next evening Ellen met Erica as usual at half-past seven outside Higham's. Erica seemed to have forgotten all about Mick. As they walked to the Cellar Bar she reported that there had been no progress on the Joe Wagstaff front after the dance. Ellen, unsurprised, said nothing.

Later, when Pete appeared with a couple of his friends, Erica suddenly remembered. 'I thought your brother was coming here tonight,' she muttered, surveying the friends and conveying to Ellen that they were not to her taste.

'I told him not to,' said Ellen.

'What did you do that for?'

Ellen gave her a look but didn't answer.

'I bet he wanted to come,' persisted Erica, ignoring the look. 'Why did you tell him not to?'

'He's my brother, Erica. Leave him alone.'

Erica lowered her head and said nothing. Ellen felt that she'd made her point. She started talking to Pete, trying to suppress the thought that he, too, was probably someone's brother and that she, too, was going to reject him, perhaps not tonight but certainly before too long. Perhaps, she thought with an inward sigh, they should all become nuns like Maria Latimer.

The Sunday morning after Christmas was a bright, bitterly cold one with a lingering frost on the ground. St Wilfrid's Church was 'perishing' in the winter when, according to Mr McCann, the cold could penetrate right through to your bones. Ellen walked home from Mass with Jennifer Chadwell. They were walking quickly, trying to get warm, and got well ahead of their mothers and Christine.

'Do you know that our Michael's going out with Margaret Latham?' said Jennifer.

'I know he was with her at our school dance.'

'Well, he's been out with her three times since then.'

Three times! This seemed an awful lot in such a short time. Ellen began to calculate: once on the Saturday night after the dance; once last night. When else? Christmas Eve?

Boxing Day? She knew that Mick hadn't been out recently but she'd thought that was because he was moping over Erica. But here was another explanation.

'She's nice, isn't she?' said Jennifer.

'Yeah . . . she's all right.'

They walked along in silence for a few moments and then Jennifer gave a little squeal. 'Oh, I nearly forgot to tell you!' she said. 'You'll never guess! Go on, try!' She waited a moment, but Ellen wasn't in the mood. 'Well . . . ' she went on, 'you know we've been talking for ages about going to live in Australia? Yeah, well now we're really going to go! It's all been decided. I'm going to leave school at Easter – and then we're off!'

Ellen stopped dead. 'Australia!' she cried. 'You're going to go and live in Australia?'

Jennifer nodded and laughed, pleased that her bombshell had been so effective. 'I know! I can't believe it myself!' she said. 'I'm not supposed to tell anyone yet, but I don't see why not.'

Ellen hardly heard anything else that Jennifer had to say. The Chadwells had been talking about going to Australia ever since Mrs Chadwell's brother and his family had emigrated there about four years ago, but no-one had thought that they really would go. And now . . . As she walked up the yard and into the house Ellen felt that the cold had, indeed, penetrated to her bones. She stood in front of the fire for a while, staring into the flames.

Her father and Mick went off to the eleven o'clock Mass and her mother and Christine came in.

'Come and eat your breakfast,' said Mrs McCann, putting the plates of bacon and eggs, which Mr McCann had cooked for them, on the table. This was Ellen's favourite breakfast of the week but she took no pleasure in it now.

'The Chadwells are going to go live in Australia,' she announced. 'Jennifer's just told me.'

Her mother and Christine were suitably surprised. Mrs McCann wondered why Mrs Chadwell hadn't said anything to her about it. Perhaps it wasn't definite. But Ellen knew that it was.

Later, when she told Mick, he said that he already knew.

'Why didn't you tell me?' she demanded.

He shrugged. 'I knew Jennifer would tell you soon,' he said. 'I didn't think you'd be that bothered.'

Ellen let out a cry of disbelief and exasperation.

Her mother, seeing that she was upset, said: 'I know you'll miss Jennifer, love. But you can always write to each other, can't you?'

'I don't know why you're so bothered,' said Christine. 'She's not your best friend, or anything. It's not the end of the world.'

Ellen left the room and went upstairs. She stood in her freezing bedroom, looking out of the window. She felt cold and empty. It is the end of the world, she thought, shivering. The other side of the world. The ends of the earth.

But it wasn't the impending loss of Jennifer that she was thinking about. Michael Chadwell was going to the ends of the earth, and she would never see him again. Her eyes filled with tears. There could be no doubting now that she was still in love with him.

And it was no consolation whatsoever to know that Margaret Latham would be heartbroken too when she found out.

PART TWO

JANUARY

1960

Until now, New Year's Eve had been a night like any other. They would go to bed at their usual times and the New Year would let itself into the McCann household unheralded. On New Year's Day – and for several days afterwards – the grown-ups would chorus: 'Happy New Year! Happy New Year!' whenever they met anyone. And Mr McCann would add 'All the best!' with a formality that Ellen always found slightly embarrassing.

But this year was different. This year, Auntie Peggy McCann and her friend Dorothy were over from America and New Year's Eve was celebrated with a big party at Auntie Annie's.

It was a wonderful party. There were lots of people there – old friends and neighbours of the McCanns as well as all the family – and the children were allowed to stay up into the small hours of New Year's Day. There was an abundance of food and drink; Uncle Jack entertained them all with his funny jokes and stories; Mr McCann sang *The Garden Where the Praties Grow*; others performed their own particular party pieces, and at midnight everyone sang *Auld Lang Syne*.

Then there was lots of kissing and hugging and New Year's wishes. 'Happy New Year!' they all said. 'Happy New

Year!' And: 'All the best!' said Mr McCann. It was very emotional because Auntie Peggy and Dorothy would be leaving in a few days time. Going all the way back to America. And when would they all see each other again?

Auntie Peggy was Mr McCann's – and Auntie Annie's and Uncle Jack's – sister. She lived in New York with her friend Dorothy Kenyon, who also came from Makerton. They'd gone to America together many years ago, before the War, when they were young women. Neither had married, but Ellen had heard people say that both had had their chances (although, sadly it would seem, not at the same time) and both (presumably on separate occasions) had rejected offers of marriage in favour of staying together.

Ellen liked to think that one of these unsuccessful suitors had been the love of Auntie Peggy's life, and that it'd broken her heart to let him go. She thought it was very silly, though, that Auntie Peggy had felt it necessary. Why had she and Dorothy felt the need to make such great sacrifices? Surely they could've stayed friends even if one or both of them were married.

Thank goodness Joan Grady would never expect such a thing of her. And if she ever did, Ellen felt it was most unlikely that she would give up Michael Chadwell.

Auntie Peggy worked as a shop assistant in a large Manhattan department store. From time to time, she would send clothes parcels to England for her nieces and nephews. These were greatly appreciated; the clothes they contained being much more colourful and luxurious than their own gloomy, post-war English ones.

A parcel from America always sent Ellen into a frenzy of delight. A while ago, included in one of them, were two Orlon jumpers, one for her and one for Christine. These jumpers were unbelievably soft and comfortable compared to their usual woolly ones. Ellen's was lemon with short sleeves and three little pearl buttons sewn on the front. She loved it so much that she hadn't been able to stop talking about it at school the day after it arrived. Joan Grady had listened dutifully to the description of this wonderful jumper, in this wonderful fibre, which had come all the way from America, but, as it was strictly for Sunday best, she could only imagine how wonderful it was.

On the following Sunday morning, however, Ellen couldn't help flaunting it in front of Jennifer Chadwell. She felt sure that no-one in Makerton had even heard of Orlon, let alone seen it – or better still, touched it. Jennifer, having been allowed (indeed commanded) to do so, was suitably impressed.

Dorothy didn't work in a department store. Having taken a shorthand-and-typing qualification with her to America, she worked in an office off Time Square. Although both their jobs seemed very ordinary to Ellen, it was generally felt that they were doing all right for themselves 'over there'. And they certainly dressed elegantly and spent lavishly when they came 'home'.

They didn't come home very often, though. It'd been many years since their last visit. Ellen had a hazy memory of going to Liverpool to meet them off the ship which, her father had told her, had taken days and days to cross the Atlantic all the way from New York. Ellen remembered crowds of people and not being able to see very much. She couldn't remember any ship, although she thought she could remember hooters sounding and whistles blowing. Later, she'd sat on Auntie Peggy's knee in the taxi on the way to Makerton, feeling a bit frightened of her loud American voice. She'd rested her cheek on the fur collar of her aunt's coat and wished that she was back home with her mother – and Christine, who was a baby at the time.

On this visit, Auntie Peggy and Dorothy had come by air for the very first time. Ellen, Michael and Christine were at school when they arrived and so couldn't go to the airport to meet them. Neither could their father who was at work.

'Did the Yanks arrive safely, then?' he asked when he got

home. He always called Peggy 'the Yank'.

'They did,' said Mrs McCann.

Auntie Peggy was staying at Auntie Annie's up at Greenside and Dorothy was staying with her own family near by. Ellen couldn't wait to see them.

They all loved Auntie Peggy. She was always laughing, always lively (in spite of the romantic disappointment), and very loud. Her voice, with an American accent that had developed on top of a naturally loud Lancashire one, resonated around their small rooms, making even the most everyday things sound dramatic and exotic.

Ellen began to imitate this accent when Auntie Peggy wasn't there. Christine found this so funny that she kept asking her to 'do Auntie Peggy again' and Ellen was happy to oblige.

'She talks like this,' she said to Jennifer Chadwell, revelling in the attention her newly acquired gift for mimicry was giving her. When she'd perfected it a bit more, she decided, she was going to try it out on Erica Latimer when they went back to school after the holidays.

For Christmas, Auntie Peggy gave Ellen and Christine a handbag each. Christine's was also a musical box. It could be wound up and then, whenever the clasp on the bag was opened, the tune of *Santa Lucia* would ring out. When the clasp was closed again it would stop abruptly. And as it wound down, the brisk pace of the rendition would get slower and slower, more and more dirge-like – until it stopped altogether and had to be wound up again. It was great fun opening and closing this bag.

On the Sunday after Christmas, Christine took it with her to church but forgot to let it wind down fully beforehand. When she opened the bag and the last few distorted bars of *Santa Lucia* escaped from it, she and Ellen got such a fit of giggles that their mother had to split them up by having one on either side of her. This strategy was only partially successful though; laughter once begun was always difficult to control and they each continued to emit odd, strangulated sounds which set them both off again. Mrs McCann, in her efforts to nudge them into silence, had to make vigorous use of both elbows.

Laughing in church was a constant problem and it featured regularly on Ellen's list of sins for Confession. She decided that one of her New Year's resolutions would be to try harder to stop doing it.

On the fourth of January, a couple of days before school started again, they all (except Mr McCann) went to Manchester Airport to see Auntie Peggy and Dorothy off. They were quite a crowd: the McCanns and Auntie Peggy in one taxi; Auntie Annie Cartwright, their Cartwright cousins and Uncle Jack in another; and Dorothy, her elderly mother, sister and two nephews in the third. Three taxis going all the way from Makerton to Manchester was an extravagance that Ellen knew she would also casually mention to Erica Latimer when she went back to school.

It was exciting to be at the airport, but also very sad. When the dreaded moment came to say goodbye, there were lots of hugs – and lots of tears. Last night, when Auntie Peggy had called to say goodbye to Mr McCann, both had shed copious amounts of tears then, too, much to Ellen's embarrassment. Mercifully, Uncle Jack was restraining himself now, only the gruffness of his voice betraying his feelings. Christine, however, caught up in the emotion of the moment, felt no such restraint and burst into loud sobs which made everyone laugh and cry at the same time.

Auntie Peggy and Dorothy blew their last kisses, gave their last waves, and then disappeared from sight. There was an awkward pause, a portentous silence. Ellen knew that everyone was wondering when they would see them again. She glanced at old Mrs Kenyon, and was overcome with sadness.

The Cartwrights decided to go straight home but the McCanns and Uncle Jack went to the observation area to wait for the plane to take off. They had to wait a long time.

Michael didn't mind as he and Uncle Jack could do some plane spotting, and Ellen didn't mind either, but Christine was bored and moaned and complained so much that Mrs McCann said she wished she'd sent her home with her cousins.

At last, the plane began to move. It inched its way on to the runway, stopped again for a few moments, and then it was off, gathering speed as it went. It hurtled down the runway and into the distance before rising slowly into the air. They all waved furiously, even though they knew that Auntie Peggy and Dorothy wouldn't be able to see them. One day, Ellen thought, when she was older, she would go on a plane like this. She would go and visit Auntie Peggy in America. She would go to lots of other places, too. And for a brief, thrilling moment, her life seemed brim-full of possibility.

The plane was just a speck in the sky now – and then it was gone. And in that moment everything changed. All the excitements and the comings and goings of the past three weeks were over; everything seemed suddenly colourless and empty. And now, when everyone else had stopped crying, Ellen's eyes began to fill with tears.

A moment later, however, her sadness turned to rage when they discovered that Christine had wandered off and was nowhere to be seen. Now they would have to spend ages looking for her – as usual. She was always getting lost. It was infuriating.

'I'll swing for her!' said Mrs McCann.

Ellen wasn't quite sure what this phrase meant. She knew it was a serious threat but could only relate it, somewhat incongruously, to a playground swing. The first time she'd heard her mother use it had been on that other memorable occasion, the summer before last, when Christine – only six years old at the time – had got lost in Blackpool. As they began their search for her now, Ellen could see that her mother was experiencing the same feelings of anger, annoyance and panic as she'd done then.

* * *

They'd set up their deck chairs on the beach. And as soon as they'd changed into their swimming costumes, Ellen and Michael went running off into the sea.

'Don't drown!' Mrs McCann called after them. 'And don't get lost!' Because in the summertime, when the beach was crowded and the tide was ever-receding, it was easy enough to get lost on Blackpool sands.

Mr McCann took Christine to the water's edge to do some paddling for a while and then they came back and began building a sandcastle. Michael returned also and lay down on the sand to dry but Ellen kept running back and forth between the sea and the deck chairs. It wasn't long before Christine wanted to go back in the water as well.

'Take her with you,' Mrs McCann said to Ellen.

'Oh . . . do I have to?'

'Yes you do,' said Christine, setting off instantly.

The tide was much further out now.

'You can watch me swim,' said Ellen, 'but don't come in too deep.'

Christine stood up to her knees in the water and watched as Ellen waded out to waist height and flailed around. Soon, though, she became bored with just watching and wanted to go back to the deck chairs and the sandcastle. Ellen was annoyed.

'I can go on my own,' Christine said.

Ellen surveyed the crowded beach. She thought they'd walked to the water in a straight line but they seemed to have veered quite a long way to the left. And they were further away now because the tide was much further out. It was funny how that happened.

'Can you see that ice-cream van over there?' she said pointing into the distance. 'There look, behind that flag where the donkeys are?' Christine nodded, but without conviction. 'There, look. You can just see my mam.' But Ellen could tell that Christine couldn't see what she was pointing at. 'Just let me have one more swim,' she said, 'and I'll take you back.'

She threw herself into the water again and swam a few

strokes out to sea. When she turned round Christine had gone. Full of foreboding, she picked her way through the throng of day-trippers and eventually arrived back at the family deck chairs. But there was no sign of Christine. Of course there wasn't!

Mrs McCann was angry with Ellen. Ellen was furious with Christine. 'She went off without me. I told her to wait. I'll kill her when we find her,' she cried.

Michael was left in charge of the deck chairs and the search began. But it was impossible; the beach was so crowded they could make very little progress, and so noisy there was no point calling out her name. Mrs McCann was getting very agitated. They decided they would get a better view from above, so they stumbled across the dry sand and up the steps to the promenade. There were trams rumbling by here, adding to their anxiety. They went to the lost children's enclosure to see if she had been handed in there, but she hadn't. A loudspeaker announcement was made, crackly and almost unintelligible, appealing for information about the whereabouts of Christine McCann, six years old, wearing a yellow swimming costume.

'I'll swing for her!' said Mrs McCann, frantic now.

Ellen's fury increased.

'Go and see if she's turned up on the sands,' her mother ordered her, at a loss what to do next.

And on her way back Ellen saw Christine sitting calmly on the steps watching the donkeys. She had, she said later, given up trying to find her family and had decided to stay put and wait to be found.

'You stupid girl,' Ellen cried. 'Where've you been? We've been looking everywhere for you! I told you to wait for me! You're in big trouble now. Just you wait till my mam gets hold of you. She's going to kill you.'

But when Mrs McCann saw Christine she ran to her and held her close.

'You silly girl,' she said. 'You've had us worried to death.'

Over her mother's shoulder, Christine gave Ellen a little

smile and then burst into tears. This was what she always did when she was in trouble.

I'll swing for her, thought Ellen.

* * *

She just knew that the same thing would happen again now, here at the airport. Her mother's relief when they finally did find her would over-ride her anger. Yet again, Christine would get off lightly.

Ten minutes later and the search was over, with Christine – as predicted – receiving only the mildest of reprimands. But when she realised that she'd missed seeing Auntie Peggy's plane take off, she burst into noisy tears.

'It-serves-you-right,' said Ellen.

The new decade had started well, and Ellen went back to school happily, with lots of tales to tell. On the bus, the first morning back, she told the others all about the New Year's Eve party; about how they had stayed up into the small hours of New Year's morning and then had had to walk home in the dark. Joan Grady listened with interest, as did Margaret Latham – who was sitting next to Ellen – but Sheila Murphy – who was sitting in front next to Joan – was not impressed.

'We always stay up that late,' she said dismissively.

'What? Till two o'clock in the morning?' said Margaret Latham.

'Yeah,' said Sheila, with a hostile sneer.

'Then on Monday my auntie went back to America and we went to Manchester airport in a taxi to see her off. In three taxis actually,' said Ellen, staring at Sheila Murphy. (Have you been in a taxi? Have you been to an airport?)

Sheila turned away, pretending not to be listening as Ellen proceeded to give an account of the trip, the airport, the planes and of Christine getting lost.

When they got off the bus and began walking to school, Ellen and Joan were side by side as usual. But Sheila Murphy kept pushing in between them and butting into their conversation. Ellen wished that Joan would tell her to get lost

– but she didn't.

The American accent was a great success with Erica Latimer and Angela Norris. Ellen had told them before Christmas about Auntie Peggy coming, and so, without having to explain why she was doing it, she just launched into the accent whenever there was a speaking opportunity. When Erica asked if she had a spare pencil she could borrow, Ellen drawled: 'Sure honey. Let me just take a peek in this liddle ole pencil case of mine.'

Erica was amused and began speaking with an American accent too. Throughout the rest of the day, choosing her teachers carefully, she even did so when answering questions in class, which caused general amusement. Ellen found this profoundly satisfying and resolved to try out the accent on Joan on the way home. But when she did, Sheila refused to be amused so she let it drop.

Ellen was beginning to feel uneasy about Sheila Murphy. She had never liked her; had always thought that she was common and a bit of a bully. But she was Joan's friend now and so had to be tolerated. It was becoming more and more obvious though that Sheila Murphy wasn't being as tolerant of her. This was probably because she was still bearing a grudge from that time at St Wilfrid's when Ellen had made everyone laugh at her.

It'd been when they'd just gone up into Miss Gaskell's class from Miss Long's. They were having hymn practice. Sheila Murphy was standing behind Ellen and Joan, and Ellen distinctly heard her sing: *'Thou who art called the parakeet'* in the Holy Ghost hymn, in spite of the fact that she had the hymn book with the words in it open in her hands. In the playground later, when Sheila was being extremely annoying about something or other, Ellen, in a state of exasperation, hadn't been able to resist bringing this to everyone's attention.

'You think you know everything, you,' she said, 'but you don't. When we were singing *Come Holy Ghost* this morning, you sang 'parakeet' when it should be 'paraclete' – *Thou who art called the Paraclete'*.

Sheila Murphy curled her lip and shrugged. Paraclete, parakeet – what did it matter?

'A parakeet's a bird,' said Ellen.

'Well the Holy Ghost's a bird,' said Sheila. 'Anyway, He is when He comes down to earth.'

'Yeah, but then He's a dove or something.'

'How do you know what kind of bird He is?'

'I know He's not a *parakeet!* All of Ellen's scorn went into her enunciation of this word. 'Parakeets,' she went on confidently, 'are all brightly coloured, like parrots – or big budgies.' She had seen pictures of them in Michael's *Book of Birds*. She knew what she was talking about.

Then Joan began to sing: *'Thou who art called the budgerigar / Best gift of God above...'* and everyone laughed.

Sheila Murphy gave Ellen a poisonous look and flounced away.

But if she was still holding a grudge, it was only against Ellen. Joan had obviously been forgiven long ago. Although they both lived on the Greenside estate, Joan and Sheila had never been particularly friendly until they'd found themselves in the same class at the Convent. But now they'd become almost inseparable. As well as spending all day at school together, Sheila called for Joan every morning and walked back to her house with her every afternoon. It was becoming clear that she wanted to supplant Ellen and become Joan's best friend in her stead.

Margaret Latham, in 1B, had made new friends very quickly. From the first day nearly, she spent all her time in school with them, and she only travelled to and fro with her old St Wilfrid's friends if their paths happened to cross.

Ellen, on the other hand, had tried to spend as much time as possible with Joan. And up till now the continual presence of Sheila Murphy hadn't been a problem. All three of them travelled to school together, and they met up at dinner times. (At first, Ellen had tried to meet them at the morning break too, but this had proved too difficult and so she'd been spending this time with Angela Norris who was in a similar position with her friends from her old primary school.) After school they would wait for one other at an agreed spot on the street, just outside the cloakrooms, before going home together. Sometimes Margaret Latham would be with them, sometimes not. When she was, she and Sheila Murphy would sit next to one another on the bus because Ellen and Joan, as befitted best friends, always sat together going home.

Throughout the first term these arrangements had worked well. Or, at least, Ellen had thought they had. Now, however, she could see that things were changing. Sheila Murphy was becoming much more assertive, much less respectful of hers and Joan's special friendship. Ellen was beginning to feel threatened.

The term was only a week old when, one afternoon after school, Ellen arrived at the meeting place a bit later than usual and there was no-one there. She hung around for a few minutes but it was obvious that Joan and Sheila had left without her. Feeling hurt and aggrieved, she walked to the bus stop as quickly as she could, hoping to catch up with them, but they were nowhere to be seen. She went home on the bus alone.

'Why didn't you wait for me yesterday?' she asked the next morning.

'We thought you'd already gone,' said Sheila.

'Why would I have done that?' asked Ellen, looking at Joan.

'Sheila said she thought she saw you walking down the road,' said Joan, 'so we hurried up but we never caught up with you.'

'That's because it wasn't me!' said Ellen. 'I wouldn't go without you. I always wait for you.'

Joan looked apologetic but Sheila just shrugged her shoulders and pulled a face.

'You should've waited for me,' Ellen said.

'Who cares, anyway?' said Sheila. 'You're making a fuss about nothing.'

A week later, Joan and Sheila said they had to stay behind for something after school, so Ellen went home on her own. The next day she waited for them as usual but they didn't show up, so thinking that they'd had to stay behind again and had forgotten to tell her, she set off alone once more. This time, though, they'd only been delayed and they caught up with her at the bus stop.

'So it's all right for you not to wait for us, is it?' said Sheila.

'I thought you were staying behind again,' said Ellen. 'I did wait for ages.'

'Well it doesn't matter because we don't care whether you wait or not. Do we?' said Sheila, turning to Joan.

Ellen turned to her too, but Joan was looking elsewhere.

When the bus came, Sheila led the way upstairs and sat down. Joan, following behind, sat down next to her. Ellen was mortified. Faced now with the choice of sitting in front of them or behind them, she opted for the latter and spent the journey watching them chatting away together. They didn't turn round once to include her in their conversation.

She couldn't believe how hurt she felt. How could Joan do this to her? I'm never going to speak to either of them ever again, she resolved. But she knew it wasn't that simple. She could travel to and from school on her own – and anyway she'd have Jennifer for company next year, wouldn't she? – but if she were to fall out with Joan and Sheila now, what would she do tomorrow at dinner-time? Who would she spend that hour and a half with? Margaret Latham had her new friends; Angela Norris had her old friends; Erica Latimer went home for dinner with Sally Wagstaff – and probably wouldn't want Ellen hanging around with them, anyway. She remembered her mother's confident words: 'You'll soon make new friends. Just wait and see.' But everyone had their own arrangements now. She had left it too late. She felt cold and sick.

The bus was approaching the Greenside stop. Sheila Murphy rose and without a backward glance headed for the stairs. Ellen thought that Joan was going to do the same but at the very last moment she turned and said: 'See you tomorrow,' just like she always did.

'Yeah. See you,' said Ellen stiffly.

Through the bus window she thought she saw Joan glance up briefly, but she could've been mistaken. She watched them walk down the path which led on to the estate. They were laughing about something, probably about her. They were becoming two of a kind, she thought bitterly. Sheila Murphy was trying to drive a wedge between them – and Joan was letting her. Joan was betraying their special friendship. And Ellen thought about Auntie Peggy and Dorothy who hadn't let anyone drive a wedge between them – not even the loves of their lives.

Later, lying awake in bed, Ellen reviewed her situation. She could see that she'd been foolish to rely so much on Joan. She should've made more friends in her own class. She went over in her mind all the groupings of girls in 1A. Could she infiltrate one of these now? Were there any threesomes that might welcome a fourth member? Her best option seemed to be Angela Norris. Perhaps Angela only went off with her old friends at dinner-times because there was no-one else available? Perhaps she would welcome an approach from Ellen? After all, they did sit next to each other and they did spend break times together. And she really liked Angela.

And then she could travel to and from school with Margaret Latham and forget about Joan and Sheila Murphy altogether. Perhaps Margaret Latham would like this, too? And she really liked Margaret Latham, too – didn't she? Yes, of course she did, she told herself, trying to dismiss the slight feeling of resentment which she had come to feel towards Margaret Latham. She knew why she felt this, and she knew it wasn't Margaret's fault. It was Miss Stupid Gaskell's fault – and that composition they'd had to write.

* * *

Miss Gaskell was the elderly teacher who taught the scholarship class at St Wilfrid's. Her authoritarian and forbidding approach came as a shock to the girls after two years of Miss Long's benevolence, and she was disliked and feared. But Ellen, a model pupil, had always managed to avoid her wrath until that stupid composition.

Once they'd sat the eleven-plus examination, the ten 'scholarship' girls were also required to submit a composition, the purpose of which was to decide 'borderline' cases, it was said. And so they'd been doing practice ones in preparation for the real thing. All had been going well for Ellen until 'A Day at the Seaside.'

'I've got a bone to pick with you, madam,' Miss Gaskell said to Ellen one morning, holding aloft their latest efforts. 'I can't believe that now, with only a week to go, you start writing like this.' She waved the papers in the air and then slapped them down on her desk.

Everyone turned to look at Ellen who began to go very red. What on earth could she have done to provoke such an outburst? Did Miss Gaskell mean her handwriting? No, she had very neat handwriting; it couldn't be that. So what had she done wrong? But she had to wait until the other nine compositions were given back, before Miss Gaskell deigned to elaborate further.

'A Day at the Seaside', she said, looking round the classroom. 'Stand up Ellen McCann and tell us all what is wrong with this.' And she began to read Ellen's composition aloud, in a low, ominous monotone. *When we go to the seaside it is nearly always to Blackpool. We go on a large, shiny coach and I always try to be the first person to see Blackpool Tower. I nearly always am. "There it is," I exclaim excitedly pointing out of the window. The next minute, though, it is on the other side of the road which makes us all laugh.'* Miss Gaskell paused. 'Well?' she said.

Ellen had no idea what was wrong with that. She stood there not knowing what to say. Miss Gaskell let the silence lengthen. The classroom, with its high windows that no-one could see out of, felt very oppressive. Several people turned round to look at Ellen. [One of these, she remembered now, was Sheila Murphy.]

'We are all waiting,' said Miss Gaskell.

'I don't know, Miss,' said Ellen.

Miss Gaskell read it out again and then threw open the question to the whole class. No-one knew what was wrong with it. It couldn't be that bad, thought Ellen, if no-one knew.

'Sit down!' Miss Gaskell barked, as if Ellen had been standing up from her own choice. 'You were asked to write about a day at the seaside,' she went on, once Ellen was seated. 'A day. A day in the past when you'd been to the seaside. A day in the past that you should have written about in the past tense. Is this the past tense? *"When we go to the seaside it is nearly always to Blackpool."* No, it most certainly isn't. It's the present tense. *"We go,* I *am,* it *is, makes"* – all the present tense. What Ellen McCann has written about is not *a* day at the seaside, a *specific* day, but *any* day at the sea side. The title of this composition was not "Any Old Day at the Seaside", was it?' She paused, and then issued her warning: 'Don't ever let me see any of you writing in the present tense again.'

Was that it then? It seemed a bit of an anticlimax. Ellen didn't know whether to be relieved or deeply ashamed. It was obvious, too, that the rest of the class had been hoping for a much more serious misdemeanour. Most of them didn't even know what the present tense was, let alone care about its misuse.

But Miss Gaskell hadn't finished yet. She began reading again: *"When we get to the promenade the tide is always in so we go for our dinner while we are waiting for the sand to appear again."* What is wrong with that?'

What was wrong with that? (Miss Gaskell couldn't possibly have known that had Ellen read it aloud herself she would've pronounced it 'promen-aid' rather than – she now realised – the more correct 'promen-ard'.)

Ellen was expecting another long, uncomprehending

silence but this time a hand went up. And it belonged to Margaret Latham.

'Yes?' said Miss Gaskell.

'Please Miss,' said Margaret nervously, 'the tide can't always be in when she goes there because tides come in at a different time every day.'

This, apparently, was the right answer. Ellen was not convinced. She'd been to Blackpool lots of times and the tide was always in when they got there late in the morning. Yes, she was prepared to concede, sometimes it was just coming in, sometimes it was right up to the sea wall, and sometimes it was on its way out, but whichever it was, they could never go straight on to the sands.

Ellen doubted whether Margaret Latham had ever been to Blackpool. Both her parents were teachers and they had a caravan which they took to France every summer. Tides might behave like that in France but she felt that she knew more about the sea at Blackpool than either Margaret Latham or Miss Gaskell put together.

Miss Gaskell went abroad on holiday too. They knew this because she'd told them that when she'd crossed the Channel the ferry fare from Dover to Calais had been more expensive than it would've been if she'd gone from Folkestone to Boulogne or Newhaven to Dieppe. She had produced a map and shown them that the shortest route was the most expensive and the longest route the cheapest. How, she had asked them, could they account for that? They couldn't, of course, but it transpired that it had to do with something called supply and demand.

Miss Gaskell held up the offending composition and made Ellen walk to the front of the classroom to get it. 'Let us hope that you are not a borderline case,' she said, thrusting it at her. 'If you are, you'll have to do better than this if you want to pass.'

She waited while they all watched Ellen walk back to her desk, and then proceeded to tell them all how uninspiring their efforts had been. More description was needed, she said, more adjectives, more interesting vocabulary. And how many times had she told them not to begin sentences with 'and' or 'then' or – worst of all – 'and then'?

Ellen's composition contained none of these stylistic lapses, and it was, in her opinion, full of detail and interesting vocabulary. Her original intention had been to write about the time Christine had got lost, but she'd decided against this, partly because she knew that Miss Gaskell wasn't a great lover of narrative, and partly because it would've been too revealing. So she'd chosen instead to write dispassionately and descriptively about a typical day at the seaside. She could have cried.

* * *

Yes, well, she wasn't a borderline case, was she? Ellen thought now, turning over in bed. And she was in 1A and Margaret Latham was only in 1B.

But she mustn't hold any of this against Margaret Latham.

A few days later, during which time the status quo had been tentatively restored, Joan was away from school. When dinner-time came round, Ellen couldn't bring herself to seek out Sheila. She queued up by herself in the dining hall and then took her tray of food over to the table where Angela was sitting with her friends. As they were on benches, room could always be made for another person if everyone budged up a bit. After they'd finished eating, Ellen tagged along with them, feeling a bit awkward and in the way, and really hoping that Joan would be back the next day. But she wasn't, and so Ellen did the same thing again. On the third day, Angela said: 'Do your American accent, Ellen' and Ellen pretended to be reluctant. But when Angela insisted, she did, and they were all amused.

On the day that Joan returned to school, Ellen went to join her and Sheila Murphy in the dining hall as usual.

But Sheila had no intention of allowing this. 'You didn't want to sit with me when Joan was away, did you? Well *we* don't want you here, now,' she said. 'You're a snob, you are. You always have been. You think just because you're in 1A you're better than us, but you're not.'

Ellen could see that it had only been a matter of time before this accusation was levelled against her. She looked at Joan, willing her to dissociate herself from this charge, but Joan said nothing. Ellen waited for a moment, her dinner tray heavy in her hands, giving her friend – her best friend – another chance to speak. Joan remained silent.

And so Ellen turned away and walked over to Angela's table. 'Hey, honey,' she said brightly. 'Is there room here for a liddle one?'

There was. The transition had been made. And it had, in the end, been quite easy. But as she laughed and chatted with her new friends, her heart was aching.

FEBRUARY

1962

For the third successive year, Erica sent Joe Wagstaff a Valentine card. And, for the first time, Ellen sent Michael Chadwell one too. It had a red heart on the front with an arrow going through it (not unlike one of Sandra Crompton's equals signs). She addressed the envelope using capital letters and a green biro that she'd borrowed from Angela Norris. She didn't write anything inside the card except a large question mark and a smaller kiss.

She didn't tell Erica that she was sending it. She just listened patiently as Erica went on and on about what she'd written in hers to Joe, and how she was hoping that this year she might receive one from him in return.

But yet again there was no card for Erica (nor – sadly – for Ellen either). Never suspecting for a moment that one of them was from Erica, Sally Wagstaff informed them that Joe had received two cards. He was, she said, maintaining that he knew who had sent them both but wouldn't say who they were. They concluded from this that he had no idea.

On the following Sunday, on the way home from church, Jennifer Chadwell told Ellen that – surprisingly – she hadn't received any Valentine cards at all this year, but that – even more surprisingly – their Michael had. 'I can't think who would've sent him one,' she said dismissively.

'Neither can I,' said Ellen. 'Our Michael got one too but his was from Sandra Crompton – as usual! She even signed it with an 'S'.' And then, before Jennifer could ask whether she'd received any herself, she changed the subject. 'Anyway, listen,' she announced. 'On Tuesday I'm going to Birmingham with Erica Latimer. We're going to stay with her grandmother for half-term.'

February was always a dull month, once St Valentine's Day had been and gone. This trip would brighten it up very nicely.

It was customary, during this half-term holiday, for Erica and her brothers and sisters to go and stay with their maternal grandmother in Birmingham. This year, however, Caroline was going to be away on a sixth-form trip and Maria had announced that she didn't want to go.

'She doesn't want to face Granny Morton,' Erica told Ellen. 'She knows what Granny'll say about her wanting to be a nun. She knows she'll try to talk her out of it. She's not a Catholic, you know. Granny I mean – not Maria, obviously.'

Ellen didn't know this. She was surprised. Did this mean that Mrs Latimer hadn't been a Catholic either? No, that couldn't be right. She must have been.

'My mother wasn't a Catholic either till she married my dad,' said Erica as though reading Ellen's thoughts.

'Oh,' said Ellen. She didn't know what else to say. Erica hardly ever mentioned her mother, and whenever anyone else did she always went very quiet.

One afternoon recently, Ellen had gone round to Church Walk after school and Granny Latimer had been there. As they'd walked into the hall they'd heard her saying to Erica's father: 'She'll make a beautiful nun. Her mother would've been proud.'

Erica stopped in her tracks. 'Would she, really?' she said.

'Yes!' said Granny Latimer, turning to face her. And then, somewhat obliquely, she added: 'She was a saint, your mother. A saint. Too good for this world.'

Erica turned abruptly and rushed up the stairs two steps at a time, leaving Ellen to follow more slowly, feeling awkward and uncomfortable.

When it became clear that Maria wasn't going to change her mind about going to Birmingham, Erica declared that she wanted Ellen to go with her instead. Her brothers alone would not suffice, she said; she needed female company. The proposition had been put to Granny Morton, Mr Latimer and Mrs McCann, and, as none of them had had any objections, it had been decided.

Ellen was both excited and nervous. She felt flattered that Erica had chosen her rather than Sally Wagstaff. But there were worries. Did she have enough suitable clothes for the trip? Would Granny Morton like her? And, most worryingly of all, what if she started her periods while she was there?

This was a constant worry these days. She was beginning to think that she would never start. She was nearly fourteen! Everyone else had started ages ago. Angela Norris certainly had. Regularly, each month, she would spend a morning or an afternoon in the nurse's room, pale and tearful, with a hot-water bottle clasped to her aching stomach. Erica had started too, but she didn't seem to suffer at all and rarely mentioned it. Even Jennifer Chadwell had started – and she was nearly a year younger than Ellen! When Jennifer had told her about this, she hadn't said that she herself hadn't started yet. She'd just let Jennifer assume otherwise. She was good at this kind of indirect deception.

At the Convent, at the beginning of the second year, each girl had been issued with a booklet entitled *Growing Up The Catholic Way*. On the cover of this was a drawing of Our Lady, wearing her veil with a halo hovering above it. The booklet dealt – very briefly – with the subject of menstruation and childbirth, and told them that sexual intercourse (Ellen liked to read these two words very slowly and deliberately: 'sex-u-al inter-course') should be avoided at all costs until they were married and wanted to have children. It didn't say what sexual intercourse was exactly, but it did contain a very interesting diagram of ovaries, uterus and vagina which Ellen found both compelling and mystifying.

She was particularly taken aback by the vagina. (How was it pronounced? She'd never heard the word spoken.) She'd been thinking of it as little more than a hole, but it was, actually, quite a long passageway. It made the prospect of menstruation all the more alarming – blood gushing down this passage rather than dripping through the hole as she had previously imagined. And the fact that it could happen at any moment, without any warning, was terrifying. How could you get on with your life in this uncertain state?

And then, once you had started, how did you cope every month? Well, obviously, people did. The school was full of bleeding girls and it catered for them accordingly. Hanging from each toilet door were brown paper bags into which you could deposit your used sanitary towels. And on the walls outside the toilets there were incinerators. She'd watched other girls using these. They would open the little drawers in the incinerators and deposit their brown paper packages inside. Then the fire would stoke up and the machines would vibrate alarmingly, sounding as though they might launch themselves into space at any moment.

She knew that when her time came she wouldn't be able to do this in public. She would have to stuff the paper bag into her satchel and take it home with her. And then she would have to slip it into the fire without her father or Michael – or even Christine, for that matter – seeing it. The whole thing was so embarrassing. The booklet exhorted them to model themselves on the Virgin Mary in all these matters. But Mary hadn't gone to school, had she, or been required to use an incinerator? Already she had her limits as a role model.

While she was packing for the Birmingham trip, her mother came into the bedroom bearing a packet of sanitary towels and a sanitary belt.

'You'd better take these, too,' she said awkwardly. 'You

never know.'

Ellen blushed and put them at the bottom of the case underneath the clothes she'd already packed. She didn't want Christine to see them.

On the Tuesday morning Mrs McCann came to Turneley Station to see Ellen off. She and Erica's father shook hands and began a polite conversation while Ellen and Erica stood waiting for the train in embarrassed silence.

Ellen had been worrying about the state of her suitcase but she needn't have – the Latimers' cases were even more battered than hers. When the train arrived they scrambled aboard and Mr Latimer heaved their luggage up on to the rack. He warned them all to be on their best behaviour and told Erica not to let her brothers put their heads out of the window unless they wanted to arrive in Birmingham with two headless corpses. As the train began to move along the platform, he and Mrs McCann began waving. Tom and James waved back but Erica and Ellen remained affectedly aloof. Once their respective parents were out of sight Erica breathed an exaggerated sigh of relief and they both began to giggle.

Granny Morton met them at New Street Station. She had a taxi waiting nearby. The streets were very noisy; there seemed to be a lot of building work going on. There were blue and cream buses everywhere and the pavements were crowded with people, many of whom were black. Ellen was fascinated and thrilled. Birmingham was a big city. It made Turneley seem small and inconsequential.

They drove out of the city centre to Edgbaston where Granny Morton lived. The taxi passed through a pair of big iron gates, crunched along a gravel driveway and stopped in front of a large, detached, double-fronted house. They all spilled out, and then the taxi crunched its way back down the drive, throwing out little stones from beneath its wheels as it went.

Inside the front door was a tiled hallway as big as a

room, with a wrought-iron staircase in the centre which swept up and round to the landing above. Ellen was impressed.

'Take your things upstairs,' said Granny Morton. 'I'll put the kettle on.'

They went up the grand staircase and the two boys disappeared down a side corridor to their room.

'That's Granny's room,' said Erica pointing. 'That one's Phyllis's. And this one's ours.' She opened the door of a large bedroom which overlooked a huge garden at the back of the house. There were two single beds in the room and Erica went straight to the one which was obviously hers when she was staying here.

'Who's Phyllis?' Ellen asked, putting her case on the other bed. Why, she wondered, did Erica never tell her about people in advance.

'She's Granny's lodger. Well, she's her friend, really. She's lived here for centuries – well, ever since Grandpa died. She's a teacher. She's nice.'

'It's a beautiful house,' said Ellen, touching the ornate marble fireplace which graced the room.

'It's Georgian,' said Erica. 'Ours is Victorian. What's yours?'

Ellen hesitated. What was hers? She'd never thought of King's Terrace in this way before. It was just old.

'It's Victorian too, I think,' she murmured and then immediately knew that this couldn't be right. If it was King's Terrace it couldn't be Victorian, could it? And there was a stone on Mrs Chisnall's house which said 1903. Oh, well, it didn't matter. Erica wasn't really interested.

The two boys were already outside in the garden by the time the girls got back downstairs. They sat down at the big kitchen table and Granny Morton poured the tea. She was a tall, handsome woman, younger looking than Ellen had been expecting – younger than Granny Latimer, anyway. Her greying hair was pinned up on her head in a rather untidy mess and she had a pair of glasses on a chain round her neck. She put these on her nose now and, lifting her head, looked down them at Erica.

'How is everyone, then?' she said. 'How is your father?'

'Fine,' said Erica. 'He's fine. Everyone's fine.'

'And Maria?'

Erica glanced at Ellen, a little smile just discernible on her lips. 'She's fine, too.'

'Hmm,' said Granny Morton. 'Tell me, how long has this nun nonsense been going on?'

The way she said 'nun nonsense' reminded Ellen of the way her own mother had reacted when she'd been told about Maria Latimer wanting to be a nun. Ellen had been surprised, expecting her mother to be impressed not annoyed. But it seemed to be the fact that Maria wanted to be a Carmelite nun – like St Thérèse, after whom their school was named – that Mrs McCann found so disturbing.

'It's been going on for quite a while,' said Erica.

'And what does your father have to say about it?'

'Not much.'

Granny Morton sniffed. 'I expect he's hoping she'll grow out of the idea. A young girl like that – wanting to lock herself away. It's ridiculous.'

'Granny Latimer thinks she'll make a lovely nun,' said Erica with another little smile. 'And if God is calling her . . .'

Granny Morton sniffed again, more loudly this time. 'Well, I hope you don't go getting silly ideas like that, too,' she said.

'We-ell . . . if He were to call me . . . ,' said Erica, smiling broadly now.

'Don't worry, He won't,' said Ellen and they all burst out laughing. Granny Morton walked over to the window and peered out into the garden. It was beginning to go dark.

'That boy is going to fall out of that tree and break his neck,' she said, knocking on the window. But the tree was at the bottom of the garden and neither Tom nor James seemed to hear.

She returned to her seat and changed the subject. 'And Maggie?' she said. 'I hear from Georgina that Maggie is a permanent fixture now.'

'She doesn't live with us if that's what you mean,' said Erica, no longer smiling. 'But yes, she's always round at our house "helping out".'

'Well, I expect your father needs all the help he can get.'

'Granny Latimer helps out. And we're all older now. We don't actually need Maggie.' Erica glanced out of the window at her brothers.

'You don't sound as though you like her,' said Granny Morton. 'I can't think why not. She was always a lovely girl. I think your father is lucky to have her.'

Now it was Erica's turn to sniff.

In their bedroom later, Ellen learned that Granny Morton had known Maggie since she was a schoolgirl. She and Erica's mother had been best friends.

'Why did Maggie come to Turneley?' Ellen asked. 'Did she come because she was . . . you know . . . already going out with your dad? Or did she just come and then they started going out with each other?' Maggie, she knew, was head librarian at the Central Library and had only lived in Turneley since getting the job there about a year ago.

'I don't know,' said Erica. 'I just wish she'd go away.'

'Why don't you like her,' said Ellen. It was always hard to get Erica to talk about Maggie and this was too good an opportunity to let pass. 'She seems nice enough to me.'

'Oh yeah! Everyone likes Maggie! Good old Maggie! Everyone likes her – except me and Maria.'

It was news to Ellen that Maria didn't like Maggie either. She wondered whether this might be because Maggie disapproved of the 'nun nonsense', too.

Erica jumped into bed and began thumping her pillow. 'We don't need a new mother,' she said. 'We don't want her – and my dad shouldn't want her either.'

Ellen tried to imagine how she would feel if her mother were dead and her father had a new girlfriend. But it was hard to picture Mr McCann with a woman like Maggie – or, indeed, with any woman other than her mother. And she remembered Joan Grady's question: 'Who would you rather die, your mam or your dad?' What if it was her dad who'd died? Would her widowed mother eventually acquire a new boyfriend? Again, it was impossible to imagine. Only women like Sandra Crompton's mother had boyfriends – 'and Mr Crompton wasn't even dead!

While they were staying at Granny Morton's they had to eat all their meals in the kitchen because the dining-room was out of use. The table in there was covered with boxes, envelopes, photograph albums and piles and piles of photographs. Granny Morton was, she said, having a big sort out.

'I've been meaning to put all these photos into albums for years,' she told them. 'It's very time consuming, but if we're going to move to a smaller place I need to be ready.' She indicated a small pile of albums. 'You can look at those. They're done, but please don't touch any of these loose photos. I'm trying to get them into chronological order and it's harder than it sounds. And you two,' she turned to the boys. 'Keep out of here altogether.' She ushered them out of the room, leaving Erica and Ellen alone.

'Are they moving?' asked Ellen, thinking what a shame it would be to leave this lovely house. 'Where are they going to go?'

'Nowhere,' said Erica. 'Granny's been talking about moving for years but she never does. When Phyllis retires. When we've all grown up. Probably never.'

The albums were full of photos of Granny and Grandpa Morton when they were young, and of their three children – Mrs Latimer and her two younger brothers.

'I've seen most of these before,' Erica said, flicking over the pages. Then: 'Oh, God! Look at this one.' She pointed to a photograph of her mother and another girl, both of them wearing school uniform. 'It's her, isn't it?'

'Oh, yeah . . . it is, it's Maggie,' said Ellen. 'They look the same age as we are now, don't they?'

'She looks stupid,' said Erica.

'No she doesn't.'

Mrs Latimer, or Anne Morton as she was then in the black and white photo, had long plaits and looked very serious and intense. Maggie, her hair loose, looked much more frivolous. She was gazing rather provocatively at the camera. Just like Erica might do, thought Ellen.

'Yes, she does. She looks silly. Just look at her,' said Erica, imitating Maggie's pose to perfection.

Ellen smiled.

'Doesn't my mother look like Maria?' Erica went on, switching her attention away from Maggie. Here, in her grandmother's house, she seemed able to talk about her mother.

Disregarding instructions, she began looking at some of the loose photos arranged in piles on the table.

'You shouldn't touch those,' warned Ellen, but Erica couldn't resist.

They seemed to be stacked in what Granny Morton hoped was chronological order. She had pencilled dates on the backs of some of them, but some of these dates had question marks next to them.

'Look. This is me,' said Erica handing Ellen a photo of her little self riding a tricycle in the garden at Church Walk. Ellen, fascinated, couldn't resist looking, either. She just hoped that Granny Morton wouldn't come back in and catch them.

There were lots of photos here of the Latimer children at various stages in their lives, from their births almost to the present day. In nearly all of them they were laughing or smiling. Mrs Latimer, smiling also, was in many of them. And then she disappeared. But, in the photos taken in the years after her death, they all continued to smile happily for the camera. It seemed a bit heartless to Ellen.

The next day, Erica took her to have a look at the university which was only a short walk away. They wandered on to the campus and walked around for a while. There was building work going on here too. Ellen looked up at the tall, red-brick clock tower as it was striking the hour and felt strangely exhilarated. 'I think I'd like to go to university,' she said. 'Perhaps I'll come here.'

'Caroline wants to come here,' said Erica, 'but I don't. I don't want to have to live with Granny. I want to go to London – or Paris.'

'You'd have to be very good at French to go there,' said Ellen. 'Better than you are now.'

'*Mais, oui! C'est vrai,*' said Erica, shrugging her shoulders and opening the palms of her hands to the sky. '*Londres* it is then.'

Ellen liked Granny Morton. She made her feel welcome, showing just the right amount of interest in her. She asked questions which were easy to answer, about school, her favourite subjects, her brother and sister. She didn't ask what her father did for a living, nor what kind of house she lived in, although Ellen had an answer for this now. It was an early Edwardian end of terrace.

Phyllis was nice too. She was a bit younger than Granny Morton but they seemed to be the best of friends. They reminded Ellen of Auntie Peggy and Dorothy. Except that Granny Morton had been married. Phyllis was a schoolteacher, 'looking forward to retirement' she kept saying. She had a car – a pale green Morris Minor – and on the Friday of their stay she took Erica and Ellen to Stratford for the day, leaving Granny Morton and the boys to their own devices.

'Everyone should visit Stratford at least once in their lives,' she boomed.

Erica sat next to her in the front passenger seat. 'Phyllis?' she said, after they'd been driving for a while and had left the city streets behind and were out in the countryside. 'Do you remember the night my mother died?'

'Yes dear, of course I do,' said Phyllis, quietly now.

'Was it out here where she crashed?'

Ellen was taken aback. She'd always thought that Mrs Latimer had died in Turneley. She was certainly buried there. Her grave was in the churchyard of St Peter's. Ellen had gone there to look at it, secretly, one Saturday afternoon ages ago, when she'd been shopping in Turneley with her mother. It hadn't been too difficult to find. It was in the shadow of the high wall that surrounded the graveyard, clearly marked for all to see. There were several other Latimers buried there too, but their headstones, with the writing carved into the stone, were old and covered in moss. Mrs Latimer's headstone was relatively new. *Anne Latimer* it said in bold lettering on the white marble. *1919 – 1956*. And underneath: *Beloved Wife and Mother*. Erica's middle name was Anne. 'I was called Erica after Grandpa Morton,' she'd told Ellen once. 'He was called Eric, of course – not Erica. And I was called Anne after Granny Latimer.' She hadn't said then that Anne was also her mother's name.

That Mrs Latimer had died somewhere else was a revelation. Ellen's heart began to beat rapidly. For some reason, she felt a bit frightened. They waited for Phyllis to reply.

'No, no,' she said after a long pause. 'I don't think it was anywhere near here.'

'Where was it then?'

'I'm not sure. Somewhere between Birmingham and Warwick, I think.'

'But it was on a country road like this?'

'Yes, I think so,' said Phyllis, slowing down slightly although she hadn't been going fast. Erica didn't speak again until they arrived in Stratford.

They had a lovely day out even though the weather was cold and dull. They walked around the town and then went down to the river where they admired the swans. Phyllis said they should come again in the summer and take a boat out. They went to look at the theatre and she said that next time they should go to see a play too. They were old enough now to appreciate Shakespeare. Listening to her saying this, Ellen got that feeling of exhilaration again – of life being full of possibilities, full of interesting and exciting opportunities awaiting her in the not too distant future. She glanced at Erica, wondering if she too was feeling that.

Phyllis said she didn't like driving in the countryside in the dark so they left shortly after lunch. Ellen wondered if it had been dark when Mrs Latimer had crashed her car. But was it her car? Would she have had the family car here in Birmingham?

'I didn't know your mother was here in Birmingham when she . . . you know?' said Ellen that night as they lay in bed.

'Yeah, she was,' Erica said. 'She was staying here. Granny had had an operation and she was looking after her.' And then, quite unexpectedly, she began to volunteer more information. 'Maria was with her too,' she said, 'and James. Maria was here because she'd got chicken pox and couldn't go to school, and James was only a baby. The rest of us were at home and Granny Latimer was looking after us.' She paused, and then, as if she were reading Ellen's thoughts again: 'It was Grandpa's car she was driving. Granny never bothered to get rid of it after he died and so we used to use it when we came here. It was old. Everyone thought there might've been something wrong with it and that's why it crashed.'

They lay there in silence for a while. Ellen thought that Erica must've fallen asleep, but suddenly she said: 'I wonder where she was going – or where she'd been? Somewhere between Birmingham and Warwick? At night-time.'

Georgina Latimer, who was in her final year at a nearby teachers' training college, was coming for tea on Saturday afternoon. After lunch, even though it was raining, Phyllis took the two boys out for a drive while Granny Morton began pottering about in the kitchen. Erica and Ellen wandered into the chilly dining room again to look at more photographs. Granny Morton had been doing some more sorting since they'd last looked.

'Look. Here's your parents' wedding photo,' said Ellen gazing at the wedding group – the bride seated beside two little bridesmaids, the groom standing behind her with the best man.

'Yeah. We've got that one on the wall at home,' said Erica, not really interested.

'I wonder why Maggie wasn't a bridesmaid?' said Ellen.

Erica shrugged. 'It was during the war,' she said, as if this explained it. They would often hear people cite the war as the reason for unusual events or circumstances. She picked up another wedding photo. This one had all the guests on it, clustered round the bride and groom. 'I've never seen this before,' she said turning it over. On the back, Granny Morton had written the names of all these guests. 'She wasn't there at all,' she said. 'Maggie, I mean. Her name's not here.' She turned the photo over again and studied it carefully.

'Hey, look,' she said. 'That's my uncle Edward in his RAF uniform. Granny said he didn't want the war to be over before he was old enough to join up but that she'd hoped and prayed that it would be. He . . .' she trailed off.

Ellen looked at her.

'He joined the RAF just before the end of the war,' she said, her voice almost a whisper now. She turned to the back of the photo again then snatched the other wedding one out of Ellen's hand and turned that over too.

'What's the matter?' said Ellen.

'Nothing.'

But something obviously was.

Ellen had never met Gina before but liked her immediately. She looked like an older version of Erica, and was very friendly – like a much younger version of Granny Morton. She seemed to be popular with the boys too. She chatted to Phyllis about her teaching practice and began to help her grandmother with the tea.

'Are we still eating in the kitchen?' she said, laughing. 'Haven't you finished sorting the photos yet, Granny?'

'It's not as easy as you might think,' said Granny Morton defensively. 'Putting them in chronological order is difficult after all these years.'

'Where are you up to then?' asked Gina.

'She's up to 1944,' said Erica. 'She's doing 1944 now, aren't you Granny? 1944.' Something in Erica's tone made them all turn to look at her. It reminded Ellen of the antagonistic way she spoke to Maggie. She began to feel uneasy.

'If you say so, dear,' murmured Granny Morton. 'Sometimes I wish I'd never started doing it.'

After tea Erica asked Gina to come and look at the photos.

'We should wash up,' said Gina but Phyllis shooed them away and they went into the dining room.

'She's done quite a lot since I was here last,' said Gina, flicking through one of the completed albums.

'Look at this,' said Erica handing her the wedding photo. Gina took it, looked at it and then put it back on the table. Erica picked it up again and thrust it back at her. 'Look at the date she's put on the back,' she said.

But Gina didn't look at the date. She just kept looking at the photo. She had gone all still and quiet.

'It says 1944.'

'Does it?'

'She must've made a mistake with the date, mustn't she? They couldn't have got married in 1944, could they? It's a mistake. She's getting muddled up.'

Gina glanced at Ellen. 'It's not a mistake,' she said.

'It must be,' said Erica, her voice rising.

Ellen was puzzled. Why was Erica so upset?

'It must be,' Erica repeated. 'Otherwise you would have been born before they got married. Three years before they got married!'

Gina said nothing but glanced at Ellen again. Ellen picked up one of the albums and tried to appear engrossed in it. There was an awkward pause.

'You know about this already, don't you?' said Erica, shocked.

'Yes,' said Gina. 'Dad and Maggie told me a while ago.'

'Maggie! What's it got to do with her?'

'It was Maggie's idea to tell me. Dad said he was going to tell me when I was twenty-one but Maggie said I should know now.'

'Who else knows?'

'No-one. Only Granny, of course . . . and Granny Latimer.'

(Granny Latimer! *'She was a saint, your mother.'* Well, obviously not all the time!)

'Why didn't they just get married when they knew she was . . . pregnant?' said Erica. 'Why did they wait all that time?' She seemed to be struggling to understand the situation. 'Was it because of the war?'

'They couldn't have got married then,' said Gina slowly, 'because they hadn't met each other then.'

'What?' Erica was shouting now.

'They didn't meet until after I was born.'

'You mean Dad isn't your father?'

Ellen gave up trying to pretend that she wasn't listening.

Granny Morton came into the room. 'What's all the shouting about?' she asked.

Erica rounded on her grandmother. 'Gina says that Dad isn't her father.'

Granny Morton took a step backwards and looked enquiringly at Gina.

'She saw the date on the wedding photo,' said Gina. 'She worked it out.'

'Oh, dear!' Granny Morton was distressed. 'Then it's all my fault.' She closed the dining-room door so that they wouldn't be overheard.

'It doesn't matter,' said Gina. 'I was going to tell them all soon, anyway.'

'I can't believe this!' Erica was getting hysterical. 'How can you be so calm about it? And if Dad isn't your real father, then who is?'

'Look, just sit down and shut up, will you?' said Gina trying to take charge of the situation. 'Nobody knows who my real father was. Apparently, she – my mother – absolutely refused to say. She never told anybody.'

Erica, who hadn't sat down, made a disbelieving noise. 'I bet Maggie knows,' she said. 'I bet you know too, Granny.'

Her grandmother shook her head. 'Don't be so aggressive, dear. And don't get so upset. It was all a long time ago.'

'I can't believe this,' repeated Erica. 'Can you?' she asked, appealing to Ellen. Ellen gave a slight shrug and lowered her eyes.

'Don't say anything to the others, yet,' said Gina. 'I'll tell Caroline and Maria myself when I come home at Easter. And the boys don't need to know until they're older, do they? Promise me you won't say anything. It's for me to tell them, not you.' Gina looked at Ellen, seeming to include her in this request. Ellen, not quite knowing how she was supposed to react, gave a slight nod of her head.

'I don't know how you can be like this about it all,' Erica persisted after a short silence.

'Because I've known for a while,' said Gina. 'I'm used to it now. There's really no need for you to get so upset. If it doesn't matter to me then it shouldn't matter to you. And I still think of Dad as my father.'

'But don't you want to know who your real father was – is?'

'Well, yes, I'm curious, but there's nothing I can do about it.'

'What about your birth certificate?'

'There's nothing on it,' said Granny Morton. 'She refused to name him. She never told a soul. It was the war. Those things happened. Now, let's forget about it and go back to the others. It's very cold in here.'

But Erica, of course, couldn't and wouldn't forget about it.

'I bet Maggie knows,' she said later that night. 'She was my mother's best friend. She must know. If I was pregnant I'd tell you. I mean I'd tell you who the father was. And you'd tell me, too, wouldn't you?'

Would I, wondered Ellen? If I wanted to keep it a secret, would I?

'And Granny Latimer. What must she have thought about it?'

'Well, your mother became a Catholic when she married your dad so I expect she was pleased about that.'

'I can't believe it! I just can't believe it! I've never thought of my mother as a sinner. Do you think she did it just once or lots of times?'

'How do I know?' said Ellen, trying not to think of Father Maloney.

'I bet Dad and Maggie sleep together. I don't think they do it at our house but I bet they do when he goes round to her flat. She's not a Catholic so it's probably not a sin for her, but it is for him. I wonder if he confesses it. Do you think he does?'

Ellen sighed. 'How do I know?' she said again. She wished that Erica would shut up and go to sleep. Somewhere, at the back of her mind, she felt uneasy about the way Erica had confronted Gina with the wedding photo. Erica hadn't known that Gina already knew about it. If Gina hadn't known, this would have been a horrible way for her to find out. She suddenly felt tired of the whole business and was glad that they were going home the next day.

On Sunday morning, Erica got out of bed and gave a cry of disgust.

'Ugh! This wasn't supposed to happen for at least another week,' she said gazing at a blood stain on the sheet. Ellen quickly checked her own sheet which, thankfully, was clean.

'And my pyjamas, too,' said Erica, annoyed but unembarrassed. 'And I haven't got any sanitary towels with me. Have you?'

Ellen reached into her case and gave the packet to Erica. She didn't know whether to offer her the belt as well, but Erica didn't ask for it.

When she was dressed she took the sheet off the bed and took it downstairs. 'I'm sorry, Granny. Look what's happened,' she said.

Her grandmother, unconcerned, handed her a bucket. 'Salt and cold water,' she said. 'And don't let those boys see it.'

So it wasn't a catastrophe. Nevertheless, Ellen was glad that it had happened to Erica and not to her.

Granny Morton sent them all off to Mass.

'Doesn't your grandmother go to church?' asked Ellen.

'No, she's not religious,' said Erica. 'I wish I wasn't religious, don't you? If my mother hadn't become a Catholic then we might not have been religious either. It would have been so much easier.'

'If Maggie marries your dad, do you think she'll become a Catholic too?'

'She won't. Not if I can help it. Marry my dad, I mean'.

After lunch another taxi arrived to take them to the station.

'Now don't forget what Georgina said to you,' said Granny Morton, kissing Erica goodbye. Erica said nothing. 'And you boys behave yourselves on the train.' She kissed Ellen too and said how nice it had been to have her to stay and that she must come again.

Erica was very quiet on the train. Ellen didn't know whether this was because of her period or because she was still brooding over the revelations of the evening before. When they got back to Turneley Station, Maggie was waiting there with Mrs McCann.

'I'm going to tell Maria,' were Erica's parting words. 'I'll see you at school tomorrow.'

On the way home Ellen told her mother all about the visit – all, that is, except for the bit about Mrs Latimer and Gina. Mrs McCann was already asking questions about Maggie's status and Ellen didn't want her mother to think that the Latimers were a disreputable family.

'I've told Maria,' said Erica the next morning.

'You shouldn't have,' said Ellen. 'You promised Gina that you wouldn't.'

'No I didn't. I didn't say anything when she asked me to promise.'

'What did Maria say then?'

'She couldn't believe it, either. She was upset. She's always thought our mother was a saint, just like Granny Latimer. Anyway,' sensing Ellen's disapproval, 'I made her promise not to tell Gina that I've told her, so there's no harm done.'

Ellen shook her head. 'Unless she breaks her promise too,' she said.

The weather had turned mild for February and the next evening, after a quick piano practice and a declaration that she had done all her homework, Ellen joined the others by the lamp-post outside the McCanns' house. She hardly ever went out these days but Jennifer Chadwell was there and she wanted to tell her about the trip to Birmingham.

They were all too old to play now and just hung around talking, although the boys always seemed to have a football with them. Ellen and Jennifer sat on the step and chatted until it got too cold for sitting. Jennifer went in, but Ellen lingered, watching Michael Chadwell kicking the ball around in the road. She went to sit on the wall, in the lamplight, and after a while he came over to talk to her.

'So Mac got another Valentine from Sandra Crompton, then,' he said. 'Did you see it?'

'Oh, yes,' said Ellen. 'Our Christine snatched it off him

and we all had a good look.'

'It wasn't written in green biro, was it?' he asked casually. Ellen's heart missed a beat. 'Green!' she said. 'No, why?' Then as an afterthought. 'Do they do green biros? I've never seen one.' And she laughed.

He laughed too and hoisted himself up on to the wall beside her.

Did he know that his card was from her?

'Did you get any?' he asked her, after a short silence. But before she could reply, Colin Hurst kicked the ball to him and he jumped down to kick it back. Then Mrs McCann chose that moment to tap on the front window and gesture for them to come in. Ellen slithered off the wall and went.

She wondered what she would have said in answer to his question. Yes, I got loads. Or the truth – no I didn't get any. Nobody loves me. But that wasn't true, was it? Michael Chadwell loved her. He knew that she'd sent him the card and was probably wishing that he'd sent her one too. Of course he loved her. Well anyway, he loved her a lot more than Joe Wagstaff loved Erica. But then, Joe Wagstaff probably didn't love Erica at all, so that wasn't saying much. She became aware of an uneasy feeling in the pit of her stomach.

The next morning she got out of bed, and there it was – a tiny blood stain on the sheet. At last! She rushed to her drawer and then down to the bathroom. When she came out, she whispered the news to her mother who was in the kitchen. Mrs McCann seemed pleased.

'What are you two whispering about?' demanded Christine.

'Never you mind,' said her mother.

Ellen gave her sister a superior smile.

'I bet I know what it is,' said Christine.

'No you don't. Just eat your breakfast and mind your own business,' said Mrs McCann. She patted Ellen on the arm.

Ellen sat down at the table, feeling both uncomfortable

and elated. She had managed it before her fourteenth birthday. But only just!

MARCH

1961

Ellen's birthday was on the fifth of March. And this year it was a significant one: her thirteenth.

During the dark winter months, when it hadn't been too cold or too wet to go outside, they'd all been congregating as usual under the lamp-post outside the McCanns' front gate. Now that she was a teenager, though, Ellen was beginning to wonder whether she was getting too old to go out to 'play' – as they still called it. But if she didn't go out occasionally then she wouldn't see much of Jennifer any more. Or of Michael Chadwell either – and that would never do.

One of her favourite activities had been watching him in church when he was an altar-boy. She'd spent many Sunday Masses worshipping him from the benches, watching entranced as he lit candles and rang bells, intoned in Latin, and fetched and carried for the priest. She'd been disappointed on those Sunday mornings when he wasn't serving at the nine-thirty Mass. But then he and Michael McCann (who'd been an altar-boy too) had grown disillusioned with these duties and had hung up their surplices for ever, thus depriving Ellen of this secret pleasure.

No, she saw very little of Michael Chadwell these days. She couldn't afford to let any opportunities be missed.

As was Ellen's custom, she allowed herself a piece of birthday cake on her birthday, even though she had given up all sweet things for Lent. Because she'd made it clear from the start that she was going to do this, it didn't count as a broken resolution. Christine, who was in Miss Long's class now and had given up almost everything for Lent this year, had a piece too, but, according to Ellen, hers was a lapse since there had been no prior announcement to the contrary.

'Oh dear!' she said to Christine. 'What would Miss Long say if she knew what you'd just done?'

Ever since Ellen herself was in Miss Long's class, one of her Lenten activities had been to do the washing-up each evening after tea. This year, however, Christine had declared that she wanted to do this instead of Ellen. A big argument had ensued, but eventually they'd agreed to do it together. Ellen would wash and Christine would dry.

Ellen had also decided to give up going to the pictures for Lent. As this had become a favourite week-end activity for her and Jennifer Chadwell it represented a very real sacrifice. Unfortunately, Jennifer refused to join her in this. She took a very moderate approach to Lent (in spite of the fact that she, too, had once been in Miss Long's class) and had no intention of giving up something as pleasurable as going to the pictures.

Erica Latimer wasn't giving up anything at all for Lent. She was very dismissive of Ellen's resolutions. 'I don't see the point of all those penances and sacrifices,' she said. 'It's just silly, if you ask me. Which you just did.'

She had been reading *The Story of a Soul*, the autobiography of St Thérèse of Lisieux, and she took it out of her satchel now and showed it to Ellen and Angela Norris. On the cover was a picture of Thérèse, the Little Flower, in her Carmelite habit, holding a crucifix and a handful of pink roses. There was a statue of her, looking just like this, in the school hall. All the girls were familiar with the story of Thérèse Martin, the motherless child who had become a

Carmelite nun at the age of fifteen and died of consumption when she was only twenty-four.

'That's what she did,' said Erica. 'And not just for Lent. She spent her whole life doing stupid little penances. Listen to this.' And in an artificially sweet little voice, she began to read a passage from the book about Thérèse's desire for suffering. Then, harshly: 'I can't stand her! I think she was a nutcase. Why couldn't she just be good without all that nonsense? You can be good without suffering, can't you? I hate her and I hate this book!'

'Why are you reading it then?' asked Ellen, a bit shocked at Erica's vehemence.

'Because Maria loves it and I wanted to see why. This is her stupid book.' Erica stuffed it back into her satchel. 'Anyway, *I* don't need to do anything for Lent because Maria's doing enough praying and sacrificing for both of us.' Maria Latimer, she'd told Ellen recently, was going to be a nun when she left school.

A little while ago, Sally Wagstaff had told Ellen that the anniversary of Mrs Latimer's death was coming up. 'She died on the eighteenth of March, five years ago,' she'd said solemnly. Ellen had looked up this date on the calendar at home. It was a Saturday, so she wouldn't see Erica on the actual day itself – which was a relief. And she wondered now if it was this impending anniversary that was making Erica rebel against the God who had taken her mother away from her.

On the Monday afternoon, a few days after her birthday, Ellen started to feel unwell. Her head was aching and her throat was hurting. She just wanted to go home and let her mother look after her. She sat listlessly through the last lessons of the day and then struggled to the bus-stop, feeling very sorry for herself. She hauled herself upstairs on the bus and slumped into a seat.

A few moments later, Joan Grady and Sheila Murphy appeared at the top of the stairs. Ellen, not as alert as usual, happened to glance at them. Realising her mistake, she turned away quickly, but it was too late.

'What are you looking at?' sneered Sheila Murphy.

Ellen stared out of the window. She was used to this kind of thing from Sheila Murphy but, unexpectedly, tears came to her eyes. She had thought that she had all of this under control, that neither Sheila Murphy nor Joan Grady could upset her anymore, but here she was, trying her hardest not to cry. She knew this was probably because she was feeling so ill, but nonetheless it unnerved her.

Over the past year she'd learned to ignore them and could even manage, when she was with Margaret Latham, to adopt a supercilious attitude towards them. But Margaret Latham wasn't with her now. And once again she found herself wishing that Jennifer had passed the eleven-plus and come to the Convent. Jennifer would have been a very useful ally on the bus.

It transpired that she had tonsillitis. She was confined to bed for a few days, missed her piano lesson and was away from school for the rest of the week. And while she was ill, Christine had to do the washing-up on her own.

On Sunday evening, however, Christine felt it was time for her sister to resume her Lenten duties. Ellen wasn't keen. The small kitchen was very chilly and she still felt fragile. But there were no pans to wash – Sunday tea was always a cold meal – so she didn't argue. She washed up as quickly as she could and then hurried back to the warm living-room, leaving Christine still drying the dishes.

The next day Ellen went back to school. She still felt weak and wobbly but didn't want to miss any more lessons. It would take her ages to catch up as it was. There would be missed notes to copy up, new vocabulary to learn, reading to do. She felt even weaker at the thought of it all.

She was dismayed to see that Margaret Latham wasn't on the bus. She felt cross with herself for feeling nervous, but she couldn't help it. She'd had a strange dream the previous night – a disturbing variation of the piano lesson dream. It'd started off, like it always did, with her setting off for her lesson, a little late as usual. As she left the backs, however, she bumped into Sheila Murphy, who, spying Ellen's music case, began to laugh.

'Where are you going with that?' she asked.

Ellen tried to ignore her and walk past but Sheila Murphy kept getting in her way, stopping her. I'm going to be very late, she was thinking, as they continued their side-stepping dance.

'You're not getting past me,' said Sheila with a sneer, spreading her arms out wide.

Ellen tried to push her out of the way but Sheila resisted her efforts so Ellen lifted her music case and swiped it across her assailant's face. She knew how much the hard leather would hurt! Sheila gave a loud cry and clutched her stricken cheek with both hands. Ellen seized her chance and began to run as fast as she could through the streets. She didn't know whether she was being followed or not. When she arrived at Mrs Walker's house, hot and out of breath, there was another surprise waiting.

'I'm afraid you're too late, Ellen,' Mrs Walker said, opening the front door. 'Someone else is having your lesson now.'

And over her shoulder, Ellen caught a glimpse of Joan Grady sitting at the piano, smiling enigmatically at her.

Through the bus window, she saw them now – Joan and Sheila Murphy – standing at the Greenside stop. But she was prepared, and made sure that this time there was no eye contact. They sat down a few seats behind her and she heard Sheila say loudly: 'There's a funny smell on this bus, isn't there?' There was a pause, and then she said: 'Oh look! She's back. That's what it is!'

Ellen felt sick. Why couldn't they just leave her alone? Why was Sheila Murphy being like this again now, after all this time? And why, why, why was Joan doing nothing to stop her? Joan never joined in the abuse, but she never objected to it either. Ellen sometimes wondered what she would do if Joan were to turn on Sheila Murphy and tell her to shut up. Would she welcome her back and be friends with her again, or would she tell her to get lost? There had been a time when she would've forgiven her. But would she now?

When they got off the bus in Turneley, Ellen let them go on ahead but Sheila Murphy, who kept turning round to look at her, was walking so slowly that she was obliged to overtake them. She went as fast as she could, trying to put some distance between them, but they quickened their pace too, until they were just behind her.

As they crossed the road to the Convent, she found herself wishing that Sheila Murphy would get run over by a car – or better still, a bus or a lorry. And she knew for certain that the next time she went to Confession and said that she had been having uncharitable thoughts *a few times*, she would only be pretending to be repentant. She wasn't going to stop thinking like this – at least not until Sheila Murphy disappeared out of her life. (She knew, too, that these thoughts were rather more than 'uncharitable' – but she couldn't imagine how Father Maloney would react if she were to confess to having 'murderous' ones.)

Feeling physically and spiritually wretched, she descended to the depths of the basement cloakroom. But Erica was pleased to see her. 'Where have you been?' she shrieked.

'I've been ill,' said Ellen. She took off her coat and hat and sat down to change into her indoor shoes. 'I'm still ill. I feel awful. I think I've come back too soon.'

'Well, I'm glad you're back,' said Erica, ignoring Ellen's demand for sympathy. 'It's no fun sitting on your own.' And then as an afterthought: 'You're not infectious or anything, are you?'

Ellen remembered that last Saturday had been Mrs Latimer's anniversary. But Erica didn't seem any different than usual, and she wondered whether the rest of the Latimer children were as unaffected. Five years, after all, was a long time.

Angela Norris was also pleased to see her, and soon she began to feel much better. She decided that she never wanted to be friends with Joan Grady again. And she would try to ignore Sheila Murphy. She would 'rise above' any further provocation, which she felt sure was what her mother would advise her to do had she known what was going on. Yes, she would show them that she didn't care. Because, suddenly, she didn't anymore. Well . . . not much, anyway.

The Lenten washing-up was ceasing to be an act of piety. Christine was getting more and more annoyed at being left alone in the kitchen every evening. She wanted Ellen to stay and help her put the dishes away.

'No, that's not what we agreed,' objected Ellen. 'We said that I'd clear the table and wash up, and you'd dry and put the dishes away. It's not my fault you're so slow.'

She had been washing the dishes the way her mother had taught her – the cups first, and then the saucers and plates leaning up against them. Sensibly, Christine had been letting these drain a bit before starting to dry them, but this, of course, meant that her sister was getting a head start. In an effort to combat this, she started drying each one as soon as Ellen put it down.

Noticing this, Ellen began to amuse herself by playing little games. She would slow down so that Christine would think her strategy was working; then she would suddenly speed up again. She could see that this was driving her sister mad. And because Christine wasn't letting the dishes drain at all, her tea towel soon got soaking wet, slowing her down further and adding misery to her fury. She kept changing her mind about whether to let them drain or not but no matter which method she chose Ellen always finished long before she did. She began to complain loudly.

'OK.' said Ellen, a few nights later, 'I'll dry then, if it'll shut you up.'

They changed positions at the sink. Christine began to wash the dishes and place them carefully on the draining board. Ellen waited for a while, allowing her to feel confident that this new arrangement would have the desired outcome. Then she leapt into action. She gathered up all the saucers into her tea towel and began to dry them as fast as she could. She dried the top of the top saucer and the bottom of the bottom one, then put the top one at the bottom of the pile and repeated the procedure until they were all dry on both sides. Then she put them straight into the cupboard on the wall instead of stacking them on the table as Christine had been doing.

She did the same with the plates and then, holding handfuls at a time, she dried the knives, forks and spoons straight into their compartments in the cutlery drawer. She dried the pans while Christine was emptying the bowl of water down the sink and wiping down the draining board. They finished at the same time.

Christine was incensed. 'You've not dried them properly,' she said.

'Yes I have.'

'No you haven't. You couldn't have.'

'Of course I could have. And look, you've left the sink in a soapy mess.'

'Well, if you're going to be that fussy,' shouted Christine, 'you can wash tomorrow, then.'

'I don't mind,' said Ellen, smiling. 'It's all the same to me. It was you who wanted to dry, remember.'

The next evening was Friday and Ellen wanted to go out, and so, as soon as they'd finished tea, she rushed into the kitchen and began to wash up even more quickly than usual. Christine ran after her and started drying the dishes using Ellen's method of the evening before, but her hands were too small and clumsy to manage it successfully. Ellen finished washing up, emptied out the soapy water, wiped round the sink and draining board and then dried her hands on the towel behind the door.

"Bye. See you later,' she said.

She opened the door to go into the living room just as

Christine threw a spoon at her. It missed and landed on the carpet at her mother's feet.

'What's going on?' demanded Mrs McCann.

'It's not fair,' shouted Christine, flapping her wet tea towel. She was close to tears. 'She's cheating.'

'How can you cheat at washing up?' said Ellen, raising her eyes to heaven.

'I'm not doing it with her anymore.' Christine was crying now. 'She can do it on her own from now on.'

'Oh dear!' said Ellen. 'What would Miss Long say about that?'

Christine threw another spoon at her.

'Oh dear, dear!' said Ellen again.

'Ellen, will you leave her alone,' said Mrs McCann, picking up the spoons and going into the kitchen.

'I haven't done anything to her,' grumbled Ellen, glancing at her father who was watching the television. She went into the front room and looked out of the window to see if anyone was out yet. There was no-one there. She sat down at the piano and played a few scales but it was cold – too cold to do any more, especially as she'd been so ill recently. She went back into the living room.

A few minutes later, Jennifer Chadwell knocked on the back door.

'We're going to the pictures,' she said. 'We're going to see Elvis. Are you sure you don't want to come?'

Ellen sighed. Of course she wanted to go. She loved Elvis. She'd seen the poster outside the cinema and had felt sad – and virtuous – because she'd thought then that she was going to forego this great pleasure. Why was Jennifer tempting her like this?

'You know I've given up going to the pictures for Lent,' she said reproachfully. 'Who else is going?'

'Me, our Michael and your Michael, Hursty and Sandra. It starts at quarter past so you'd better make your mind up quick.'

Twice before, Ellen had resisted Jennifer's invitations,

but . . . this was *Love Me Tender*. And this time Michael Chadwell was going too. 'OK. I'll come,' she said.

'Oh dear!' said Mrs McCann who was pottering about in the kitchen. 'Oh dear, dear!'

'I don't care!' said Ellen. 'I've been ill. I need cheering up.'

'Well, you can take Christine with you,' said her mother. 'She needs cheering up, too.'

Ellen was indignant but didn't want to protest too much in case her mother mentioned her short piano practice. And anyway, their Michael could help look after her.

She rushed upstairs and studied herself in the dressing-table mirror. Erica had given her some blue, translucent eye-shadow for her birthday which she hadn't used yet. She smeared a tiny amount on each eyelid, admired the effect, back-combed her hair a bit more at the top, and sped downstairs. Christine was already waiting with her coat on. Ellen could see that she'd noticed the eye-shadow straight away, but she didn't say anything. Mrs McCann didn't say anything either, but made a slight, disparaging sound instead.

Love Me Tender was on at the Plaza. Ellen wished that it had been on at the Rex instead. The Rex was Makerton's posher cinema with its mock marble columns, gilt paintwork and red velvet curtains and upholstery. The Plaza, in contrast, was dull, dingy and badly in need of refurbishment. Every Saturday afternoon the (misnamed) children's matinées were held there. These were rough, rowdy affairs where merely surviving the queue to get in was an achievement in itself. Whenever Ellen and Jennifer went to one of these matinées they would pay the extra threepence to go upstairs where the risk to life and limb was slightly less than in the bear pit below. It was much less rowdy in the evenings, though.

When Ellen, Christine and Jennifer got there, the boys and Sandra Crompton were already waiting in the queue outside.

'I thought you'd given up the pictures for Lent,' Mac said to Ellen. Sandra Crompton and Colin Hurst, neither of whom were Catholics and to whom this statement was meaningless, turned to stare at her.

Ellen glanced at Chad. 'I'm making an exception – for Elvis,' she said. 'It's not a sin, you know.' But it felt like one.

The queue moved forward and they neared the ticket office window.

'Let's try and get on the back row,' said Sandra Crompton, looking at Mac.

'You can if you want,' said Jennifer, 'but we're not paying a shilling. We're going in the ninepennies.'

'My mam said you've got to look after Christine with me,' Ellen said to her brother, just in case he wanted to go on the back row too. His former hostility towards Sandra Crompton seemed to be fading a little these days.

'No, she didn't,' said Christine.

'Yes, she did.' ('I have told lies, *once or twice* since my last confession.')

They bought their ninepenny tickets and were ushered to seats halfway down the cinema. Ellen was desperate to sit next to Chad but somehow Jennifer got between them. Sandra Crompton, she noted, was sitting expectantly between Mac and Colin Hurst.

The lights went out and they watched the Pathe News, the Pearl and Dean advertisements and the trailer for next week's film.

'Can you see properly?' Ellen whispered to Christine.

'Yes, thank you,' Christine whispered back, on her best behaviour now.

Then it was the interval and everyone, except Ellen and Christine, wanted choc ices. Jennifer got up to get them.

'Sit in my seat,' Ellen said to Christine, moving into the seat next to Chad that Jennifer had just vacated. 'You'll be able to see much better here.'

'I'm all right where I am,' said Christine.

'No, you're not,' said Ellen. She turned to the others. 'She can't see properly where she is.'

'Yes, I can,' said Christine, 'but I'll move if you want to

sit next to Chad.' Ellen could have murdered her.

Chad got up. 'She can sit here,' he said, 'in between you and your Michael.' He waited while Ellen and Christine stood up too, then he moved down the row a bit and was just going to sit down next to Ellen when Jennifer came back bearing the choc ices.

'Hey, get up,' she said. 'I'm sitting next to Ellen.'

The lights began to dim.

'Will you lot settle down,' said a middle-aged usherette, flashing her torch along their row.

'Come on, move,' hissed Jennifer and to Ellen's dismay Chad obeyed her. Once again she found herself sitting between Jennifer and Christine, only this time they were on opposite sides of her.

The film began and soon Ellen was lost in the American Civil War story of the Reno brothers, the stolen money and the shared sweetheart. Christine whispered to her that Colin Hurst was holding Sandra Crompton's hand. Ellen glanced along the row, feeling annoyed. If Michael Chadwell had been sitting next to her, perhaps he would've been holding her hand now, too. She wondered if her brother was upset that Sandra had chosen Colin Hurst instead of him. How sordid their little romances were compared to hers!

The ending of the film was too much to bear. Elvis, having been shot dead, was being buried. Ellen's eyes were so full of tears that she could hardly see the screen. Christine began to sob quietly, and even Jennifer was sniffing slightly. Then a ghostly picture of Elvis singing '*Love Me Tender*' was superimposed in a corner of the screen. It was heartbreaking. Christine's sobs were loud and uncontrollable now and people were turning round in their seats to smile at her.

The lights came up. Ellen blinked away her own tears, Jennifer blew her nose loudly, but Christine was inconsolable.

'Shut up, will you?' said Mac, embarrassed. 'It's only a film.'

'Leave her alone,' said Ellen, taking her sister's hand as they edged their way out of the row.

When they got outside, Sandra Crompton and Colin Hurst promptly disappeared into the night. The others began to walk home together.

'That was so sad,' said Jennifer, laughing now. 'I cried my eyes out.'

Ellen, still holding Christine's hand, didn't trust herself to speak. They turned into the dark backs and Jennifer began to sing *Love Me Tender* causing Christine, who had been slowly regaining control of herself, to begin howling again. Once safely inside the house, Ellen burst into tears too. She didn't know whether she was crying for Elvis or for herself and Michael Chadwell. It was all so tragic. And when Mrs McCann saw the tears and heard the cries, she thought for a moment that they'd been fighting again.

Ellen did some serious pondering in bed that night. Why had Chad let Jennifer make him change seats? Had he done it reluctantly, or was he not bothered where he sat? Did he like her or not? This was the crucial question. Should she ask Jennifer to find out? No, she couldn't do that, it would be too embarrassing. And what if the answer was no? What would she do then? Would it make any difference to the way she felt about him? She thought about Erica and her slow-burning, hidden passion for Joe Wagstaff. No, it was better to leave things as they were.

She turned over and tried to go to sleep, but there was something else on her mind – the broken Lenten resolution. She'd said that it wasn't a sin, going to the pictures, but was it? Giving things up for Lent was optional, she knew that, but if you said you weren't going to do something and then you went and did it, was that wrong? Was it wrong 'in the eyes of God'? How was one to know? God, she thought, was a bit like Michael Chadwell – unfathomable. And some people, like Erica, hadn't given up anything for Lent. Surely it was better to have tried and failed than not to have tried at all? Which reminded her of something she'd heard her mother say. 'Better to have loved and lost than never to have loved at all.'

Tried and failed, loved and lost. She drifted off to sleep

thinking about Michael Chadwell again.

The next evening Ellen and Christine washed up together again and Ellen stayed in the kitchen to help put the dishes away. There was only a week of Lent left now and she had resolved to salvage what she could from the wreckage of her good intentions.

There were only a few days of term left too. Sheila Murphy was still being a nuisance on the bus, but once Ellen was safely in school everything was fine. And getting better.

In their English lesson, they were studying *Lochinvar*. Sister Monica, who was Scottish and passionate about poetry, pronounced 'Lochinvar' with an exaggerated 'ch' sound and read the poem aloud with great gusto. When she came to the lines:

For a laggard in love and a dastard in war
Was to wed the fair Ellen of brave LoCHinvar

there was a bit of a stir. Firstly because of the rather risqué word 'dastard' (whatever it meant) and secondly because of 'fair Ellen'. Erica nudged Ellen, who smiled self-consciously.

When the lesson was over and Sister Monica had left the classroom, Erica stood up and began to recite the lines again in her best Scottish accent:

For a laggard in love and a bastard (more giggles) *in war*
Was to wed the fair Ellen of brave LoCH-CH-invar.

Ellen stood up too and smiled and bowed graciously to the assembled company. Everyone laughed. She felt a surge of happiness. She belonged here; her friends were here; she didn't care about Joan Grady any more. She really didn't.

For the rest of the day Erica kept calling her 'the fair Ellen'.

She took the poetry book home with her and read the poem again that evening. She imagined herself as 'the fair Ellen', waiting for the young Lochinvar to ride to her rescue (a bit like Michael Chadwell had done that night in the backs when the dog had attacked her). It was so romantic.

The following morning, in the cloakroom, Erica made an

important announcement: 'I'm not going home for dinner next term. I'm staying in school, where you'll have the pleasure of my company. I'm not having school dinners, though,' she said, shuddering at the thought, 'so you "fair Ellen", will have to bring packed lunches.'

Ellen was thrilled. 'OK.' she said. (There would be a battle to be fought here with her mother – but she would win it.) 'I'll ask Angela if she wants to change too.'

'Well even if she doesn't, you still have to,' said Erica.

'Is Sally going to stay too?'

'I don't know,' said Erica, shrugging. 'I haven't told her yet.'

They made their way to the school hall for assembly. The hymn that day was *Come Holy Ghost, Creator Come*. Ellen knew that Joan and Sheila Murphy were in their line a little further back from where she was standing. Just before the Paraclete line she turned round deliberately and caught Joan's eye. For a brief second, she felt a deep sadness. She knew that Joan was looking at her because she too was remembering the incident at St Wilfrid's. But Joan had made her choice. Ellen shifted her attention to Sheila Murphy, and as they all sang *'Thou who art called the Paraclete'* she gave her a bold, sneering smile before turning back to face the front.

'Who're you looking at,' whispered Erica who was standing behind her.

'No-one,' said Ellen.

No-one at all.

Miss Long's *pièce de résistance* was reserved for Good Friday. They could, she told her little girls every year, preserve a silence for the three hours between twelve and three o'clock – the hours when Jesus was dying on the cross. Ellen had done this the year she was in Miss Long's class and it'd been so difficult that she'd never tried it again since. But now that it was Christine's turn she decided to do it with her. It would, she hoped, make up for the outing to the pictures – 'in the eyes of God'.

Together they struggled through the three hours. Mrs McCann kept commenting on how peaceful it was, and Michael kept trying to make them speak, but they didn't. At quarter to three they left the house to go to the Good Friday service. The church bells were tolling solemnly as they made their silent way to St Wilfrid's. They entered the church feeling very holy and very pleased with themselves. And then three o'clock struck, the service began and their silence could be lifted.

Christine opened her handbag to take out her prayer book . . . and *Santa Lucia* made another bid for freedom. She snapped the bag shut as quickly as she could, but the damage had been done. Having been pent up for three hours, they couldn't help themselves and were overcome by a fit of giggles so furious as to be frightening. And it was a long service; there were several recurrences.

When they came out of church, their mother had plenty to say. 'You're a disgrace, the pair of you!' she cried. 'On Good Friday of all days!'

They tried to look repentant.

She took Christine by the arm and shook her. 'How many times have I told you about that bag? I'm going to take it off you and put it away.' And then, turning to Ellen: 'As for you! You're old enough to know better. You're thirteen now.'

APRIL

1963

It had been a very cold winter, but now it was spring and Ellen was feeling full of its promised joys.

School holidays could sometimes be boring, but, gratifyingly, the Easter one this year was going to be filled with activity. On Easter Tuesday they were going on a school trip to the Lake District for a few days, and then, a few days after they got back from that, Ellen and Erica were going to Southport for a Beatles concert. Erica had made all the arrangements for this outing and already they were savouring to the full the anticipatory delights it afforded them. Perhaps an encounter with the Beatles at the stage door? Love at first sight. Their lives taking off in a whole new direction! Ellen's favourite Beatle was George Harrison; Erica oscillated between John Lennon and Paul McCartney. 'I'll have either,' she said magnanimously. 'Or both.'

But something else was looming on Erica's horizon, casting a long, dark shadow over the otherwise happy days ahead. Her father and Maggie were getting married. She arrived at school one morning just before the end of term, full of this devastating news.

'It's on Saturday the twenty-seventh of April!' she said, taking off her hat with a flourish. 'They must've known for ages but they only condescended to tell us last night. I can't believe it!'

'It's not such a surprise, though, is it?' said Ellen. 'They've been going out for ages.'

'Yes, I know. But getting married! She'll be living with us all the time then. She'll be my stepmother!'

They moved out of their cloakroom and into the crowded area where the toilets and hand basins were situated. Erica began to back-comb her hair vigorously in front of the large mirror which ran the length of one wall.

'It's awful,' she lamented. 'I think I'll have to run away.'

'No you won't,' said Ellen making a few quick adjustments to her own hair before moving away from the mirror.

The bell rang for the beginning of school; three urgent rings which Erica, busy with her back-combing, ignored.

'Come on, girls, hurry up! The bell's gone,' said a prefect, trying her best to disperse the throng. 'Stop talking and go to your classrooms!'

A slow exodus began, the narrow basement stairs causing a bottleneck as usual.

'And that means you, too, Erica Latimer,' the prefect added.

Erica, looking like a scarecrow now, turned away from the mirror, pointed at her head and gave the older girl a long, insolent stare. Then she turned back and began to smooth her hair into shape, slowly, as if she had all the time in the world.

'Granny Morton'll be pleased,' she continued. 'She's always approved of Maggie.'

'Erica!' shouted the prefect. 'Did you hear what I said?'

'Pardon,' said Erica. 'Did you say something?'

Ellen sighed. 'Come on, let's go,' she said. Prefects could demand lines and hand out detentions. Erica, however, seemed intent on provocation until Caroline Latimer, also a prefect, hove into view, at which point she changed her mind. She smiled sweetly, first at the prefect and then at her sister, picked up her satchel from the floor and followed Ellen up the steep stairs into the heart of the school.

'Granny Latimer won't be so pleased, though,' she said when they got to their classroom. 'She thought the world of my mother. You'd think it'd be the other way round, wouldn't you?'

Yes, you would, thought Ellen. She had been reading *Rebecca* recently and had a sudden vision of Granny Latimer as Mrs Danvers, full of hostility towards the new wife and defending to the death the memory of the first, beloved, Mrs de Latimer.

A week later, thirty fourth-year girls and six teachers assembled at Turneley station to catch the train to Kendal. When they had signed up for this trip, Ellen had been worried that Joan Grady and Sheila Murphy might be going too. But thankfully they weren't – walking in the Lake District obviously not being Sheila Murphy's idea of fun. Margaret Latham, however, was going, even though she'd been to the Lake District many times before with her parents in their caravan (without ever making a detour to Blackpool on the way there or back, thought Ellen). Margaret and her friend Kathleen were going to be sharing a room with Ellen, Erica, Angela Norris and Sally Wagstaff.

When the train arrived and they had settled into their compartment Erica immediately began to bring Ellen up to date with the happenings of the past week. The others, of course, were listening too.

'They're getting married in church,' she said. 'I thought she'd been married before but apparently not – she was only living with someone so she's not actually divorced or anything. Anyway, it'll be in church but only a short service. They're not having a Nuptial Mass because Maggie's not going to convert. Granny Latimer's not pleased about that!' She turned to Ellen and said accusingly: 'I told you she wouldn't be.'

'I never said she would be,' said Ellen. (She imagined

Granny Latimer, lurking unseen by Anne's grave, brooding darkly as she watched the newly-weds emerge, happy and smiling, from the church.)

'Then there's going to be a small party at our house and then they're going away for a few days – somewhere or other,' continued Erica, feigning forgetfulness.

'Paris,' said Sally helpfully.

'Then they'll come home and we'll all live unhappily ever after.' Erica shuddered dramatically.

'Are you going to be bridesmaids?' asked Angela.

'No! Can you imagine that? All four of us? No, it's going to be a "small, discreet affair" – to quote my wicked stepmother-to-be. She's having a friend of hers to be her matron-of-honour, nothing fancy. But . . .' and Erica was off again.

Maggie, she said, had been having a huge row with her brother ('we never even knew she had a stupid brother'). She turned to Ellen again. 'He's called George, by the way, but Hunter not Harrison.' Apparently, this brother, for some unknown reason, didn't want to go to the wedding but Maggie wanted him to give her away ('I wish he would'). They'd been arguing about this on the phone for ages the other night and when they'd finished shouting at each other Maggie had put the phone down in tears. Erica sounded pleased with this bit. 'Anyway, it's all sorted now and he is coming after all.'

Outside the station at Kendal there was a coach waiting to take them on to Keswick. The route took them through the beautiful lakeland countryside and they kept exclaiming at the scenery as they went along. They caught a glimpse of Lake Windermere, then drove through the town of Ambleside and on past tiny Rydal Water to Grasmere. There were daffodils everywhere, inspiring Erica to recite Wordsworth's poem and getting the last lines of the verse wrong in the process.

'*Beneath the lake, beside the trees / Fluttering and dancing in the breeze,*' she declaimed.

'Beneath the lake?' said Sally, giggling.

'Yeah. Wordsworth must've been stoned on opium when he wrote it.'

They continued on – past gloomy Thirlmere, with Helvellyn towering above it – and eventually arrived in Keswick where they were staying in a large boarding-house which catered specially for school parties.

They struggled up three flights of stairs with their luggage, to room number eight.

'Look, you can see the lake from here!' said Margaret.

'Oh yeah,' said Ellen, joining her at the window. 'We've got a lovely view.'

'Bags me the top bunk,' said Sally, heaving herself up on to the one nearest the window. Erica dived on to the one underneath.

'I can't stand heights,' she said. 'I'll stay down here.'

'You'll be no good on a mountain, then, will you?' said Ellen, climbing inelegantly on to another top bunk.

'If I fall down a mountain and break my leg, then I won't have to go to this dreadful wedding, will I?' said Erica. 'It's something to think about.'

'Yeah, but you might break your neck instead,' said Ellen, wishing that Erica would drop the subject of the wedding. Margaret and Kathleen must be bored to death with it, she thought. They didn't really know what it was all about. They didn't know anything about the Latimers.

After the evening meal they were allowed to go out for a while. Some of the girls went into the town but the inhabitants of room eight decided to go for a walk by the lake instead. Miss White, whose love of the Lake District was infectious, recommended they go to Friar's Crag.

'Keep an eye on the time, though,' she said, pointing them in the right direction. 'It'll be dark soon. And don't fall into the lake!'

It was beautiful at Friar's Crag. In the fading evening light the mountains rose up around them, silhouetted against the dark blue sky. Below them, the lake, with its little wooded islands, was silvery and still with just an occasional lapping sound on the shore. They stood by the fir trees, momentarily lost in awe.

Ellen, looking out over the water, had that same quivering feeling she'd had at the airport when Auntie Peggy was going back to America. The feeling that life was full of possibilities, that there were so many places to see. And here she was now, seeing one of them. 'It's so beautiful,' she said quietly, feeling that she could stand there for ever.

But it was going dark quickly now and the air had turned chill, so they didn't linger for much longer. As they neared the boarding-house they could see a group of four boys sitting on the steps of the house next door, smoking.

'Hello, girls,' said one of them, in a pronounced Liverpool accent.

Margaret and Kathleen, slightly flustered, went straight in, followed closely by Sally who had just started going out with her boyfriend Steve and didn't want to complicate matters. Erica, Ellen and Angela stayed out for a while, chatting.

The boys were about seventeen or eighteen and in the sixth-form of their school in Liverpool. Erica told them that they were sixteen. Two of them had Beatle haircuts, which made them quite irresistible, and Erica and Ellen arranged to meet them in the town the next evening. Angela said she might join them, she didn't know yet.

The next three days were spent walking. The teachers and a few of the girls (Sally Wagstaff and Margaret Latham among them) had proper walking boots but the rest had to make do with their school outdoor shoes. They were split into two groups and set off on different walks on different days. On the first day they took a ferry across the lake and did a gentle walk around part of the lakeside before taking another ferry back to Keswick. This was to break them in.

The next day they went to Walla Crag. At the start of the

ascent, Ellen and Erica got left behind because they had to stop so that Erica could put on another pair of socks over the ones she had on already. She hadn't put this second pair on before they left the boarding-house in case 'anyone' saw her looking too clumpy.

'Come on, hurry up,' said Ellen, watching the rest of the group disappearing into the middle distance.

Miss White had hung back to make sure they were all right, but now she was stepping up her pace to catch up with the others. Ellen and Erica toiled along in her wake. As they climbed higher the wind became stronger. It was warm in the sunshine but much cooler when the sun went behind the scudding clouds. This meant that they were either too hot or too cold, and they had to keep stopping with ridiculous regularity to put their anoraks on or to take them off again. The gap between them and the main group was widening.

'Why do they have to go so bloody fast?' said Erica, gasping for breath. 'I'll kill Sally and Margaret when we catch up with them.'

'If we ever do catch up with them,' panted Ellen. 'Even Angela's way ahead of us. What's the matter with us? Why are we so slow?'

'Don't talk, just walk!'

Eventually, those in the vanguard stopped to eat their sandwiches. But by the time Ellen and Erica reached them, most had finished and were preparing to set off again.

'Don't even think of leaving till we're ready,' said Erica throwing herself on to the ground and taking her packed lunch out of the duffel bag which she and Ellen had been taking turns to carry. Miss White laughed and took out her camera. She began taking lots of photos – of the scenery and of the girls.

Sally had a blister on her heel and had to have a plaster put on it. Erica was unsympathetic. 'It serves you right for walking so fast,' she said.

On Friday, their last day, they crossed the lake again and climbed Catbells. They were stiff from yesterday's climb but the effort was worth it. The views from the top were wonderful. They could see almost all of Derwentwater spread out below them, and, in the distance, Bassenthwaite Lake. Miss White took some more photos of them all, with the wind whipping their hair all over the place.

After tea, back at the boarding house, they were almost too tired to make the effort to go out again, but Ellen wanted to go to Friar's Crag again before they left the next day.

The boys from Liverpool had gone home that afternoon. They had said goodbye to them the night before, after a second evening spent walking around the town with them. Angela had joined them on the first evening but hadn't liked the boy allocated to her and so hadn't gone again. Ellen's boy had a girlfriend back in 'the Pool' and had made it quite clear that there was no future for them, but he hadn't been averse to a bit of handholding and kissing and neither had she. Erica, however, had high hopes for hers. He was called Neil. He'd offered her a cigarette the first evening and, with a defiant look at Ellen, she'd taken it and smoked it with hardly a flinch. He'd promised that he would ring her when they got home and that he would come to Turneley to see her. She'd allowed herself a few tears when they'd parted.

'I think I'm in love,' she'd said to Ellen as they went back indoors.

'What about Joe Wagstaff, then? Do you like Neil more than you like him?'

'Well, no!' Erica had said witheringly, 'Of course not! Don't be stupid! You know that Joe is the love of my life. But I can't make him ask me out, can I? And I'm not going to be a nun while I'm waiting.'

The conversation had ended there as Sally had been in the bedroom. But thinking about it later, Ellen had decided that this was how she felt about Michael Chadwell, too. If he ever asked her out, she would go. Of course she would. But she couldn't wait for ever.

On the day they were going to Southport, Ellen went round

to Erica's house earlier in the afternoon so that they could spend some time getting themselves ready for the evening ahead.

'I think,' said Erica, poring over her Beatles magazines, 'that we should change our hairstyles.' She went over to the dressing table and began to brush out her back-combed hair. This done, she took her comb, parted her hair down the middle and combed it flat, giving herself a much deeper fringe than she'd had before.

'What do you think?' she asked, turning round to face Ellen. It was a dramatic transformation. 'Do yours.'

Ellen had been trying to grow her hair long for some time now. Her mother had wanted her to keep it short, but Ellen had rebelled and refused to have it cut anymore. It was a slow business though. She'd been dismayed to read somewhere that hair only grew half an inch a month. That was only six inches a year, not counting the shorter layers which had a lot of catching up to do! It would be a long time before her hair was as long as Erica's.

She took the comb from Erica and began to flatten her own hair. 'It's too shaggy,' she said, surveying herself in the mirror. 'These side bits need to be longer.'

'They'll grow,' said Erica. 'Come here and let me cut you a proper fringe.'

Once this was done, there was no going back. Erica snipped at her own fringe too and was pleased with the result.

'Neil'll like it,' she said confidently. 'And so will the Beatles! Maggie, on the other hand, will probably hate it, so I'm going to have it like this for the wedding – and the wedding photos.'

They set to work on their faces – applying brown eyeshadow, lots of mascara and pale pink lipstick. And then they were ready.

There were two shows in Southport that evening but they had to go to the earlier one because the last train back to Turneley left before the later one was due to end. This wasn't ideal, but it would have to do.

Their seats were on the second row of the concert hall, on the left hand aisle, with an excellent view of the stage. The place was packed and as soon as the curtain went up the screaming started. The Beatles, being top of the bill, were last on, which meant a long wait. The compère kept mentioning them every time he came on to introduce other people, thereby fanning the flames of an already vastly over-heated audience. Ellen felt a bit sorry for these other acts; no-one was really listening to them. When at long last the Beatles did bounce on to the stage, there was uproar. There they were – in their grey, collarless Beatle suits, their forward-flopping hair shining in the spotlights.

'Hello!' shouted John Lennon and the decibels rose even higher. Then they started to play and there was pandemonium. Ellen didn't know whether she was screaming or not. She couldn't hear anything except this great wall of hysterical sound. Only occasionally could she hear a snatch of a familiar song. And whenever the screaming did subside for a few seconds it only took one or more of the Beatles to shake his head and go 'ooh… ooh' for it to start up again even louder than before.

'*Love, love me do!*' they sang – and the audience did.

The girls were sitting so near the stage that they could exchange looks with them. For one breathless moment, Paul seemed to be looking straight at them. Ellen could feel Erica next to her reacting to this. She glanced around behind her. It was a grotesque scene; people out of control, their mouths open, their faces contorted, shouting, screaming, crying. Girls were fainting and having to be carried out. It was frightening, but so very exciting.

Wave upon wave of sound washed over her, rising and falling, rising and falling, like a series of the crescendo and diminuendo markings on her piano music. For a few strange seconds, the noise in her ears seemed to diminish, as if she were suddenly under water. She felt as if she wasn't breathing, couldn't breathe. Then the volume returned and she joined in the screaming as something to do to retain her grip on consciousness. When George Harrison began to sing *Do You Want To Know A Secret?* she thought, for a moment, that she was going to die. She felt close to tears but, mindful of the mascara, just managed to control herself.

It was a bit of a relief when suddenly it was all over. The Beatles waved to the audience and left the stage. The lights in the auditorium brightened. Slowly people began to leave, many still sobbing. Erica, Ellen noticed, had black streaks of mascara running down her cheeks.

They wanted to go to the stage door – this was the bit they'd been imagining for the past few weeks (the door opening, being invited in) – but when they got round to that part of the building there was already a large crowd there, and they had a train to catch that they dared not miss. This practicality hadn't featured in their imaginings, but reality bore down upon them now and so, reluctantly, they turned away and set off for the station.

'You've got black streaks all down your face,' said Ellen when they were on the train.

'I don't care,' said Erica. 'Did you see Paul looking at me?' Her voice was husky from all the screaming.

'He wasn't looking at you. He was looking at me.'

'He was probably admiring our hair,' said Erica, laughing. She took out her hanky, put some spit on it and attempted to wipe the mascara off her face. 'He's probably at the stage door now, looking for us.'

'Yeah. And when he can't find us he'll be too upset to do the second show!'

'They'll have to cancel it!'

'And they'll have to say why and it'll be in the papers and then we'll . . .'

And off they went with wild abandon. They laughed so much that when they got off the train at Turneley, they were exhausted.

'I'll see you on Thursday,' said Erica, saying goodbye to Ellen at the Makerton bus-stop. 'And keep your hair like that. I'm definitely keeping mine like this. I can't wait to see everyone's faces when they see it.'

'I'll have to put it up for my job,' said Ellen who, since her fifteenth birthday a few weeks ago, had been working on Saturdays in Teller's cake shop on Makerton High Street.

'Don't talk to me about Saturday!' said Erica, referring yet again to the dreaded wedding.

But when they went back to school on Thursday, once the subject of the new hair styles was out of the way, that was all that Erica did talk about for the next two days. Ellen would be glad when it was all over, although she knew that Erica would still go on and on about Maggie – probably for ever.

Erica issued strict instructions for Ellen to ring her on the Sunday morning after the wedding for a post-mortem on the proceedings. 'Ring on your way home from church,' she said.

Ellen didn't want to do this. She knew that it would be a long conversation and that she would be starving and longing to get home to the bacon and egg breakfast that her father always had ready for them on Sunday mornings. 'No, I'll go home and have my breakfast first,' she said.

The phone box was outside the post office. Ellen dialled the number and pressed the coins into the slot. Erica must have been waiting in the hall because she answered the phone immediately.

'At last!' she said in a low voice. 'Where've you been?' Then, without waiting for a reply: 'Listen, I've got to talk to you. Face to face, I mean. You've got to come to Turneley this afternoon. You'll never guess what's been happening here. I can't wait to tell you.'

Ellen gazed out through one of the phone box's dirty little panes of glass. A woman was posting a letter and a man was walking past with a fierce looking black dog on a lead. Whatever it was, she thought, couldn't it wait till tomorrow?

'I've got to tell you today. It can't wait till tomorrow,' said Erica, as though Ellen's thought had been transmitted down the phone line. She was still speaking in a low, urgent

voice, obviously not wanting to be overheard by anyone in
the house which, Ellen knew, would be fuller than usual with
all the wedding guests. Granny Morton would still be there
with Phyllis. And so would Gina, who was a teacher now and
lived in Birmingham, too.

'OK,' she said with a sigh. 'Shall I come round to yours?'

'No! It's crazy round here. I'll meet you in the park at
half past two – that bench by the lake. I'll see you then. Bye.'

Ellen walked back home wondering what had happened.
Something out of the ordinary, it would seem. Whatever
'ordinary' was in Erica's world.

Turneley Park was in its springtime glory. Near the big
entrance gates, which had the words 'Jubilee Park 1897'
written into their wrought-ironwork, there was a beautiful
carpet of bluebells. The trees were newly in leaf, the flower
beds freshly planted. Everywhere there were daffodils,
clinging on to their last vestiges of bloom. Several different
kinds of ducks were swimming on the ornamental lake,
gliding up and down and to and from the little island in the
middle. Two families of ducklings were following their
mothers – all in a row except for a tiny one that had got left
behind.

Erica was sitting on the designated park bench watching
them. She was leaning forwards slightly, hugging herself to
keep her unfastened coat wrapped around her. She was
wearing fish-net stockings and shiny black patent shoes. She
turned her head as Ellen approached and Ellen thought how
striking she looked with her hair curtaining her face and her
grey-blue eyes dark with eye make-up.

'There you are!' said Erica impatiently.

'I'm not late,' Ellen said, and smiled as the nearby Parish
Church clock corroborated this statement by striking the half
hour. She sat down, prepared for a tirade about the wedding.

'You'll never guess what I'm going to tell you,' Erica
began. She paused for effect. Ellen maintained an expectant
silence. 'Maggie's brother,' she intoned, and paused again.

'Maggie's brother,' she repeated, 'is Gina's father!'

Ellen was taken completely by surprise. 'What?' she gasped. 'No! How? What do you mean?'

Erica seemed pleased with this reaction. 'Yes,' she said, nodding her head. 'George Hunter is Gina's father. And that's why he didn't want to come to the wedding.'

There was a short silence while Ellen struggled to assimilate this information. 'Did Maggie know?' she asked.

'No! She was just as amazed as the rest of us. Everyone's going mad back at home. Granny Morton and Phyllis are still there, and so is Gina.'

'Is *he* still there?'

'No. He left last night.'

'But . . . but . . . why did nobody know? What did he say? What did Gina say? What's he like? God! I can't believe it!'

A family with a small boy and a baby in a pushchair had stopped in front of them to feed the ducks. The toddler was shrieking and the ducks were quacking in alarm. Erica got up and Ellen followed her. As they began walking round the lake, Erica began answering these questions.

'Well . . . he's middle-aged, about my dad's age, grey hair, tall, quite handsome,' she said, settling into her narrative. 'He arrived right at the last minute yesterday, in this big black car. He drove up just as we were on our way to church. Maggie had been thinking that he wasn't going to get here on time and she was cross with him.

'So we didn't get introduced till after the service. He knew Granny Morton, of course, and he'd met my dad before, too – at Grandpa Morton's funeral, but that was years ago. So there we all were, outside the church, and it was: "This is Tom. This is James." "Pleased to meet you." "And this is Gina/ Caroline/ Maria/ Erica". "Pleased to meet you," and all that nonsense. If we'd known then, we'd have watched a lot more closely when he was introduced to Gina, but of course we didn't know. Then there were photos and then we went back home.

'Well . . . everyone was eating and drinking and laughing

and talking. Then my dad gave this really awful speech about how Maggie had come into his life, after all the sadness of before, and transformed it in a way he would never have thought possible.' Erica pulled a face. 'Granny Latimer cried. Granny Morton had a little quiver. I was nearly sick!

'No-one was watching George Hunter to see how he was reacting – because like I said, we didn't know. Then he, George that is, gave a little speech about what a great person Maggie is; about how she too had suffered heartache in the past (I don't know what that was all about!) but that now she'd found true happiness with my father – and his lovely family – which was something she thought she'd never have. And then he started getting all upset which was *so* embarrassing. Of course, we thought he was getting all emotional about his sister. We didn't know then that . . .'

Erica trailed off. She stopped walking and picked up a piece of gravel from the path. She examined it for a moment and then threw it, with some force, into the water, startling the ducks who began quacking loudly and swimming round in frantic circles. A woman standing nearby turned to look at them disapprovingly.

'What's she looking at?' said Erica. The church clock struck three.

'Never mind her,' said Ellen, walking on. 'Go on, what happened next?'

'Well . . . a bit later on, I was coming downstairs and I saw him and Maggie standing in the hall, by the front door. They were arguing again. She was saying something like: "Nice speech, so why did I have such a job getting you here?" then I couldn't hear what they were saying till Maggie started going: "What on earth are you talking about?" Then he took his wallet out and handed her something. She took one look at it, then she saw me watching them, and she dropped it on the floor and ran into the kitchen. He went after her. And I picked it up.' Erica stopped walking again. She turned to Ellen, holding an imaginary object in her hand. 'It was a photo,' she said. 'A photo of Gina when she was a little girl.

She must've been about five or six. Granny Morton's got the same one.'

'Oh, God!' breathed Ellen. 'What did you think then?'

'Nothing,' said Erica. 'I had no idea what to think. Then my dad came looking for Maggie and he saw me standing there with the photo and he took it off me and went into the kitchen too. Then after a bit they went upstairs, all three of them – my dad, Maggie and George. Anyway, they were up there for ages and then they sent James down to get Granny Morton. Then they sent for Gina.'

'Oh, God!' Ellen exclaimed again. 'George, Georgina!'

'Yeah, I know,' said Erica. They walked on in silence for a while. Ellen was trying to imagine how Gina must have felt – must still be feeling. And Mr Latimer! And Granny Morton! They must've spent years wondering about this, and now they knew. And Maggie was Gina's aunt!

'Then it was time for my dad and Maggie to leave,' Erica went on. 'There were other people in the house, not just family, so they were trying to pretend that nothing had happened, but you could tell that something was wrong. Anyway, they left and then other people began to go too, and so did George. You could see he was upset. He said something to Granny Morton, then he kissed Gina on the cheek, said goodbye to the rest of us and got into his car and went.

'When there was just us left, Gina told us. Granny Latimer cried – again – and Granny Morton told her it wasn't the end of the world. Then Tom got all upset because nobody'd told him and James about Dad not being Gina's father in the first place. James wasn't bothered though.' Erica began to laugh. 'So you can see,' she said, breaking into a broad Lancashire accent. 'A good time was 'ad by all, at our Maggie's weddin'!'

They looked round for another bench to sit down on, but the park was full of people now, enjoying the spring Sunday afternoon, and they couldn't see a vacant one anywhere. Instead they went to sit on the steps leading up to the elevated bandstand in the centre of the park. From there they saw Maria and Claire Wagstaff coming in through one of the side gates.

'Do you think Maria's telling Claire, now?' asked Ellen, watching them. Erica shrugged. 'Did Claire know about Gina, anyway?'

'I don't know. Who knows what Maria tells her.'

'Does Sally know?'

'I haven't told her, but she might know if Claire knows.'

'What exactly did Gina tell you, then?'

'She said that George Hunter was married with a small child – a little boy – when he started . . . started seeing . . . started having an affair with my mother. He was six years older than her and Maggie. Maggie knew nothing about this. Neither did Granny or Grandpa Morton. It was at the beginning of the war. It didn't last long because he was in the army and had to go away. Maggie was away too, in London. When he left he didn't know that my mother was having a baby. The next thing he heard, years later, was that she was getting married to my dad. And the first time he saw her again was when Grandpa Morton died. He was back from the war then and he took his mother to the funeral.

'That was when my mother told him about Gina – and gave him that photo. She made him promise never to tell anyone, never to say anything about it. He'd had another child then, too – so Gina's got two half-brothers. I suppose we're all half-sisters and brothers to her too. It's funny that. Anyway, he's divorced now.'

They sat in silence, trying to digest all this. After a while, Erica said that they should each go home. 'We'll be in time for *Pick of the Pops*, if we hurry,' she said, 'and I want to see if the Beatles are at number one. I'm sick of thinking about all this.'

But Ellen had another question. 'Will Gina see him again?' she asked.

'I don't know. I should think she probably will. He still lives in Birmingham, or somewhere near there . . . Oh . . .

Oh!' She leapt to her feet. 'Oh God! Oh, bloody hell!'

'What?' Ellen stood up too, alarmed at Erica's agitation.

'I've just remembered something! Yesterday, when George was leaving, Granny Morton said to him to drive carefully. She said: "It's a long drive back to Warwick." Warwick! He lives in Warwick!'

Ellen looked blank.

'Remember what Phyllis said that time in the car. About my mother. That she'd crashed "somewhere between Birmingham and Warwick"!' Erica put both hands to her head as if trying to keep hold of this revelation.

Ellen bit her lip. Yes, she did remember now. And she also remembered what Erica had said later. *'I wonder where she was going – or where she'd been? Somewhere between Birmingham and Warwick? At night-time.'* Well, now they knew what she'd been doing. She'd been to see George Hunter! But why?

Ellen sat on the bus going home, her head in a whirl. There were so many unanswered questions. Was the night of the crash the first time that Mrs Latimer had seen George Hunter since her father's funeral eight years before? Or had she been seeing him whenever she could ever since then? Had their affair still been going on? Had she still been in love with him? Had she always been in love with him? Had she never really loved poor Mr Latimer?

She wondered whether Mr Latimer, on his honeymoon with Maggie, was thinking these same things, was asking himself these same questions. Or had he always known that on the night she died Mrs Latimer had been to see another man? He wouldn't have known who it was, but he might've known that she'd been to see someone. He knew she had a past. There had always been Gina there to remind him of that.

And George Hunter? Had he always loved Mrs Latimer? Was that why he was divorced now? Could it really be possible that they'd been continuing their affair, secretly, for all those years?

What would Maria think when Erica gave her this latest piece of information? Maria, who had only been a little girl, with only Phyllis and an invalid grandmother to look after her, the night her mother died. Maria, with the chickenpox scars on her beautiful face. Scars she would carry with her for ever.

And what would Granny Latimer think now, if she knew what Erica and Ellen thought they knew? (*'She was a saint, your mother. A saint.'*) A lot of saints had been sinners first. But had Anne Latimer been a sinner first and last – and never a saint in between?

'Now, what was it that couldn't keep till tomorrow?' asked Mrs McCann when Ellen got home.

Ellen stared at her for a moment. She wasn't going to tell her mother any of this. But if she'd been intending to, it would have been a daunting task.

'Not much,' she said.

'How was the wedding, then?' Angela Norris asked at school the next morning.

'Interesting,' said Erica, and she and Ellen started to laugh.

'What's so funny?'

But Erica didn't want to say anything more. 'You wouldn't believe me if I told you,' she said.

But she did have something else to tell Ellen. When she'd told Maria about the Warwick connection, she said, Maria had told her something interesting too. The night of the crash hadn't been the only time that Mrs Latimer had gone out on her own after dark during that stay in Birmingham. Maria could remember several other occasions, too. This seemed to prove beyond doubt, as far as Erica was concerned, that her mother had been seeing George Hunter. Maria, she reported, found this unthinkable. 'She doesn't want to believe it, but I think she does, really. I wonder what everyone else thinks?'

A few days later, Ellen happened to be round at Church Walk when Granny Morton rang to see how they were all getting on.

'Where do you think my mother was going, the night she died?' Erica asked her.

'I expect she was seeing one of her friends,' said Granny Morton.

It seemed to Ellen, who was sitting on the stairs next to Erica, her ear pressed to the receiver, listening in to the conversation, that the word 'Warwick' was hanging heavily in the ether.

'She still knew a few people round and about,' went on Granny Morton. 'She always tried to keep in touch with them whenever she could, whenever she was down here.'

'There you are, then!' said Erica, putting down the phone.

PART THREE

MAY

1964

May was the month of Mary, of Whitsun and Walking Day. This year, though, and much more importantly, it was the month the Chadwells were leaving for Australia. On Tuesday the nineteenth, so Jennifer had informed Ellen, they would be sailing from Southampton on a ship called the *Fairstar* which take four weeks to get there. And as this departure date crept ever nearer, the despair that Ellen had been feeling since last Christmas, when she'd first found out they were going, was turning to desperation.

A few weeks ago, Michael Chadwell had broken up with Margaret Latham. He'd told Mick that there was no point continuing with the relationship; he would be gone soon, it was better to end it now. But, thought Ellen when Mick told her this, he'd known from the start that he was going away. So why had he bothered going out with Margaret Latham in the first place? Probably because she'd given him no choice. She'd always been the driving force.

Mick also said that Chad had been finding her much too intense and was just using Australia as an excuse to finish with her. Even if he hadn't been leaving, he would probably have finished with her anyway.

'Oh,' said Ellen, her heart lifting.

Margaret was heartbroken. On the bus going to school the following Monday morning, she told Ellen (who didn't say that she knew already) what had happened, then burst into tears. Ellen tried her limited best to console her, while Christine, who was sitting behind them, looked on with great interest.

'He's probably just trying to be sensible,' said Ellen. 'He probably thinks it's better to finish now than to have things drag on and then end. If there's no future in it . . .'

'She's right,' said Christine from behind, bringing all the wisdom of her twelve years to bear on the matter. 'It's for the best.'

But Margaret was inconsolable. She was in love with Michael Chadwell, and as far as she was concerned, she said, there was no obstacle so great that it couldn't be overcome if only he felt the same way. Privately, Ellen agreed with this. He just doesn't love you, she thought.

'He doesn't love me!' wailed Margaret.

'No, I'm sure he does!' said Ellen. 'He's just trying to do what's best. You don't think so now, but you'll feel differently in a few weeks time. And anyway . . . ' (she tried not to finish the sentence but couldn't resist it) 'you haven't been going out with him for that long, have you? Only a few months . . . a few weeks really.'

'*Sixteen* weeks!'

'Well . . . it's not as if you've been in love with him for years, is it?' Ellen said, turning and glancing at Christine who was watching intently and nodding wisely. She felt herself blushing.

The hymn in morning assembly was *I'll sing a hymn to Mary*. Ellen stopped singing and studied her hymn book. Lately, probably because she was revising for her O-levels, she'd found herself becoming increasingly preoccupied with the use of language and she brought her analytical powers to bear now on the second verse. It was a very tricky one, rendered almost incomprehensible in its sung form:

> *O Lily of the Valley*
> *O mystic Rose, what tree*
> *Or flower e'en the fairest*
> *Is half so fair as thee?*

'*O mystic Rose, what tree | Or flower . . .*' This, she could see now, was an example of *enjambement* – where the sense of the words carried on beyond the end of one line and into the next. So if you were reciting it, you would slide across the line ending. You would say 'what tree or flower . . . ?' But when you sang it, pausing at the end of each line, it didn't make sense: '*. . . what tree* (long hold, new breath) / *Or flower e'en the fairest . . .*' - it sounded like 'what tree?' And that *e'en*. It was 'even', of course! For years she'd been singing '*in* the fairest'. And she was pretty sure that lots of other people were making the same mistake.

The hymn came to an end, but she didn't close the book. Hymns were full of *enjambements* and other archaic constructions, she thought, leafing through its pages and feeling learned (that is learn-ed, not learnd). For example, the refrain of another popular May hymn:

> *In this thine own sweet month of May*
> *Dear Mother of my God I pray*
> *Do thou remember me.*

There were no *enjambements* to spoil the sense here. But that last line, '*Do thou remember me*', was a command, not an interrogative. Well, perhaps not so much a command – that wouldn't be the correct way to speak to the Mother of God – more of a request: 'Please remember me' not 'Do thou remember me?' where Mary might well, if she were so inclined, answer, 'Yes, Ellen, I remember thee well'.

The distractions she was experiencing now, when praying or singing hymns, were not the usual drifting-off-into-daydreams kind. They were much more literary and grammatical in nature. Take another example. When saying the *Hail Mary*, punctuation was crucial. All her life, she realised now, she'd been saying '*blessed is the fruit of thy womb Jesus*'. As if Mary's womb was called Jesus! Whereas, with a comma after 'womb', it made perfect sense. Jesus was the fruit of her womb, not the womb itself.

'Pray, Father, give me your blessing' was another one! 'Pray' meaning 'please', not an instruction to the priest, telling him to pray! She smiled to herself. Pray, Father, give me your blessing, for I have sinned. I have allowed grammar, punctuation, archaic and poetic devices to distract me from my prayers – *lots of times*. This, she thought, would be a new and unusual sin for confession. And not one to be shared with Jennifer Chadwell, either!

And Father Maloney would say: 'You must fight against this, my child. Think of the Virgin Mary. And for your penance say three *Hail Marys*.'

'Oh no, Father. Pray, not *Hail Marys*. Do thou give me some other prayers instead.'

Erica's sixteenth birthday was on the seventh of May, which this year happened to be Ascension Thursday – a Holy Day of Obligation and therefore a holiday from school. She'd toyed with the idea of having a party, but since the Latimer residence contained so many undesirables, she'd abandoned the idea.

It was Sally Wagstaff's birthday later in the month, anyway, and she was definitely having a party, so there was always that to look forward to. And, of course, Joe was bound to be at Sally's party – if not for the whole evening then at least for part of it. He did live there, after all. He'd been very elusive of late but quite recently, to Erica's great delight, he'd started frequenting the Cellar Bar again. And so the torch that she always carried for him had been refuelled and was burning brightly once more.

To mark her birthday she had decided that she and Ellen, Pete (with whom Ellen had been going out since the Christmas dance) and a friend of Pete's called Paul, should go to Manchester, in the evening, to see *Becket*. She'd chosen this particular film because she'd heard from Sally that Joe had seen it and thought it was great.

Maggie wanted her to have a family birthday tea first, but as they would have to leave early to get to Manchester this had been scaled down to sandwiches and birthday cake at four o'clock. Mr Latimer wouldn't be there but Maggie had arranged to finish work early so that she could be. 'Please don't go to any trouble on my account,' Erica had said haughtily, but Maggie had remained unruffled. Her policy these days, Ellen had noticed, seemed to be to counter Erica's hostility with affability. Maria, Tom and James had been instructed to be present – 'no arguments, please!' Granny Latimer had been invited, too, and so had Ellen.

Earlier in the afternoon, the two girls were in Erica's bedroom, waiting for the appointed hour. Since Maria had taken up residence in Gina's old room on the top floor, the whole room belonged to Erica and she had been gradually spreading herself out in the extra space. She'd been given a record-player for her birthday and she'd placed it on top of what had been Maria's chest of drawers. All her records from downstairs were stacked up next to it. Ellen wished that she too could have a bedroom all to herself, away from Christine's watchful and judgmental eye.

Taking great care with the new stylus, Erica put her Rolling Stones EP on to play. 'I hope Joe doesn't get to hear that I'm going out with Paul Dawson tonight,' she said, settling herself on her bed.

'He'd be eaten up with jealousy if he did find out, wouldn't he?' said Ellen who was reclining on the spare bed.

But Erica was impervious to sarcasm where Joe Wagstaff was concerned. She began to sing *Happy Birthday Sweet Sixteen* over the top of Mick Jagger, changing the pronouns as she went along: *'I've turned into the prettiest girl he's ever seen . . . '*

If there had been a pillow on Maria's abandoned bed, Ellen would have thrown it at her.

'There're lots of songs about being sixteen, aren't there?' mused Erica. 'There's *She Was Only Sixteen*, and that one in *The Sound Of Music*, what's it called? I think the Beatles should have had sixteen instead of seventeen in *I Saw Her Standing*

There.'

'Seventeen scans better,' said Ellen. 'It needs three syllables – se-ven-teen.' (This was becoming a habit!)

'They could sing 'si–ix–teen,' said Erica.

'Next year you'll be glad they didn't.'

There was another song about being sweet sixteen – one that someone had sung at that New Year's Eve party, years ago when Aunty Peggy was home from America – that contained the phrase: *'the lovelight in your eyes'*. Ellen had particularly thrilled to this. She'd been nowhere near sixteen at the time, but she remembered how she'd gazed into her dressing-table mirror the next day and seen the lovelight in her own eyes, for Michael Chadwell.

She didn't mention this song to Erica. Instead she said: 'Sweet sixteen and never been kissed,' which was something her mother would say from time to time, whenever an occasion merited it. This made them laugh now. It sounded so old-fashioned, and so very inappropriate. They were long past such sweet innocence.

Erica had bought herself a birthday present which she produced now and showed to Ellen. It was a box of Tampax. She opened it, took out the instruction leaflet and spread it out on the bed. Ellen went over and knelt on the floor to look at it with her. There was a diagram on it which they studied carefully. It was very similar to the one in the booklet they'd been given in the second year, only more three-dimensional.

'Hey, do you remember those books?' said Erica. 'I've still got mine somewhere.' She went over to her bookshelf and began searching for it. It took a while to find. 'Here it is; *Growing Up The Catholic Way*. Listen to this,' she said, settling herself back on her bed: *'Never talk to boys about this. Never let them touch your body. Always behave in the way the Blessed Virgin Mary would have behaved.'*

They burst out laughing and began to speculate, in detail, about how Mary – complete with halo – might behave on a night out in Turneley, having to deal with some of the boys they knew. It was all very funny – and slightly blasphemous – but they didn't care.

'Well, anyway,' said Ellen, calming down after a while, 'I don't suppose she'd use Tampax either. It's probably a sin.'

'Do you think it is?' said Erica, poring over the diagram again. 'Maggie uses them. I've seen them in her bag. But then, she's not a Catholic, is she?' She took a tampon out of its wrapper and studied the section in the leaflet which dealt with insertion. 'I'm going to give it a try anyway.'

She made a tunnel with the fingers of her left hand and pushed the applicator into it. 'It doesn't look that difficult,' she said. 'And it'll be good practice for the "real thing".' She exerted some pressure with her right thumb and gave a triumphant little laugh as the tampon slid effortlessly from its cardboard container and landed on the bed. 'Do you want to try one?' she asked, offering the box to Ellen.

Ellen gazed at its contents for a moment, as though they were chocolates and she was trying to decide which one to choose. Then she took one and put it in her bag.

At four o'clock they were all sitting round the big table in the Latimers' dining room. Maggie – straight from work and all made-up and elegantly dressed – was making a big effort, and Granny Latimer was smiling benignly at everyone. But the two boys were obviously there under duress, and Maria had her usual air of abstraction about her. The sandwiches were for Erica and Ellen because they wouldn't be having anything else later, but Tom and James, ever hungry, ate some too. Maria sat silently, waiting for the cake.

Although she was a frequent visitor here now, Ellen always felt slightly uncomfortable in Maria Latimer's presence. Maria always ignored her. She never looked her in the eye or spoke to her directly: she made Ellen feel invisible. But there was one advantage to this. Ellen could scrutinise her with impunity. There would never be any need to look away hurriedly should their eyes meet, because there was very little chance of this ever happening. She sometimes felt that it would be perfectly possible to hold a microscope up to Maria and examine her in minute detail, and still not attract her attention.

Metaphorically, she did this now. Maria didn't look well. She was very pale and thin, all mournful eyes and sharp cheekbones beneath the long brown hair which hung around her face like a nun's veil. She seemed to be cold, huddled in a baggy brown jumper which looked as if it might be one of her father's. She had made no effort to dress up for this birthday tea.

Maggie lit the sixteen candles on the cake that Granny Latimer had baked and they all sang *Happy Birthday*. The boys, obliged to sing, did so loudly and disruptively. Granny Latimer, Maggie and Ellen sang nicely, but Ellen couldn't hear Maria at all, although her lips were moving. Erica put her hands on her heart, pretending to be touched by this tribute, and then blew out the candles, in instalments and with a great deal of exaggerated huffing and puffing.

'You didn't do it all in one go,' said James. 'That means you can't make a wish now.'

'Yes I can,' said Erica, closing her eyes. 'There! A wish! I've made one.'

'It won't come true, though,' James insisted.

'Oh yes it will,' said Erica. Her eyes darkened. 'It most certainly will!'

Ellen could see that the wish had Joe Wagstaff written all over it.

They each had a slice of cake and a cup of tea. Maria, Ellen noticed, ate hardly any of her cake. She kept breaking off tiny pieces, but she was only giving the illusion of eating. Most of her slice remained on her plate.

('Is Maria all right?' she asked Erica later. 'She doesn't look very well.'

'Doesn't she?' said Erica in an offhand manner. 'She's always praying and fasting, that's why. She's really going for the nun thing again, you know. We thought for a bit that she'd gone off the idea but she's definitely back on it now. In a big way. She's talking about not doing her A-levels. She says she's leaving school at the end of term and going into her stupid bloody convent. Of course, *she* didn't say "stupid bloody", that was me.')

'Now do be careful in Manchester,' said Maggie as they were leaving. Erica raised her eyes to heaven. 'We're not little kids,' she said.

'Things can happen to grown-ups, too,' said Maggie. 'Who are these boys you're going with?'

Erica heaved a great sigh. 'Does it matter?' she said. 'If we were staying in Turneley you wouldn't be so nosey.'

'Yes, but you're not,' said Maggie. 'And I expect Ellen's mother was concerned too, wasn't she?'

Ellen smiled and nodded.

'Yes, but you're not my mother, are you?' Erica muttered, under her breath but audible enough to be heard. Then, in a normal tone: 'We're going with two little dickey birds, if you must know. One named Peter, who's Ellen's boyfriend. And one named Paul, who's definitely not mine.'

Sometimes, Ellen felt a bit guilty about Pete. For months she'd been happy enough spending her Friday and Saturday evenings with him; mostly in the Cellar Bar with Erica and her succession of boyfriends, sometimes at the pictures, or, very occasionally, at someone's house. She liked him, she really did. But the truth was, he liked her much more than she did him – and they both knew it.

In February, knowing that he would certainly send her one, she'd sent him a small, rather unenthusiastic Valentine card – and he'd been delighted with it. Margaret Latham had sent a much larger one to Michael Chadwell. She'd shown it to Ellen before she sent it, and on the day itself had also shown her the one she'd received from him in return. Ellen had noted with satisfaction that it was not unlike the one she'd sent Pete, both in terms of size and the rather vague sentiments it contained. There could be no doubt that it was far inferior to the one – written in green biro – that she herself had received the year before.

Having a steady boyfriend like Pete, though, did mean that she didn't have to keep going out with one boy after another, as Erica was doing these days. It was much less exhausting. Much less *risqué* too. You always had to be careful with boys. It didn't do to excite passions in them that couldn't easily be controlled. You had to be on constant alert, ever ready to repel invasion, without seeming too forbidding.

'The thing to do is this,' said Erica confidently. 'If he keeps trying to touch your . . . bosom . . . then take his hand, or hands, and put them on your bottom. Your bottom at the back, that is, obviously. Your . . . buttocks! But if he's trying to put his hand up your skirt, then take the said hand and put it on your bosom.'

Ellen wasn't convinced that this was a foolproof strategy. It seemed to her that it could easily be open to misinterpretation, but she had to acknowledge that Erica had more experience in these matters than she did.

'If you're lying down,' Erica continued, 'then cross your legs and let your thigh muscles take the strain.' Ellen pretended to be taking notes. 'My thigh muscles,' Erica added, 'are as hard as iron after last night.' They both giggled.

'If all else fails,' she said on another occasion, after an evening when 'all else' seemed to have done just that, 'there is something else you can do to defuse the situation.'

She proceeded to enlighten Ellen as to the precise nature of this 'something else', and to demonstrate exactly how to do it – and deal with its consequences. It made Ellen think of Sandra Crompton. Erica referred to this activity as 'taking matters into your own hands', a phrase which amused them greatly. And whenever they heard anyone else using this expression in other contexts, they were reduced to paroxysms of mirth.

Pete, however, always anxious to maintain her good opinion of him, rarely overstepped the mark and Ellen was thankful that she hadn't, as yet, needed to bring this new measure into play. If only because she couldn't imagine having to confess such a thing. What would she say? I have been immodest, Father? No, that was far too vague. I have taken matters into my own hands! Would Father Maloney have any idea what she was on about? What, she wondered, did Erica say?

When asked, though, Erica said she didn't say anything. Her Confessions, few and far between these days, were very selective. 'There's no point shocking the priest, is there? Anyway, it's none of his business. And . . . if you think about it, it's not really a sin. Well . . . OK,' she conceded, reacting to Ellen's cynical smile, 'even if it is, it's only a little one, because it's done to stop the Big One being committed.'

Ellen was amused by Erica's logic. 'Taking matters into her own hands', it would seem, was a weapon in her armoury, to be deployed in the battle to preserve her virginity!

Impure, unchaste – intact.

It was a good night out. There could be no faulting Joe Wagstaff's taste in films and, of course, they loved being in Manchester. It was so much more sophisticated than Turneley. It made Ellen feel – just like she'd felt that time in Birmingham – that there was a wider world out there calling to her, and it was exciting. But, she thought sadly as they were walking to the station, it was this same wide world that had called to the Chadwells and soon now, in answer to that call, they would be sailing away far beyond her horizon – expanding though that might be. She felt her heart contract.

She sat on the train, unresponsive beneath the arm that Pete had placed around her shoulder, and watched Erica with Paul. Erica had a gift for attracting boys, and a seemingly endless need to do so. They would fall under her spell, oblivious to the warning signs that seemed so obvious to Ellen. She would give them the impression (out of all proportion to what any intelligent person might reasonably expect) that she found them utterly irresistible, whereas the reality was that they meant little or nothing to her. Then later, when she abandoned them, they would get upset and angry.

Ellen had seen this happen so many times before. It was what would have happened to Mick if she hadn't intervened. And Paul was heading down this same path to disaster right now. *Fly away Paul,* she thought, fly away before it's too late. You're going to get hurt.

But then, so too was Pete. Soon now, very soon, she would be telling him to *fly away, Peter.* She readjusted herself slightly under his grasp and wondered if he would do so of his own accord if he knew what she was thinking right now. If he knew how she was feeling about Michael Chadwell?

Michael Chadwell who was going to fly away – far, far away – and who would probably never come back. And she knew that no matter how badly Pete was going to get hurt, nor how much Margaret Latham was already hurting, theirs was nothing compared to the pain she was in now. Pain that would continue to intensify in the days to come. The Chadwells were leaving in less than two weeks time, and no-one knew just how much her heart was breaking.

Jennifer had been keeping Ellen up to date with the emigration proceedings. The Chadwells were going to Sydney which was where Mr Chadwell's brother and his family had been living for the past four years. Until they could get a house of their own, they would stay with them. Mr Chadwell, a garage mechanic here, had a similar job waiting for him 'down under'. Michael would continue with his electrician apprenticeship and Jennifer, who had just left school at Easter, was going to train to be a hairdresser in her auntie's salon. Mrs Chadwell, who worked part-time at the Makerton Bakery alongside Mrs McCann, had nothing fixed up yet. She was just going to wait and see what Australia had to offer her.

They were going on something called the Ten Pound Scheme which meant that that was all they had to pay to go there but if they didn't stay for at least two years then they would have to pay the full fare to the Australian government – as well as the full fare to come home.

They were going to rent out their house in Turneley

Road for a while, just in case they didn't like it in Australia ('but we will') and wanted to come back ('which we won't'). They were going to sell it later when they knew for sure that they had settled there. Some of their belongings were about to be sent on ahead of them, but most of their furniture was going into storage until they got a house of their own.

The voyage itself was going to be a great adventure. They would be sailing through the Suez Canal and docking at all kinds of exotic places before crossing a vast expanse of ocean to their new continent. Ellen pored over her school atlas and traced the route with her finger until it came to rest on Sydney. She was familiar with the map of Australia. She'd been introduced to it a long time ago at St Wilfrid's. Miss Gaskell had had a penchant for geography and had equipped her girls with an impressive knowledge of the subject which, if retained, would prove useful when they went out into the wider world.

They knew all the continents; all the individual countries of North and South America; and – for some obscure reason which Ellen could no longer recall – where the Juan Fernandez Islands were. They could locate Rhodesia and Ceylon on a map of the world, both places where Miss Gaskell's brothers had once lived or were now living. And the royal tour of Australia in 1954 had given Miss Gaskell an abiding interest in the Antipodes.

Ellen could still remember the names of three big Australian rivers; the Murray, the Darling and the strange sounding Murrumbidgee. She knew the Australian states and roughly where the cities were – Perth and Fremantle, Adelaide, Melbourne, Canberra, Brisbane and, of course, Sydney. And also Alice Springs, which had featured in a film that Miss Gaskell had been to see. She could sing *Waltzing Matilda*, a particular favourite of Miss Gaskell's, and consequently knew what a swagman and a billabong were, although – along with a coolibah tree – she couldn't quite visualise them.

She also knew a couple of verses of *The Wild Colonial Boy*, but this had nothing to do with Miss Gaskell. This was a song that often got sung at family gatherings, usually to Uncle Jack's piano accordion accompaniment.

'Dad,' she'd asked once, 'do you think Miss Gaskell knows *The Wild Colonial Boy?*'

'She probably knew his father,' Mr McCann had replied.

And Ellen had thought this was very funny.

The days passed.

Ellen spent hours every night in bed going over in her mind all the past interactions between herself and Michael Chadwell. That special bonfire night, and the night they'd gone on the Big Wheel, and all the other times, hanging around outside, under the lamp-post or sitting on the wall, when she'd been certain that she was in love with him and he with her. Why had they never expressed this love? Perhaps if she hadn't started going to Turneley at the weekends; if she hadn't started going out with other boys . . . ?

If she had known that he would be going away now, would she have done things differently, she wondered? 'Where there's life there's hope,' Mrs McCann would say. But was there any hope for them now? If he knew how she felt – assuming that he felt the same, of course – perhaps he wouldn't go. Or . . . even if he did go, perhaps he wouldn't stay. But how was he to know how she felt? He knew she was going out with Pete. Several times over the past few months he and Margaret Latham had been at the bus stop in Turneley when she and Pete had been there too, saying goodnight. He probably thought she was in love with Pete.

On the other hand, he had finished with Margaret Latham. Was this a last ditch attempt to . . . to what? Perhaps he was waiting for a similar gesture on her part. Should she make it clear how she felt? She could tell Mick, or Jennifer? Although why they didn't already know – or at least suspect – was beyond her. What was the matter with them all?

The Chadwells were planning to leave Makerton late in the

evening of Saturday, the sixteenth of May. They were going to spend that night and the next – Whit Sunday – with relatives in Manchester where they would say their goodbyes to Mrs Chadwell's family. Then, on Whit Monday, they were going to travel by train to Southampton where they would board the *Fairstar* which was due to set sail the next day.

On their last evening they were going to have a farewell party for all their friends and neighbours. When Margaret Latham heard about this she told Ellen that she was thinking of going too, to say her final (and no doubt tearful) goodbyes to Michael. 'Do you think I should?' she asked.

Ellen shrugged.

This party, as it turned out, was on the same night as Sally Wagstaff's.

'It's going to be the best one we've ever been to,' Erica enthused, as if they'd been to hundreds. 'And it'll be so easy to get to! Just across the road! You can stay the night at our house if you want, so you won't need to worry about buses and things.'

Ellen braced herself. 'I'm not going,' she said.

'Not going! What do you mean you're not going?'

'I can't go. These people who live near us are emigrating to Australia and they're having a farewell thing on that Saturday night and I've got to go there.'

'What? Can't you get out of it? Sally's party'll be much better.'

'I've got to go to it. I've known them all my life.' Why, Ellen wondered, was she pretending to be reluctant? Why didn't she just say that she'd much rather go to the Chadwells' party than to Sally's?

'Is Pete going with you?'

'No! Definitely not!'

'Well I'm sure you could get out of it, if you tried,' persisted Erica.

'No, I couldn't. I've got to go.'

'Well, couldn't you go there first, and then come on to Sally's later?'

Ellen shook her head. She didn't want to think about 'later'. It was much too painful. Right now she couldn't contemplate anything beyond the moment of farewell.

Departure day dawned.

Early that morning, Ellen walked down the High Street to Teller's wondering how she was going to get through the day. But now that it was here at last, she felt excited as well as sad. One way or the other it would be a decisive day. Either Michael Chadwell would leave without anything further happening between them, or something momentous would occur that evening. Either of these possibilities would be hard to bear, but Ellen was pinning all her hopes on the something momentous.

She arrived at the shop and donned the unflattering blue nylon overall and horrible white cap that she was obliged to wear. The fair was in Makerton, and it was also a Bank Holiday weekend, so they would be busier than usual. Time always passed more quickly when they were busy, and before she knew it she was on her way home for dinner.

As she was walking up the backs, she ran into Michael and Jennifer who were in the process of carrying chairs from the Hursts' house to their own, ready for the evening. Ellen was acutely conscious of her overall and wished that she'd taken her hair down before coming home. But at least she wasn't wearing the stupid cap.

'Can't stop. See you later,' said Jennifer, staggering under the weight of the two chairs she was carrying, one turned upside down on top of the other. Michael, carrying an identical load, hovered. Ellen's heart started beating fast.

'Yeah, see you later,' she called after Jennifer, but keeping her eyes on him.

'Are you coming tonight, then?' he asked, his voice husky. Ellen nodded. 'I thought you might be going to Turneley,' he said, 'what with it being Saturday night.'

Ellen shook her head. 'No!' she said. 'It's your last night! I couldn't miss your last night, could I?' She paused, willing him to understand the singularity of the pronoun.

He smiled, and her heart stopped its hammering for a second and stood still.

'I'll see you later, then,' he said and she nodded again. He turned away and she opened the back gate and stumbled up the yard, quivering all over.

In the middle of the afternoon, Erica phoned her at the shop. She knew this was against the rules but from time to time she did it anyway. Mrs Downes, the manageress, took the call in the back room and after a brief conversation called Ellen away from the counter.

'It's your friend,' she said, handing over the phone. 'She shouldn't be ringing you at work, you know. Don't be long.'

Ellen took the receiver. 'Hello,' she said, carefully. Mrs Downes was still within earshot, ready to curtail the call at the first sign of frivolity.

'It's me,' said Erica, unnecessarily. 'Are you absolutely sure about tonight? It's going to be a great party and you really should be coming to it and not to some boring old family thing. It's not too late to change your mind. Go on, say you'll come.'

Ellen hesitated, conscious that Mrs Downes was listening. Interpreting her hesitation as a sign of weakening resolve, Erica said: 'Go on! Come! You want to, I know you do.' The silence lengthened. 'Are you still there?'

Mrs Downes turned and went back into the shop.

'Erica, listen!' Ellen hissed. 'I've told you not to ring me here. I'm not going to Sally's, so don't keep going on about it. Just go and enjoy yourself. You don't need me there. Now please go away!'

Erica groaned. 'OK, if you say so. Wait a minute, though. Are you coming out tomorrow afternoon? Give me a ring tomorrow morning.'

'No! I don't know! I'll see you on Monday at Walking Day, anyway. Goodbye.'

'I'm glad you're not going out tonight,' Mrs McCann said to

Ellen at tea-time. She meant going out to Turneley. 'You should be here to say goodbye to the Chadwells. Jennifer's been a friend of yours for a long time, even though you've gone your separate ways.'

The phrase made Ellen shudder.

'And Chad too,' chimed in Christine

'Yes, and Michael, too,' agreed Mrs McCann. 'I think our Michael's going to miss him a lot.'

Yes, he will, thought Ellen, because although Mick was still at school and Michael Chadwell was working, they hadn't yet 'gone their separate ways'. Until now, that was. Now all the Chadwells were going their separate ways. A lot of people were going to be upset tonight, she realised. They were all saying goodbye to friends and neighbours. But her loss would be the greatest of all. Her loss was incomparable.

'Can I stay up till they go?' asked Christine.

'There's a taxi coming for them at ten,' said Mrs McCann, not quite answering the question.

Less than four hours left! Ellen went upstairs to get ready. She changed her clothes and then knelt down at the dressing-table mirror to do her make-up. Christine came in and sat down on her bed.

'Stop watching me! You're putting me off!' said Ellen, trying to apply eye-liner with a shaking hand. No mascara tonight, she decided, anticipating tears. She combed her hair, which annoyingly had a slight wave in it from having been up all day, and then stood up for a final, full-length look in the mirror on the inside of the wardrobe door.

'You look nice,' said Christine suddenly.

Ellen gave a small, uncertain smile, not quite knowing how to handle this unexpected compliment.

'Much nicer than Margaret Latham's going to look,' continued Christine, giving Ellen a meaningful stare. Then she leapt off the bed and looked at herself in the mirror too. 'But nowhere near as nice as me!' she said, laughing – and the moment passed.

The Chadwells' house looked strange, stripped of its personal possessions. Most of the furniture was still there, but the big mirror that used to hang over the fireplace was gone, as were the pictures that used to adorn the walls. Squares and oblongs of lighter coloured wallpaper marked where they'd been. The mantelpiece and sideboard were clear of ornaments. It was just a house now, no longer a home. Looking round, Ellen wondered how much more sadness she could bear.

All the men were in the front room. Colin Hurst, who had just arrived, looked Ellen up and down and then swaggered in to join them. Mr Chadwell, in Australian mode already, was opening bottles of beer and handing them round.

'Mam says pour some drinks for the ladies,' said Jennifer, putting her head round the door. She grabbed hold of Ellen and pulled her out of the living room and into the hall which was full of suitcases down at the end near the front door.

'I can't believe we're finally going!' she said. 'I'll write to you all the time. And send you photos. Promise me you'll write too.'

'Course I will,' said Ellen. 'We'll always be friends no matter where we are.' As she was saying this, an image of Joan Grady flashed across her mind. But she'd known Jennifer all her life; they'd grown up together; it would be different. Tears filled her eyes, and Jennifer, seeing them, started to get weepy too.

'No, stop it!' she said, laughing. 'Don't set me off!'

Ellen laughed too, trying to get a grip on her emotions. They went back into the kitchen. More people were arriving now, among them some of Jennifer's old school friends, bearing little going-away presents. Jennifer went out into the yard with them. Ellen lingered, looking around for Michael, but there was no sign of him, nor, she noted grimly, of Margaret Latham either.

She stood in the kitchen doorway, watching her mother taking fairy cakes out of a big cake tin and putting them on to plates. She'd baked them specially for the party. The small kitchen was overflowing. Food, containers, plates and glasses

were everywhere and when Mrs McCann had finished she
hesitated, unable to find a resting place for the cake tin in her
hand.

'Here,' she said giving it to Ellen. She groped in her
cardigan pocket. 'Here's the key. Run home with this tin.
There's no room for it here and I don't want it getting lost.'

'Oh, can't Christine do it?' sighed Ellen. But Christine
was nowhere to be seen so, reluctantly, she obeyed.

On her way back she bumped into Mick and Margaret
Latham at the Chadwells' gate. Margaret was looking very
tragic.

'Do you think Michael'll mind me coming?' she asked.

'No, I'm sure he won't,' said Mick, mechanically,
indicating that this wasn't the first time she'd asked him this
question.

'He might,' said Ellen, wanting to slap her. 'But never
mind, you're here now.'

'Perhaps I should go home.' Margaret was on the verge
of tears. (Goodbye, then! Nobody's stopping you!)

'Don't be silly,' said Mick. 'He won't mind. Nobody'll
mind.'

They went into the house, and there was Michael, talking
earnestly to Christine. As soon as she saw him, Margaret gave
a funny little sob.

'I hope you don't mind me coming . . .' she said
tremulously. 'I just wanted to come and say goodbye.'

Ellen's urge to slap her intensified.

'No, come in. It's all right,' Michael said. 'Help yourself
to something to eat.' He gestured vaguely at all the food and
then he took Mick by the shoulder and propelled him into the
front room.

Through the open door Ellen could hear her father
saying: 'Here he is – the wild colonial boy!' She hoped he
wasn't going to start singing, but it must have been too early
in the evening because no song followed. She had always
loved *The Wild Colonial Boy* and now, of course, it was more
poignant than ever.

'At the early age of sixteen years' she sang in her head.
He left his native home
For Australia's sunny shores
He was inclined to roam.

Michael was seventeen (which didn't scan so well – too many syllables . . . unless you left out the word 'years', which she would do the next time she sang it) but that was irrelevant. Her throat tightened, and even though she was only singing in her head, she was unable to continue.

Margaret was talking to Jennifer now, asking her if it was all right for her to be there. (Oh, shut up, shut up!)

Michael came back into the room and walked over to Ellen. For a long moment they looked at each other. There was definitely no time for shyness now; no time for pretend denials. Very little time left at all!

'Come on,' he said, holding out his hand.

They crossed the room, went through the kitchen and out into the yard. Ellen tried not to look at Margaret Latham as they went past her. She could feel other people watching them too – Mick, Jennifer, her mother, Christine. I don't care, she thought. I've waited years for this. Nothing is going to stop me now.

They closed the yard gate behind them and stepped into King's Terrace. Ellen glanced at the side wall, and smiled. There was nothing chalked on it now, but there should have been. 'Ellen McCann equals Michael Chadwell. True.'

Once outside, they hesitated. The faraway sounds of the fair came drifting towards them through the warm evening air.

'Shall we have a quick ride on the Big Wheel?' asked Michael, smiling.

Ellen smiled back and nodded. Hand in hand they scampered across Turneley Road and half walking, half running made their way to the market place. As they stood in the queue for the Big Wheel Michael put his arm round her, and Ellen, who had been in other arms since the last time he'd done this, knew at once that this was where she really belonged.

'Do you remember the last time we did this?' he asked.

'Yeah. Course I do. You were frightened.'

'No, I wasn't. It was you that was doing all the screaming.'

'That was just to make you feel better!'

Soon it was their turn to clamber on board. How different it was from that last time! It was still light and so not quite as romantic as October would have been. But as they went round and round, soaring into the air, swooping down to earth and then up again, she with her head on his shoulder, he with both arms round her now, it was more than enough.

When the ride was over, she said: 'Elvis was singing too, and I really thought you were going to kiss me. But you didn't – and then we had to get off and that was that.'

They still hadn't kissed, but this wasn't the right place. They began to thread their way through the crowd and off the fairground. As they passed the roll-a-penny stalls, Ellen looked for Hilda Millington, but she wasn't there. They crossed the main road and made their way along a side road to the rec. As they went past the phone box on the corner by the post office, Ellen wondered briefly how Sally's party was going. The light was beginning to fade now, and the noise from the fairground was fading into the background too. A man, out walking his dog, was coming along the dirt track towards them. The dog had bounded off over the rough grass and he was whistling to it and calling its name. They waited until he had gone past before they stopped walking and stood with their arms around each other.

They kissed, gently at first, and then, holding each other even closer, with more urgency. There had been other arms and other kisses – but nothing had prepared Ellen for this. It was beyond anything she had ever felt before. They broke apart and looked searchingly at each other, both a little frightened by this access of passion.

'Oh!' Michael whispered.

She made a small, inarticulate sound, and then they were

kissing again.

'I love you, Ellen,' he said.

'I love you too. I've always loved you. You do know that, don't you?'

'What shall we do now?' he asked. But they both knew the answer to this. 'Where shall we go?' he said, looking across the deserted rec.

Ellen slid her hand into her skirt pocket. 'Let's go to our house,' she said. 'I've got a key and there'll be no-one there.'

They hurried along the dirt track that brought them out on to Turneley Road. Praying that no-one would see them, they crept past the Chadwells' house, down the backs and into Ellen's yard. Once inside they stopped and kissed again.

'What time is it?' said Michael, looking at his watch.

It was ten to nine. Ellen opened the door and they went inside. She slipped the catch on the lock so that no-one else could get in even if they had another key. She hesitated for a moment before leading him into the front room. The street lamp had just come on outside, casting a subdued light through the net curtains and giving the room a rather unreal atmosphere.

They were acutely aware that time was running out for them. Ellen slipped her hands under his t-shirt and he pulled it off over his head and dropped it on to the piano stool. He began unbuttoning her blouse and while he was doing this she began unfastening his belt. She was desperate to ensure that there were no misunderstandings at this eleventh hour. Surely he knew now that he had her full permission. She straightened her arms and her blouse fell to the floor. She reached behind her back and unfastened her bra, and he slipped it off.

'Oh, Ellen,' he said, pulling her towards him.

She could feel his watch strap against her bare skin. She pulled away and sat down on the couch to remove her shoes. And then, standing up slightly, she slipped off her knickers and pushed them out of sight under a cushion. She felt a bit embarrassed doing this, but she didn't want there to be any unseemly fumbling.

They were both still half dressed but they could wait no longer. They lay down on the floor and she folded her arms around him, holding him close. She guided him into what she hoped was the right position. There was no time for hesitation now. She wanted him so much. She had waited so long.

'Oh, Ellen, Ellen,' he kept saying.

She gave a little cry of pain and he paused, but she held him even closer, not wanting him to stop. She loved him so very much. She never wanted to let him go . . .

When he gave a convulsive cry and pulled away from her she could no longer contain her tears. They lay in each other's arms, knowing that very soon now they would have to part.

'I love you,' he whispered. 'Don't cry.' But he was crying too.

Time was passing, passing. They got up and began to get dressed. Ellen glanced outside. All was quiet. There was no sign of the taxi yet. 'You go on,' she said. 'I won't be long.'

She let him out of the back door and went into the bathroom. She gazed at herself in the mirror, overwhelmed by what had happened. I'm not a virgin any more, she thought. *'In this thine own sweet month of May'*, I, Ellen McCann have sinned. But how could this be a sin? There was no time for further reflection though. She flushed the toilet, tidied herself up as best she could and left the house, locking the door behind her.

The taxi had just arrived and was parked in King's Terrace outside the Chadwells' side gate. Mr Chadwell and some of the other men were carrying suitcases out and putting them into the boot. People were gathering on the pavement outside. She couldn't see Michael anywhere. But Margaret Latham was still there, in spite of everything. When she saw Ellen, she scowled and turned away.

The pavement was crowded now. The time had come for the last goodbyes. Hands were shaken, backs patted, cheeks kissed. There seemed to be an order of precedence to this – acquaintances first, the more important people left to the last.

Mrs Chadwell, moving through her friends and neighbours, had started to cry. 'Goodbye, love,' she said, kissing Ellen on the cheek.

'Goodbye,' whispered Ellen. 'Goodbye.'

The tears were infectious and soon everyone was either laughing or crying or both. Christine was getting very upset, and so was Jennifer. She came over and put her arms around Ellen.

'Don't forget to write to me,' she wept.

'I won't,' said Ellen, hugging her friend.

'And why didn't you tell me about you and our Michael?'

Ellen shrugged, trying to smile through her tears. She could see Michael now, moving from person to person. She shrank back against the wall and watched him. He shook hands with Colin Hurst, then he gave Christine, who was sobbing loudly now, a kiss on both cheeks. He turned to Mick. They shook hands and looked at each other awkwardly – something more was obviously needed. Michael drew Mick towards him and thumped him on the shoulder blade; Mick reciprocated. They were still nodding at each other wordlessly when Margaret Latham, who had been standing with Mick, suddenly threw her arms round Michael's neck and burst into noisy tears.

'Goodbye,' he said, awkwardly, trying to disentangle himself from her embrace. Over her shoulder, he looked pleadingly at Mick who stepped in and took charge of the weeping girl.

Jennifer and her mother were already in the taxi. Mr Chadwell was about to get in too.

'Goodbye, goodbye!' everyone began chanting. 'Good luck! *Bon voyage!*' And Mr McCann called out: 'All the best! All the very best!'

Everything was happening so quickly now.

'Come on, lad. In you get. You don't want to get left behind!' someone joked, and suddenly all eyes were on

Michael Chadwell.

'Where's Ellen?' he said, looking for her amongst the crowd.

She was still standing against the wall, the palms of her hands pressed against the bricks. He moved towards her and she stepped forward into his arms for the last time.

It was a long kiss, different from the earlier ones, desperate in a different way. She was aware that everything had gone quiet, that everyone was watching them, but she didn't care. She clung on to him, not wanting to let him go.

'I love you, Ellen McCann,' he whispered.

'I love you, Michael Chadwell.'

'I'll come back,' he said, kissing her one last time. He began to pull away. After he had slipped out of her grasp she continued to hold her empty hands out to him. He turned and got into the taxi.

The engine started up and everyone began waving and chanting again, some bending down to see into the taxi. It began to move slowly away. The younger ones followed it, waving and shouting goodbye. Ellen stepped into the road and saw Jennifer's tear-stained face through the back window. At the road junction the taxi halted for a moment before turning left into Turneley Road. And then it was gone.

No-one spoke for a moment.

'Well, it's what they wanted. Good luck to them!' said Mr McCann, breaking the silence.

People began to disperse. Margaret Latham was still in tears and Mick, with an exasperated look at Ellen, said he would walk her home.

'Come on, let's get you home too,' said Mrs McCann, drying her own eyes and putting her arm around a distraught Christine. 'And you as well,' she said tentatively to Ellen.

Ellen, who was still standing motionless in the middle of the road, turned suddenly and rushed down the backs. She let herself into the house and went into the front room where she stood looking out of the window, struggling to control herself. She wanted to be alone, to throw herself on the floor and cry until she could cry no more. But she couldn't do this yet.

She stayed there until she heard Christine going up to bed, then she went back into the living room. The television was on and her father was sitting watching it. She sat down – carefully – and joined him. Her mother was pottering about in the kitchen. No-one spoke.

After a while Mick came in. 'Did you have to do that, tonight?' he said to Ellen. 'Margaret's really upset. I've just had to go all the way home with her.'

Ellen stiffened but said nothing, continuing to stare unseeingly at the television screen.

'We're all upset,' said Mrs McCann, coming out of the kitchen and handing Ellen a mug of cocoa. 'Let's not make matters worse.'

Ellen gazed into the depths of her drink and wondered how much worse matters could possibly get.

Christine was asleep when she went up to their room. Ellen, suppressing her tears, lay in bed waiting for everyone else to come upstairs. She heard her father's heavy footsteps, and then shortly afterwards the lighter ones of her mother. Ages afterwards, Mick followed them. She waited a while longer until she thought everyone must be asleep, and then she got up, opened the door carefully and crept down the stairs. She went into the front room, closed the door quietly behind her and pulled the piano stool in front of it.

The light from the street lamp was shining into the room and throwing shadows on to the walls. She sat down on the couch and wrapped her arms around herself. Rocking to and fro, she began to cry. But her tears did nothing to ease the pain. She got up and went to the window, but it was no use looking out any more. He wasn't there. He would never be there again. The taxi had disappeared round the corner and he had gone. 'I'll come back,' he had said. Come back, now, she cried. Please, come back to me!

She knelt down on the floor, where earlier they had lain together, and wondered what he was doing now. Was he lying awake, missing her too? Wanting her, aching for her, like she was for him? Oh, Michael, Michael!

She thought she heard someone coming down the stairs and scrambled to her feet. There was an armchair in the chimney recess and she went and crouched down on the floor behind it. She'd hidden herself here once before, years ago, to read the bit in *Little Women* where Beth died. She'd wanted to savour it, to read it over and over and cry her eyes out without anyone seeing her or laughing at her. She was much bigger now, though, and this space was too small to be an effective hiding place. Nevertheless, although she knew that no-one was coming she continued to sit there, with her knees drawn up to her chin. The grief she had felt for Beth March back then was nothing compared to the grief she was feeling now, she thought. And she wept and wept until she had no more tears left.

She didn't know how she was going to bear this pain, this yearning. She wondered if it would've been better if nothing had happened between them. The regret would've been unbearable, but the loss would have been less. Or was it 'better to have loved and lost, than never to have loved at all'? Yes it was, she decided, because in spite of all this pain and suffering, she would always have this night to sustain her. She had held him in her arms. He had been hers completely. He had told her that he loved her, and she had told him that she loved him too. And she did. She would always love him. But now he was gone and she might never see him again.

Gradually, the tears subsided. 'I'll come back,' he'd said and she would cling to this promise. After all, he wasn't dead (like Beth had been). He wasn't lost to her in that way. 'Where there's life, there's hope', her mother would say. And there was life, and last night she had lived it to the full. Nothing could change that; nothing would ever make her regret it.

Next morning, when Mrs McCann came to get them up for Mass, Ellen turned over in bed to face the wall. 'I'll go this evening,' she muttered, and her mother accepted this without further comment.

When she came downstairs later, there was only Christine there. Mr McCann had gone to church and Mrs McCann had gone to help Mrs Hurst do some clearing up after last night's party. Mick was still in bed.

Ellen sat at the table, her hair obscuring most of her swollen face, and tried to eat the bacon and egg breakfast her father had cooked. The radio was on in the background, playing requests for loved ones who were far from home. Christine started clearing away the breakfast things.

Mick came down and got his breakfast from the kitchen. It was supposed to be keeping warm under a low grill but Christine had deliberately turned it off. Muttering about this, he sat down at the table. Ellen got up and went to sit in her father's armchair, taking her cup and saucer with her.

'I couldn't believe you and Chad last night,' said Mick. 'Why did you have to go off with him like that when you know how Margaret feels about him?' Ellen said nothing. 'Were you deliberately trying to upset her or something?'

'Shut up!' said Christine, standing in the doorway. 'You don't know what you're talking about. You don't know anything, you.'

'Oh? And you do, I suppose?'

'Yes, I do. I know more than you. And Chad wasn't even going out with Margaret Latham any more. He'd finished with her, in case you'd forgotten.'

'No, I haven't forgotten.' Mick looked across at Ellen. 'But you knew how upset she'd be. You shouldn't have done it. And just in case *you've* forgotten – you *are* going out with someone. You've got a boyfriend. I wonder what he'd think about this?'

Ellen shook her head.

'Well anyway, she won't forgive you in a hurry, so don't think she will,' said Mick.

Ellen got up to put her tea back on the table, the cup rattling loudly in the saucer as she did so. 'I couldn't care less about Margaret bloody Latham!' she said. 'I don't care what she thinks or what she feels!' Her voice was rising with each word. 'Christine's right – you don't know what you're talking about.' She rounded on her brother, letting him see her tear-ravaged face now. 'Shall I tell you something?' she cried. 'Shall I?'

He didn't answer.

'Well I'm going to anyway. *I've* been in love with Michael Chadwell ever since I was a little girl. I've been in love with him for years. I've spent years . . . And she's only known him for a few weeks. And it's me that he loves, not her. And now he's gone! He's gone to the other side of the world and I might never see him again and I . . . I . . . I can't stand it! And all *you* can do is keep going on about Margaret this and Margaret that. Well I don't care! I don't give a damn about her! All I care about is . . .' Ellen gave a cry of pain. The tears were flowing down her face now. 'So just shut up, will you?' she yelled. 'Just shut up, shut up!'

Mick looked stunned. He sat there, slowly taking in what she had said. He looked uneasily at Christine who gave him her most disdainful look and shook her head in disgust. Ellen fled from the room and rushed upstairs.

She stayed in her bedroom all afternoon. And she didn't ring Erica. She deliberately walked straight past the phone box on her way to and from the evening Mass. She sat in church, her eyes all red and swollen, and tried not to cry any more.

She didn't go to Communion. She hadn't fasted for the requisite time, but she couldn't have gone, anyway, because 'in the eyes of God' she'd committed a mortal sin. A mortal sin for which she could go to hell! But how could it be a *mortal* sin? Murder was a mortal sin! But so too was missing Mass on Sundays. It didn't make sense. How could these offences be equally grave? Who decided these things? And how could what had happened last night be any sort of sin at all?

She wasn't going to confess it. Not because she didn't

have the words. This time it was very straightforward. I have had sex-u-al inter-course, *once*. No, she wouldn't go to Confession and say that she was sorry, because she wasn't. Nor could she promise not to do it again, because if Michael Chadwell were to come back ('I'll come back,' he'd said) then she knew that she would.

She wasn't going to spend any more time questioning these things now, but somewhere in the recesses of her soul she felt that her faith had faltered.

The next day, Whit Monday, was Walking Day in Turneley. Every year on this day, the Catholic parishes in the town, in a mass affirmation of faith, turned out in all their Whitsun glory to parade through the streets. There were brass bands, pipe bands and choirs. There was an abundance of beautifully dressed children: little boys with shiny red ties and sashes; girls carrying bouquets – the older ones hanging on to ribbons suspended from tall banners, and the younger ones holding on to horizontal bars festooned with flowers. There were processions of religious societies and sodalities – the Children of Mary, the Knights of St Columbus. The whole parade, which was watched by crowds of people, took about two hours to go by. And when the weather was fine – as it was today – it was a wonderful spectacle, a popular Bank Holiday day out.

Every year the girls from the Convent 'walked' too. Immaculately turned out in their summer uniform (green dresses, brown blazers and beige summer hats), they marched in four house lines behind the school banner. And every year until now Ellen and Erica had taken part. But this year they'd decided not to; it would be too embarrassing to be seen in their school uniforms in public.

It was, however, Christine's first Turneley Walking Day and she was very excited about it. She set off early, leaving her mother, Auntie Annie and her cousin Maureen Cartwright to follow on later. Ellen had said that she wasn't going but at the very last minute she changed her mind. The town centre was closed to traffic and they had to get off the bus at the stop before Higham's and walk the rest of the way.

All the different parishes 'walked' from their respective churches around the town and assembled in the market square. When all were present, and when the Protestant Parish Church clock struck eleven, there was a mass singing of *Faith Of Our Fathers* before the grand procession got under way. In the past, Ellen had always found this thrilling. She'd arranged to meet Erica here for this today, but she was feeling very fragile and didn't think she could stand listening to a blow by blow account of Sally's party, so she decided not to go to the square at all but to stay with her family instead. She would make up some excuse for Erica's benefit later.

They took up their positions at her mother's favourite vantage point across the road from the Convent. It was exciting when the procession first came into view but after a while Maureen Cartwright began to get bored and restless. She kept asking when they were going to see Christine. Eventually the school banner appeared and there she was, smiling because she'd seen them, but trying not to turn her head to look at them as she marched past. Ellen watched Angela Norris and the rest of her classmates go by, and she looked for Maria Latimer too – but she didn't seem to be there.

The procession ended back at the market square where it had started. Ellen was sent there, through the crowded streets, to collect Christine and take her to the café next door to Higham's where it'd become an annual ritual for them to have dinner while they were waiting for the buses to start running again. They were about to go into the café when Ellen saw Erica waving to her from the other side of the road. Her heart sank.

Erica fought her way across. 'Where have you *been?*' she cried, landing at Ellen's side. 'I waited for you for ages!' Ellen was about to make an excuse but Erica didn't wait for one. She seemed much too excited to be angry. 'You'll never guess what happened on Saturday night!' she said.

Ellen flinched slightly and said nothing. Christine took hold of her arm in a gesture of support and understanding.

'Go on! You'll never guess. Not in a million years,' said Erica again.

'Do you really want me to make a futile attempt then?' asked Ellen, but Erica failed to register the hostility in her tone.

'Da – dah,' she said loudly, flinging her arms out in a dramatic gesture, oblivious to the crowds around them. 'Only me and Joe Wagstaff! I can't believe it! I'm going out with Joe Wagstaff! At long bloody last!'

It was, indeed, unbelievable. Once again Ellen's eyes filled with tears.

It was half-term so for the moment Ellen was spared the ordeal of having to listen to all the details of Erica's triumph. She spent the next day, Tuesday, sitting in the front room, pretending to be revising for the impending O-level exams. But she couldn't stop thinking about Michael Chadwell. She wondered what he was doing now, and what he was thinking about. She tried to imagine Southampton docks and the ocean-going *Fairstar* which, according to Jennifer, used to be called something else, but had been newly refitted and was now a luxury liner. This was going to be its maiden voyage under its new name.

'Do you think the Chadwells will have left by now?' Christine asked at tea-time.

'They'll probably be sailing on the evening tide,' said Mr McCann from his armchair.

If there is an evening tide tonight, thought Ellen, trying not to think of Margaret Latham.

She tried to imagine the scene. The sea would be crashing against a harbour wall (like it did against the sea-wall at Blackpool when the tide was in). And then the tide would turn, carrying the huge ship out of the harbour and into the English Channel. There would be crowds of people on the quayside to see it off, waving and calling goodbye to their loved ones. The Chadwells would be on deck waving too, but to no-one in particular because they'd already said all their goodbyes.

Ellen wished she could be there. The abrupt disappearance of the taxi on Saturday night had been awful. How much more romantic it would have been to watch as the ship drifted slowly away into the sunset. She could picture herself, her hair blowing gently in the breeze, standing there until the *Fairstar* was no longer visible and she was the only person left on the quayside. Michael would still be on deck too, all alone, clutching the rail and watching the coastline recede further and further into the distance. The sun would disappear over the horizon and darkness would fall.

How very beautiful! How unbearably sad!

But life went on.

On Wednesday morning a furniture van came to the house in Turneley Road and took the Chadwells' furniture away. In the afternoon another one arrived and some new people moved in.

On Thursday afternoon Ellen went to Turneley to meet Erica. They went for a walk in the park and Erica told her all about last Saturday night. It seemed that Joe had been out when the party started and, as the evening wore on and he still hadn't appeared, Erica had been in despair, thinking that it was going to be yet another big disappointment. But then, in he came! He looked round the room, walked straight over to her and began dancing with her! And that had been that!

It seemed, to say the least, too good to be true. Ellen had a strong sense of foreboding.

But Erica was ecstatic. 'It's going to be great,' she enthused. 'We can do lots of things together, the four of us.'

'Ah!' said Ellen. 'Well, no we can't. There's something I've got to tell you too.' She paused. 'I'm going to finish with Pete.'

'No! You can't do that! Why?'

'Because . . .' Ellen shrugged. How could she explain it to

Erica? How, indeed, was she going to explain it to Pete?

'No! You're being silly. Don't go and spoil things. It's ideal as it is – me and Joe, you and Pete. You can't finish with him!'

'I have to. I can't carry on going out with him just for your convenience. Not when I . . . when I don't . . . want to.'

Erica was outraged: 'I don't know what's the matter with you,' she said. 'You've been acting funny all week.'

No, you don't know what's the matter with me, thought Ellen. And I'm not going to tell you, either. 'There's nothing the matter with me,' she said. 'I just don't want to go out with him anymore, that's all.'

On Friday night, when he met her outside Higham's, she told Pete. She couldn't tell him the real reason so she said that she didn't want to go out with anybody at the moment; she just wanted to concentrate on her exams. Then she thought this might be misleading – she might be giving him the false hope that once the exams were over things could go back to normal – so, to make it very clear, she added: 'I don't want to go out with you ever again.' And then, to soften the harshness of this: 'I'm very, very sorry.'

Pete was visibly hurt. He didn't say anything, didn't try to dissuade her. It was almost as if he'd been expecting it. They walked the rest of the way to the Cellar Bar in a miserable silence. Once there, he retreated into a corner and Ellen bought herself a glass of orange juice and went to sit with Erica and Joe. She felt awkward being with them, but it would be an opportunity to study Joe Wagstaff (who barely acknowledged her arrival) at close quarters.

'So you've done it, then,' said Erica, shaking her head. 'She's just gone and finished with Pete,' she said to Joe. 'Go and talk to him. Look, he's over there all by himself. He's obviously upset.'

'He'll be all right,' said Joe, glancing over at Pete. 'He'll get over it.'

Ellen narrowed her eyes. 'Of course he will,' she said.

'I'm very easy to get over.'

Erica gave her one of her I-don't-know-what's-the-matter-with-you looks but Ellen just gave her a level stare in return and then settled down to scrutinise the new lovers.

Erica was looking very attractive and Joe Wagstaff – she had to admit – was very handsome. But search as she might she could find little evidence that he was in any way besotted with Erica. He laughed when she was being funny – and sometimes when she wasn't; he gave her cigarettes and lit them for her; he allowed her to touch him possessively, which she did all the time, but he didn't reciprocate. He didn't put his arm round her or hold her hand.

Ellen, who had known passion, could detect none here. Not on his part anyway. If Erica were to finish with him now, she thought, he would have no trouble getting over it. He might even be relieved. Her sense of foreboding intensified.

On the first day back at school after the half-term holiday, Ellen and Christine got on the same bus as Margaret Latham. As soon as they appeared at the top of the stairs Margaret looked away pointedly and stared out of the window. Ellen hesitated a moment and then led Christine further down the aisle, away from her. She sighed as she sat down. Soon the whole top deck of the bus would be filled with people she'd fallen out with! Still, she consoled herself, she wouldn't have to bother about Sheila Murphy and Joan Grady for much longer. It was most unlikely that either of them would be staying on into the sixth form. Margaret Latham would be, though. Ellen sighed again.

'She's just being silly,' said Christine. 'Go and talk to her. She probably wants to be friends with you again now.'

But Ellen didn't want to talk to Margaret yet. She didn't want to talk about Michael Chadwell because if she did they might both burst into tears.

JUNE

1964

June – an otherwise pleasant enough month – was always blighted by exams. For Ellen, particularly so this O-level year. Christine, too, had her first end-of-year exams at the Convent and was taking them very seriously. And although Mick was taking his end-of-year sixth-form exams rather less so, there was, nonetheless, a subdued atmosphere in the McCann household. But this was only partly due to exam pressures; it had been like this ever since the Chadwells' departure. Ellen had barely spoken to Mick, and neither had Christine, whose sisterly solicitude was still in evidence.

Ellen's days were filled with revision and exams. She was trying her best to concentrate, but it was difficult. Time and again she would find herself drifting off into her own private world of heartbreak. But no-one else could tell the difference.

Erica, on the other hand, wasn't trying at all. She didn't seem a bit bothered about her exams. All she cared about was Joe Wagstaff. He, too, had exams – he was in the middle of his A-levels – so they only saw each other at weekends but, with him or without him, he was all she could think about.

'I can't wait for these stupid exams to be over,' she said as they were waiting outside the school hall for their second maths paper. 'I know I'm going to fail them all.'

Ellen said nothing. Erica was clever; she would pass all her exams, perhaps not brilliantly but certainly adequately. And all this public sighing over Joe Wagstaff was getting on her nerves.

'I want to leave school, anyway,' Erica went on. 'If Joe goes to university in September, I want to go with him. Not to university, obviously, but I'll get a job in the same place and we can see each other all the time. Perhaps we'll go to London. You can come and visit us.'

Erica was being ridiculous. Ellen looked at Angela Norris and raised her eyes to heaven in disbelief. 'Does Joe know about this?' she asked, her little sneer implying that if he did he wouldn't think it was such a good idea.

'Not yet. It'll be a nice surprise for him,' said Erica, choosing to ignore Ellen's tone.

She's frightened, thought Ellen. She knows there's something not quite right. She knows it's not going to last. She's going to do something stupid.

For the duration of the examination period the Convent girls only had to go into school on those days and at those times when they had an actual exam. Late one Wednesday morning, Ellen was on her way home when Sandra Crompton got on the same bus. She knew that Sandra had been working in Woolworth's in Turneley for some time now, but so far she had managed to avoid her. This, however, must be her half day.

After a few seconds of rather rude deliberation, Sandra sat down next to her. Ellen's heart sank. It'd been a long time since they'd last spoken.

'So! You're still going to school then?' Sandra said, trying (but not too hard) to veil her contempt by feigning surprise.

'Obviously,' said Ellen, hearing herself sounding like Erica.

'You must be going to leave soon, though?'

'No.'

'You're going to stay at school for even longer?'

'Yeah.'

'What for?'

'Because I want to.' (Because I don't want to end up working in Woolies like you.)

Sandra sniffed. 'I haven't seen your Michael about for ages,' she said. 'Is he still going to school too?'

'Yes.'

They travelled in silence for a while until Sandra suddenly remembered something. 'Hey!' she said gleefully. 'I saw you and Michael Chadwell on the fair the other Saturday!' She made it sound as though she'd witnessed something shameful.

'Oh.'

'Are you actually going out with him now? I always knew you fancied him.'

'No, I'm not – actually.' Ellen's heart contracted. 'He doesn't live here anymore. He's gone away. The whole family's gone away.'

'Oh?' Sandra was interested. 'Where've they gone then?'

'Australia.' (To the other side of the world! To the ends of the earth!)

The Chadwells would be nearing Fremantle now. Indeed, they might even have arrived there and had their first taste of Australia before sailing on to Sydney.

'Australia! Blimey!' Sandra was impressed. 'Oh well! I never did like that Jennifer Chadwell.'

Ellen stared out of the window, not trusting herself to speak. For the first time since the Chadwells had left, she was experiencing a keen sense of loss for her friend – 'that Jennifer'. Her eyes filled with tears. Yet again.

The days passed. There were only a few exams left now.

On the last Monday morning, Ellen arrived at school for their second Latin paper, and was taken aback to find no sign of Erica. Had she decided not to finish her exams? Was she really intending to leave school like she'd been threatening to do? It would be just like Erica to do something stupid like that.

The hall was almost empty. There were only a handful of girls doing Latin and they were scattered alphabetically around the room. Over in one corner there were a few older girls doing an A-level exam. One of them was Claire Wagstaff. I wonder what she thinks about Erica and Joe, thought Ellen. Perhaps Erica was with Joe now? But it was more likely that he, too, had an exam this morning and was busy doing it and not thinking about Erica at all. Ellen tried not to think about her either; tried not to keep wondering where she was or what she was doing. She needed to focus on her Latin.

The big clock over the door at the front of the hall was ticking audibly. The time came and passed when, even though late, Erica would still have been allowed to sit the exam. She had definitely missed it now. There was going to be trouble.

Ellen looked round the room. The sun was shining through the high stained-glass windows, creating streams of dust beams in the air and reflecting patches of colour on to some of the desks and parts of the floor. There were two large statues at the front of the hall, one on each side of the dais: on the left, St Thérèse, the Little Flower; on the right, the Little King. Around the hall were little niches set in the walls, housing other statues.

Standing in one such niche, near where Ellen was sitting, was one of Our Lady. Our Lady of Grace. She was wearing a white dress and veil and a blue cloak with a gilded lining. Her arms were slightly outstretched by her sides, the palms of her hands facing forwards. She was standing on a serpent. Her eyes were modestly downcast. She looked very demure – pure and chaste. The Virgin Mary, thought Ellen. *The Virgin of all virgins.* She glanced across the room at another statue of Mary holding the baby Jesus in her arms. Mary the Virgin Mother. She looked away and went back to her exam paper.

Every so often, vague sounds drifted in from the rest of the school. No bells were rung while there were exams in progress, nor were the younger girls allowed to go anywhere near the hall or any of the other exam rooms. Nevertheless, you could always tell when there was a lesson change or when it was break time.

Ellen stretched her legs out under the desk and looked round the room again. As she was doing so the door at the top of the hall opened quietly and a little first year girl slipped in and handed something to the invigilating teacher who was sitting at the lectern on the dais. Ellen watched the girl go out again, and then returned to her translation. She was pleased with her work. It was going well in spite of everything.

A gradual hush marked the end of break. Someone got up to get an extra piece of paper; someone else sneezed loudly, causing a few muffled snorts of amusement and an admonitory look from the dais. Then quietness descended again. After a while, piercing the silence and making them jump, the teacher informed them that the A-level candidates had an hour and five minutes to go, but the Latin candidates had only another five minutes left. This announcement was followed by the usual panic-stricken flurry, but Ellen had already finished.

She read through the last bit she had written and then sat back, satisfied. A patch of light from one of the windows was casting a red stain on her closed answer book. Feeling Mary's gaze upon her, she glanced up at the statue again. And she wondered, as she did so many times each day, where the Chadwells were now and what Michael was doing. Soon Jennifer would be writing to her. And Michael? Would he write to her too?

'Stop writing!' said the teacher. 'Leave your answer books on your desks and go out quietly. Remember that some girls are still working. Ellen McCann?' she looked round inquiringly. She didn't know who Ellen was. 'Can I have a word, please?'

Ellen turned round and exchanged startled looks with Angela. What was this about? She went over to the dais.

'Sister Marie-Pierre would like to see you in her office straight away,' whispered the teacher, holding up the note she'd been given. Ellen's heart missed a beat. Instantly she thought of Erica.

The Headmistress's office was on the first floor, tucked away down a short corridor, away from the hustle and bustle of the school's main highway. Feeling very apprehensive, Ellen knocked on the door. She'd only been in this room once before, last year with Erica. And on that occasion they'd been in trouble.

Instead of walking back to school from La Maison after their last games lesson, they'd caught a bus. This, as they well knew, was strictly forbidden, but they'd been messing about and were last out of the changing room and in grave danger of being late back to school – and not for the first time. When the bus appeared, just as they were approaching the bus stop, it seemed the solution to their problem. But they were seen getting off it and were duly reported.

Sister Marie-Pierre had made a big fuss. For some reason, returning to school on the bus was a major crime. She'd made it very clear that such flouting of the rules would not be tolerated under any circumstances. Retribution of a terrible nature would be visited upon them if they were caught doing this again. Did they understand? Trying not to giggle, they'd said yes Sister, they did.

'You'd think catching a bus was a mortal sin,' Erica had said when they were dismissed. 'Stupid cow! Stupid holy cow!'

'Sit down, Ellen,' said Sister Marie-Pierre now. 'I'm afraid I have some bad news for you.'

Ellen swallowed hard. It's Erica, she thought. She's done something stupid. But it wasn't Erica.

'It's Maria Latimer,' the headmistress said solemnly. Ellen felt a momentary flash of relief which disappeared instantly at her next words. 'I'm afraid she died last night.'

The shock was immense. Ellen could see now why people were always asked to sit down before they were told bad news. Died! How? Why? What had happened? How could she have died? She opened her mouth but no words came out.

Sister Marie-Pierre said nothing more by way of explanation. Instead, she said: 'I'm telling you now in case you were intending to go round to their house, to see what had happened to Erica, perhaps?' Ellen nodded. 'I don't think you should go, not for a few days at least. The family, as you can imagine, are very upset.'

(Ellen pictured Maria lying dead in the little attic bedroom. Mr Latimer, Maggie, Erica and the boys were kneeling around her bed. Granny Latimer was there too. They were all weeping.)

'Do you have an exam this afternoon?'

'No, Sister.'

'Well then, go home now, Ellen, and pray for her soul. And pray for the family too, at this difficult time.'

Ellen nodded again and left the room in a daze.

Angela was hovering outside, waiting to hear what this was all about.

'Maria Latimer's dead!' Ellen told her. 'Don't ask me how. That's all I know.' She thought about Claire Wagstaff, still doing her exam in the hall. She didn't know yet. She too would be sent for soon and told the dreadful news. Maria was her best friend.

'What are you going to do now?' asked Angela.

'I don't know. I wonder if Sally knows anything else. I wonder if she's in school.'

They asked around, but no-one had seen Sally.

Ellen decided to go home as she had been told to do. She sat on the bus, her mind racing. How could Maria have died just like that? She must have been all right last Friday, otherwise Erica would've said something. What could've happened over the weekend? Ellen felt uneasy. I knew she wasn't well, she thought. She was so pale and thin at Erica's birthday tea. And she remembered how Maria had been pretending to eat. Had she fasted herself to death? Was that possible? The last time she'd seen Maria was in school last week. Even though it'd been a very warm day, she'd been wearing her cardigan, huddled into it as though she were cold. Why had no-one else noticed that there was something wrong with her?

Ellen had no exams for the next two days and so it was Thursday morning before she went back to school. She went early, hoping to see Sally Wagstaff, but Sally wasn't there. Perhaps she'd already finished her exams.

When Ellen's exam was over, however, Sally was waiting for her outside the hall. She wasn't in school uniform; she'd only come in to see Ellen, she said. She grabbed hold of her and steered her away from Angela and into a quiet corner.

'You've heard about Maria then?' she said.

'I know she's dead but I don't know any details. What happened?'

'She was found dead on Monday morning,' Sally said. She lowered her voice to a whisper. 'Lying by her mother's grave!'

Ellen stared at her in complete incomprehension. 'What? She was found in the graveyard – dead? How, though? I mean why was she dead?'

Sally shook her head. 'I don't really know,' she said. 'It's all a bit of a secret at the moment. They're not saying much. But . . .' she looked at Ellen, her eyes widening in horror. 'I did hear that she was found lying in a pool of blood! She'd been there all night.'

The two girls continued to stare at each other while Ellen tried to make sense of this.

'Are you saying she was murdered?' she said. 'In the churchyard? Next to her mother's grave?' It sounded unbelievable.

Sally shrugged. 'I don't know. That's all I know.' And then: 'Anyway, Erica wants you to go round to her house this afternoon.'

'Oh, God!' said Ellen. 'What am I going to say to her? Have you seen her? Have you spoken to her?'

'Not really. She rang this morning to ask me to tell you

to go round, that's all.'

'What about your brother? And Claire? Have they seen her? Have they been round?'

'I don't think so. Claire's devastated. We all are,' said Sally, beginning to get tearful. Ellen put her arm round her and stopped asking any more questions.

She didn't want to go round to the Latimers' house. She felt totally out of her depth. What would she say to Erica? How would Erica be? How would she be if it were Christine who had died? (She thought fleetingly of Jo March in *Little Women*.) Would Joe Wagstaff be going round to comfort Erica? Probably not.

'I'm her best friend,' she said to Angela. 'I should go round if she wants me to, but I'm scared. I don't know what I'm going to say to her.'

It was Maggie who answered the door. Ellen stood there uncertainly.

'Come in, Ellen,' she said, attempting a small smile. 'Erica's in her room. Go on up.'

The house was very quiet. No-one else seemed to be in, which was a relief. Ellen took a deep breath and knocked on Erica's bedroom door.

'There you are!' said Erica, opening the door and ushering her into the room. 'I thought you were never coming!' Ellen felt slightly reassured by the familiarity of this welcome.

One of the curtains on the big bay window was drawn, shading part of the room and leaving the rest of it bathed in sunlight. Erica's bed was in the shade and she sat on it now and waited for Ellen to sit down too. Ellen hesitated. She usually sat on Maria's old bed when she was here, but she wondered now whether this would be inappropriate. But it hadn't been Maria's bed for a while, so she perched on the edge of it and felt the warmth of the sun on her back.

'How are you?' she asked awkwardly. Erica was pale and looked slightly dishevelled from lying down, but there were no signs of tears.

'What do you know?' Erica asked, ignoring this inquiry.

'Not much,' said Ellen. 'Just that she was found near your mother's grave.' She didn't like to mention the pool of blood.

'We didn't even know she wasn't here on Sunday night,' said Erica. 'She was always up in her room on her own. We just thought she was in bed. And then on Monday morning, when we were all getting ready for school and work and things, a policeman came to the door and told us – well he told my dad and Maggie.

'Some woman had been walking through the churchyard and saw her lying there. They called the police and an ambulance but she was already dead. The priest knew who she was, of course, and the police came round to tell us.' Erica paused and shuddered. 'It was awful,' she said. 'Really awful.'

'How . . . what . . .?' Ellen hesitated, but she had to know. 'Sally said something about a pool of blood.'

Erica got up and came to sit next to her. Close up, Ellen could see the dark shadows under her eyes.

'That's what I have to tell you,' she said. 'They did a post-mortem. She was having a baby, Ellen! They said she'd had a haemorrhage and bled to death. They said she was between three and four months pregnant and she had a miscarriage and bled to death!'

'Having a baby! Maria! Maria was having a baby? No, she couldn't've been!'

'Well, she was. And nobody knew. And now she's dead and nobody has any idea whose baby it is . . . was. Except the father, of course. He must know.' Erica got up and went back to sit on her own bed. 'She was going to be a nun,' she said. 'It was all decided. She wasn't going to go back to school next year to finish her A-levels. She was going to go into her stupid convent in August instead. She said she'd made up her mind once and for all this time and wasn't going to be talked out of it again.' Erica gave a hollow laugh. 'And now they're all wishing they'd let her go last year, when she wanted to – and then this wouldn't have happened.

'But she was pregnant!' she went on. 'So why was she going ahead with all the arrangements? She couldn't go and be a bloody nun if she was having a baby, could she? She must've known she was, mustn't she? But none of us had any idea. My dad is beside himself. He keeps saying he's a doctor, he should've noticed, he should have realised something was wrong. But none of us noticed, did we?'

Ellen didn't say anything. She'd noticed that something wasn't right. She'd even mentioned it to Erica a few weeks ago. But no, she hadn't suspected that Maria was having a baby! Not Maria! It was inconceivable!

'What about Claire? Does she have any idea who the father is?'

Erica shook her head. 'She doesn't know about it yet – about her being pregnant, I mean. Nobody knows except us – and now you. Even Granny Latimer doesn't know exactly what happened. Nobody wants to tell her. It'll break her heart. She thinks Maria was a saint – just like she thinks my mother was a saint.' Erica gave another empty little laugh.

'And Granny Morton? Does she know?'

'I don't know. I don't know what they've told her. She's coming up for the funeral next week, anyway. And everybody'll know soon because there's going to be an inquest or something, and it'll probably be in the paper.'

Maggie knocked on the door and came in bearing tea and sandwiches on a tray. 'Try to eat something,' she said to Erica. She smiled at Ellen and asked how her exams were going.

'All right, thank you,' said Ellen. 'I've nearly finished now.'

'Well I've definitely finished,' said Erica. 'I'm not doing any more now, not after this.' But, Ellen noted, she didn't mention leaving school.

Maggie went away and they began to drink their tea.

'I can't think who the father could be, can you?' said

Erica, toying with a sandwich. 'But it's all I can think about and it's driving me mad. She didn't go out or anything. She hardly knew any boys. And why would she . . . you know . . . if she was going to be a nun? It doesn't make sense.'

'Perhaps . . .' said Ellen, searching for a viable explanation. 'You don't think she could have been . . . raped, or something, do you?'

'I don't know. I've been thinking all kinds of things.'

They sat in silence for a while and then Erica began again. 'When she found out about my mother and George Hunter . . . well, before that really. . . when she first found out about Gina . . . she was really upset. And then, when we found out about George Hunter and we thought that he and my mother had been seeing each other even after she was married to my dad, she was even more upset. She wanted to think that our mother was perfect, and she obviously wasn't. So I don't understand why she would have . . . you know, sinned herself in the same way.'

'Perhaps,' said Ellen, 'she went to your mother's grave because she thought your mother would understand. She wouldn't think it was such a dreadful sin because it was one she'd committed too.' She wondered how understanding her own mother would be if she knew about her and Michael Chadwell. Thank goodness she didn't know. And thank goodness too that she wasn't pregnant now like Maria had been! Pregnant. The word sounded so harsh and unforgiving. It wasn't one that they used at home. There, people would lower their voices and say 'she's expecting'. She wondered what words she herself would use when she told her mother about Maria – as she would have to do, later.

Erica was about to say something else, but then changed her mind and said instead: 'I just wish she was here so we could ask her. I just really wish she was here.'

Thinking that Erica might be about to cry, Ellen changed the subject slightly. 'Have you seen Joe?' she asked.

'No. I haven't been out, and he hasn't been round yet.'

Typical, thought Ellen. But what, she wondered, would

Joe Wagstaff say and do when he finally did see Erica? How would he comfort her? How could anyone comfort her?

The news of Maria's death was all round the school now. There were no assemblies because the hall was still being used for exams, but prayers were being said in classrooms and in the chapel. 'Let us pray for the repose of the soul of Maria Latimer,' the girls were entreated. And so: *'Eternal rest give unto her, O Lord,'* they prayed. *'And let perpetual light shine upon her. May she rest in peace. Amen.'*

Ellen, though, wasn't thinking about Maria's soul. She was thinking about her body, resting, not in peace, but in a pool of blood in the dark graveyard. She wondered if Sister Marie-Pierre and the rest of the teachers knew how Maria had died. She studied their faces but if they did know they weren't giving anything away.

Sally, however, knew all about it now. She expressed her dismay and disbelief to Ellen. Claire, she said, was ab-solutely shocked. She just couldn't believe it. She'd had no idea. And she had no idea who the father might be, either. She was really, really upset that Maria hadn't confided in her. Maria had been her best friend.

But best friends don't know everything, Ellen thought. Maggie hadn't known about her best friend and her own brother; and Erica didn't know anything about her and Michael Chadwell. And just for a moment, she wondered whether Erica might be keeping secrets from her, too. It was possible, she conceded – but she doubted it.

Ellen saw Erica again a couple of days before the funeral. She called round after school and they went for a walk to the park, carefully avoiding St Peter's churchyard on the way.

Everyone knew now about Maria's baby, Erica said, but no-one had any idea who the father could be. No-one knew what to think. It was a mystery. There had been some kind of an inquest but there was going to be a proper one at some future date 'to establish the cause of death'.

'What does that mean? They know what the cause of death was, don't they? She had a miscarriage,' said Ellen, confused

Erica said nothing.

They walked along, deep in thought.

'Do you think . . . ?' Ellen ventured.

'Yes, I do!' said Erica, nodding vigorously. 'I think she was trying to get rid of the baby. That's what you were going to say, wasn't it? And I think it's what my dad and Maggie think too.'

'And she went to your mother's grave because she didn't know where else to go?'

Ellen tried not to think about how Maria might have gone about inducing a miscarriage. Gin, hot baths, jumping up and down . . . knitting needles? All things she'd heard about obliquely. But would Mrs Latimer have been understanding about that? After all, she hadn't got rid of Gina when she'd found herself in a similar situation. But then . . . she hadn't been going to be a nun, had she?

'And I also think,' said Erica, sitting down on a park bench, 'that she was trying to kill herself as well as the baby. And that's what this inquest thing is about. To decide if she committed suicide or not.'

Ellen arrived home later to find two postcards from Port Said propped up against the mirror on the sideboard. They had arrived that morning. One was from Jennifer, addressed to 'Miss E. McCann', saying what a great time they were having on board ship and sending love and regards to everyone from everyone. On the front of the card, set in an oval frame in the centre, was a picture of the gleaming white *Fairstar*. It was surrounded, one in each corner, by four different interior views. It all looked very grand.

The other postcard, addressed to 'Ellen McCann', was from Michael. This one had a picture of moonlight on the water, with a ship in the distance sailing towards the horizon. On the back, in green biro, he'd written: 'I think about you all the time. I love you. x.'

Christine watched her as she read the cards. 'They're from Port Said, wherever that is,' she said, letting Ellen know that she'd read them both. Everyone else had probably read them too.

'It's pronounced Port Side, not Port Sed,' said Ellen, taking refuge in pedantry to hide her embarrassment. 'It's in Egypt, near the Suez canal.' She placed Jennifer's card back against the mirror and took the other one up to her room.

She read it over and over again. 'I think about you all the time.' She gazed at the picture, imagining him standing on the deck in the moonlight, sailing further and further away from her, their beautiful night together fading further and further into the past. 'I think about you all the time. I love you. x.'

He had proclaimed his love to the world. And she wondered what she would say to him when she had an address to write to. But whatever she did say, it would be in a letter, for his eyes only.

Maria's funeral was on the last Wednesday morning in June.

Ellen had asked for permission to attend and went from school with Sister Marie-Pierre and a group of Maria's friends from the Lower-Sixth. They were ushered into benches near the back of the church and Ellen, bringing up the rear, managed to get an aisle seat. The organ played slowly and quietly while they waited for the service to begin.

The priest – in his black chasuble and stole – and the altar boys walked down the side aisle to stand at the church door to wait for the coffin to arrive. When it did, the organ leapt into life and the congregation rose to its feet and began singing *Sweet Heart Of Jesus*. Ellen tried to join in, but found that she couldn't. She clutched the side of the bench and turned sideways to watch the funeral procession make its way down the main aisle.

Maria's coffin was carried by four undertakers. There was a spray of pink roses on top of it. Behind it walked Mr Latimer with Granny Morton, who was holding a handkerchief to her face. Maggie followed, holding the arm of a weeping Granny Latimer. Ellen's heart turned over. Gina came next with her boyfriend, then Caroline and James, and Erica and Tom. Erica glanced at Ellen as they went past. She was dressed all in black, with a black mantilla over her head. She looked very pale and strained. Among the rest of the official mourners were the Wagstaffs — Sally with her parents, and Claire and Joe. Claire, in tears, was clutching her brother's arm for support. Joe had his head bent too and Ellen couldn't see his face.

The Requiem Mass began. The priest said a few careful words about Maria: a tragedy . . . so young . . . God in His merciful forgiveness . . . resting now in His house in the afterlife, just as she had wished to do in this life. The sound of weeping from the front of the church was very audible. And, surrounded by Maria's sobbing classmates, Ellen found herself shedding tears too. She wondered if Erica was doing the same.

When it was time for Communion, she watched as Mr Latimer escorted his mother to the altar rails. They were followed by the rest of the Latimer children except for Erica who remained sitting on the bench with Maggie and Granny Morton. Erica's disaffection with God was now complete; she couldn't even go to Communion at her sister's Requiem Mass.

Ellen, too, sat down while the girls around her joined the queue for the altar rails. She hadn't been to Confession since her night with Michael Chadwell and, until and unless she did, she wouldn't be going to Communion either. She wondered if Maria had confessed her sin and been forgiven. Perhaps the priest on the altar knew the answer to that. Perhaps that was what he'd meant by 'merciful forgiveness'.

But Maria couldn't have confessed her final sin or sins — if, indeed, she had committed them. Not to a priest, anyway. She might have made a sincere Act of Contrition though, lying there in the graveyard. And Ellen, who had never really liked Maria Latimer, felt a sudden surge of compassion for her now. She would pray for the repose of her soul; she would do Erica's praying for her. *Requiescat in pace.* May she rest in peace.

The service ended. The choir began singing *Hail Queen Of Heaven* and the mourners began to follow the coffin as it was carried out of the church. Ellen watched them again as they filed past. Mr Latimer, who seemed to have aged visibly since Ellen had seen him last, kept glancing from right to left, acknowledging the congregation. Everyone else, including Erica, had their heads down.

And then Ellen saw Joe Wagstaff. He was walking in the middle of his two, quietly weeping sisters and the look of pain on his face shocked her. Perhaps she'd been misjudging him, she thought. Until this moment, it hadn't occurred to her that he, too, might be deeply affected by Maria's death. After all, the two families were very close. And all the time she'd been blaming him for not looking after Erica.

'Mother of Christ, Star of the Sea / Pray for the sinner, pray for me,' she whispered, feeling compassion for all of them now.

The bright sunshine was dazzling when they stepped outside the church. The weather was certainly not in mourning for Maria Latimer. No pathetic fallacy here, thought Ellen, remembering the cold, grey day last November when Mrs Chisnall had been buried.

Sister Marie-Pierre shepherded her pupils to a position in the churchyard slightly away from the family mourners. Many of the girls were holding on to each other, weeping. Ellen, a stranger among them, felt very alone.

The sight of the open grave was too much for everyone to bear. How could they help but think about Maria, lying here that night, dying. And now her coffin was being lowered into the gaping hole which was also her mother's grave. The anguish of the family, looking down and confronting their double loss, was too dreadful to watch.

Ellen closed her eyes. A triple loss, really, she thought, and opened them again to look around beyond the periphery of the crowd. Was there someone else here, lurking in the shadows of the churchyard, behind a tree perhaps? Someone who might be paying his last – anonymous – respects to Maria Latimer and their unborn baby? She and Erica had speculated about this. But she couldn't see anyone.

The altar boys departed and people began to move away. Some went to say a few words to the priest and to Mr Latimer before leaving. Sister Marie-Pierre was one of them. She knows, thought Ellen, watching her take Mr Latimer's hand and speak earnestly to him.

The girls were told to make their way back to school but Ellen asked if she might speak to Erica first. She hovered uncertainly, not wanting to get in the way. The older members of the family were moving away now, too. There were black cars waiting for them in the road outside the churchyard, even though it was only a short distance back to the house.

Ellen saw Erica walking around the grave to where Joe Wagstaff was standing with Claire and Sally. She went over to join them.

'Did you see anyone?' Erica asked her.

Ellen shook her head.

'If you're talking about the father,' said Claire, 'we'll probably never find out who he is now.'

They all looked down into the open grave where Maria's coffin lay covered in flowers and handfuls of earth.

'Well, if I ever do find out who he is, I'll kill him!' said Erica and, for the first time in Ellen's presence, she began to cry. She made a small movement towards Joe but he turned and walked away.

Ellen, forgetting her compassion for a moment, gazed scornfully at his retreating back. She was about to put a consoling arm around Erica when, with tremendous force, the revelation hit her. She froze with horror and for a second couldn't believe what she was thinking. She looked at the others, but they were too locked in their grief to notice her reaction, let alone to suspect what was causing it. But it was so obvious to her now. A series of images flashed through her mind. She knew she was right.

It was Joe Wagstaff! He was the father of Maria's baby!

She walked back to school, trying to decide what to do next. Should she tell someone? Should she tell Erica? Would Erica believe her? What would happen when everyone found out? What would they do and say to Joe Wagstaff? And what would happen if she told them and she was wrong? But she wasn't wrong, was she?

She spent the afternoon torturing herself with these questions. After school she decided to go back to the churchyard to have another look at Maria's grave now that it would be filled in and covered with flowers. Several other girls were doing the same and so Ellen, not wanting to join them, wandered around for a while, reading the inscriptions on other graves, until they had gone. Then she stepped over to Maria's grave and bent down to read the cards attached to the wreaths and bunches of flowers that had been placed on the mound of fresh earth.

There was a large wreath of white lilies from the school, with a formal message written by Sister Marie-Pierre. She couldn't see anything specifically from Erica, but the ones from other members of the family and from friends were so personal and intimate that it felt wrong to be reading them. There was a wreath of pink roses from 'the Wagstaff family'. 'To dearest Maria,' it said on the card. 'We shall all miss you so very much. Rest in Peace.' Claire and Sally had added their individual names to the general family signature.

Granny Latimer had addressed one: 'To my darling little angel'. Ellen wondered what she was thinking about Maria now. But it was the one from Mr Latimer that she found the most heart-rending. It was attached to a simple wreath of white flowers and it said: 'May God bless you, my beloved little girl. Forgive me. Your loving and heartbroken Daddy.' Ellen was so overcome that she couldn't read any more.

She stood up. And then, through her tears, she saw it – a single red rose that had been placed at the top of the grave, near the headstone. It wasn't a cultivated flower like all the others. Its stem was uneven. It looked as though it might have been picked by hand from a rosebush – from one of the rosebushes in the park, perhaps.

Ellen stared at the red rose. He must have come back this afternoon to place it here, she thought. She looked round, but the churchyard was empty now. He had been and gone. But, as she passed the church on her way out, she saw that he hadn't gone. He was standing in the porch. He must have been waiting for all the girls to leave. She began walking towards him, not yet knowing what she was going to say. When he saw her coming over to him he turned away, just as he had turned away from Erica earlier, but this time there was no escape except into the sanctuary of the church. He rejected this option and turned back to face her, trying to appear confident as usual. He didn't know yet that she knew.

She took off her hat – and immediately wished that she hadn't. Joe Wagstaff was very familiar with the Convent school uniform, so why did she feel at a disadvantage wearing it in his presence? Especially now when she had the upper hand?

'I know,' she said as she closed in on him. He leaned back slightly and attempted a little, bemused frown. She held his gaze and repeated her assertion. 'Don't pretend you don't know what I'm talking about,' she said. 'I know it's you.'

Slowly his expression changed. He began to look lost and frightened. Then, to her consternation, he turned, put both his hands against the wall of the church and bowed his head between them. Ellen didn't know what to do, so she just stood there and waited. Her feelings towards him kept changing by the second – dislike, annoyance, pity, sympathy. Was he crying? And if so, who was he crying for, himself or Maria?

After what felt like an age, and without changing his position, he said: 'How do you know?'

She shrugged, but he couldn't see this.

'Who else knows?' he asked.

'I haven't said anything to anyone else, if that's what you mean,' she said.

'Are you going to?'

'I don't know.'

There was another long pause.

'Please don't,' he said, turning round to face her. 'Please don't tell anyone. Please, I'm begging you.'

She had no idea what she was going to do. But now – for the very first time in their acquaintance – she had his full attention.

'We need to talk about this,' she said, 'but not here, not now.'

He would tell her everything, and then she would decide what to do next.

JULY

1966

The end of the school year was fast approaching, bringing with it the end of Ellen's schooldays. Her A-level exams were over. Now it was just a matter of waiting for the results to come out in August and then her future would be decided. If they were good enough she would go to university. If they were not . . . well she wasn't going to think about that.

She wondered if Erica would come into school to see her before the end of term. She hadn't come back to school last September and when Ellen had rung up to see what was happening Maggie had told her that Erica was staying with Granny Morton for a while. Just before Christmas she'd rung again but Maggie had said that Erica wasn't in. 'Please tell her I rang,' she'd said – but Erica had never responded.

Then one evening a few months ago, when she and Christine had been on their way home from the pictures in Turneley, they'd seen Erica coming towards them, clinging on to the arm of some boy whom Ellen hadn't recognised. She had a cigarette in her hand, despite the fact that she'd always maintained that it was 'common' to smoke in the street. But then, the boy she was with was 'common' too. Ellen's heart sank. She and Christine slowed to a stop, ready to speak to her, but Erica reacted as though Ellen were an acquaintance

227

she could barely be bothered to remember.

'Oh, hello . . . er?' she said vaguely. Ellen glared at her in silence. 'Sor-ree!' Erica drawled. 'We can't stop.' She gave an affected laugh and then staggered into a shop doorway and proceeded to drape herself around her companion.

'What's the matter with her?' said Christine as they walked on to the bus stop. 'Do you think she's drunk?'

'She's just being an idiot!' said Ellen, deeply hurt and angry. 'A bloody stupid idiot!'

And that was the first and last time Ellen had seen her since last August. But she'd continued to think that – eventually – Erica would come to her senses, that she wouldn't just let their friendship fade away like this, after all these years. Now, though, as the end of term drew ever nearer, she wasn't so sure. Time was running out.

She tried to convince herself that Erica was a troubled person who, perhaps, needed allowances to be made for her. Maybe she herself should take the initiative – again – and go round to Church Walk one afternoon after school, before it was too late. But she knew that she wouldn't because in some ways it would be a relief to leave the Latimers and all their dramas behind. She would be starting a new life soon, anyway, in a new place, with new friends. So perhaps it was for the best, as her mother would say (as indeed she had said after she'd inquired about Erica recently).

But all the same . . . a best friend . . .

'Are you going to cry?' asked Christine as they were travelling to school on the bus on the last day of term. 'I know I will when I'm leaving. I cried when I left St Wilfrid's.'

'I don't know,' said Ellen. 'I might.'

'I definitely will,' said Margaret Latham. 'I always cry during the leavers' assembly anyway – and whenever I have to say goodbye to anyone.'

'Do you really?' said Christine, giving Ellen a look.

'I'll be sad, but I'm glad at the same time,' said Ellen. 'It's a strange feeling.'

Later that morning the whole school crowded into the hall for the leavers' assembly. Those who were leaving – some fifth formers as well as sixth formers – stood in horizontal rows at the front; the rest of the school stood in their usual vertical lines behind them. Hymns were sung and prayers – 'especially for those girls who won't be returning in September' – were said. It was at this point that the weeping began.

Sister Marie-Pierre gave her usual leavers' speech. In the past, when they hadn't been the ones who were leaving, this speech had always sounded pompous and cliché-ridden, but now, to Ellen and her friends in their emotionally overwrought state, it was poignant and inspiring. The headmistress spoke about their schooldays and the happy times they had had here at the Convent; about how they had grown up into fine young women who would go forth into the world and make it a better place because they would be taking with them the values and virtues that the school had instilled in them.

Ellen wondered what Erica was doing now, having already gone forth. Not being virtuous, that was for sure. She sighed. She'd been trying not to think about Erica at all, but now that the last day had arrived she knew that she really wanted her to put in an appearance. But if she didn't, well . . .

As invariably happened on such occasions, someone fainted and had to be carried out. Shortly afterwards, one after the other, two more girls did the same. This made Ellen think about Erica again. It would have amused her. 'Wouldn't it be funny,' she'd said once, after a previous fainting outbreak, 'if mass hysteria broke out and we all went down one after another, like dominoes, and there was only Sister Marie-Pierre left standing, talking to herself?' Yes, it would be funny, thought Ellen, but she wasn't smiling now.

The assembly was nearly over. It finished with a rousing rendition of the school song which proved to be the final emotional straw. Fighting back her own tears, Ellen glanced along the row and saw Margaret Latham weeping openly into her hanky.

A few days ago, on the way home from school, Margaret had (at long last) broached the subject which, it would seem, was still dear to her heart.

'Do you still hear from Jennifer Chadwell?' she asked casually, trying to sound as though she was just making conversation and was only mildly interested in the answer to her question.

Ellen was taken off guard. 'Yeah, from time to time,' she said awkwardly.

'Does she like living in Australia?'

'Yeah, she loves it.'

'And . . . Michael?' Margaret was clearly embarrassed.

'Yeah. They all seem to like it there.' Ellen said, deliberately choosing to misunderstand the question. She knew very well that Margaret was asking her whether or not she was still in touch with him. 'Their house in Turneley Road's just been sold so they're obviously not planning to come back.' She paused. 'As a family, that is,' she couldn't help adding.

The Chadwells had been in Australia for just over two years now. The crucial second anniversary had been and gone. They could come back to England now, if they wanted to, without having to repay their outward fares, and, although there had never been anything in any of Jennifer's letters to suggest that they might, Ellen had been hoping that they would. But a For Sale sign had gone up outside the house, and now there was a Sold notice stuck across it too. So that was that. They had gone for ever.

Although her hopes for the family's return had been dashed, she was still trying hard to cling on to her other hope that one day – any day – Michael would come dashing back on his own, like young Lochinvar, to claim his 'fair Ellen'. There would be a knock on the back door, or a ring on the front doorbell. She would glance in the mirror as she went to answer it. (She would, of course, be looking her very best.) Suspecting nothing, she would open the door and he would be standing there, suntanned and smiling. Disbelief would be followed by joy. And before too long there would be a glorious repetition of their last night together. And then . . . ? What? But that didn't matter. Opening the door was all that mattered. Opening the door and seeing him standing there, smiling.

For over two years now she'd been tending her broken heart. And whenever she'd begun to think that she might have cried all her tears for Michael Chadwell, a poem or a song would come along to prove otherwise. When *The Carnival Is Over*, sung by The Seekers, came out last autumn, she felt that it might have been written especially for them. It brought back all the unbearable sadness of their parting. She didn't want their carnival to be over. 'I'll come back,' he'd said. But now, after all this time, did she still believe that he would? She would always love him though. Until she died.

Yet . . . there was no escaping the fact that sometimes now, when she went to answer that knock on the door or that ring on the bell, it wasn't always Michael Chadwell who was standing there.

They filed out of the hall and went back to their classrooms. At twelve o'clock the rest of the school was dismissed for the summer, but the leavers were having a party later in the afternoon and so they hung around, waiting for it to begin.

This was Erica's last chance – but there was no sign of her. She's not going to come, thought Ellen sadly. She doesn't want to see me again. She's never forgiven me for not telling her about Joe Wagstaff. And she never will.

* * *

Ellen had arranged to meet Joe Wagstaff on the Friday evening after Maria's funeral. She'd chosen the venue for this meeting very carefully. It was to be at The Plough, an old pub that had recently (according to the local newspaper) 'undergone structural alterations and a major refurbishment' and was now considered by some to be smart and sophisticated. It was strategically situated halfway between

Turneley and Makerton, about a mile or so from the Greenside estate and near the slipway for the new motorway. It would be just right for their encounter. No-one they knew would see them together; no-one would know that she was underage.

She arrived slightly late so that he would be the one waiting for her. She was determined to retain her advantage over him. She'd dressed carefully for this meeting too, in her turquoise dress and Sunday-best navy and white houndstooth-check coat. She wanted Joe Wagstaff to take proper notice of her now.

They greeted each other awkwardly. He held the door open for her and she led the way in. The place was nearly empty although it was past eight o'clock. He ordered half a pint of bitter for himself and she asked for a vodka and tonic. This was what she and Erica drank on the very few, nerve-wracking occasions when they ventured into pubs. She was feeling a bit nervous now but was confident that she could pass for eighteen. After all the events of the past few weeks, she certainly felt older and wiser than her sixteen years.

They went to sit in a booth in a secluded corner. She slipped her coat off and placed it on the seat beside her. Joe was wearing his leather jacket. He took his cigarettes and a lighter out of one of its pockets and offered her one. Ellen shook her head. She couldn't risk a cigarette. She might get one of those little coughing, choking episodes which sometimes accompanied her smoking efforts. He lit one for himself and then looked directly at her.

'How did you know?' he said. 'How did you find out?'

He was looking pale and strained, but there was no denying that he was very handsome. He and Maria would have made a beautiful couple, she thought. But then, he and Erica were a striking couple, too. And perhaps people were thinking that she and Joe, sitting here now, also made a lovely couple.

'I don't know,' she said, returning his gaze. 'It just came to me – in the churchyard after the funeral, when you walked away. Suddenly it seemed so obvious. I don't know why other people haven't realised it too.'

'Well they haven't,' he said, lowering his eyes and flicking ash into the ash-tray on the table. 'I should've said something straight away, as soon as I found out she was dead – and pregnant. But I didn't. I was too shocked. And it's too late to tell them now.' He looked up at her again.

'I don't think it is,' Ellen said. 'There's going to be an inquest or something. There'll be lots of questions asked. Wouldn't it be better if you owned up now, before they find out anyway? Someone's bound to realise that it had to be you.'

'Why does it have to be me? No-one found out about us before she died. No-one suspected anything then, so why would they now?'

'Because they're looking for answers. They're desperate to find out. They won't let it rest until they do know.'

Joe stared into his glass and shook his head helplessly.

'And anyway, who else could it have been?' Ellen said. 'Her dad? Tom? The priest?' She'd intended these suggestions to sound preposterous, but now that she'd voiced them they sounded sinister – not totally beyond the bounds of possibility. Were other people thinking such things, too, she wondered? Harbouring such corrosive suspicions? 'I really do think you should tell someone,' she went on. 'Why don't you tell Mr Latimer? It might not be as bad as you think. In many ways it'd be a relief for them to know that it was you because they're probably thinking all sorts of horrible things.'

'They'd blame me for her death – and I couldn't bear that,' he said. 'It's bad enough that she's dead . . .' He lowered his head, struggling to control himself.

Ellen felt deeply sorry for him. Had he loved Maria just like she loved Michael Chadwell? She wanted to comfort him. To put her arms around him, perhaps.

'Anyway, I don't think they will find out,' he said. 'Unless you tell them. Unless you put the idea into their heads.' And then, suddenly altering his tone: 'But you can't prove it. It would only be your word against mine.'

Ellen smiled and shook her head. She had rehearsed this conversation many times over the past two days, but now he was departing radically from her preferred script.

'I think you should tell someone,' she said quietly, 'but if you're not going to, then . . .' She paused.

'Then you'll tell them? Is that what you're saying? You'll tell Erica?'

Ellen gave a non-committal shrug. 'Erica's my best friend,' she said. 'She'd never forgive me if she knew I was keeping something like this from her. But . . . I'm not your enemy, Joe. There's no need to be so hostile. I just need to know what happened between you and Maria before I decide what I'm going to do.'

There was a long silence. Joe stubbed out his cigarette and gazed deeper into the depths of his beer glass, lost in thought.

Ellen watched him carefully. 'I can see you're very upset,' she said. 'You were in love with Maria, weren't you?'

He lowered his head further and she thought he might be going to cry. She glanced round but they were private here, no-one could see them. She reached across the table and put her hand on his arm.

'Did you know, before she died, that she was pregnant?' she asked.

Without looking up, he shook his head. 'No! No, I didn't!' There was another long pause before he continued: 'First there was the shock of her death, then the shock of finding out that she'd been pregnant. That's when I should've said something, I know. But I didn't. I just couldn't believe it. I was . . . I was angry with her. Why hadn't she told me? She should've told me. But then . . . I hardly saw her during those last few weeks, because I was . . .' he trailed off and shook his head again.

'Going out with Erica,' said Ellen, finishing his sentence and removing her hand from his arm. 'What on earth made you start going out with Erica?'

He looked up at her and she could see that he was going
to talk. It would probably be a relief for him to tell someone
all about it. And that someone was going to be her. A
profound feeling of satisfaction swept over her.

'Because I was so angry with Maria,' he said, angry again
now. 'I thought we . . . I thought she'd given up that stupid
idea of hers about being a nun. I thought when we'd . . . I
thought she . . . But no, suddenly she started it all off again
and I was so angry . . . and hurt . . . and I told her that I'd
had enough, that I never wanted to be bothered with her
again, she could go and be a nun for all I cared. And I went
to Sally's party, and there was Erica as usual, and I just . . .'

Poor Erica! But Ellen would think about her later.

'So you'd been going out with Maria for a long time,
then?' she said, trying to grasp what he was saying.

'Sort of. Well, ever since we were little kids, in a way. She
and Claire were best friends. She was always round at our
house. And then, when we got older . . .' He smiled. 'She was
so beautiful and I really liked her, and I was beginning to
think she liked me too. But just when I thought,' he smiled
again, wryly this time, 'just when I was going to ask her to go
out with me, she suddenly announced that she was going to
be a nun. So I backed off.' He held up his hands and leaned
back in his seat. 'But as time went on,' he said, leaning
forwards again, 'she still seemed to like me, so I suppose I
never really lost hope. And she seemed so . . .' he trailed off
again.

(Un-nunlike, thought Ellen, mentally finishing his
sentence again, remembering how Maria had looked that
Saturday night, years ago, when she'd seen her going to the
fair with Claire and Joe.)

'Then it all started to get serious with the nun thing
again. After Easter last year she started saying she wanted to
leave school and go into this . . . this stupid enclosed convent
place where she'd never be seen again!'

(After Easter last year! After Mr Latimer and Maggie's
wedding. After they'd found out that George Hunter was

Gina's father, and that Mrs Latimer had been to see him on the night she died. But why would this have re-ignited her desire to be a nun, Ellen wondered?)

'Everybody was trying to talk her out of it – well, everybody except her grandmother. They were all saying she should wait and do her A-levels first and then see if she still felt the same way. They were all hoping she'd change her mind if she gave herself a bit more time.

'Claire didn't want her to go and she tried really hard to get her to agree to stay on at school. Maria was round at our house one day and Claire told her that she should stop being so stubborn and listen to what people were saying to her. No-one wanted her to go just yet. Even that headmistress nun didn't want her to. Then Claire went out of the room and Maria asked me what I thought she should do. And I said: "I don't think you should go. Not now, not in two years time, not ever. But you already know that," I told her. "I don't know why you're even asking me. You know how I feel about you." And she didn't say anything. She just looked down in that way that she had and I couldn't tell what she was thinking. But the next thing I heard was that she'd decided to go back to school.'

He smiled at the memory. 'I thought then that I could change her mind altogether. And then I thought I had changed it, because just before Christmas last year we started going out with each other. But she wanted it to be a secret. She said she needed to be sure about giving up the nun thing and didn't want anyone to know about us yet.'

(Just before Christmas. Ellen remembered Erica saying: 'Sally says she thinks he's got a girlfriend . . . but she's always saying that.' And she remembered the school dance and Maria in Joe's arms, dancing slowly and sadly to the sound of Ray Charles.)

'It was quite exciting, meeting in secret,' Joe went on. 'We'd go for walks, go to the pictures. Sometimes we'd even sneak out when everyone else had gone to bed. We've got this shed at the bottom of our garden. No-one can see it from the house and we'd go there sometimes. I thought we were happy. I know I was. I loved her and I thought she loved me.' His voice began to falter. 'Do you want another drink?' he asked, standing up quickly.

Ellen shook her head. She needed to keep her wits about her, as her father would say. She watched him go to the bar.

It was all beginning to make sense now. Maria, up in her attic room, hadn't been withdrawing from the world as everyone had thought. On the contrary, having her own room was part of her plan for going out with Joe Wagstaff in secret. 'We didn't even know she was out,' Erica had said, referring to the night Maria had died. But if Maria had been in love with Joe, why had she persisted with the idea of becoming a nun? It was this that didn't make sense to Ellen. And it couldn't have made sense to Joe either.

He came back with another half pint and began talking again straight away. He wanted to tell her everything now. She felt another surge of satisfaction.

'After the first time we . . . slept together, I thought that was it, that she'd tell everyone she'd changed her mind and didn't want to be a nun anymore then we could stop hiding and go out properly. But she didn't want to do that. I don't know why. And every time I brought it up she just got all upset. She said she wasn't ready yet, so we just carried on as we were.'

He looked straight at Ellen. 'I didn't make her do anything she didn't want to do,' he said. 'I didn't take advantage of her – if that's what you're thinking.'

Ellen shook her head. 'It's not what I'm thinking,' she said. But what did he mean by the 'first time' and 'we just carried on'?

'So you . . . slept together more than once?' she asked, feeling embarrassed to be talking to him about this.

He nodded. 'Yeah. The first time was New Year's Eve. At our house. My parents had gone away for New Year and Maria was staying with us. Claire thought she was sleeping in our spare room, but she wasn't. She was with me. And there were other times after that.

'Then, about Easter, when I thought everything was fine, she suddenly started saying it was all a mistake, that she did want to be a nun after all. She said she couldn't help it – God was calling her! I couldn't believe it! She said all the arrangements were being made, she was going into her convent in August, and she really meant it this time. I tried to talk her out of it but she wouldn't listen. And when I kept going on about it, she refused to discuss it with me. Then she wouldn't even see me anymore.'

'Easter? You said this was at Easter? Do you think she knew then that she was pregnant?'

Joe shrugged. 'If she did, she didn't tell me. I had absolutely no idea.'

'But she must have known that she was, mustn't she?' said Ellen. 'She must at least have suspected that she was. So how could she have gone ahead with her arrangements? It doesn't make sense, does it?'

Maybe . . . she thought, struggling for an explanation, maybe Maria had seen her pregnancy as God's way of punishing her for abandoning her so-called vocation. Perhaps she'd thought that if she went ahead with her plans to go into her convent God would forgive her and everything would be all right – it would just turn out to have been a false alarm. But then, as time went on and it'd become obvious that everything wasn't all right, she'd decided to . . . to what? To get rid of the baby? If that's what she'd done; they couldn't know this for certain. And then, when the miscarriage – or the abortion, if that's what it was – was happening, perhaps she'd decided to let herself die too, by staying out in the churchyard instead of seeking help.

The dying, though, could have been accidental. She might not have been aware of the danger she was in. Or she might have been too weak to do anything to save herself. They would never know now what she had intended.

Ellen wondered if the pregnancy could have been God's way of pointing out to Maria Latimer that she wasn't meant to be a nun. After all He did move in mysterious ways. Only this time – in His infinite wisdom – He'd been a bit too subtle!

They sat in silence, each deep in thought, entangled in unanswerable questions.

Then Joe began to speak again: 'On the evening of Sally's party I went over to their house and made her talk to me. But I couldn't get her to change her mind. And I was so angry with her! I told her that she'd been messing me about. I said I didn't care anymore, that she could go and bury herself away if that's what she wanted to do!' He was struggling to control himself again. 'And that's exactly what she did, isn't it? Buried herself away!' He gave a bitter laugh and turned his head away.

Ellen hesitated a moment. 'Do you think,' she asked, watching him closely, 'that she . . . just had a miscarriage, or do you think she . . . deliberately tried to get rid of the baby?' Had he thought about this possibility? Or the possibility that she might have been trying to kill herself too?

He put his head in his hands.

'I don't know,' he said. 'That's what people are wondering, isn't it? What do you think?'

'I don't know. She could've done anything. She must've been desperate.'

'She should've told me about it,' he said, getting upset again. 'Perhaps if I hadn't been going out with Erica . . . ? That must've really hurt her. That's why I did it, really – to hurt her. But if I'd known she was having my baby, I would never have done that. I'd have . . .'

'What? What would you have done?'

This was a crucial question. Joe looked at her helplessly.

'Would you have told someone?' she asked. 'Told Mr Latimer, or Maggie, or Claire? Because if you would've told them then, why can't you tell them now?'

There was another long silence. He looked wretched.

'It's not your fault that she died,' said Ellen, her heart going out to him. 'I'm sure they won't think that.'

He shook his head. 'I know I should've told them,' he said. 'But I didn't. And now it's too late.'

This was where the conversation had begun.

'I don't think it is,' said Ellen.

They stared at each other for a moment.

'There's something else I want to know,' she said, leaning back in her seat. 'What are you going to do about Erica?'

He gave a little groan. 'I don't know.'

'You do know that she's madly in love with you, don't you? She always has been. But you're never going to be in love with her, are you? I don't even think you like her very much.'

'I should never have started going out with her,' he said. 'I know that. But I do like her. It's just so hard to be with her now when all she wants to do is talk about Maria. I've hardly seen her since it happened. I know I should finish with her but I don't want to hurt her now when she's so upset.'

'But you'll hurt her soon, you know you will. And she's been talking about leaving school and going with you to wherever it is you'll be going to university.'

'Oh, God!' said Joe.

'You really shouldn't have started all this in the first place.'

'I know, I know! You think I should finish with her now, then?'

'Yes, I think you should, before she does something stupid. She'll be heartbroken but . . .' Ellen shrugged. (I'm heartbroken, too). 'Anyway, it's your decision.'

She looked around. The pub had filled up. A group of men, standing at the bar, kept bursting into raucous laughter. Someone had fed the juke box and Cilla Black was belting out *Anyone Who Had A Heart* so loudly that they were having to raise their voices now in order to make themselves heard. The intimate atmosphere had gone. Ellen glanced at her watch.

'I've got to go,' she said, standing up. Joe stood up too. 'I really do hope you decide to tell the Latimers,' she said, slipping on her coat. 'I think they deserve to know the truth. But it's your decision. I won't say anything.'

As they walked past the bar, Ellen was surprised to see that Frank Chisnall was among the noisy group of men there. He was turned slightly away from her and she had to look twice to make sure that it was him. He'd sold his mother's house recently and everyone had thought that he'd gone back to London, or wherever it was he'd come from, but it would seem that he hadn't. Her mother, she knew, would be interested in this sighting.

Observing that Ellen was looking at Frank, one of his mates nudged him and said: 'Ey up, you've got an admirer!'

There was a burst of lewd laughter, causing Ellen to blush. Frank turned and took a moment to recognise her. When he did he nodded and smiled at her and she smiled back, hoping that he wouldn't speak to her in front of Joe. Seeing her smile, his companions began to push Frank towards her, whooping suggestively as they did so.

'Ger in there, Frank, lad!' one of them said loudly.

'Give over,' said Frank. 'Take no notice of this lot, love,' he said to Ellen. He had that cocky look about him.

Joe stepped forward, put a protective hand on her arm and steered her away from the bar and out through the door. She blushed again.

Outside, it was going dark and there was a faint curve of moon in the sky. They stood for a moment, embarrassed again.

'I'll walk you to your bus stop,' Joe said, looking in both directions, trying to locate where it was. The pub was in between two stops.

They crossed the road and Ellen turned to the right, towards the one which was slightly further away but on a much nicer stretch of road. There were hedgerows and fields on both sides here – a little bit of surviving countryside between the motorway roundabout in one direction and the sprawl of the Greenside council estate in the other. It was a familiar stretch of road to Ellen, one she travelled along all the time, on the bus to and from Turneley, but she had never been here on foot before. It felt strange to be walking along it now with Joe Wagstaff at her side. Strange and unreal in the fast fading light. In the dusk; in the twilight.

The pavement was narrow and uneven. They walked along in silence, concentrating on not bumping into each other. When they got to the bus stop, Ellen said: 'If you do decide to tell them, please don't say anything about me. Erica would never forgive me if she found out I already knew and hadn't told her.'

'I won't . . . That's if I do decide to tell them.'

Ellen nodded. 'You don't need to wait,' she said. 'Look, there's your bus coming the other way.'

'Right,' said Joe. 'I'll see you around . . . and thanks.'

He sprinted across the road and leapt on to the bus. Ellen kept watching it until it disappeared from sight.

'I saw Frank Chisnall when I was coming home tonight,' she told her mother when she got in. 'He was coming out of that pub – you know the one, just past Greenside, near the motorway?'

'Oh,' said Mrs McCann, interested. 'He's stayed around then. Well, well!'

Ellen went upstairs and read her postcard from Michael Chadwell again. And she thought about the red rose on Maria Latimer's grave, symbolically conveying the same message: 'I think about you all the time. I love you. x.'

'Where've you been?' asked Christine, sitting up in bed.

'Nowhere. Just to see Erica,' she said, getting undressed.

'All dressed up like that? Did you go out somewhere?'

'No.'

'Hmm. Very strange!'

Ellen got into bed and turned to face the wall. She didn't want to talk. She had a lot to think about. She tried to imagine what the last few weeks of Maria Latimer's life must have been like. She must have been really frightened when she realised she was having a baby. Would she really have gone into her convent in that state? Had she really loved Joe? What would he have done if he had found out that she was pregnant? He was planning to go to university. Would they have got married?

She wondered what she herself would've done had she too been pregnant. Her mother would've gone mad, that much was certain. And then what would have happened? She would've had to leave school, of course. Would she have been sent away like that girl who lived at the top of King's Terrace? She'd disappeared for a while and then she'd come back and carried on with her life as if nothing had happened – except that her boyfriend had started going out with someone else in the meantime. Presumably her baby had been adopted.

She thought about Mrs Latimer, who had kept her baby but had refused to divulge the identity of its father. Would she have done the same – *if* she'd been pregnant? Or would she have said that it was Michael Chadwell? Would she have told him?

There was enough material here for nights and nights of fantasising on this subject, and she settled down now to make a start. Tonight she would begin with her refusal to divulge the name of the father.

'It doesn't matter,' she would say. 'I'm not going to get married, so it doesn't matter who he is.'

Erica, of course, would think it was Pete. She would think that was why Ellen had finished with him. But no-one would suspect that it was Michael Chadwell, would they? (Christine, in the other bed, gave a little snorting snore.)

Perhaps she would write and tell him. Or perhaps not. Anyway, at some point, Mick would write to him and mention that Ellen was having a baby but wouldn't tell anyone whose it was. What would he do then? Would he come back as quickly as he could? Would he be able to? Would she want him to? She would be huge by this time so it might be better if he were to come back just after she'd had the baby. She wondered whether Michael would prefer a boy or a girl.

Over the next few nights she spent many hours elaborating on this fantasy. The actual reunion was the climax of every version and she imagined it in a variety of ways. Sometimes she knew that he was coming and was prepared. At other times, it was a complete surprise – which was wonderful, but a bit risky because she wanted to be looking her best. At first, she imagined herself standing with the baby in her arms when he walked in. But then she would have to put it down for their passionate embrace, so perhaps it might be better to have the baby lying in its cot or pram nearby? She wanted everything to be perfect.

'Why didn't you tell me?' he would cry. 'You knew I would come as soon as I heard.'

And then what? Because this was the problem. Try as she might, the happiness-ever-after bit was never quite satisfactory. She persisted with it for a while, and then abandoned the pregnancy story altogether. It had been an enjoyable diversion, but thank goodness it was only a fantasy. Thank goodness it wasn't real!

From now on, if Michael Chadwell were to come back at all, it would have to be just for her.

'You'll never guess what's happened now,' Erica said, flouncing into the cloakroom the following Monday morning. It was her first day back at school since Maria's death. Ellen's heart skipped a beat. What had happened?

'Joe's only gone and finished with me!' Erica took off one of her shoes and hurled it across the floor. She seemed more angry than upset.

'Oh, no,' said Ellen, trying to sound surprised. 'Has he? Why?'

'I don't know! He kept going on about not wanting to have a girlfriend at home when he was going away to university. So I said I'd go with him if he wanted. But he said he didn't want that. So I said we could keep things casual, but he didn't want that either. I don't know what's the matter with him. What am I going to do?' She retrieved her shoe and stuffed it into the shoe rack. 'I can't believe it. Not after I've waited all this time. And at a time like this, too.'

Ellen tried to look sympathetic. 'What a shame!' she ventured. (So he hadn't told them, then.) She felt disappointed.

'A shame!' cried Erica. 'It's more than a shame! But I don't think he really means it. He's just frightened about getting serious, that's all. He said he really likes me, so I'm not going to get upset about it. He'll come round, I know he will.' She glanced at Ellen. 'Don't look at me like that! He *will* come round, just you wait and see. I think I know him better than you do.'

* * *

The leavers' party had finished, all the goodbyes had been said, and, with an inevitable sense of anticlimax, the girls began to drift away – leaving school for the very last time. Ellen scanned the street outside, but there was no sign of Erica. I might never see her again, she thought sadly, and then the sadness turned to anger. If Erica Latimer can't be bothered to keep in touch, then why should I get upset, she thought? She can get lost, for all I care.

She and Margaret Latham set off on their last journey home together. Margaret was going off to France next week for her summer holiday. Then, in September, she would be going to a teachers' training college. She was going to be a primary school teacher. Ellen had no idea what she herself wanted do after university (provided that she got in). It was, she thought, much more exciting not to know. But then, Margaret Latham had always been a bit boring, hadn't she? A bit predictable.

To her surprise – and now that it was too late – she suddenly found herself regretting that she hadn't been friendlier with Margaret over the years. All through their schooldays she had been a benign presence on the sidelines of Ellen's life. Her only crime (apart from knowing about tides) had been falling in love with Michael Chadwell. And now, apart from the odd 'hello' in the street, they might never speak to each other again. She deserved better.

'Why don't you come round to our house when you get back from France,' Ellen heard herself saying as she stood up to get off the bus.

Margaret looked surprised. 'OK,' she said, smiling. 'We'll have our exam results by then. Our fates will be sealed.'

Ellen went upstairs to get changed. She hung her blazer in the wardrobe and put her hat on the shelf above it. She wouldn't be needing them again. And in time, they and other items of her uniform would become Christine's.

She had been expecting to feel pleasantly sad on this, her last day of school, but she hadn't been prepared for this awful feeling of emptiness that was engulfing her now. Since she had stood here all those years ago, admiring her new school uniform in this same wardrobe, so many people had gone from her life – Joan Grady (although that had happened a long time ago); Jennifer Chadwell ('your friend, Jennifer', who had recently transmuted into 'your mate, Jen') who was never going to come back from Australia; Michael Chadwell, too, of course, who probably wouldn't either. And now Erica.

AUGUST

1965

With very little advance warning, Auntie Peggy and Dorothy decided to come 'home' again for three weeks this summer. It was five – nearly six – years since their last visit and they felt that if they left it any longer they would be too late to see Dorothy's mother, old Mrs Kenyon, who was getting frailer by the day now. According to Mr McCann, she was 'at death's door', which was sad, but she'd had 'a good innings'. As long as Dorothy got back in time to see her one last time, it was all part of the natural order of things.

'I didn't know she played cricket,' Christine had said, and every time Dorothy's mother was mentioned after this she would seize an imaginary bat and execute an elegant stroke with it. Ellen found this very amusing.

While Mrs Kenyon had spent the past five years growing very old, the McCann and Cartwright children had spent them growing up. Which surely was to be expected, Ellen thought. But Auntie Peggy greeted them all with such exclamations of surprise and wonder that you would think they'd done something amazing and quite out of the ordinary. 'No! This can't be Michael! He's taller than his father now! Oh, my word!' And: 'This young lady must be Ellen! Well-I-never!' Then Auntie Peggy uttered an even greater shriek of disbelief and everyone looked at Christine who was the cause of this.

'Yes, she's certainly shot up recently,' said Mrs McCann proudly, as if she were personally responsible for all this growing.

'Yeah, I woke up one morning and I'd grown six inches in the night,' muttered Christine, squirming uncomfortably under their collective gaze.

Auntie Peggy and Dorothy had changed a bit too, but no-one commented on this. Ellen wondered what they would say if she were to exclaim: 'Oh my goodness, Dorothy, you've put on a bit of weight, haven't you?' Or: 'Auntie Peggy! I hardly recognised you with all that grey hair!'

Looking critically at her aunt, it seemed to Ellen that it wasn't just her hair that was less colourful now. She was altogether a little less loud, a little less exciting than she'd seemed before. She and Dorothy were getting old too. Younger people grew up; older people grew even older and died. As Mrs McCann had said when Mrs Chisnall was dying: 'You'll be old, yourselves, one day.' It was a fact of life.

But death, she knew, was no respecter of age. Not everyone lived to be old. Erica's mother hadn't; Maria Latimer hadn't. Nor had Joan Grady's father who'd died of a heart attack a few months ago. He'd 'dropped dead' suddenly at the age of forty-four, bowled out before his time.

When Ellen heard about this, she remembered Joan asking her who she would rather have die, her mother or her father. And she wondered if Joan's choice of the latter had come back to haunt her now.

Ellen had been intending to work full-time in Teller's for part of the holidays, like she'd done last summer, but now she rearranged her weeks so that she could spend time with Auntie Peggy and the rest of the family. Mick also had a holiday job, in the Makerton Bakery, but he considered himself too grown up for picnics in the park or trips to the sea-side and so he carried on working.

One day, Auntie Peggy took Ellen, Christine, and Maureen Cartwright to Manchester to do some shopping.

'I want to buy each of you something nice,' she said, brushing aside the polite objections of Mrs McCann and Auntie Annie. 'It's only once in a while, for heaven's sake!'

This was true. The parcels from America had stopped coming long ago. Times had changed and there was no need for them now. But Auntie Peggy still liked to treat them.

After buying some new clothes for Maureen and Christine they went to the department store café for something to eat.

'Well now, isn't this nice?' said Auntie Peggy, settling herself down at the table amidst all their carrier bags. 'Ellen's turn after we've eaten. Something to make the boys sit up and take notice, eh?'

Ellen managed a dutiful little smile.

Auntie Peggy surveyed her eldest niece for a few moments and then said: 'I must say I'm surprised you're not courting yet – a beautiful girl like you.'

Ellen blushed, Christine snorted, and Maureen Cartwright giggled.

'Well, I guess there's plenty of time for all that,' Auntie Peggy continued. 'What with you planning to go to college and all.'

'I have had boyfriends,' said Ellen defensively.

'She has,' Christine confirmed, nodding her head vigorously.

'I just don't happen to have one at the moment, that's all.'

'And that's because . . .' Christine paused for effect, 'her heart is in Australia.'

Maureen Cartwright, who hadn't really been listening until now, took notice of this and turned to look at her cousin. Ellen narrowed her eyes and looked menacingly at Christine.

'Well it is,' said Christine. 'There's no point denying it.' She turned to her aunt. 'Her boyfriend went to live there. It was all very tragic – and very romantic.'

'You don't say!' boomed Auntie Peggy.

'It was a long time ago,' said Ellen.

'Yes, but you've not been out with anyone else since, have you?'

Ellen shrugged.

'I bet . . .' Christine went on, feeling safe to say this with Auntie Peggy there. 'I bet he's been out with other girls, though. I bet he has another girl-friend now.'

'He probably has,' said Ellen, pausing as the waitress appeared and began unloading the contents of her tray on to their table. 'Like I said – it was a long time ago.' She picked up her knife and fork and began to eat her dinner, but the edge had been taken off her appetite.

It had been a long time ago; and it had been a long time too since she and Michael Chadwell had last exchanged letters. After their initial outpourings of love and longing, a silence had fallen between them. This was as much Ellen's fault as his. It was hard to know what to write about anymore. Would he be interested in her sixth-form life, for example? Probably not.

Jennifer provided her with all the family news, writing in detail about life in their Sydney suburb. She talked about her own boyfriends, but so far she hadn't said anything about Michael and his girlfriends. This could be because he hadn't had any, or because he had but she was sparing her friend's feelings. And, in her grimmest moments, Ellen knew that one day Jennifer would write and tell her that Michael was engaged to some Australian girl whose existence she'd failed to mention before.

But thoughts such as these were too painful and not to be dwelt upon. 'I'll come back,' he'd said, and she continued to cling on to this hope. One day there would be that knock on the door, that ring on the bell . . .

'Well. You'll be lucky to get through life without having your hearts broken at least once,' said Auntie Peggy looking solemnly at all three girls. Maureen Cartwright giggled again.

'I'm sure you're right,' said Christine, her eyes on Ellen.

Ellen was thinking about Auntie Peggy's lost love. Had there been a Michael Chadwell in her past? Someone who had left; someone whom she had hoped would come back one day? Someone who never had. And had she spurned others while she'd been waiting for the one who never came? She would grow old now with only Dorothy for company. They had no children – only nephews and nieces, and these were on the other side of an ocean. And Ellen realised that the admiration she had always felt for her aunt was turning into pity.

As they were finishing their meal Auntie Peggy returned to the subject of shopping. 'What about that suede jacket, then?' she said. 'Would you like that?'

Ellen was embarrassed. The jacket Auntie Peggy was referring to was very expensive. They'd always assumed that Peggy and Dorothy were rich, but something she'd overheard her father say recently made her hesitate now. 'It's all show,' he'd said. 'They've not been over for such a long time because they can't afford it. They're not as well off as they'd like us to think.'

But it was a beautiful jacket – soft dove-grey suede – and she would like it very much.

'Yes, I think you would,' Auntie Peggy said, beaming.

'It's very expensive,' said Ellen.

'Yeah, it is,' said Christine.

'Never mind that,' said their aunt. 'Who else do I have to spend my money on?'

A few months ago, Ellen had been admiring a similar jacket in her mother's catalogue. That one hadn't been real suede, though, but a much more affordable suedette. She'd been on the point of ordering it . . . and then she and Erica had seen someone in the street wearing an imitation leather jacket which Erica had poured such scorn on that Ellen had been totally unnerved. It was, apparently, fake, cheap and nasty. As soon as she'd got home she'd told her mother that she'd changed her mind, that she didn't want the jacket after all because it was suedette and therefore vulgar. Instead, she would save up for the real thing, which, she'd made quite clear, wouldn't be found in her mother's catalogue.

This jacket, though, was definitely the real thing.

Once Ellen became its proud owner she couldn't wait to show it off.

Erica was full of admiration and jealousy when she saw it. 'It's fab,' she said, stroking it. 'I wish I could have one. You are lucky. I can't even afford a new pair of stockings at the moment.'

'Well, you should get a holiday job and then you'd have some proper money of your own,' said Ellen who sometimes resented her friend's life of leisure. Erica had never had a Saturday or a holiday job. She'd always preferred genteel poverty to toil of any kind.

'I am going to get a job soon,' she said. 'A proper job, I mean. I'm going to leave school. I can't bear the thought of going back for another year.'

'Don't be silly!' said Ellen who had heard all this before. 'What would you do? Work in a shop? You'd hate it, I'm telling you.' She had worked in Teller's long enough to speak with authority on this subject. 'It's soul-destroying.'

'Anything would be better than school,' insisted Erica, whose soul, perhaps, had already been destroyed.

It hadn't been a good year for her. In addition to the A-level subjects she was studying, she'd also had to do the two O-levels she'd missed the previous year, and re-sit maths which she'd failed. She should have done these O-levels last November – she had, after all, done all the work for them – but she'd opted instead to do them the following summer, a decision she later came to regret. They'd hung over her all year, blighting any enjoyment she might otherwise have derived from her A-level studies, and she hadn't been able to settle at all.

She hadn't wanted to take the exams in November, she'd said, because that was when Maria's inquest was due to be held. It would, she'd insisted, be too distracting, too distressing.

* * *

She'd been expecting to be present at the inquest but when the time came Mr Latimer was very firm. Only he, Maggie and Claire Wagstaff were to attend. It was just a formality and the sooner it was over the better. There was no need for Erica to take time off school. He would report back to the family afterwards.

Erica was furious. 'It's all right for Claire to take time off college,' she fumed. 'I hate my dad.'

'Claire was her best friend,' said Ellen.

'Yes? And I was her sister!'

'Your dad and Maggie can speak for the family.'

'Whose side are you on?'

Ellen ignored this remark.

The findings of the inquest were interesting.

'This is what they *say* happened,' Erica told Ellen, her tone indicating that she disagreed with the verdict.

Apparently, the post-mortem examination had revealed that Maria, as well as having suffered a miscarriage, also had a sprained ankle and bruising on her face and body consistent with a very recent fall. It had been suggested that she was on her way to visit her mother's grave and had entered the churchyard by climbing over the high wall that surrounded it. A short cut, maybe – unusual, but possible. On the street side of the wall there was a bench near a bus stop. She could have used this bench to climb up without too much difficulty. Then she could have fallen off and hurt herself, and this could have triggered the miscarriage.

No conclusion had been drawn as to whether or not she'd been aware that she was pregnant. Her plan to enter a convent would seem to indicate that she hadn't been aware of, or hadn't been able to accept, her condition. Either way, no-one else knew – neither family nor friends (Claire Wagstaff had confirmed this).

There was nothing to suggest that she had deliberately thrown herself off the wall to harm either herself or her baby (assuming she'd been aware that there was a baby). The verdict was accidental death.

'She threw herself off,' said Erica. 'Of course she did! Why would she have been on that wall in the first place? It isn't a short cut. And climbing on walls wasn't the sort of thing she would do.'

Ellen, thinking about Joe and Maria sneaking in and out of houses in the dark, wasn't so sure. Perhaps it was exactly the sort of thing Maria had got used to doing. But had she fallen off the wall accidentally? That was the question.

'Or,' continued Erica, 'perhaps she was with "him" and he pushed her off.'

'Now you're being silly,' said Ellen.

'Am I? And how could she have not known that she was over three months pregnant? She must've known.'

'Well,' said Ellen, wondering why she was trying to convince Erica that the verdict was sound when she too found this part hard to believe, 'you do hear of cases where people give birth without realising that they're pregnant. It's not impossible.'

'Yes, but if Maria had . . . slept with someone, then that would have focussed her mind on the possibility, wouldn't it? No, it's a stupid thing to say. Of course, she knew. And she threw herself off that wall. She must have done.'

After school they went round to the church to check out the feasibility of this theory. They located the bench a few yards from the bus stop. As there were a few people waiting there, they loitered until a bus came and took them away. Unobserved now, Erica gave Ellen her satchel to hold and with great ease, if not much elegance, stepped on to the bench and hauled herself up to sit on the wall. She leaned down and took hold of both their satchels while Ellen struggled up to join her.

The drop on the graveyard side of the wall was much greater than on the road side.

'You'd definitely hurt yourself if you fell off here,' said Ellen, clinging on to the wall, just in case.

'Yeah. But you wouldn't stand up here, would you? You'd sit down like we're doing and you'd turn round,' Erica was demonstrating as she spoke, 'and then lower yourself down. *Voilà!*' she said, landing at the side of a grave.

'If she did fall,' said Ellen, 'she'd have landed on those stones there.'

They stared at the probable landing place for a moment. Ellen's eyes moved on to Mrs Latimer's grave. Would Maria have picked herself up and limped over to it? Or had she dragged herself along the ground? More questions. But no real answers – only probabilities and possibilities.

'Well I think she definitely threw herself off,' said Erica. 'She wouldn't have fallen.'

'She might have,' said Ellen, standing up gingerly. 'She might have felt faint, you know. In her condition.'

Erica shook her head. She wasn't to be convinced. 'Come on down,' she said. 'I can't climb back up there.'

Ellen eased herself carefully to the ground and they made their way out of the graveyard, stepping round and over graves as they did so. Ellen glanced at Maria's grave as they went past. There were fresh flowers on it – but no red rose.

'Granny Latimer puts those there,' said Erica, pausing for a moment. 'I don't think anyone else comes here now except her.'

'Don't they?' said Ellen.

'Nobody else can bear to.'

Erica was also bitterly disappointed that the identity of 'him' hadn't come to light.

'My dad and Maggie don't seem bothered about it anymore,' she complained. 'They don't seem to care.'

Ellen thought about this and concluded that Joe must have told them after all. Perhaps that was why Mr Latimer hadn't wanted anyone else to go to the inquest. So who else would know? Probably Claire. Possibly Granny Latimer and Granny Morton. Maybe Gina and Caroline, and Mr and Mrs

Wagstaff. But surely not Sally. Nor the boys.

And most definitely not Erica.

As the Christmas holidays approached, Erica was already planning the next stages in her campaign to win back Joe Wagstaff. When he came home from university in December, Sally happened to mention that he'd been to the folk club that was held every Wednesday evening in a pub near the market. Consequently, the next week, Ellen and Angela Norris were commandeered into accompanying her to the upstairs room of this shabby, old-fashioned establishment – called, rather grandly, the Market Square Hotel.

The room was crowded when they arrived. Joe Wagstaff was already there with a group of his old school friends, one of whom was Pete. This was awkward for Ellen – she hadn't seen Pete since the summer – but Erica was overjoyed. She went straight over to their table, grabbed a stool and placed it as close to Joe as she could.

'Hi, everyone!' she cried. 'Make room for three more little ones.'

Ellen and Angela had no choice but to squash in and join them, too. Joe's mates were obviously pleased at this development, but he himself seemed less so. He glanced at Ellen and gave a little shake of his head. She smiled. It was no use him looking pleadingly at her, she thought. Erica was irrepressible; there was nothing she could do about her.

She turned to Pete, the smile still on her face. 'Hi,' she said, and was relieved when he smiled back. But she declined his offer to buy them drinks; she didn't want there to be any misunderstanding here.

She was hoping that sometime during the evening she might have a word with Joe. She wanted him to confirm what she had been thinking. And every now and then she caught him looking at her, as if he, too, wanted to say something. But it wasn't to be. Even in the intervals between folk songs, the place was so noisy that they had to shout to make themselves heard. Intimate conversation was impossible. And she could hardly lean across the table and bellow: 'Did you tell Mr Latimer that you were the father of Maria's baby?' No, she wasn't going to find out tonight whether or not he had owned up. But if he had, she thought, looking across the table, she really wished that Mr Latimer had seen fit to tell Erica too, so that all this Joe Wagstaff nonsense could have been stopped once and for all.

Last July, when Joe had finished with her, Ellen had expected Erica to be devastated. Instead, she'd coped with the break-up surprisingly well. Reverting almost instantly to the patterns of her original obsession, it was as if she'd never been out with him at all, as if those few summer weeks had never happened. And it occurred to Ellen that Erica preferred it this way: to be forever in pursuit, forever on the brink, of happiness.

'I think Joe was glad to see me last night, don't you?' Erica said in school the next day. They were in their form-room packing their satchels for the morning's lessons. 'I think he might want to go out with me again. What do you two think?'

'We-ll, he made his escape pretty quickly,' said Angela. 'He could've walked home with you if he'd wanted to, but he didn't, did he?'

'That's because he was with all his mates. No, I definitely think I'm making progress again on the Joe Wagstaff front.'

Angela shrugged and gave Ellen a what-can-you-do-with-her look. But Ellen was losing patience.

'No,' she said. 'You're not making any progress at all. He doesn't want to go out with you. He definitely doesn't. And if you really think he does, then you're bonkers.'

'How would you know? You're always so negative about Joe.'

Ellen groaned. 'And you're always so ridiculously positive. Even when there's nothing at all to be positive about. If you think he was showing the least bit of interest in you last night, then . . .' But what was the use?

'That other boy was though,' said Angela. 'That Alan.

You could go out with him.'

Erica gave Angela a withering look.

'Look, forget about Joe Wagstaff,' said Ellen. 'You're driving us mad. Just forget about him, please!'

Erica gave her a pitying look. 'What do you mean, forget about him?' she intoned tragically, placing the palms of her hands on her bosom. She grabbed hold of Ellen and shrieked: 'Nelly! I *am* Joe Wagstaff!'

'Erica Latimer and Ellen McCann! Will you make less noise please!' said their form-mistress, looking up to see what was going on.

Shaking with laughter, they tried to look as contrite as possible.

* * *

Gina Latimer was getting married on the twenty-first of August and, seeing that she and Caroline were going to be bridesmaids, Erica had decided to defer any decisions about her future until after the wedding.

'He's coming – George Hunter,' she told Ellen. 'But he's not giving her away, even though he's her real father.'

'Of course he's not,' said Ellen, shocked at the idea. 'It would be really awful if he did – for your dad I mean.'

'The Wagstaffs are coming too, and I can't bear the thought of you-know-who seeing me in my bridesmaid's dress. It's awful. I look really stupid in it. Like a little girl.' She turned to Ellen. 'Why don't you come to the church on Saturday and then you can see what I mean?'

It was the last weekend of Auntie Peggy's stay, but instead of saying no to Erica as she'd been intending to, Ellen heard herself agreeing to go.

The day of the wedding was grey and overcast but – as people kept saying over the course of the afternoon – at least the rain was holding off. Inside though, the church was brightly lit and adorned with an abundance of flowers. Ellen, wearing her new suede jacket, slipped in and sat near the back, carefully avoiding the place she had sat in last year at

Maria's funeral.

She could see Granny Latimer sitting at the front with Maggie – and a man who must be George Hunter. Behind them were Granny Morton and Phyllis who had come up from Shropshire, where they were living now, having finally sold the big house in Birmingham. The Wagstaff family were several benches further behind. Ellen hadn't seen Claire Wagstaff for ages, nor Joe since last Christmas at the folk club. And Sally, she noted, had Steve with her.

Tom and James were ushers, guiding the guests to their allotted places. Ellen hadn't seen Tom Latimer for a while either – he always seemed to be out whenever she went round to Church Walk these days – and she was amused to see that he, too, like Christine, had 'shot up'.

She studied the backs of the heads of the groom and the best man. The groom was called Martin. He was, according to Erica, quite nice, and everyone quite liked him – except for Gina, of course, who obviously liked him a lot! Both he and Gina were teachers and they'd moved away from the Midlands and had been living in London for nearly a year now.

The organ struck up, and the congregation rose to its feet as the bride and her father entered the church. Gina was wearing a long, white, empire line dress with lace sleeves. A short veil was attached to her upswept hair, and she was carrying a spray of white flowers. Mr Latimer, Ellen thought, was looking very proud to be giving away one of his 'beloved little girls'. Only this one wasn't really his.

The organ was at full strength now as they began their walk down the aisle. Caroline and Erica followed behind them, identically dressed in short, pale blue dresses and white shoes. They were carrying small posies of flowers in their white-gloved hands and their hair, with more white, artificial flowers woven into it, was piled high on their heads. Erica, catching Ellen's eye as she walked past, pulled a face. Ellen responded by raising her eyebrows in mock horror before smiling sweetly back at her.

The Nuptial Mass began. This must be the first time in ages that Erica has been to church, Ellen thought. Even before Maria's death she'd been a very unenthusiastic Catholic, hardly ever going to Confession or Communion. Now, she hardly ever went to Sunday Mass either. And she'd begun to do things like deliberately eating meat on Fridays as an ostentatious, defiant gesture. Her lapse was almost total.

Ellen herself hadn't gone to Confession or Communion for a long time after her night with Michael Chadwell. But then, nearly a year afterwards, she'd decided to make her Easter duties.

'Pray Father, give me your blessing,' she'd said, 'for I have sinned. It's eleven months since my last confession. . . I have had sex-u-al intercourse, *once*.'

Father Maloney, obviously shaken by the eleven month gap, asked when this act had taken place, and seemed encouraged to learn that it had been so long ago. She didn't tell him that her partner in sin had been beyond reach since then. The priest said that she should resolve never to do such a thing again before matrimony, and took her silence as acquiescence. She said the Act of Contrition: '*Oh, my God, I am sorry, and beg pardon for all my sins . . .*' and that was that. But had she been forgiven, she wondered? Because she wasn't sorry. She would never be sorry. Making love with Michael Chadwell had never been a sin – not in her eyes anyway.

The next day she went to Communion and waited for a thunderbolt from heaven to strike her, but none did. She knew she was being hypocritical. But it kept her mother happy. And she didn't really care.

She had to agree with Erica that a lot of it was silly. How could eating meat on Fridays be a sin? It seemed so trivial. And why did women have to cover their heads in church, too, she thought, as the mantilla she was wearing now slipped on to her shoulders. She didn't put it back on again, and wondered if this was a sign that she, too, was lapsing.

When the ceremony was over the bridal procession made its way out of the church. Ellen couldn't help thinking about the last time she'd stood and watched these same people walking along this aisle. This time, though, they were all smiling and happy. She remembered Joe Wagstaff's stricken face and looked at him now as he walked by. He turned slightly and smiled at her. He was wearing a suit and a dark blue tie. She wondered if Erica had seen him yet, all dressed up like this.

Outside, the wedding party began to pose for photographs. Standing on the sidelines, Ellen was able to get a good look at George Hunter now. Yes, she could see that he was Gina's father. They had the same blue eyes – but then Mr Latimer had bluish eyes too. No, it was something more intangible.

Lost in thought, studying Gina and her two fathers, she didn't notice Joe Wagstaff walking towards her until he arrived at her side.

'Hi,' he said, smiling again.

'Hi,' she said back, noting with pleasure that his eyes had flickered over her suede jacket. She glanced around. Should she ask him now about telling Mr Latimer? But just as she was about to do so, Erica, momentarily released from her bridesmaid duties, came bounding over.

'Hi, Joe,' she gushed. 'Don't look at me in this grotty dress!'

'OK, I won't,' he said with a grin, and turned and walked away.

Erica sighed. 'What were you talking about?' she demanded.

'Nothing,' said Ellen.

'What did he say?'

'Nothing.'

'He didn't mention me then?'

'No.'

'He looks gorgeous though, doesn't he? Perhaps I'll ask him for a dance later.'

The photographs had all been taken and the guests were preparing to leave for the reception. As Gina was about to get into the first of a line of cars waiting by the church gate, she stopped and said something to her new husband. Holding up the skirt of her dress, she turned and went into the graveyard. Everyone watched from a distance as she laid her spray of white flowers on her mother's grave. On Maria's grave. A little murmur ran through the crowd. Ellen looked at Joe Wagstaff but his face was turned away from her.

'Ring me tomorrow morning,' ordered Erica as she hurried off.

Ellen waited until they'd all departed and then she, too, made her way to the grave. As well as Gina's spray, Granny Latimer's usual flowers were there in the container.

There was no red rose.

Obeying orders, Ellen stopped at the phone box on the way home from church the next morning.

'It's not even half past ten yet,' Erica complained when she came to the phone. It was obvious that she'd only just got out of bed. 'I thought you'd be ringing later.'

'I'm on my way home from church. I can't come out to the phone box again because I've got to help my mother. We're having lots of people round for tea this afternoon.'

'But I need to see you this afternoon. I've got something really important to tell you.'

Oh no! Not Joe Wagstaff again, thought Ellen. What had happened now? Some little sign that Erica thought he had given her? Some tiny little thing to keep her hopes alive?

'I can't this afternoon,' she said. 'I've just told you. My auntie's going back to America tomorrow and we're having a big family tea-party.'

'Make some excuse. I've got to tell you this.'

'No, I can't. Tell me now. No don't! There's someone waiting for the phone.' Ellen turned round in the phone box so that she was facing away from the woman who was waiting impatiently outside.

'Oh, God! Listen, you've got to come round – just for half-an-hour.'

'Erica! I've told you, I can't! You're not the only one with a family, you know.' Ellen was getting annoyed.

'Well if your bloody family had a telephone then we could talk properly without all this stupid phone box business, couldn't we?'

Ellen recoiled. 'I'll see you on Wednesday afternoon,' she said stiffly.

Erica, realising perhaps that she'd offended Ellen, changed her tone. 'No,' she said. 'Come round tomorrow for tea. I'll tell you then.'

'I can't. I'm working tomorrow. Some of us have to, you know.' Ellen put the phone down with a bang and went home to her breakfast, still smarting from Erica's attack. But she would forget about her now and concentrate on her own family instead, because after today she wouldn't see Auntie Peggy and Dorothy again for a very long time. They deserved her undivided attention.

After breakfast Mrs McCann, Ellen and Christine began preparing the house and the food for the tea-party. The two girls vacuumed and dusted the front room and were about to begin on the living room when the front doorbell rang.

Mrs McCann was in the kitchen baking. 'Who's that?' she muttered, making it clear that visitors would not be welcome right now.

Christine went to answer it, leaving Ellen to react in the way she always did whenever the front doorbell rang. Her heart began to race. It might be Michael Chadwell. It wasn't impossible.

Christine came back into the room with an annoying little smile on her face. 'It's someone for you,' she said coyly.

Ellen's heart began to beat even faster. 'Who is it?' she asked, feigning only mild interest.

Christine continued to smirk suggestively. 'Go and see,' she said.

Oh God! It couldn't be! Ellen glanced in the mirror over the sideboard. She had no make up on yet. A couple of hours later and she would be looking her best, but she would have to do. She swallowed hard and went to the front door which Christine had left half open.

She opened it wider – and there was Joe Wagstaff, standing there smiling at her.

'What are you doing here?' she asked, surprised and acutely embarrassed.

'Well . . . I wanted to talk to you yesterday, but I didn't get a chance. So here I am now.' He gestured towards his father's car that was parked in the road behind him.

'Oh,' said Ellen. But the doorstep was obviously not the place for this conversation. 'Come in, then.'

He stepped into the small vestibule. She closed the door and then tried, without touching him, to get past him and into the narrow hallway which seemed to be getting ever narrower by the second.

'We can talk in here,' she said, opening the front room door and ushering him in ahead of her. Christine was loitering by the living-room door, with that silly smile still on her face. Ellen gave her a quick, dismissive wave of the hand and followed Joe into the room, making sure to close the door firmly behind her.

'Sit down,' she said, with a vague gesture.

He looked at the small couch and then at the armchair in the chimney recess, before choosing the former. He sat down, taking up more than half the space, and spread his right arm out along the back of the couch. He seemed perfectly at ease. Confident. Cocksure?

Ellen sat down on the piano stool, at a slight angle so that she was facing him. She moved slightly and her elbow caught the piano keys, producing an unexpected discord which startled them both. Clumsily and with a loud bang, she closed the piano lid.

'Do you play the piano?' he asked, his eyes wandering over the framed certificates on the wall above it.

'Only with my elbows these days,' she said, attempting levity. 'I used to have lessons when I was younger.' Maria Latimer, she remembered, had been an accomplished pianist.

Ellen glanced nervously round the room. It was clean and tidy, all ready for the afternoon visitors. But it was so small! Compared to the rooms in his house it must seem like a cupboard, she thought. And the ornaments on the mantelpiece – presents for Mrs McCann, from the children when they were younger – looked so cheap and silly. What must he be thinking? Was he surprised that she lived here, in a house like this?

'How did you know where I lived?' she asked. Surely he hadn't asked Erica for her address – not that Erica would even remember it!

'Pete gave me your address,' Joe said, 'and I stopped and asked someone the way once I got to Makerton.'

'Right,' said Ellen, nodding her head.

She sat waiting for him to speak.

'I know I should've told you ages ago,' he said, 'but before I went to university last year I did go and see Mr Latimer. I told him about me and Maria and we had a long talk. He was very understanding and – you were right – he was relieved to find out.'

Ellen nodded again. 'I thought you must have,' she said.

'He asked me to go to the inquest. He said my evidence would help to clarify things. We agreed that we'd tell Maggie and my parents and Claire. He said that no-one else from the family would be at the inquest and so they didn't need to know about me. He said he'd tell Maria's grandmothers that his mind had been put at rest on this matter, and that would be all that was necessary. There would be no need to name names. I didn't tell him that you knew.'

'How did Claire take it?'

Joe pulled a face. 'Well . . . she couldn't believe it, at first. She couldn't believe that she hadn't known anything about it. And she was very upset that I hadn't told her straight away – when Maria died. But she calmed down . . . eventually.' He paused. 'When we came out of the inquest,' he said, 'Mr Latimer told me that I shouldn't blame myself for what'd happened. He said Maria had been a very disturbed girl and that he should've been a better father and seen it at the time.'

'Poor Mr Latimer!' Ellen hesitated: 'Do you blame yourself?' she asked.

'I don't think so. Not anymore.'

She wanted to ask him if he was still in love with Maria. But she didn't.

The sound of the vacuum cleaner could be heard coming from the other room. Feeling that some explanation for this Sunday labour was called for, Ellen said: 'We're getting ready for a family tea party this afternoon. My auntie has been over from America and she's going back tomorrow.'

'I'd better go then,' said Joe, getting to his feet.

Ellen stood up too. 'Well, thanks for telling me,' she said. 'It's a pity though that Mr Latimer didn't tell Erica as well, and then she might leave you alone. She still goes on and on about you.'

'Yeah, I know. I had hoped that she'd have got over it by now, but you should've seen her yesterday at the wedding reception.'

Ellen grinned. 'Yes, I can imagine!'

'Do you think I should tell her now and put a stop to it? Do you think that would be a good idea?'

Ellen thought it would definitely be a good idea. 'Well . . . it's your decision,' she said. 'But if you do, then just remember not to tell her that I know already. She'd go absolutely berserk if she knew that – especially after all this time. She'd never forgive me for not telling her straight away.'

'I'll think about it, then,' he said.

They were standing now in the middle of the room, just where she and Michael Chadwell had stood on that May evening last year. If it had been Michael at the door, she thought, looking at Joe – he would take her in his arms now. And how she still yearned for this! It was so awful to long for someone and not be able to have them – which, presumably, was how Erica felt about Joe. And was it how he felt about Maria? But there was no hope for him and Maria. So if it was hope that kept the longing alive, might it not fade away –

given time?

Ellen made a move and they manoeuvred themselves out of the room and back down the narrow hallway to the front door.

'I'll see you around,' Joe said, just like he'd said that night at the bus stop last year. He took two strides and was out on the pavement. Ellen watched as he got into the car, reversed into the backs and then back on to the road. She watched as he drove past the Chadwells' old house, halted for a few seconds and then turned right on to Turneley Road.

After the car had disappeared she stood there for a moment longer, remembering how she had watched the Chadwells' taxi stop there too, before it had turned in the other direction – left – and out of sight.

'I'll come back,' he had said.

('I'll see you around.')

Ellen went back into the front room. It was, she thought, a perfectly adequate room, and if her house wasn't good enough for Joe Wagstaff, well . . . hard luck. It might not be big – it might not have a telephone! – but it was nothing to be ashamed of. She realised though that it wasn't Joe Wagstaff she was annoyed with. It was she who had been uncomfortable and embarrassed, not him. It was she who ought to be ashamed of herself.

She went back into the living room and told Christine and her mother that her visitor was just someone who had called to say hello – one of Erica's ex-boyfriends.

'Oh, was that Joe Wagstaff?' said Christine. 'It was, wasn't it? He's lovely, isn't he?'

Ellen shrugged.

'He is,' insisted Christine. 'In fact, I'd go as far as to say he's excessively handsome!'

'Exceedingly handsome,' said Ellen. 'I mean, it's "exceedingly" not "excessively".'

'Exceedingly handsome, then.'

'Handsome is as handsome does,' said Mrs McCann, diving into the oven.

Christine raised her eyes to heaven. 'What's she going on about, now?' she said to Ellen.

That night, for the first time in ages, Ellen had the piano lesson dream again.

She decided that she wanted to resume her lessons, and so she went to see Mrs Walker.

'I know I can play the piano a bit,' she said to her, 'but I want to be a more accomplished player.'

Mrs Walker seemed unconvinced, but agreed to a trial period during which Ellen must do plenty of practice and never be late for her lessons.

When she started to practise again, Mrs Chisnall (who was still alive) was delighted. 'I always liked to hear you play, love,' she said. 'You're much better than Christine.'

But then Mrs Chisnall changed into old Mrs Kenyon (who now seemed to be living next door) and Dorothy asked Ellen not to practise because her mother was sick and the sound of the piano was disturbing her.

She was about to go for her next lesson when Erica rang (it would seem that now they had a telephone too). Erica kept on and on talking. Ellen kept trying to end the conversation, but . . . inevitably she was late for her lesson. Mrs Walker shook her head sadly and closed the door in her face.

I'll never be as accomplished as Maria Latimer now, thought Ellen bitterly, as she slunk home and put the music case away for the last time.

Wednesday was half-day closing at Teller's and so in the afternoon Ellen, still feeling slighted, went round to Erica's. There was no-one else in the house when she got there. They went into the kitchen and Erica made coffee for them both. They had taken to drinking coffee lately, feeling that it was more sophisticated than tea. Neither of them mentioned their last, fraught telephone conversation.

'Has your auntie gone, then?' Erica asked, trying to sound interested.

Ellen nodded.

'Well,' said Erica, eager to get on with her news. 'You'll never believe this.'

I probably won't, thought Ellen. Not if it's something to do with Joe Wagstaff. But it wasn't.

'George Hunter gave Gina a wedding present,' said Erica solemnly, and then paused for effect.

'Wow!' said Ellen. 'That is hard to believe!'

'No, listen! It was a cheque for five hundred pounds! I saw it when she was opening her cards. But that's not what I'm on about. It was signed G. E. Hunter!'

Ellen waited. There had to be more.

'So I asked Maggie what the 'E' stood for, and do you know what she said?'

Ellen looked vague. 'I don't know. . . Ethelbert?' she ventured. 'No? Ethelred, then.'

Erica had a pained expression on her face as Ellen went through a list of names. 'Edgar? Edward? Ernest? . . . Eric?'

'Yes!' she cried. 'Eric. George Eric Hunter!'

Ellen waited again.

'That's what I wanted to tell you! Don't you see? Eric, Erica! I think he's my father, too!'

Ellen burst out laughing. 'Don't be silly!' she said. 'Anyway, I thought you said you were called after your grandfather.'

'Yeah, that's what I was told. But . . . don't you see?'

'No, I don't.'

'Look! My grandfather died on the twenty-seventh of July 1947. And George Hunter went to his funeral, remember. And I was born on the seventh of May 1948. They could easily have . . .'

'What? At your grandfather's funeral!'

'Well . . . not at the actual funeral. But she probably stayed with Granny Morton for a few days afterwards. They could easily have done it then.'

'But,' protested Ellen, determined to reject this new theory, 'your father would have been there too, wouldn't he –

at the funeral? It's just as likely that he's your father – which of course he is. This is a stupid conversation. Why do you want George Hunter to be your father all of a sudden?'

'I don't *want* him to be. I just think he is. You know what my mother was like?'

'No, I don't. And neither do you. We don't know anything for certain – except about Gina. Your mother might not have been seeing him that night . . . the night she died. She might've been visiting a girl friend – like your granny said. We don't really know. We're just . . . guessing.'

'Well, *he* would know,' said Erica. 'About that night, and about me. I'm going to ask him and then we'll know for certain.'

'You wouldn't know for certain. Even if they . . . did it, it wouldn't prove he was your father,' said Ellen. 'You're just jumping to conclusions. If his middle name was Thomas or James, would you think they were his too?'

'Yes, I would.'

'Perhaps all of you are his,' said Ellen. 'Have you thought of that?'

'Perhaps we are,' said Erica, ignoring the sarcasm.

'You're not really going to ask him, are you? He'll say he's not, even if he thinks he might be. He'll think you're after his money. Is that what this is all about? You want a suede coat like mine?'

Erica was not amused.

'But if he was, that would make Maggie your auntie!' went on Ellen, laughing. '*You're not my mother,*' she said, imitating Erica's constant cry. '*No,*' she continued, pretending to be Maggie, '*but I am your aunt!*'

'Oh, very funny,' said Erica. 'I wish I hadn't told you now.'

'Just forget about it,' Ellen said, serious again. 'Don't go and do something you might live to regret.'

But she knew that Erica wouldn't forget about it. And later, after she'd considered more carefully what Erica had told her, she had to concede that, improbable though it was, it was not impossible. If Mrs Latimer had felt the same way about George Hunter as she, Ellen, felt about Michael Chadwell, then . . .

But what would be gained by Erica pursuing this? And what would be lost if she insisted on doing so?

Disobeying instructions, Erica rang Ellen at work the next afternoon. Mrs Downes, frowned and tutted as usual.

'I just thought you might like to know that I've failed all my exams,' Erica announced.

'Oh,' said Ellen. 'What a drag! But I can't talk now.'

'OK then. I'll see you tomorrow night. Go back to your cakes!'

On Friday evening they met outside Higham's as usual but were at a loss what to do with themselves. They were outgrowing the delights of the Cellar coffee bar and occasionally they went into the proper bar there instead, but they didn't really like doing that. And so when there was no folk club, no dancing, no parties, nothing on at the pictures that they wanted to see, they invariably ended up in Erica's bedroom listening to records.

They made their way to Church Walk now, through the park. It was that lovely time of evening when the light was mellow and the air hushed. It always filled Ellen with sadness, reminding her of times past and the ends of summer days.

'Turneley's so boring,' said Erica, breaking into her wistfulness. 'I'm going to leave school and go and live in London with Gina and Martin.'

'No you're not,' said Ellen, sighing loudly. 'They wouldn't want you, anyway. Why do you keep on saying stupid things like that?'

'Do you know, that's all you say to me these days – that I'm stupid. Well, I'm obviously too stupid to pass my exams, so I might as well leave.'

'I didn't say you were stupid,' said Ellen. 'I said you were *being* stupid, which isn't the same thing.'

'I'm not *being* stupid. I'm *being* realistic. I don't want to stay on at school. I don't want to go to university. And I don't want to stay at home with people who aren't even my parents.'

Ellen clutched her head. 'Don't start all that again, please!' she groaned. 'You're driving me mad!' The pleasant melancholic feeling had left her now and she was beginning to wish that she'd stayed at home.

When they arrived at Church Walk, Mr Latimer and Maggie were in the kitchen. He had just come in from the hospital and she was dishing up a meal for him. He greeted the two girls and began to eat. Ellen smiled and said hello; Erica said nothing. She put the kettle on and put coffee into two mugs.

'You've heard the bad news, then,' Mr Latimer said to Ellen. He turned to Erica. 'Have you decided yet which subjects you're going to re-sit?'

Erica glanced at Ellen. 'I'm not,' she said. 'I'm going to leave school. It's pointless staying on. I'll only fail my A-levels as well, so I'm going to leave and get a job.'

'Oh, Erica!' said Maggie, banging a saucepan into the sink and pouring cold water into it.

'You're being too pessimistic,' Mr Latimer said. 'Why don't you forget about the Latin and the geography and re-sit the maths in October? And you won't fail your A-levels if you knuckle down and work hard next year.'

'I don't want to. I'm going to leave.'

'We'll see about that,' said Maggie.

'Well, it's not up to you, is it?' said Erica. She gave Ellen a level stare. 'You can't stop me. You're not my mother.'

Ellen raised her eyebrows and shook her head.

'I'm in no danger of forgetting that fact,' snapped Maggie, letting herself get annoyed, which was unusual for her these days. 'But you should listen to your father.'

'Yes, well . . .' said Erica, looking at Ellen again. '*He's not my father,*' she mouthed silently. Ellen held her breath. 'He can't stop me either,' Erica said out loud. 'You were going to let Maria leave school, weren't you? So why can't I?'

'Yes, and that was a mistake I don't think we would want to repeat,' said Maggie.

'I think we should talk about this when you've calmed down and had a chance to think about it more carefully,' said Mr Latimer.

'I am calm,' said Erica. 'It's Maggie who's getting in a state. But I'm not going to change my mind, and you can't stop me – either of you.'

Ellen was feeling very uncomfortable. She'd witnessed many exchanges between Erica and her father and Maggie over the years, but this one felt very dangerous. 'Your dad's right,' she said. 'You need to think about it a bit more.'

'My dad . . .!' said Erica, and gave a harsh little laugh. The coffee was made now and, carrying both mugs, she walked out of the kitchen.

Ellen followed her. 'I think I'm going to go home,' she said as Erica started up the stairs. 'I can't stay here listening to any more of this.' She opened the front door and stepped outside.

Erica put the mugs down on the floor and followed her, letting the door close behind them. 'No, don't go yet,' she said. 'It's only early. It's all right. I wasn't really going to say anything about George Hunter.'

'Weren't you? I don't know what you're going to say next, and I don't think you do either. You've got to stop all this silly nonsense, Erica, before you do say something you'll regret.'

'There you go again! First I'm being stupid, now I'm being silly.'

'Well, you are.'

Erica went to sit on the garden wall and Ellen – reluctantly – went to join her. A red sports car had pulled up across the road outside the Wagstaffs' house and they watched as Sally and Steve got out of it. Sally waved to them and Steve nodded curtly. Ellen waved back but Erica just sat there glowering. Sally and Steve disappeared into the house.

'She's probably going to marry that stupid idiot,' Erica

muttered. And then, looking across at the Wagstaffs' house: 'I wonder if Joe's home?'

Ellen made an exasperated little noise.

'What was that for?' protested Erica. 'Am I not even allowed to mention his name now?'

'I wish you wouldn't. It's so boring. You're living in a fantasy world all round. George Hunter . . . Joe Wagstaff.'

'No I'm not! You weren't there at the wedding reception last Saturday. You didn't see what Joe was like. It's only a matter of time before . . . He still likes me. I know he does.'

'He doesn't. Believe me, he doesn't.'

'How do you know? You think you know everything, don't you?'

'I know that Joe Wagstaff will never go out with you again, Erica,' Ellen said quietly. 'He should never have gone out with you in the first place. It was a terrible mistake. You've got to accept that now and stop clinging on to something that's all in your mind. You really do have to forget about him.'

Erica attempted to laugh. 'I'm not listening to you,' she said. 'You don't know what you're talking about.'

'Oh yes, I do. I know exactly what I'm talking about.' Ellen took a deep breath. (She was going to do it: she was going to tell Erica.) 'He never wanted to go out with you, at all. It was Maria he wanted. He was in love with her. He was the father of her baby.'

There was a chilling silence.

Erica stared at Ellen, a scornful look of disbelief fading rapidly from her face. Then: 'You're lying!' she screamed. 'You're lying! How can you say such a thing?'

'Because it's true,' said Ellen. There was no going back now. 'He told me so himself.'

'He told you! He told you? When did he tell you?'

'Last year. After Maria's funeral.'

'Last year!' Erica leapt off the wall. 'He told you last year,' she shouted, 'and you never told me? Why didn't you? Oh, you bitch! You bloody bitch!'

For a moment Ellen thought that Erica was going to hit her, but instead she began to walk off down the road. Then she turned abruptly and came back.

'Why did he go out with me, then?' she said. 'It doesn't make sense.'

'He'd quarrelled with Maria – because of the convent business. He was angry, and you were there. He shouldn't have done it, but he did.'

'I don't believe any of this!' Erica began to cry.

'Yes, you do. And I think you knew at the time that something wasn't quite right, didn't you?'

'And you've let me . . . ? All this time. How could you?'

'I thought once he'd finished with you, you'd get over it and that would be that. I didn't know you'd be like this. You've got to forget about him, Erica, once and for all.'

'Don't you tell me what I have to do! You're a traitor! I hate you!'

Erica rushed up the path, but the front door was closed and she couldn't get back into the house. She rang the bell with one hand and hammered on the door with the other. Mr Latimer flung it open, alarmed by all the racket. Maggie was right behind him.

'What on earth's the matter?' he asked.

'Ellen's just told me that Joe Wagstaff was the father of Maria's baby,' Erica shouted.

'Come inside,' said Mr Latimer, stretching out his hand to her. But Erica, seeing the look on her father's face, stepped out of his reach.

'Oh, God!' she shrieked. 'You know already, don't you? You've known all along, haven't you? Everyone has – except me.'

'Come inside,' Mr Latimer said again, taking hold of her this time. 'Go home Ellen. We'll sort this out.'

And so Ellen, with her heart pounding and Erica's screams echoing in her head, turned and walked away.

A week after Auntie Peggy and Dorothy had left, old Mrs

Kenyon, her innings over at last, lay down her bat and died. Dorothy, all those miles away across the sea, couldn't be at the funeral. If only her mother had gone two weeks earlier, people said, then she could have been there. But that would have spoiled their holiday, so it was probably better this way.

Ellen thought it was all very sad. It would be a long time before Dorothy could come back and visit her mother's grave. And the next time she and Auntie Peggy did come home, everything would be different. Because nothing stayed the same for ever. People grew up; people died. People went away – far, far away.

People grew apart.

SEPTEMBER

1966

Ellen's throat was aching with the effort to suppress her tears. She knew that the woman sitting opposite was looking at her. She probably thinks I'm upset about my boyfriend, she thought, not my mother. Or . . .

As she sat there, staring out of the train window but not seeing anything anymore, Ellen realised that she'd been hoping, right up until the last moment, that Erica would make an appearance and they would be reconciled at last.

Last week she'd bumped into Sally Wagstaff in Turneley. It'd been a long while since she'd last seen her and Sally couldn't wait to tell her that she and Steve were getting engaged in a few weeks time. Wondering how Erica had reacted to this news, Ellen said how fab that was. She told Sally that she herself was about to go to university.

'I'm off to Birmingham next week,' she said.

'To Birmingham? Really?'

Sally also said that she hadn't seen Erica for ages. She didn't think she was still at home, but if she did see her she would tell her that Ellen was leaving soon.

But, of course, nothing had come of this.

Margaret Latham, however, had called round, like Ellen had suggested she should. She'd only just returned from France and was very suntanned. The skin on her nose was peeling slightly which Ellen found oddly attractive. Both of them were pleased with their exam results.

Margaret was bound for her teachers' training college in Liverpool and she and Mick began to exchange addresses and talk about meeting up at one of the student haunts he'd been raving on about. Christine looked at Ellen and, behind their backs, began to pull a series of funny faces. Ellen smiled. Yes, she thought, it would indeed be funny if . . . But no! Mick wouldn't want Michael Chadwell's cast off girlfriend. . . . would he? Christine was now pretending to be sick, and Ellen's smile widened.

The train began to slow down and the elderly man got up and attempted to remove his suitcase from the luggage rack. Ellen wondered if she should give him a hand as he wasn't very tall. But he was only elderly, not old, and might be offended, so she sat and watched him struggle. It was a relief when he finally managed to grasp its handle and haul it down on to the seat. The train pulled into the station and, still struggling, he removed himself and his case into the corridor.

Ellen glanced up at her own suitcase on the rack above her head. It was the same one she'd taken to Granny Morton's all those years ago, and to the Lake District, too. It'd been old and shabby then, and was even more so now, but it would have to do.

Her trunk, however, which was still in her bedroom at home, was brand new. It was a dark blue one with metal corner edges and fasteners. It closed with a metal clasp and there was a little padlock and key to lock it into place. This was locked now – the key was in her purse – and the trunk was going to be sent to her university hall of residence sometime in the next few days.

There was another key in her purse, too – one for the black and gold metal money box in which she kept Michael Chadwell's postcard and the letters he'd sent her from Australia. The money box was one of the first things she'd packed, but just before she'd locked the trunk ready for its journey, she'd changed her mind and had returned it to the drawer where it'd always lived. She was making a new start, she'd told herself. She didn't need to take it with her.

Thinking about this now, she was overcome with regret. It contained all she had left of Michael Chadwell. How could she have left it behind? It felt like a betrayal of their love. Their carnival might not yet be over. He might still come back. But deep in her heart she knew he wouldn't. They would *'never meet again'*. The tears brimmed over now and ran down her face. And this time she was weeping for her lost boyfriend. She stared unseeingly out of the window, making no effort to hide them. The woman opposite could look all she wanted.

Gradually, she regained her composure. She would think about the future, not the past. Her social life, ever since Erica had gone, had been abysmal. She'd hardly been out in the evenings at all, other than with Christine and, very occasionally, Angela Norris. But all this would change now. And she was looking forward to continuing her studies.

Her mind wandered back to the very cold day last January when she'd gone for her interview at the university. She'd thought that when it was over she might walk round to have a look at Granny Morton's old house. But she hadn't gone – and she probably wouldn't go in the future either. Some other family would be living there now: someone else would be sleeping in the bedroom she'd shared with Erica; some other boys would be climbing the trees at the bottom of the garden. It was all just a memory.

She thought about the interview itself. She had been interrogated by two lecturers who had questioned her about her literary likes and dislikes and about her expectations of university life. And why, they'd asked her, was Birmingham her first choice?

She'd rambled on a bit, somewhat tritely, until suddenly she'd heard herself telling them about her childhood visit there with Erica. She'd told them how they'd walked around the campus pretending to be students; about how she'd been inspired by the atmosphere of the place and how, since then, she'd always equated the idea of university with Birmingham. 'And so, when I came to apply, it was at the top of my list,' she'd said. And they'd smiled – and she'd known that she'd said the right things.

The train was slowing down again, approaching the railway junction at Crewe.

The woman sitting opposite Ellen stood up. 'This is where I change,' she said. She began assembling her belongings and then opened the sliding door and stepped into the corridor, leaving Ellen all alone.

Crewe was a large station with many platforms. Ellen sat and listened to the incomprehensible announcements coming over the loudspeakers and watched all the people getting on and off trains. Where had they come from? Where were they going to? Two middle-aged women entered her compartment and sat down opposite each other by the door.

After a few more minutes the train began to move again, and as it gathered speed her sadness began to evaporate. She was getting nearer and nearer to her destination. Fields and trees and houses were flashing by. She would be there soon. And then her new life would really begin.

She shifted the focus of her gaze away from the landscape outside and on to her own reflection in the window. 'Why was Birmingham your first choice?' they'd asked her. And she'd told them the tale about herself and Erica. But what she hadn't told them, she thought, staring at her face in the glass, was that Joe Wagstaff was a student at Birmingham.

She stood up and changed seats. And now, with her back turned on Turneley, she could see where she was going.

ABOUT THE AUTHOR

Rosaline Riley was born and grew up in Lancashire. She now lives near Streatham Common in South London.

For many years she was a literature tutor in the Lifelong Learning Department at the University of Warwick where she specialised in teaching 20th century and contemporary novels.

Clad in Armour of Radiant White is also available on Kindle.

Also by Rosaline Riley:

The End of the Road. A novel about family relationships, friendship, betrayal and deception.
The wise, we are told, forgive but do not forget. But is forgiveness ever really possible when some things are impossible to forget?

Available on Kindle and in paperback.

ISBN: 978-0-9932122-0-8

Website: www.thecommonreadercommonwriter.pathline.co.uk

Printed in Great Britain
by Amazon.co.uk, Ltd.,
Marston Gate.